Ask Again, Yes

MARY BETH KEANE

MICHAEL JOSEPH
an imprint of
PENGUIN BOOKS

MICHAEL JOSEPH

UK | USA | Canada | Ireland | Australia
India | New Zealand | South Africa

Michael Joseph is part of the Penguin Random House group of companies
whose addresses can be found at global.penguinrandomhouse.com

First published in the United States by Scribner, an imprint of Simon & Schuster, Inc. 2019
First published in Great Britain by Michael Joseph 2019
001

Interior design by Alison Cnockaert

Printed and bound in Great Britain by Clays Ltd, Elcograf S.p.A.

A CIP catalogue record for this book is available from the British Library

HARDBACK ISBN: 978–0–241–41090–5
OM PAPERBACK ISBN: 978–0–241–41091–2

www.greenpenguin.co.uk

Penguin Random House is committed to a
sustainable future for our business, our readers
and our planet. This book is made from Forest
Stewardship Council® certified paper.

For Owen and Emmett

prologue

—

July 1973

FRANCIS GLEESON, TALL AND thin in his powder blue police-man's uniform, stepped out of the sun and into the shadow of the stocky stone building that was the station house of the Forty-First Pre-cinct. A pair of pantyhose had been hung to dry on a fourth floor fire escape near 167th, and while he waited for another rookie, a cop named Stanhope, Francis noted the perfect stillness of those gossamer legs, the delicate curve where the heel was meant to be. Another building had burned the night before and Francis figured it was now like so many others in the Four-One: nothing left but a hollowed-out shell and a blackened staircase within. The neighborhood kids had all watched it burn from the roofs and fire escapes where they'd dragged their mat-tresses on that first truly hot day in June. Now, from a block away, Fran-cis could hear them begging the firemen to leave just one hydrant open. He could imagine them hopping back and forth as the pavement grew hot again under their feet.

He looked at his watch and back at the station house door and won-dered where Stanhope could be.

Eighty-eight degrees already and not even ten o'clock in the morning.

This was the great shock of America, winters that would cut the face off a person, summers that were as thick and as soggy as bogs. "You whine like a narrowback," his uncle Patsy had said to him that morning. "The heat, the heat, the heat." But Patsy pulled pints inside a cool pub all day. Francis would be walking a beat, dark rings under his arms within fifteen minutes.

"Where's Stanhope?" Francis asked a pair of fellow rookies also heading out for patrol.

"Trouble with his locker, I think," one said back.

Finally, after another whole minute ticked by, Brian Stanhope came bounding down the station house steps. He and Francis had met on the first day of academy, and it was by chance that they'd both ended up at the Four-One. In academy, they'd been in a tactics class together, and after a week or so Stanhope approached Francis as they were filing out the classroom door. "You're Irish, right? Off the boat Irish, I mean?"

Francis said he was from the west, from Galway. And he'd taken a plane, but he didn't say that part.

"I thought so. So's my girlfriend. She's from Dublin. So let me ask you something."

To Francis, Dublin felt as far from Galway as New York did, but to a Yank, he supposed, it was all the same.

Francis braced for something more personal than he wanted to be asked. It was one of the first things he'd noticed about America, that everyone felt at ease asking each other any question that came into their minds. Where do you live, who do you live with, what's your rent, what did you do last weekend? To Francis, who felt embarrassed lining up his groceries on the checkout belt of the Associated in Bay Ridge, it was all a little too much. "Big night," the checkout clerk had commented last time he was there. A six-pack of Budweiser. A pair of potatoes. Deodorant.

Brian said that he'd noticed his girl didn't hang around with any other Irish. She was only eighteen. You'd think she'd have come over with a friend or a cousin or something but she'd come alone. It seemed to him she could have at least found a bunch of Irish girls to live with. God knew they were all over the place. She was a nurse in training at Montefiore and lived in hospital housing with a colored girl, also a nurse. Was that the way it was for the Irish? Because he'd dated a Russian girl for a while and the only people she hung around with were other Russians.

"I'm Irish, too," Stanhope said. "But back a ways."

That was another thing about America. Everyone was Irish, but back a ways.

"Might be a sign of intelligence, keeping away from our lot," Francis said with a straight face. It took Stanhope a minute.

———

At graduation, Mayor Lindsay stood at the podium and from his third row seat Francis thought about how strange it was to see in person a man he'd only ever seen on TV. Francis had been born in New York, was taken back to Ireland as an infant, and had returned just before his nineteenth birthday with ten American dollars and citizenship. His father's brother, Patsy, had picked him up from JFK, taken Francis's duffel from his hand and thrown it on the backseat. "Welcome home," he'd said. The idea of this teeming, foreign place as home was mystifying. On his first full day in America, Patsy put him to work behind the bar at the pub he owned on Third Avenue and Eightieth Street in Bay Ridge. There was a framed shamrock over the door. The first time a woman came in and asked him for a beer, he'd taken out a highball glass and set it down in front of her. "What's this?" she asked. "A half beer?" She looked down the row at the other people sitting at the bar, all men, all with pints in front of them.

He'd shown her the pint glass. "This is what you want?" he'd asked. "The full of it?" And understanding, finally, that he was new to the bar, new to America, she'd leaned over to cup his face, to brush the hair off his forehead.

"That's the one, sweetie," she'd said.

One day, when Francis had been in New York for about a year, a pair of young cops came in. They had a sketch of someone they were looking for, wanted to know if anyone at the bar recognized him. They joked around with Patsy, with Francis, with each other. When they were leaving, Francis mustered up some of that American inquisitiveness. How hard was it to get on the cops? How was the pay? For a few seconds their faces were inscrutable. It was February; Francis was wearing an old cable sweater that had been Patsy's, and felt shabby next to the officers in their pressed jackets, their caps that sat rightly atop their heads. Finally, the shorter of the two said that before becoming a cop he'd been working at his cousin's car wash on Flushing Avenue. Even when it all went automated, the sprayers would get him and in the winters he'd end the day frozen through. It was too brutal. Plus it was a lot better telling girls he was a cop than telling them he worked a car wash.

The other young cop looked a little disgusted. He'd joined because his father was a cop. And two of his uncles. And his grandfather. It was in his blood.

Francis thought about it through that winter, paying more attention to the cops in the neighborhood, on the subways, moving barricades, on television. He went to the local station house to ask about the test, the timing, how it all worked and when. When Francis mentioned his plan to Uncle Patsy, Patsy said it was a sound idea, all he needed was twenty years and then he'd have his pension. Francis noticed that Patsy said "twenty years" as if it were nothing, a mere blink, though at that moment it was more than the length of Francis's whole life. After twenty years, as long as he didn't get killed, he could do something else if he wanted. He saw his life split up into blocks of twenty, and for the first time he wondered how many blocks he'd get. The best part was he'd still be young, Patsy said. He wished he'd thought of it when he was Francis's age.

———

After graduation, his class had been split into groups to do field training in different parts of the city. He and thirty others, Brian Stanhope among them, were sent to Brownsville, and then to the Bronx, where the real job began. Francis was twenty-two by then. Brian was only twenty-one. Francis didn't know Brian well, but it was comforting to look across the room at muster and see a familiar face. Nothing, so far, had happened the way they'd been told things would happen. The station house itself was the exact opposite of what Francis had imagined when he decided to apply to the police academy. The outside was bad enough—the façade chipped and peeling, covered in bird shit and crowned in barbed wire—but inside was worse. There wasn't a surface in the place that wasn't damp or sticky or peeling. The radiator in the muster room had broken in half and someone had shoved an old pan underneath to catch the drips. Plaster rained from the ceiling and landed on their desks, their heads, their paperwork. Thirty perps were pushed into holding cells meant for two or three. Instead of being paired with more seasoned partners, all the rookies were sent out with other rookies. "The blind leading the blind," Sergeant Russell had joked, and promised it would only be for a little while. "Don't do anything stupid."

Now, Gleeson and Stanhope walked away from the smoldering building and headed north. From the distance came the clang of yet another fire alarm. Both young patrolmen knew the boundaries of their precinct on a map, but neither of them had seen those boundaries in person yet. The patrol cars were assigned by seniority, and the eight-to-four tour was heavy with seniority. They could have taken the bus to the farthest edge and walked back, but Stanhope said he hated taking the bus in uniform, hated the flare-up of tension when he boarded through the back door and every face looked over to size him up.

"Well, then let's walk," Francis had suggested.

Now, with rivers of perspiration coursing down their backs, they made their way block after block, each man with stick, cuffs, radio, fire-arm, ammo, flashlight, gloves, pencil, pad, and keys swaying from his belt. Some blocks were nothing but rubble and burned-out cars, and they scanned for movement within the wreckage. A girl was throwing a tennis ball against the face of a building and catching it on the bounce. A pair of crutches lay across their path and Stanhope kicked them. Any building with even a partial wall left standing was covered in graffiti. Tag upon tag upon tag, the colorful loops and curves implied motion, suggested life, and taken together they looked almost violently bright against a backdrop that was mostly gray.

The eight-to-four tour was a gift, Francis knew. Unless there were warrants to be executed, there was a good chance all would be quiet until lunch. When they finally turned onto Southern Boulevard, they felt like travelers who'd crossed a desert, grateful to be on the other side. Where the side streets were nearly empty, ghost-like, the boulevard was busy with passing cars, a menswear store that sold suits in every color, a series of liquor stores, a card shop, a barber, a bar. In the distance, a patrol car flashed its lights at them in greeting and rolled on.

"My wife is expecting," Stanhope said when neither of them had said anything for a while. "Due around Thanksgiving."

"The Irish girl?" Francis asked. "You married her?" He tried to re-member: were they engaged back in academy when Stanhope had told him about her? He counted toward November—just four months away.

"Yup," Stanhope said. "Two weeks ago." A city hall wedding. Dinner on Twelfth Street at a French place he'd read about in the paper; he'd had to point at his menu because he couldn't pronounce anything. Anne had to change her outfit last minute because the dress she'd planned on wearing was already too tight.

"She wants a priest to marry us once the baby comes. We couldn't find a parish that would do it quickly, even seeing her belly. Anne says maybe she'll find a priest who can bless the wedding and baptize the baby on the same day. Down the road, I mean."

"Married is married," Francis said, and offered his hearty congratulations. He hoped Stanhope didn't see that for a second there he'd been trying to do the math. He didn't care, really, it was just a habit brought from home, a habit he'd lose, no doubt, the longer he stayed in America. People went to Mass in shorts and T-shirts here. Not long ago he'd seen a woman driving a taxi. People walked around Times Square in their knickers.

"You want to see her?" Stanhope asked, taking off his hat. There, tucked inside the lining, was a snapshot of a pretty blond woman with a long, slim neck. Next to it a Saint Michael prayer card. Also tucked in the lining was a photo of a younger Brian Stanhope with another guy.

"Who's that?" Francis asked.

"My brother, George. That's us at Shea."

Francis had not thought to put any photos in his hat yet, though he, too, had a Saint Michael prayer card folded in his wallet. Francis had asked Lena Teobaldo to marry him on the same day he'd graduated from academy, and she'd said yes. Now he imagined that would be him soon, telling people there was a baby on the way. Lena was half-Polish, half-Italian, and sometimes when he watched her—searching for something in her bag, or peeling an apple with her knuckle guiding the blade—he felt a shiver of panic that he'd almost not met her. What if he hadn't come to America? What if her parents hadn't come to America? Where else but in America would a Polack and an Italian get together and make a girl like Lena? What if he hadn't been at the pub the morning she came in to ask if her family could book the back room for a party? Her sister was going to college, she told him. She'd gotten a full scholarship, that's how smart she was.

"That'll be you, maybe, when you graduate from high school," Francis had said, and she'd laughed, said she'd graduated the year before, that college was not in the cards for her but that was fine because she liked her job. She had a head of wild curls, brown shoulders above some strapless thing she was wearing. She was in the data processing pool at General Motors on Fifth Avenue, just a few floors above FAO Schwarz. He didn't know what FAO Schwarz was. He'd only been in America for a few months.

"People keep asking me if we're going to stay in the city," Stanhope said. "We're in Queens now, but the place is tiny."

Francis shrugged. He didn't know anything about the towns outside the city, but he didn't see himself in an apartment for the rest of his life. He imagined land. A garden. Space to breathe. All Francis knew was after the wedding he and Lena would stay with her parents to save money.

"You ever heard of a town called Gillam?" Stanhope asked.

"No."

"No, me neither. But that guy Jaffe? I think he's a sergeant? He said it's only about twenty miles north of here and there are a lot of guys there on the job. He says the houses all have big lawns and kids deliver the newspapers from their bicycles just like in *The Brady Bunch*."

"What's it called again?" Francis asked.

"Gillam," Stanhope said.

"Gillam," Francis repeated.

In another block, Stanhope said he was thirsty, that a beer wouldn't be the worst idea. Francis pretended not to hear the suggestion. The patrolmen in Brownsville drank on the job sometimes but only if they were in squad cars, not out in the open. He wasn't a coward but they'd only just started. If either of them got in trouble, neither of them had a hook.

"Wouldn't mind one of them sodas with ice cream in it," Francis said.

When they walked into the diner, Francis felt the trapped heat wafting at him despite the door having been propped open with a pair of bricks. The elderly man behind the counter was wearing a paper hat that had gone yellow, a lopsided bow tie. A fat black fly swooped frantically near the man's head as he looked back and forth between the policemen.

"The soda's cold, buddy? The milk's good?" Stanhope asked. His voice and the breadth of his shoulders filled the quiet, and Francis looked down at his shoes, then over at the plate glass, which was threaded with cracks, held together with tape. It was a good job, he told himself. An honorable job. There'd been rumors there wouldn't even be a class of 1973 with the city slashing its budget, but his class had squeaked through.

Just then, their radios crackled to life. There'd been some morning banter, calls put out and answered, but this was different. Francis turned up the volume. There'd been a shot fired and a possible robbery in progress at a grocery store located at 801 Southern Boulevard. Francis looked at the door of the coffee shop: 803. The man behind the counter pointed to the wall, at whatever was on the other side. "Dominicans," he said, and the word floated in the air, hovered there.

"I didn't hear a shot. Did you?" Francis said. The dispatcher repeated the call. A tremor jumped from Francis's throat to his groin, but he fumbled for his radio as he moved toward the door.

Francis in the lead, Stanhope right behind him, the two rookies unsnapped the holsters on their hips as they approached the door of the grocery. "Shouldn't we wait?" Stanhope asked, but Francis kept moving forward past a pair of payphones, past a caged fan that stood beating the air. "Police!" he shouted as they stepped farther inside the store. If there'd been any customers there when the robbery was taking place, there was no sign of them now.

"Gleeson," Stanhope said, nodding at the blood-sprayed cigarette cartons behind the single register up front. The pattern showed the vigor of someone's heartbeat: blood that appeared more purple than red reaching as far as the water-stained ceiling, settling thickly on the rusted vent. Francis looked quickly to the floor behind the register, and then followed the grisly path down aisle three, until finally, lying in front of a broom closet, a man sprawled on his side, his face slack, an astonishing amount of blood in a growing pool beside him. While Stanhope called it in, Francis pressed two fingers to the soft hollow under the man's jaw. He straightened the man's arm and put the same two fingers to his wrist.

"It's too hot for this," Stanhope said as he frowned down at the body. He opened the fridge next to him, removed a bottle of beer, popped the cap off by striking it against the end of a shelf, and chugged it without taking a breath. Francis thought of the town Stanhope had mentioned, walking in his bare feet through cool, dew-damp grass. There was no predicting where life would go. There was no real way for a person to try something out, see if he liked it—the words he'd chosen when he told his uncle Patsy that he'd gotten into the police academy—because you try it and try it and try it a little longer and next thing it's who you are. One minute he'd been standing in a bog on the other side of the Atlantic and next thing he knew he was a cop. In America. In the worst neighborhood of the best known city in the world.

As the dead man's face turned ashen, Francis thought about how desperate the man looked, the way his neck was stretched and his chin pitched upward, like a drowning man craning for the surface of the water. It was only his second dead body. The first, a floater that had risen to the surface in April after a winter in New York Harbor, was not recognizable as a person, and perhaps for that reason it was barely real to him. The lieutenant who'd taken him along told him to get sick over the side of the boat if he wanted to, but Francis said he was fine. He thought of what the Christian Brothers had said about a body being merely a vessel, about the spirit being the pilot light of one's self. That first body, a water-logged piece of meat hauled up, dripping, onto the boat's deck, had parted with its soul long before Francis had laid eyes on it, but this one—bit by bit, Francis watched it depart. In the old country someone would have opened a window to let the man's spirit fly out, but any souls

10

let loose here in the South Bronx would be free only so far as they could bat around four walls until, exhausted, they wilted in the heat and were forgotten.

"Prop that door, will you?" Francis called. "I can barely breathe."

Then, Francis heard something and froze. He placed a hand on his gun.

Stanhope looked at him, wide-eyed. There it was again, the whisper-soft sound of a sneaker on linoleum, listening to them as Francis listened back, three human hearts pounding in their cages, another lying still. "Step out with your hands up," Francis called, and then, all at once, they saw him: a tall and gangly teenager in a white undershirt, white shorts, white sneakers, hiding in the narrow space between the refrigerated case and the wall.

———

An hour later Francis was holding the kid's hands, rolling each finger in ink and then on the card, then four fingers together, then the thumb. First the left hand, and then the right, and then the left again, three cards total—local, state, federal. After the first card there was a rhythm to it, like an ancient dance: grasp, roll, release. The kid's hands were warm but dry, and if he was nervous Francis couldn't detect it. Stanhope was already writing up his report. The grocer had died well before the ambulance arrived and now here was the killer, his hands as soft as a child's, his fingernails well tended, clean. The kid's hands were loose, pliable. By the third card the kid knew what to do, began helping.

Later, after all the paperwork, the older cops said it was customary to take a guy out for his first arrest. The arrest had been credited to Francis, but they took Stanhope, too, bought him round after round while he told the story differently each time. The kid had stepped out and threatened them. The blood was dripping from every wall. Stanhope had blocked the exit while Francis wrestled the perp to the ground.

"Your partner," one of the older cops said to Francis. "He's creative."

Stanhope and Francis looked at each other. Were they partners?

"You're partners until the captain tells you otherwise," the older cop said.

The cook came out of the kitchen carrying plates piled high with burgers, told them it was on the house.

"You going home already?" Stanhope said to Francis a little later.

"Yes and so should you. Go home to your pregnant wife," Francis said.

"The pregnant wife is why he's staying out," one of the others cracked.

———

It took an hour and fifteen minutes by subway to get back to Bay Ridge. As soon as Francis walked in, he stripped to his boxers and climbed into the bed Patsy had crammed into his living room for him. Someone had called the kid's mother. Someone else had driven him to Central Booking. He'd said he was thirsty, so Francis had gotten him a soda from the machine. The kid gulped it down and then asked if he could fill the can with water from the tap. Francis went to the bathroom and filled it. "You're a fool," one of guys in plainclothes had said. He still had to learn everyone's name. Who knew? Maybe the grocer had done something bad to the kid. Maybe he deserved what he got.

Patsy was out somewhere. Francis called Lena, prayed she'd pick up and he wouldn't have to go through her mother.

"Did something happen today?" she asked after they'd chatted for a few minutes. "You don't usually call this late." Francis looked at the clock and saw it was near midnight. The paperwork and the beers had taken longer than he'd thought.

"Sorry. Go back to sleep."

She was silent for so long he thought she had.

"Were you afraid?" she asked. "You have to tell me."

"No," he said. And he hadn't been, or at least he hadn't felt what he understood fear to be.

"What then?"

"I don't know."

"Try to keep it outside yourself, Francis," she said, as if she'd been listening to his thoughts. "We have a plan, you and me."

GILLAM

one

GILLAM WAS NICE ENOUGH but lonely, Lena Teobaldo thought when she first saw it. It was the kind of place that if she were there on vacation she'd love for the first two days, and then by the third day she'd start looking forward to leaving. It didn't seem quite real: the apple trees and maples, the shingled houses with front porches, the cornfields, the dairy, the kids playing stickball in the street as if they didn't notice their houses were sitting on a half acre of grass. Later, she'd figure out that the kids played the games their parents had played growing up in the city. Stickball. Hopscotch. Kick the can. When a father taught a son how to throw a ball, he marched that boy to the middle of the road as if they were on a block tight with tenements, because that's where he'd learned from his father. She'd agreed to the trip because it was something to do and if she'd stayed in Bay Ridge that Saturday, her mother would have made her bring food to Mrs. Venard, who'd never been right since her boy went missing in Vietnam.

Her cousin Karolina's dress was hanging on the hook behind Lena's bedroom door, altered and ready for Lena to wear in just six days' time. She'd gotten her shoes, her veil. There was nothing more to do other than wait, so when Francis asked if she wanted to take a little trip to check out a town he'd heard about through a guy at work, she'd said sure, it was a beautiful fall day, it would be nice to get out to the country for a few hours, she'd pack a picnic lunch. They unpacked that lunch on a bench outside the public library, and in the time it took to unwrap their sandwiches, eat them, sip all the tea from the thermos, only one person entered the library. A northbound train pulled into the station and three people got off. Across the town square was a deli, and next to it a five-and-dime with a stroller parked outside. Francis had driven them in Lena's father's Datsun—her brother Karol's copy of *Led Zeppelin IV* stuck in the tape deck. Lena didn't have a driver's license, didn't have the first idea how to drive. She'd assumed she'd never have to learn.

"So? What do you think?" Francis asked later as they eased back onto the Palisades Parkway. Lena opened the window and lit a cigarette.

"Pretty," she said. "Quiet." She slipped off her shoes and put her feet up on the dashboard. She'd put in for two weeks of vacation time— a week before her wedding plus a week after—and that day, a Saturday, was her first day of the longest stretch of days she'd had off in three years.

"You saw the train? There's also a bus that goes to Midtown," he said. She thought it a random piece of information until it hit her like a kick in the shin that he wanted to live there. He hadn't said that. He'd said only that he wanted to take a spin in the car, check out a place he'd heard of. She thought he only wanted a break from all the wedding talk. Relatives from Italy and Poland were already arriving, and her parents' apartment was packed with food and people every hour of the day. No one from Ireland was coming but some relation of Francis's who'd emi-grated to Chicago had sent a piece of Irish china. Francis said he didn't mind. It was the bride's day anyway. But now she saw he had a plan in mind. It seemed so far-fetched she decided not to mention it again un-less he brought it up first.

———

A few weeks later, the wedding over and done with, their guests long departed, Lena back at work with a new name and a new band on her finger, Francis said it was time for them to move out of her parents' apartment. He said that everyone had to tiptoe through the narrow living room if Lena's sister, Natusia, was in there with her books. Karol was almost always in a bad mood, probably because the newlyweds had taken over his bedroom. There was nowhere to be alone. Every moment Francis spent there, he said, he felt like he should be offering to help with something, do something. Their wedding gifts were stacked in corners and Lena's mother was always admonishing everyone to be careful, think of the crystal. Lena thought it was nice, a half dozen people sitting down to dinner together, sometimes more, depending on who stopped by. For the first time she wondered if she'd known him well enough to marry him.

"But where?" she said.

They looked on Staten Island. They looked within Bay Ridge. They climbed walk-ups in Yorkville, Morningside Heights, the Village. They walked through houses filled with other people's things, their photos displayed on ledges, their polyester flower arrangements. On all those visits, Lena could see the road to Gillam approaching like an exit on the freeway. They'd socked away the cash gifts they'd gotten at the wedding plus most of their salaries and had enough for a down payment.

One Saturday morning in January 1974, after he'd worked a midnight tour plus a few hours of overtime, Francis got to Bay Ridge and told Lena to get her coat, he'd found their house.

"I'm not going," she said, looking up from her coffee with her face set like stone. Angelo Teobaldo was doing a crossword across from her. Gosia Teobaldo had just cracked two eggs onto a skillet. Standing six foot two in his patrolman's uniform, Francis's face burned.

"He's your husband," Angelo said to his daughter. A reprimand. Like she'd left her toys scattered on the carpet and forgotten to put them away.

19

"You keep quiet," Gosia said, motioning for him to zip his lip. "We're having breakfast at Hinsch's," she announced, extinguishing the flame under the skillet.

"Let's just go see, Lena. We don't have to do anything you don't want to do."

"Oh, sure," Lena said.

An hour and twenty minutes later, Lena pressed her forehead against the glass of the passenger window and looked at the house that would be theirs. There was a brightly lettered For Sale sign outside. The hydrangea that would flower in June was just a clump of frostbitten sticks. The current owners were home, their Ford was in the driveway—so Francis kept the engine running.

"What's that? Are they rocks?" Toward the back of the property were five huge rocks, lined up by Mother Nature hundreds of millennia ago in ascending order, the tallest maybe five feet high.

"Boulders," Francis said. "They're all over this area. The realtor told me the builders left some as natural dividers between the houses. They remind me of Ireland."

Lena looked at him as if to say, So *that's* why you brought me here. He'd met a realtor. His mind was made up. The houses on that street—Jefferson—and the surrounding streets—Washington, Adams, Madison, Monroe—were closer together than the houses farther from town, and Francis said that was because these houses were older, built back in the 1920s when there was a tannery in town and everyone walked to work. He thought Lena would like that. There was a porch out front.

"Who will I talk to?" she asked.

"To our neighbors," he said. "To the people you meet. You make friends faster than anyone. Besides, you'll still be in the city every day. You'll have the girls you work with. The bus stops right at the end of the block. You don't even have to learn to drive if you don't want to." He'd be her driver, he joked.

He couldn't explain to her that he needed the trees and the quiet as a correction for what he saw on the job, how crossing a bridge and having that physical barrier between him and his beat felt like leaving one life and entering another. In his imagination he had it all organized: Officer Gleeson could exist there, and Francis Gleeson could exist here. In academy, some of the instructors were old-timers who claimed they'd never in their thirty-year careers so much as drawn their weapons, but after only six months Francis had drawn several times. His sergeant had just recently shot a thirty-year-old man in the chest during a standoff beside the Bruckner Expressway, and the man died on the scene. But it was a good kill, they all said, because the man was a known junkie and had been armed. Sergeant hadn't seemed the slightest bit concerned. Francis had nodded along with the rest of them and gone out for drinks when their tour was over. But the next day, when someone had to meet with the man's mother and the mother of his children to explain to them what had happened since they wouldn't leave the waiting room for anything, it seemed to Francis that he was the only one who felt rattled. The man had had a mother. He'd been a father. He hadn't always been a junkie. Standing by the coffeepot and wishing the women would go the hell home, it was as if he could see the whole rest of the man's life—not just the moment he'd foolishly swung around while holding his little .22.

And though he told Lena none of this, only that work was fine, things were busy, she sensed the thing he wasn't saying and looked at the house again. She imagined a bright row of flowers at the foot of the porch. They could have a guest bedroom. It was true that the bus from Gillam to Midtown Manhattan would take less time than the subway from Bay Ridge.

———

In April 1974, just a few weeks after they packed a rental truck and moved north to Gillam, a local physician completed an internal exam in his little office beside the movie theater and told Lena she was nine weeks along. Her days of running for the bus were numbered, he said. Her only job now was to eat right, to keep her mind peaceful, to not spend too much time on her feet. She and Francis were walking around the house looking for a place to sow a tomato plant when she told him. He halted, baffled.

"You know how this happened, right?" she asked with her most serious expression.

"You should be sitting," he said, dropping the plant and grabbing her by the shoulders, steering her to the patio. The previous owners had left behind two rusted wrought-iron chairs, and he was glad he hadn't thrown them away. He stood, then sat across from her, then stood.

"Should I stay here until November?" Lena asked.

She stopped working at twenty-five weeks because her mother was driving her crazy, saying all those people rushing through the Port Authority Bus Terminal might elbow her, might knock her down. On the day she fitted the dustcover over her typewriter for the last time, the other girls threw her a party in the lunchroom, made her wear a baby's bonnet they decorated with ribbons from the gifts.

Home all day with more free time than she'd ever had in her life, she'd only begun to get to know the elderly couple who lived in the house to the right of theirs when the woman died of bladder cancer, and her husband just two weeks later of a massive stroke. For a while, the empty house bore no sign of change and Lena began to think of it as a family member whom everyone had forgotten to tell. The wind chime they'd hung from their mailbox still tinkled. A pair of work gloves lay on top of their garbage can as if someone might come back and pull them on. Eventually, the edges of their lawn began to look craggy. Newspapers swollen with rain, bleached by the sun, made a pile at the top of their driveway. One day, since no one seemed to be doing anything about it, Lena went over and cleared them away. Every once in a while a realtor would lead a couple up the driveway, but none of it seemed to go anywhere. At some point Lena realized that she could go a whole day without speaking or hearing a single human voice if she kept the TV turned off.

Natalie Gleeson was born in November of 1974, one month to the day after Francis and Lena's first wedding anniversary. Lena's mother came to stay for a week but she couldn't leave Angelo alone any longer than that. The man couldn't so much as boil water for tea. She said she was coming to help Lena, but she spent most of the day leaning over the bassinet and cooing, "I'm your busha, little one. It's very nice to meet you."

"You take the baby out every day, no matter the weather, and you walk around the neighborhood for one hour," Gosia advised her daughter. Natalie was asleep in the pram with a wool blanket packed around her. "Look around at the trees, at the nice even sidewalks. Wave to your neighbors and think about what a lucky girl you are. What a lucky baby she is. She has a drawer full of clothes already. Francis is a good man. Repeat it to yourself again and again. Go into the shops. Tell them your name and that you just moved here. Everybody loves a new baby."

Lena began to cry. When the bus approached, she felt a wild temptation to climb aboard behind her mother, take the baby in her arms, leave the pram on the sidewalk, and never return.

"When you were born, I used to daydream about leaving you with Mrs. Shefflin—remember Mrs. Shefflin? My idea was I'd ask her to watch you while I ran out for a carton of milk and then I'd never come back."

"What? Really?" Lena said, her tears instantly drying. It was so unexpected she started laughing. Then she was laughing so hard she was crying again.

———

And then, on the Friday of Memorial Day weekend 1975, Lena was nursing Natalie in the rocker upstairs when she looked out the window and saw a moving truck come to a stop outside. She'd just learned she was pregnant again, two months gone already, and her doctor had joked that her Irish husband had almost given her Irish twins. The realtor's sign had been removed a few weeks earlier, and now that she thought about it, she remembered Francis saying something about the house having finally sold. Lately she felt so tired it was hard to hold a thought in her head.

She rushed down the stairs and out onto the porch with Natalie tucked into the crook of her arm. "Hello!" she called out to her new neighbors, and later, when she recounted the meeting to Francis, she said she was afraid she'd said something corny and made a bad impression. Natalie was still hungry, and was sucking on her little fist.

A blond woman in a pretty eyelet sundress was walking up the driveway carrying a lamp in each hand.

"You bought the house," Lena said. Her voice was an octave too high. "I'm Lena. We just moved here last year. Welcome! Do you need any help?"

"I'm Anne," the new neighbor said, and Lena heard traces of a brogue. "That's Brian, my husband." She smiled politely. "How old's the baby?"

"Six months," Lena said. Finally, on the first warm day of the year, there was a new person to admire the baby, to offer a finger for Natalie to grip. She wanted to ask a thousand questions at once. Where had they moved from, how long had they been married, what made them choose Gillam, how did they meet, what kind of music did they like, what part of Ireland was Anne from, did they want to come over for a drink later, once they'd unpacked?

Anne was very beautiful, Lena noted, but there was something else about her, too. Once, at work, when Lena was passed over for a promotion, her boss Mr. Eden had said that it was no reflection of Lena's performance, it was just that the other woman had more presence, and the promotion would mean greeting clients. Lena had no idea what he meant but she didn't want to seem stupid, so she accepted his explanation and went back to her desk. It was her accent, maybe. Too Brooklyn. Maybe it was her habit of fixing her hair at her desk after lunch. One time she'd gotten a strand of celery caught between her molars and for the life of her she couldn't get it out with her tongue, so she'd jammed her finger into her mouth and coaxed it out with her fingernail. Now she wondered if presence was the thing her new neighbor had, if it was something a person had to be born with and could never be learned.

Anne glanced over her shoulder at her husband as she put her hand flat against her own stomach, and lowered her voice. "She'll have company in a few months."

"How wonderful!" Lena said.

Brian Stanhope, who had not yet said hello, was crossing the lawn behind them just then and heard what his wife said. He staggered as if he'd tripped on something, and instead of approaching the women as it seemed he was about to do, he turned sharply and kept unloading the truck. Lena asked Anne if she felt tired, if she'd been sick. It was all normal, she said. Every pregnancy is different. Keeping crackers by her bed might help. If she ever let herself get hungry, she'd end up feeling sick all day. Anne nodded but the advice seemed to slide right by her, and she didn't seem to want to discuss it with Brian listening. Lena remembered that she hadn't heeded much advice either. Every woman learns on the job.

Eventually, Brian came over to them. "I work with Francis," he said. "Well, I used to. Until a few weeks ago I was in the Four-One."

"You're kidding," Lena said. "What a coincidence!"

"Not really," Brian said, grinning. "He's the one who told me about the house. He didn't say?"

Later, when Francis got home, she wanted to know why he hadn't told her they were coming. She could have made a welcome party, had food ready. But he had told her, he insisted. He said the house sold, she said, but not that it sold to his friend.

"Well, I don't know about friend," Francis said.

"You work with him. You eat meals with him. You've known him since academy. Weren't you partners for a while? He's your friend," Lena said.

"I'm sorry," Francis said. "I forgot. He got transferred. I haven't seen

25

him in a few weeks." He pulled her to his chest. "What's the wife like? They lost a baby, did I tell you that? A stillborn, I think. Probably going on two years ago now."

Lena gasped and thought of Natalie's warm belly rising and falling in her crib upstairs. "How awful." She recalled with horror the advice she'd offered, how silently Anne had taken it.

———

Lena paid attention to her neighbor's belly to see how it was growing, but she wore everything so loose—oversized nursing scrubs on work-days, and on her days off peasant blouses and skirts so long they almost skimmed the ground. Lena often watched Anne hurry to her car in the mornings, keys in hand, and felt a small flame of jealousy for the other woman's freedom. Sometimes she'd go out to the mailbox when she saw that Anne was outside and try to approach her, to start a conversation, but most times Anne just gave Lena a light wave and went in. A few times, when she saw Anne's car was in the driveway, she'd gone to their door and knocked but no one ever answered. Once, she stuck a note in their mailbox asking if they wanted to come to dinner some Saturday night—they could name the date—but got no reply.

Francis said maybe they'd never gotten the note. Maybe the mailman had taken it. "Can you ask Brian?" Lena asked.

"Listen," Francis said. "Don't worry about it. Some people don't like to make friends so close. I can understand that, can't you?"

"I understand completely," Lena said, then took Natalie into her arms and went up to their bedroom to sit on the edge of the bed.

———

Summer came and went. Brian was outside raking their yard one Satur-day when Lena spotted Francis chatting with him on the narrow strip of grass between their driveways. Francis was laughing so hard he had to bend over a little to catch his breath. Sara was born, another healthy girl, except this time around Lena couldn't rest when the baby rested because Natalie was there, too, unsteady on her feet and always toddling toward the stairs. Eventually a full nine months went by since the Stanhopes had moved in, and no matter how early the pregnancy had been on the day they arrived, baby Stanhope would have been in the world by then. Never had Lena detected crisis from next door, the house cloaked with the kind of sadness a lost baby would bring. One day, after arriving home from the grocery store, both babies wailing from the backseat, Lena stood at the open trunk of the car considering the dozen bags she had to get inside when she glanced up and found Anne staring at her from the end of their front porch. Lena had learned to drive but she wasn't confident about it. The only route she'd dared so far without Francis was to the grocery store and back. She was afraid she'd done something wrong and Anne had seen.

"Hello!" Lena called over, but Anne turned her back and went inside.

———

When it was almost Sara's first birthday, Lena observed that Anne's belly appeared to be growing. She badgered Francis to ask Brian next time he saw him.

"Ah, come on," Francis said. "They'll tell us if they want to tell us."

But one day it must have come up. Lena was sewing a button onto one of Francis's shirts when he came into the kitchen to wash his hands. Without turning from the sink, he said she was right, the Stanhopes were indeed having a baby. Being a man he hadn't gotten a single detail, but Lena knew Anne must be close to her due date when her car stayed in their driveway all day and she no longer seemed to go to work. Lena waited for the right time, the right day, and then she put Sara in the playpen, turned on the television for Natalie, folded up the old baby swing, and trudged across the snow-dusted driveways to the Stanhopes' front door. Anne seemed taken aback by the gesture, and though she didn't invite Lena in, she did ask if she wouldn't mind demonstrating how to unfold it, how to use the straps. Lena, thrilled, took off her mittens to open it on the Stanhopes' porch, to show her how to unsnap the fabric if it needed to be washed, how to drape it around the frame and secure it. As they talked, Anne, who was wearing only a thin wool cardigan, said she was due the following week, and Lena told her what she hadn't even told her mother yet, that she was pregnant, too. Since she estimated her own due date was about six months behind Anne's, she figured the Stanhope baby could occupy the swing for six months—which the manufacturer had printed as the maximum age anyway—and then Anne could pass it back. They could pool what they had and try to help each other. Anne was going to stay home with the baby for a while and then decide about work. She liked working, she told Lena, as if it was a confession, and Lena, feeling an opening, told her that she understood, that being home with a baby was more difficult than it looked from the outside, more difficult than it seemed like it should be.

"If you need anything—if Brian isn't home when the time comes—or anything at all, you know where to find me." As she crossed back over the driveways, she thought: It was just that we got off on the wrong foot. She thought: She probably lost that baby and couldn't face me, having two. She thought: Maybe I offended her somehow, without realizing, and now it's all water under the bridge.

Peter was born less than a week later, nine pounds ten ounces.

"It was gruesome," Brian said to Francis.

"As far as I know they're all like that," Francis said. And then: "You didn't see . . . that time when . . . ?"

"No, no. It was nothing like this. They knew, you see, beforehand."

"I didn't mean to—"

"Not at all. It's fine."

Anne held her son on her lap for the ride home from the hospital, and when she carried him into the house, the corner of his thick blue blanket flapped in the bitter February wind. Lena had Natalie and Sara scribble "Welcome Home" drawings, then left them outside the Stanhopes' door, weighted down with a poppy-seed loaf she'd baked that day.

The next morning, while Francis was waiting for the teakettle to boil and Lena was ladling oatmeal into bowls, the sound of the doorbell rang out. The wind had rattled the house all night long, and the morning news said it had brought down tree limbs all over the county. Francis thought the doorbell had something to do with that, someone wanting help, someone alerting them to something, a downed wire, a closed road. Instead, he opened the door to find Anne Stanhope wearing a beautiful ankle-length camel hair coat buttoned to the throat, and holding the baby swing. She was wearing bright red lipstick but there were dark circles under her eyes. "Here," she said, holding the swing out to him.

"Is everything all right?" Lena asked over her husband's shoulder. "Is the baby all right?"

"I can take care of my own baby," Anne said. "And I can bake for my own husband."

Lena went silent, wide-eyed. "Of course you can!" she said finally. "I just know it's hard in the beginning so I thought—"

"It's not hard at all. He's a perfect baby. We're fine."

Francis found purchase inside the exchange long before Lena. "Well, thanks a lot," he said, taking the swing and beginning to shut the door, but Lena stopped him.

"Wait a second. Just wait a second. I think there's been a misunderstanding. Keep the swing," she said. "The baby will nap in it. Really. We're not even using it."

"Are you listening?" Anne said. "I don't want it. If I need something for my son, I'm fully capable of buying it."

"Fair enough," Francis said, and this time closed the door. He tossed the folded swing toward the couch, where it bounced off the cushion and clattered to the floor. While Lena stood openmouthed in the middle of the living room, a wooden spoon in her hand, he shrugged and said: "It's him I feel sorry for. He's a nice fella."

"What in the world did I do to her?" Lena asked.

"Not a thing," Francis said, already headed back into the kitchen to his tea and his newspaper. "Something's not right." He tapped the side of his head. "Just don't bother with her anymore."

———

Six months later, Kate was born into the swampy humidity of August. Lena always said she couldn't nurse Kate because as soon as they were skin to skin they'd both get so sweaty she'd slip right off. She gave up after only a day or two, and when Francis was on midnights he'd come home, drop his things by the door, and give Kate her first bottle of the day. It was such a break for Lena, and it was so sweet to see father and daughter staring at each other over the bottle while she drank, that Lena wished she'd bottle-fed all three. "You're a dote," Francis would say to the baby when she finished, and then flip her to his shoulder for a burp.

Peter, six months ahead, was eating cereal and applesauce while Kate was naked on her belly, learning to hold the weight of her own head. Later, they'd both wonder when their brains first registered the presence of the other. Could Peter hear Kate cry when the windows of both houses were open? When he learned to stand up to the porch railing, did he ever see Kate's sisters pulling her along the sidewalk in their Radio Flyer and wonder who she was?

———

For the rest of her life, when asked to recall her earliest memory, Kate would remember watching him run around the side of his house with a red ball in his hand and already knowing his name.

two

THE SNOW WAS SUPPOSED to skirt Gillam, was supposed to swing across the Hudson to Westchester County, over Connecticut, and then out to sea. But by the time Mrs. Duvin told her sixth grade class to open their social studies textbooks, they could all smell it coming in the heavy, steel-glinted air. Peter wrote "1988" in his notebook, even though they were fully two months into 1989. The radio left on a low volume in the faculty lounge carried the news that the storm had changed course and now the towns west of the Hudson could expect another twelve inches on top of the nine they'd gotten over the weekend. "Snow!" Jessica D'Angelis said, bolting upright at her desk and pointing to the window that faced the teachers' parking lot. Mrs. Duvin flicked the classroom lights on and off to remind them to collect themselves. Then, as if she'd forgotten why she'd come over to the light switch in the first place, she stood in the darkened classroom and looked over her students' heads to the sky outside.

When the PA popped to life, they could all hear Sister Margaret breathing into the microphone. "Due to the coming storm, classes will be dismissed at noon today. Your parents have been notified. Children who take the bus will begin lining up at eleven fifty-five."

Kate found it difficult to sit still on a normal day but with a snow-storm scuttling the classroom routine—they had to retrieve their lunch boxes from the lunch shelf and return them, uneaten, to their back-packs; they had to go over the vocab words at ten o'clock since they wouldn't be there at one fifteen—it was as if she'd lost the power of hearing. Peter could feel her frenetic buzzing all the way from his seat, two rows away. Mrs. Duvin was still talking at the front of the class-room, rapping on the blackboard, telling them not to move a muscle until her say-so while Kate was shoving folders and marbled notebooks into her bag, twisting around in her seat to get a better view out the windows. She wanted to make an ice rink in her backyard, she was say-ing to Lisa Gordon, who Peter could tell was trying to ignore her, or at least not be seen by Mrs. Duvin to be engaging her. Her dad had given her the idea, she said.

"Kath-leen Glee-son!" Mrs. Duvin said, isolating each part of Kate's name so there were four separate rebukes. But instead of sending her out into the hall like she usually did, she just gave her a pleading look and then pointed at the clock. At precisely 11:55, Kate, Peter, and the other bus kids were walking down the hall. Kate was swinging her backpack, walking on the toes of her navy bucks as if at any moment she might break into a sprint. When they got outside she slid across a patch of black ice, arms wheeling like in a cartoon.

Peter followed close behind her as they bumped down the aisle of the school bus to the emergency exit row. She paused at their seat to let him slide past—since kindergarten he'd been sitting by the window. As always, Peter threw his backpack to the floor and then slid down until his knees jammed up against the vinyl back of the seat in front of them. Kate knelt facing backward so that she could see and talk to everyone.

"You beat John this morning," Kate said as she settled in beside him. "Was he mad?" The boys played wall ball every morning while the girls clustered in groups to watch. Once, at the beginning of the year, Kate took position alongside the boys, and when one of them asked what she

32

thought she was doing, she looked around like it was the most obvious thing in the world, like it was a completely normal thing for her to join the game when in fact in all the years they'd been at St. Bartholomew's no girl had ever played before. She was fast, which kept her in for a few minutes, but the boys were stronger and, of course, gunning for her. She fumbled. She fumbled again. In no time she had three strikes and was standing at the wall with her hands flat against the brick while they pelted her in the butt, one by one. John Dills took a running start and threw from such close range that Peter winced and Kate took one hand off the wall to clutch the spot where she'd been hit.

"You're such a dick," Peter said when John returned to his spot, snickering. The girls looking on glanced between Kate and the boys and didn't know whom or what to root for. When it was his turn, Peter threw lightly, the ball barely brushing the back of Kate's legs, and they called him on it. "It's a stupid rule," he said, refusing to throw again, but strangely, Kate was the one most annoyed about it. "Why didn't you throw it for real?" she fumed later, glancing left and right to make sure no one could hear them. He was afraid he'd hurt her, he'd stammered. She didn't speak to him for the rest of the day.

"Hey, Kate," he said now. A thought had occurred to him when Mrs. Duvin was putting the homework on the board, of his mother coming into his room at dawn to look for something on his bookshelves. She'd been worked up about something through breakfast. He knew better than to ask. But then, several hours later, when everyone in class bent over their papers to copy what Mrs. Duvin was writing on the board, he drew a line between that morning and the last time he'd seen the model ship she'd given him after dinner the week before. It wasn't his birthday yet. Christmas had just passed. It was as seaworthy as any real ship, his mother had said proudly, an exact replica in miniature of Sir Francis Drake's Golden Hind, every mast and sail as it was on that great ship, everything historically accurate down to the long beak, the pintle and gudgeon rudders. His mother ignored his father when he asked how much it cost. His father looked at the box it had arrived in, examined the postage marks, looked for a packing slip. It was heavy, solid. Not a toy, exactly, but what?

"You know that model ship I showed you the other day?" Peter asked. "Do you remember if we left it outside?"

"No," Kate said. "Why? Can't find it?"

"No. And I think my mom was looking for it this morning."

Kate dropped down to sit on her heels. "We had it by the rocks. Oh, but then we floated it. Was that the same day?" There was a pile of snow that had melted in the sun, and they'd placed the gleaming wood boat in the narrow stream that flowed from the top of Kate's driveway to the street.

"I think I had it after that."

Kate turned, her wide hazel eyes looking at him steadily. It was like watching choppy water go smooth as glass. There was a time—kindergarten or first grade—when one of them might have idly taken the other's hand to crack the knuckles, to measure the breadth and length of their fingers against each other, to lock fists and declare a thumb war, and even then he could feel something in her settle, go still, when he had her full attention. But they'd gotten too old for thumb wars. She brushed her hair from her face and tucked it behind her ears. The others were calling her from the back of the bus. "Will you get in trouble?"

"No, it's fine," Peter said. He had a scab on his knuckle and he pried up the edge with his fingernail.

"But we'd better find it," she said.

Peter shrugged. "Yeah."

Over the years, whenever the subject of Peter's parents came up, Kate studied him and was uncharacteristically quiet. Only once, when they were sitting out by the rocks—Kate wearing black wool tights on her head so she could pretend the legs were two long ponytails that reached her waist—had she hinted that she noticed anything was different about his mom, compared to other moms. That day, they'd looked up in unison as his mother drove up the street. They watched her park her car, hurry into the house without looking left or right or saying hello to anyone. Kate's mother was outside pulling weeds. Mr. Maldonado was painting their mailbox post. Two houses down Mr. O'Hara was digging a hole to plant a sapling and had invited the kids on the block to help fill it in when he'd gotten the tree in place.

"Why is your mother like that?" Kate asked that day. The yards were small, shaded by heavy trees. Peter knew by the cracks of light between the branches and the rising chorus of cicadas that it would soon be time for all the kids to go inside. He had been hoping Mr. O'Hara would call for their help before his mother came home.

"Why is my mother like what?" Peter answered after a moment. They were in second grade, had just made First Holy Communion. Peter opened his hands as if in prayer, leaned over the tall grass between the two largest boulders—impossible to reach with a lawn mower no matter how hard Mr. Gleeson cursed and rammed his up against the crevice—and bringing his palms together he caught a grasshopper. He held the wings together with his thumbs so Kate could look at it more closely, and when he brought his hands to her face he could feel her warm breath on his wrists. They'd spent the summer trying to catch one, and there one was, sitting right beside them when they'd just about given up.

"Like she is. You know."

But he didn't know, really. And neither did Kate. So they let the subject drop.

———

After Central Ave. came Washington, then Madison, then Jefferson, and once the bus rumbled past the Berkwoods' pine tree, Peter could see his own driveway.

"We're gonna have a war," Kate said as she leaned into him to get a better look out the window. Half the kids had taken out their lunches and fished out the snacks. The bus smelled like potato chips and Hi-C. "Two teams. Twenty minutes to make ammo and then the war begins."

The bus bounced them up and down, jolted them forward and back. Branches, sky, and then he saw it: the maroon of her car. Beside him, he knew Kate spotted it, too.

"Okay, well, you'll ask, right?" Kate said. "You might be allowed."

"Yeah," Peter said.

They tumbled down the bus steps, one after the other, into the afternoon. "See ya maybe," Peter said, hitching his backpack up on his shoulder. The clouds were backlit, phosphorescent. Kate stood there for a moment like she'd forgotten something, and then she ran up her steps and into her house.

———

He found her in the near dark of the kitchen, pulling the yellow skins off a pile of chicken drumsticks. The cuffs of her shirt kept brushing the raw meat. "You can do this, can't you?" she said without turning around. It was twelve twenty in the afternoon. They wouldn't eat dinner for another six hours. She usually twisted her hair away at the top of her head when she was cooking, but today her hair was loose around her face, stringy. He tried to read what was coming in the set of her shoulders. He put down his backpack, unzipped his coat. She'd not eaten anything at dinner the night before, and he'd watched his father glance at her as he told a long, drawn-out story about something that had happened at work. He made himself a drink and then rattled the ice cubes around the bottom of the glass. She had a way of cringing and closing her eyes as if against the sight of something too painful to look at straight on, except it was just Peter, just his father. They were just sitting at a table. Just talking about stuff that had happened to them that day.

"Mom's not feeling great," Brian Stanhope said when she finally went upstairs to lie down. He seemed to not notice her leaving, but once she was gone he made himself another drink and then broke open a baked potato, dropped a slice of butter on the steaming white inside. "She's on her feet all day, you know? Not like an office job." He reached for the salt.

"You're on your feet all day, too, right?"

"Ah, not all day," Brian Stanhope said. "And it's different for women. They need—I don't know."

Peter wondered if the way his mother acted sometimes was related to the reason Renee Otler was allowed to go to the bathroom in the middle of assembly even though no one was ever allowed to go during assembly. Kate wouldn't talk about it on the bus. When they were alone out at the rocks, she said that he better not tell any of the boys, but Renee had gotten her you-know-what on the playground the day before and the school nurse had showed her how to use a pad. She was the first of the girls, as far as Kate knew. "I'll probably be last," she added as she pulled her T-shirt tight across her chest and frowned at what she saw there.

When Kate said "pad," Peter felt a shock go through him and he could feel his face burn. Kate tilted her head with interest. "You know about periods, right?"

———

"Sure. Just like this?" Peter said now, pulling at the edge of the slippery chicken skin. The kitchen was so dark that Peter had trouble making out the bowls she'd set up on the table: eggs beaten in one, a pyramid of breadcrumbs in another. As she made her way upstairs to her bedroom, he tried to find the rhythm that she seemed to have when she made their dinner. He oiled the baking sheet, as he'd often seen her do, lined up the breaded chicken drums. He could hear the kids assembling outside. He washed his hands, and as he listened to the soft tick-tick-ticking of the gas stove heating up, he stood at the back door and glimpsed Larry McBreen's red-and-blue striped jacket as he stomped along the cut-through behind the Gleesons' house. The Maldonados would be out.

Kate's sisters. The Dills. The Frankel twins, who went to public school. Everyone.

When he found that ship, he'd go up and show her that he had it, that he'd not lost track of it. She'd been so excited to give it to him. Together they'd read the certificate that had come with it, and she said she'd bring him to the library to find a book on Sir Francis Drake, or about woodworking, or about shipbuilding, or all three. That night, when he went to the fridge to get out the carton of milk, she'd pulled him toward her like she used to when he was five or six, and whispered that it had cost six hundred dollars, plus another seventy-five for shipping. Then she made her eyes big, as if she let the information slip out by accident and had not, in fact, been dying to tell him, and by that he knew he should never tell his father. She'd seen it in a catalog one of her patients had left behind at the hospital and decided Peter had to have it. When she'd pictured having a son, she'd always pictured him playing with things like that ship. It was made in London, she continued, her eyes full of delighted mischief as if he knew what that meant. She'd lived in England for nearly two years, a long time ago. They had the loveliest things there, she told him. What had gotten into her head about New York? She couldn't remember. A job? Some notion that it would be better than England? She'd told him all of it before. It was her favorite subject when she was in a talkative mood. He got a restless feeling when she spoke of those years. It was a tragedy, clearly, from her view, that she'd left one life and ended up in another. A path had diverged in a wood and she chose the one she'd regret forever. And yet there Peter was, very glad to have been born, listening to her, thinking she looked prettier than the other mothers when she dressed up a little and washed her hair. Anyway, she said, smiling faintly. She was so happy he liked the ship because that said something about him, it really did. It said something about his taste and his intelligence. And then, when she went to work on Monday morning—the only morning she had to leave before his bus—he'd brought it outside to show Kate and he hadn't seen it since.

The thing was, the ship was fun to look at, but after a few days of looking, there was not much more to do with it. It floated, just as she promised it would, but when they sent it sailing down Kate's driveway with the rushing meltwater, it had gotten a pair of scratches that ran parallel to the hull. He'd pulled off his mittens and rubbed at the scratches with his thumb, but there they were, glaringly obvious in the polished mirror finish of the wood. Kate wanted to send it downstream again, this time with an old Barbie on board, but he was afraid it would get more scratches. So he'd put it somewhere safe. But where?

The quiet of the house when she kept to her room was not the peaceful silence of a library, or anywhere near as tranquil. It was, Peter imagined, more like the held-breath interlude between when a button gets pushed and the bomb either detonates or is defused. He could feel his own heartbeat at those times. He could track his blood as it looped through his veins.

His father seemed to go on with life as if his mother were merely at work, or at the store. He didn't seem to notice when she began to skip meals, when her teeth became dull and thick with plaque, when her posture changed. Even if she stayed mostly up in her bedroom for three, four, five days, his father still ate his cereal standing at the sink. He still read the headlines of the *Post* out loud. When he reached for the little paper package of ground coffee and found it empty, he still said to Peter, "We're out of coffee," and then he'd go write it on the list Anne kept on a pad by the telephone, as if she'd merely stepped out. When Peter was little—first and second grade—his father sometimes spoke to her before he left for work, shutting the door to their bedroom so that Peter wouldn't come in. "Look out for your bus, buddy," he'd say, and Peter—bundled in his winter coat, his backpack straps securely looped across both shoulders—would keep an eye on the clock over the table. When the little hand was nearly on the eight and the big hand was between nine and ten, he knew to go stand outside.

Then, around third or fourth grade, Peter noticed his father didn't go in and talk to her anymore. Sometimes he'd glance up the stairs before he left for work. Sometimes he'd say goodbye and then circle back, as if there was something he'd forgotten. It occurred to Peter that his father actually liked these periods where she disappeared to her room for a few days. He seemed lighter, more relaxed. He sat on the couch after work and left his drink on the coffee table. One night he told Peter that it was his thirty-sixth birthday, and Peter felt terrible that probably no one had said happy birthday to him all day, but his father didn't seem to mind. He let Peter have toaster waffles for dinner. He watched basketball on TV and stayed up all night. The drone of the television at three o'clock in the morning was somehow more upsetting to Peter than the fact that his mother hadn't come downstairs in a week, and Peter would wake up disoriented, panicked, like he'd slept through his alarm and missed the bus. Sometimes, he'd bring his pillow to the hall and wait. She went to the bathroom, he knew. She would lean over the bathroom sink, put her mouth on the lime-scaled faucet, and take long slugs of cold water before heading back to her room.

"Mom," he'd say when she stepped out, and she would stop, put her hand on his head, completely unsurprised to find her child lying in the hall in the middle of the night. He'd remind her—two weeks ahead of time, a month—he had a birthday party to attend, a present to buy, a family tree project at school he needed her help on. He'd inform her that he'd eaten a grape jelly sandwich for both breakfast and lunch, hoping to draw her out. But she'd just close her eyes as if the sound of his voice was abrasive, and retreat again to the cave of her room until she was ready to emerge.

And when she did emerge after a few days, she usually emerged as Peter's favorite version of his mother. She'd been tired and needed rest, Peter figured, and she'd gotten it. Often, after seeing only dim glimpses of her for days, he'd wake to the smell of bacon and eggs, pancakes. She'd greet him softly and then she'd watch him eat while she smoked a cigarette and blew the smoke out the back door. She was calm. Serene. Like a person who'd been through a harrowing experience and was relieved to have arrived on the other side.

Maybe she was coming down with something, Peter thought as he put the chicken in the oven and searched the pantry for what might go along. A can of green beans. Something to make her happy. Maybe she'd caught the flu. He'd go up to her bedroom door and tell her it was all done. No need to worry. He could bring her a plate later or she could come down, whatever she felt like doing. He'd just gotten out a saucepan when he heard his father open the door. "Anne?" he called out, and then "Oh," when he crossed into the kitchen to find Peter.

"School got out early."

"Where's Mom?"

"Resting," Peter said. "I was just—" He held up the can of beans.

"We'll do that later, buddy. That'll just take a minute when we're ready to eat."

Peter put the can down. He left the saucepan on the stovetop for later. "Well, then can I go out to play for a while? Some of the kids—"

"I saw them. Go on. Have fun."

"The chicken is—"

"I'll take care of it."

———

The first shot of war had not yet been fired. The teams had assembled on the wide stretch of flat yard beside the Maldonados' house. Kate saw him first. "We get Peter!" she called, and every head turned. "Did you find it?" she asked when he took his spot beside her. They'd drawn boundaries— one team would fire from behind the grove of trees, the other from behind Mr. Maldonado's Cadillac.

"Not yet," he said.

A snowball exploded on the front hubcap of the Caddy. In an instant, Peter, Kate, and the rest were returning fire, the cold burning their hands, their cheeks, while under their coats their bodies grew warmer. As Kate gathered as many snowballs as she could, Peter crouched beside her, hammering them at the other team faster than she could make them. His nose running, his cheeks stinging, he forgot about the ship, about his mother, about the chicken drums he hoped his father would remember to take out of the oven. Kate was laughing so hard she fell face-first into a pile of snow.

Their side ran out of ammo. When half their team broke off to build up a store again, the ones who kept fighting got pelted, had to go lie down in the graveyard. "This sucks," Kate's sister Natalie said after a few minutes. "I'm going inside." When she stood up and walked across the battlefield, skirting the dead bodies like they were nothing, the game collapsed and the battlefield became just a yard again, the soldiers became kids. One by one, the others emerged from cover and headed home. The snow began to fall in earnest.

"You coming?" Sara said to Kate as she headed for their front door. The three Gleeson sisters crisscrossed traits. Kate looked more like Natalie, but Natalie had dark hair and was at least four inches taller than Kate. Sara and Kate were both blond, but other than those two details they didn't look at all alike. All three of them spoke with their hands, like their mother. "In a minute," Kate said.

"You going in?" Kate asked Peter when it was just the two of them left.

"I guess," he said.

"My mom made hot chocolate. We could take a thermos to the rocks."

"I better not."

"Okay," she said, looking past him to his house, to the upstairs window where his mother was looking down at them. "It's your mom," Kate said, offering an uncertain wave. Then she dropped her hand and waited, as if giving Peter's mother a chance to wave back. "My mom?" Peter wheeled around, cupped his hand to his eyes.

"That's your room, isn't it? Your window?" Kate asked.

———

By the time he stripped off his wet mittens, hat, scarf, coat, and boots and bounded up the stairs to his room, the ship was in bits. Some things came off easily as they were made to do in case they needed replacement. The jib, the boom, the crow's nest. But the entire hull was in splinters. Seeing the raw, broken-open insides of wood that had been varnished to a shine was like seeing something naked and vulgar, and Peter had to look away.

"It was in the garage," she said evenly. "It was just sitting there on the lid of the garbage can."

"I know," Peter said, astonished. He felt dizzy, confused. "That's where I left it." It came to him now in full color: hearing the hollow rumble of the school bus's engine coming around the corner, running into his garage with the ship to place it somewhere safe until his return.

"You left it where it could slide right off and fall? You left it where it could get damaged? Why?"

"I was playing with it. I wanted to show it to Kate. You know, because I liked it. I really liked my present, Mom. And then I left it there because I heard the bus." Peter looked at the wreckage strewn across his comforter and felt a roar come into his head. His mother put her fingertips to her temples and stood.

"Why would you want to show that girl? Why would you take it outside?"

"I don't know. I just wanted her to see it."

"Well that'll learn you." She crossed the room and slapped him hard across the mouth. "And that'll learn you."

Peter staggered back, his face numb at first and then, on a delay, his left cheek felt as if stung by a thousand needles. He touched the corner of his mouth with his tongue to search for blood. As he clutched his cheek, he looked around at his books, his poster of the solar system. What was he meant to learn? He really tried to see it. He felt like he was breathing through a straw.

"But you broke it," he said. "It was okay when you found it. And then you smashed it." His voice felt thick as he spoke and the pressure in his head was so heavy he was afraid something would burst. "You said it cost all that money. It didn't get broken where I left it." He felt wild all of a sudden. He flew to his bed and whipped the comforter and blankets off, and all the little bits of ship that hadn't already been scattered went flying. He toppled the tower of books on his desk. He threw a basket of Magic Markers he kept on a shelf. He went to his windowsill and grabbed the snow globe she'd given him when he was just a kindergartner. Santa flying his sleigh high over the Empire State Building. He held it over his head.

Brian came running up the stairs to Peter's room, still holding the remote control of the TV.

"What the hell is going on?" He saw the shipwreck. "Christ."

Anne gathered her robe around her. "Ask him. Ask him how he treats nice things." She came over to Peter and shoved him. "Ask him." Another shove. "Ask him."

"Stop it, Anne," Brian said, pulling her away. "Stop." He threaded his fingers behind his head and stood at the window for a moment with his back to them. When he turned he said, "Okay, Pete." He began opening Peter's dresser drawers. He grabbed underwear, an undershirt. Sweats. He pushed everything into Peter's chest and told him to shove it all in his backpack.

His mother watched them. "What are you doing?" she demanded.

"You did this," Brian said calmly. "The way you act. You did this."

As Peter followed his father down the stairs, they heard her shrieking after them, though the words were sheared off as soon as Brian closed the front door.

Having to wait for the car to warm up cut down on the drama of their exit, and already, the adrenaline that had left Peter breathless had slowed. His cheek still stung but it was better now. It didn't feel right, leaving her alone in the house with that stunned expression on her face, and he circled back to the idea that there'd been a misunderstanding of some kind. There was a piece of the story either she was missing or he was.

Next to him, fiddling with the heating vents so that they were all pointed toward the windshield, his father was caught up in some private riptide that Peter could feel only faintly. Brian banged the steering wheel with the heel of his hand. He did it again. The snow was already thick on the street and mailboxes, the battle scars the kids had left on the Maldonados' side yard already made smooth again. Once they could finally back out of the driveway, the car fishtailed toward their mailbox, and then all the way down the block. His father leaned forward over the steering wheel to better glimpse the road in between frantic sweeps of the wiper blades. They turned onto Madison, onto Central. A plow flashed its lights at them and passed by, followed by a salt truck. Up ahead they could see that Overlook Drive and its steep hill had been barricaded. All the traffic lights in town had been changed to flashing yellows so that no one would consider stopping short for a red and spinning out of control. Peter was clutching his backpack so hard his hands began to cramp.

His father let the car roll to a stop in the middle of Central Avenue. Everything around them was the perfect stillness of a black-and-white photograph, a ghostly hush that settled over the parked cars, the abandoned playground, the gazebo on Central that hosted jazz quartets on summer Fridays and now held nothing but silence. The wipers beat on.

"Damn it," he said.

"Pretty bad out," Peter said.

"Yeah."

"Where are we going?"

His father rubbed his eyes.

"I just need to think for a sec, buddy."

A blue car appeared in the distance and moved toward them. Peter didn't recognize it as Mr. Gleeson's car until it was right beside them.

Both men rolled down their windows, and the snow swept into the car like the storm had just been waiting for a chance to scoop them up.

"The roads are a mess!" Mr. Gleeson shouted. "Everything all right?"

"Fine! We're fine!" Peter's father answered. It was his cop voice. Sure of itself. Full of authority.

"Is that Peter? Where you guys heading?"

"Wanted to rent a movie!" Peter's father said. "We'll be stuck inside from the looks of things."

"Everything's closed," Mr. Gleeson said. "Parkway too." For a moment Peter thought Mr. Gleeson was going to get out of his car and come peer into theirs.

"We're too late then! Waited too long!" Peter's father shouted with sort of a goofy look on his face, like he'd been caught doing something he'd be teased about later on. The snow was belting him in the face and immediately turning into beads of water against his warm skin.

"Take it easy!" Mr. Gleeson shouted into the whirling storm.

"Will do!" shouted Peter's father.

With the windows rolled up again, the car seemed even more quiet. The storm whistled and every once in a while a gust blew a drift from the ground so that it looked as though snow was falling up and down and every which way. They remained idling in the middle of the street.

Eventually, Peter's father gestured toward the auto shop on the corner. "Flat roof," he said. "You see? He's already got at least a foot up there. I'd shovel that off before morning if I were him."

"Wouldn't it be dangerous to go up there in this storm?" Peter asked.

"Sure, but if he doesn't want it to collapse." Brian shrugged, placed his hands on the wheel at ten and two.

Peter looked building by building to check for flat roofs. Pies-on-Pizza. Nail Fetish. Heads You Win Beauty Parlor. All closed.

"I can't have friends over," Peter said without looking at his father. "Ever. I can't have them in there. Even when she seems fine."

"No, that's true."

"Why?"

"Your mom, she's just—I don't know. She's sensitive. She gets worked up. But trust me—some kids? They've got it worse than you, my friend. Worse by a mile. Some of the things I've seen you don't even want to know."

"But—"

"Look. You have a lot. You know what I was doing at your age? I was working. I was delivering papers. My mother? She drank all day long, Pete. You're probably not old enough yet to know what that means. She put booze in her coffee, in her orange juice, everything. By your age I was getting calls from the neighbors, from the grocery store, 'Hey, come collect your mother, Brian, she's in bad shape.' And she'd be kissing me—'So sorry, sweetie'—and then I'd have to let her pretend she was helping me with homework so she wouldn't feel so bad about it."

"But you said she brought you and your friends to the Polo Grounds that time. That she bought tickets for everyone."

His face softened as he thought back, and after a moment he nodded. "That's right. I told you that? Yeah, it was me, your uncle, and a couple kids from the building. One time—did I ever tell you this?—she signed a test my friend Gerald failed. It was snowing just like today and he carried the test in his hand the whole walk home. It was all rumpled and wet, with a big red F over his name. He needed a parent signature, and he was so scared about it he came to our apartment first to think out a strategy. She must have been listening because she told him to hand over the test so she could take a look. Next thing she's signing his mother's name big and bold right across the top of the page. 'Don't worry so much,' she says to him. Then she gave us money to go buy ourselves a candy bar. Our teacher never even questioned it."

"Your friends liked her."

"They loved her. I wish you could have known her."

Then he put on the car's hazards and slowly, slowly drove back home.

three

ON NEW YEAR'S EVE 1990—the year Kate and Peter were in eighth grade—Anne Stanhope walked up to the deli counter at Food King and took a number. She looked beautiful. Her coat was long and narrow. She was without a hat on that cold day but her scarf—a tartan plaid—was looped twice around her neck. Mrs. Wortham, who worked in the podiatrist's office in town, was also waiting and noted the height of Anne's heels—four inches, maybe more, dainty things, especially considering the slush and salt-coated streets outside. She thought, Oh, well, she must have come from work, some people don't get the day off, and then she remembered that Anne Stanhope was a nurse. Maybe she's going to a party, Mrs. Wortham decided. After taking her number from the spool of tickets and without saying hello to anyone, Anne stood off to the side like the others who were waiting for one of the hair-netted employees to turn the dial on the counter. "Forty-three!" was called. "Forty-four!" One by one various residents of Gillam stepped forward and spoke their orders across the tall glass display. A pound of smoked ham, thickly sliced. A half pound of provolone. The store was crowded that day. People had worked through their Christmas leftovers and wanted a fresh start for the new year. Anne Stanhope held the number fifty-one.

Forty-five, forty-six, forty-seven. Johnny Murphy, who'd been sent to the store by his mother, spotted one of his old high school baseball coaches. Home on break from his first year at college, Johnny greeted the older man warmly and stood at the counter blocking the way until someone joked that Mr. Big-Time Pitcher had better shove over. He'd gone to college on scholarship, and the whole town had followed his senior year wins over neighboring towns that were wealthier, had better facilities. Number forty-eight forgot the list his wife had written before sending him off, so he hemmed and hawed up there until he settled on London broil and a pound of German potato salad. Forty-nine and fifty were called up together, to opposite ends of the counter. It was busy now, the numbers ticking by more quickly because the manager had sent help to get through the midday rush.

Next thing Anne Stanhope knew, everyone who'd been waiting alongside her seemed to be ordering, or seemed to have ordered already. There were people who'd come after her—she couldn't have described them; she felt merely a gathering presence beside and behind her—who now had their meats and cheeses and salads and were on their way. Only Anne Stanhope remained. The employees behind the counter were so busy that the dial was at fifty-two and then almost instantly at sixty. Sixty-one was called. People stepped around her, in front of her, and she felt—right down to her fingertips—a kind of quickening. The gathering of momentum was familiar, though she hadn't felt it in a while—her heart and her pulse and some wild fury coming together in a rhythm that gained force and speed the longer she stayed quiet, the more she looked around and noticed. Her peripheral vision sparked and distorted the edges of everything so that when she turned quickly to look at something, it moved just out of sight. And even while everything inside her body seemed to speed up, everything outside of her body—the movements of the other shoppers, the reaching and lowering of boxes and packages into carts—slowed. A carton of milk had a wet drip gathering along the cardboard seam. The tip of an old man's nose was so vein threaded it looked blue, and when he went to rub it she saw the delicate hairs inside his nostrils, every bit as private as hair in any other part of the body. In the distant front of the store, the automatic doors wheezed open, and she could feel the cold air racing down the aisle to slide under the collar of her coat. She could see that the people around her didn't care that she'd been missed. She took a step back and saw in vivid color—because her mind was that sharp at moments like this, everything spotlighted so that details she'd overlooked were now glaringly obvious—that in fact they'd orchestrated her exclusion for private, petty reasons that weren't worth trying to understand. They smirked and nodded and gave each other signals. They'd banded together and decided that number fifty-one would get skipped.

She stepped out of her heels to get a better sense of what was happening, to defend herself if need be, and in one nimble motion she bent and swept the shoes from the floor, tossed them in her basket. She unwound the scarf from her neck.

"Wait!" she called out, raising her hand like a grade-schooler who'd just thought of the answer. She pushed forward to the counter.

"Are you all right?" a woman standing nearby asked. "You can't take off your shoes."

"Why can't I?" Anne snapped, turning on the woman to study her. The woman's lips were rubbery, untrustworthy, and she had shades of laziness in her expression that Anne found disgusting. Some distant part of her recognized the woman as a Eucharistic minister at St. Bartholomew's, and she was amazed she'd never noted how revolting she was before this. This woman had put her filthy fingertips on the host, the body of Christ, and Anne had taken it into her mouth. She felt her stomach rise and a crawling at the back of her throat. She put a fist to her pursed mouth and willed herself not to vomit.

"Stop!" she shouted when the feeling passed. Everyone from the seafood case to the imported cheeses stopped talking and looked. She held up her ticket and stepped forward. "It's my turn." There was something pathetic in her voice—she could hear it as if she were listening to someone else—and in case they thought she was going to cry she repeated herself, louder, with more determination. But in the few short steps she took to the counter—she felt the cold of the linoleum floor on her bare feet as twin cramps at the bottom of her calves—she forgot what she wanted or why she was there, only that every single person in her vicinity had plotted against her.

"How dare you," she said to the elderly man standing in front of the pasta salads. And then: "Stop looking at me."

"I'm very sorry," the man said, stepping aside. "Please go right ahead."

"Stop looking at me," she repeated.

"I'm not. I wasn't. There's no need to raise your voice, honey," he said softly, and everyone understood he was trying to placate her, that this was a situation that could go a hundred different ways and he was trying to get it to go the calmest, easiest way possible. "I'm very sorry about that. It was an honest mistake but now you go right ahead."

"Stop looking at me," she shouted at him, and then she swung around and shouted it in the general direction of the rest of the store. The taller of the two hair-netted women behind the counter asked her in a firm tone to please lower her voice, while the other called the manager. Anne turned slowly in a circle, taking in everything and everyone, and then she walked over to the pyramid of crackers—stone ground, whole wheat, sesame, plain—and bumped it with her hip. When it toppled she wrapped her arms around herself and squeezed her eyes shut. There'd been a dozen people standing around but now there were two dozen. More. No one said a word. "Stop looking at me," she said at a normal volume. Then she covered her ears and began to howl.

Over the loudspeaker, someone paged the manager for a second time.

———

Peter, who'd opted to wait in the car listening to the top one hundred countdown, had just looked at the dashboard clock when he heard an ambulance in the distance. When it seemed that the siren couldn't get any louder, it got just a little bit louder until it pulled up to the front of the supermarket and went abruptly silent. He watched in the side-view mirror for a moment, and then he turned and watched out the back windshield of the car. There were people gathered and the EMTs were waving them back. A police cruiser pulled up behind the ambulance. A second cruiser approached from the south lot. Peter had been at Food King once when a man had a heart attack. The man had been holding a gallon of milk, and though Peter hadn't seen him fall, he'd seen the gallon container glug-glug-glugging milk from its throat, spreading down the dairy aisle while the man on the ground clutched his shoulder. His father had pulled him away before Peter could see what happened next. Thinking about it, Peter wondered why he hadn't thought of the man again until now. Death was something for grown-ups to worry about but, still, he knew that when his time came he didn't want it to come at Food King. Janet Jackson was up for the second time, and Peter slumped down in his seat. He didn't see how they'd get through all one hundred songs before midnight, as the DJ had promised. When he looked up an old man he recognized as Chris Smith's grandfather was standing at the driver's side window. Mr. Smith made a cycle motion with his fist and Peter rolled down the window.

"It's Peter, right? You know me? My grandson is in your class? Listen. Your mom wasn't feeling well in the store. Nothing to worry about but they're going to take her over to the hospital. Can I give you a lift home? I'm glad I spotted you."

Peter blinked at Mr. Smith for a moment, and then he got out of the car so fast that he left the keys in the ignition. "What happened?" he asked, looking now at the crowd at the front of the store in a different light. He began jogging through the parking lot. When he saw that someone was being carried out on a stretcher, he began to run.

"Mom?" he called from the back of the crowd that had gathered. She bucked when she heard his voice, and one of the EMTs stumbled. "Peter!" she shouted, her voice thin with urgency, and Peter felt every face in the crowd turn to look at him. They stepped back so that he could make his way. "Quickly!" she shouted to him, but he didn't know what she meant. He noticed that a third EMT was carrying her shoes and her scarf. The tips of her fingers looked bluish and cold, and her hair was parted differently than it had been when she walked away from the car. He wondered if they'd forced her onto the stretcher, and if she'd fought them. Her coat was draped over her like a blanket. "Quickly!" she shouted again, her eyes wild and locked on his, but he froze in place, having no idea what to do. The same faces that had turned to look at him now turned away. The coat shifted and he saw that her hands were strapped down. Her ankles, too. He began to shiver. They lifted her into the back of the ambulance and a police officer waved everyone back, including Peter.

"Peter! Quickly!" she shrieked.

Peter looked at the officer blocking his way. "That's me," he whispered. "I'm Peter. Can't I go in there with her?"

"Peter," Mr. Smith said, coming up beside him. "Why don't I take you home and you can call your dad from my house. Mrs. Smith will make you a sandwich." But he lived with Chris, Peter remembered, and then Chris would know, and then their whole class would know. His shoulders were quaking so violently now that he knew everyone must be noticing. Mr. Smith put an arm around him, but that only made it worse.

The police officer asked, "You're her son?" He introduced himself as Officer Dulley.

"Yes," he said.

Officer Dulley asked him for his full name and address, and when he didn't answer, Mr. Smith gave the officer Peter's full name and told him he was pretty sure the Stanhopes lived on Jefferson. That, yes, Peter lived with his mother. Yes, his father was in the picture. They were talking about his dad now. Officer Dulley disappeared inside the ambulance for a few minutes and then came back. No one seemed in any rush to get anywhere.

"Did she have a heart attack?" Peter asked when he returned.

"No," Officer Dulley said, without indicating if whatever did happen was better or worse.

"What precinct is your dad in?" Officer Dulley asked, but Peter couldn't remember. It was right there in his brain but he couldn't come up with it.

"He's on the job, right?"

Peter nodded.

It was decided that he would hang out at the Smiths' house until they got in touch with his father.

"Wait," Peter said, stepping away from Mr. Smith's hand on his shoulder and watching as the ambulance doors closed. "I want to go with her." But they were already pulling away from the curb.

"She's fine, Peter. She'll be fine."

"Well, then can't you just drop me off at home?" The ambulance paused at the intersection at Middletown Road and whooped the siren twice to let the other cars know it was going to drive through. "My dad will be home pretty soon."

"Are you sure that's what you want?"

"I'm sure."

On the short drive Mr. Smith said it was a tiring time of year, really, when a person thought about it. It was a happy time of year, sure, with all the family and the celebrating but overwhelming, too, for some people. For a start, look at all the money being spent. "Plus it's different for women," he added, "they always feel like everything has to be just so with the dinners and the entertaining. You need this bowl to match this bowl. You need this spoon. Used to be people made gingerbread cookies and got maybe one present, but these days things are different." Then he looked at Peter like that explained everything. Peter felt like telling him that he and his father had put up their tree. He alone had baked cookies when the day came for the class bake sale. He'd just followed the directions on the package and they'd turned out delicious, then he'd put them in a shoebox like he'd seen the other kids' moms do. When his mother came home, she snapped at him that he'd forgotten to line the box with foil or wax paper. Who would want a cookie from a box shoes had been sliding around in? She made it sound as if he'd stored the cookies inside a public toilet. All those ingredients wasted. He'd used the last of the butter. She slammed the fridge. The last of the brown sugar. She slammed the cabinet door. But then, when she saw the baking sheet and bowls washed and drying on the counter, she stopped ranting, and it was as if an invisible hand had been clapped over her mouth. She ran her fingers along the table and found they came up clean. She stood before the shoebox and selected a cookie from the top of the pile. He waited. He watched. Finally, she said quietly that they were so good it would be a shame anyway to sell them for only twenty-five cents apiece. They were extraordinary.

"We'll keep these for ourselves," she said. "Tomorrow I'll get some from the bakery for you to sell at school."

"What happened in the store?" he asked Mr. Smith as they rounded the corner onto Jefferson. "Did someone say something to her? Was someone rude?"

"I don't know," Mr. Smith said. "I really don't."

"She's just sensitive," Peter said.

As they drove down Jefferson, Mr. Gleeson was outside pulling a garbage can to the curb. He looked up at Mr. Smith's car and watched it slow to a stop at Peter's driveway. "Is that Francis Gleeson?" Mr. Smith asked, leaning over the steering wheel. He sounded relieved.

The two men spoke at the end of the driveway while Peter retrieved the key from under the rock and went into his house. They were still talking even after Peter poured himself a glass of water and went up to

56

his bedroom. He chugged the water with his back to the window and counted to forty. When he turned around they were still there, except they'd turned their backs to his house, as if they knew he might try to read their lips and figure out what they were saying.

———

She had a gun in her handbag. She hadn't taken it out, she hadn't even mentioned it, but they found it in the ambulance when they were going through her things. All she wanted was the secret weight of it hanging off her shoulder, cold and solid when she rummaged through her bag for her wallet. She hadn't planned on using it. She couldn't even imagine using it. It was just a thing to have. A thing that would surprise people, if it came to it, a thing that surprised her when she remembered it was there and what it was made to do. But the EMT who spotted it handed her whole bag over to the cop like it was on fire. "Your husband, he's on the job?" the cop asked, holding Brian's little off-duty five-shot away from himself like it was contaminated. "Local or city?" He popped open the cylinder. "Jesus Christ," he said, and tilted the gun so that five bullets slid neatly into his palm. Anne Stanhope refused to answer. Once she'd stopped howling in the store, she was unable to speak. She had no interest in speaking. Speaking was a habit she'd gotten into years ago, in the distant past, and now that she'd stopped she felt no desire to start again. It was pointless anyway—all the blah-blah-blabbing and, still, no one understood each other. The EMT came at her with a small plastic cup at the bottom of which a large yellow and white pill rolled around. He lifted her head to place a pill on her tongue, and she spit it back at him.

"Why'd you have this in your bag today, Anne?" They were idiots, she thought. Each one more idiotic than the last. They had no brains for nuance. They had no conception of a way of thinking that was different than their own. "Your husband. He left this at home?" They assumed

Brian was at work, but Brian wasn't at work. He was at the garage not a mile away from Food King, hoping the mechanic there could squeeze six more months of life out of his Chevy. He'd left the gun where he always left it when he was off duty—on top of the bookcase in the family room. Yes, he was supposed to be wearing it but he couldn't be bothered. He was in Gillam. Why would he need it? Anne would have had it back on the bookcase without him ever realizing it was gone.

———

In the fluorescent light of the hospital corridor, in full view of any person who might happen down the hall, they unstrapped her from the gurney and lifted her onto a hospital bed. Someone rolled her over and someone else tugged down her pants until she could feel her bare behind was exposed for the world to see. She began laughing. They told her to be still so she wagged her behind a little to show them she didn't care. Someone pushed a needle into her and she noticed she was sobbing. She didn't remember that she'd stopped laughing. She turned her face to the mattress so they wouldn't see. Now the sheet under her face was damp and would stay damp until they changed the bedding or moved her again. Someone put thick socks on her bare feet.

When they moved away from her, she figured she had two or three minutes. Maybe less. It all depended on what they'd given her. The cop was hovering around the nurses' station, the attending physician was with another patient—so she summoned all her strength and stood from the bed. It felt as if they'd attached lead weights to her wrists and ankles. She had a lead anchor strapped to her chest. She moved down the hall and had the same feeling she'd had as a kid trying to run in water. Right. Left. One. Two. Working hard but not getting anywhere. She'd grown up swimming at Killiney Beach, the stones in the water there rattling around inside the waves like bones in a bag. Diving under, you risked getting pummeled. Her mouth was hanging open and her lips were dry.

One foot in front of the other she made it to the end of the hall and slipped out through the swinging doors. They still had her shoes, her coat, her bag, but at home she had more shoes, she had another coat. When she reached the lobby, she put her hand on the reception desk for a moment to catch her breath, and the attendant didn't even notice she was there. When she stepped outside there was a cab waiting, and she had just enough strength left to open the door and collapse onto the smooth bench seat, the most comfortable seat she'd ever sat upon. It was warm in the cab, and the driver caught her eye in the rearview as if he'd been waiting for her. She knew then that everything had turned around since the supermarket, and now the world was falling over itself to win back her favor.

"Gillam," she said. "One-se-ven-one-one Jeff-er-son Street." She said it slowly, as if speaking to a child. She knew she wouldn't be able to repeat it. She closed her eyes and slept.

———

It was Francis Gleeson's face she saw next. His stubbled jaw was different from Brian's. He had a nice face, really. Not as handsome as Brian's but nice enough. Dependable. A big Irish head like a cabbage. He was holding her tight. She wanted to ask him about the sound of the waves in Galway, if it was the same bag of bones as in Dublin. He'd tried to talk to her about Ireland once. Early, early, early on. Lena Gleeson was spilling over in those years between the breasts and the belly and the wet-mouthed babies hanging from her. But now Anne wished she'd been kinder. He was carrying her easily, and just as if he entered her house any day of his life, he continued past the threshold, all the way upstairs, and laid her on her bed. She decided if he tried to rape her she'd just let him and deal with it later because she didn't have the strength to fight. She tried to tell him there was money for the cab in her wallet, but her mouth didn't work. And she had no wallet. Her feet were so cold.

———

Peter thought he and his mother might be able to keep the whole thing from his father if they thought it out and worked together. She hadn't told him what to do, but he figured they had time; he knew his father wouldn't find it unusual to come home to her asleep upstairs. But then, after carrying his mother up the stairs, Mr. Gleeson didn't go home like Peter expected him to. "Your mother's resting," he said, and asked if Peter would like to go over to his house for a while. Kate wasn't home but Peter could watch a movie with Natalie and Sara. When Peter refused, Mr. Gleeson just sat down on the Stanhopes' porch step and waited. Peter couldn't remember if he'd turned off the car ignition or if it was still up there idling in the Food King parking lot, still ticking off the top one hundred hits of 1990. Then the police officer who'd been asking Peter all those questions at Food King showed up; he'd headed straight to 1711 Jefferson Street as soon as Anne was discovered missing from the hospital. Mr. Maldonado was outside taking down his Christmas lights even though it was after dusk by then, and Peter watched him look over at Officer Dulley in his navy uniform.

Officer Dulley and Mr. Gleeson talked on the lawn, and when Brian finally came home, Peter watched from the window as they spoke to him, and then stepped aside as he rushed into the house and swept his hand back and forth, back and forth across the top of the bookcase. Mr. Smith phoned to make sure Peter was okay. As soon as he'd gotten home and told his wife everything that had happened, his wife had reprimanded him for dropping Peter off, for leaving him alone when it would be dark soon, what a thing for a boy to cope with by himself. "Slow down," Brian Stanhope said, stretching the phone cord as far away from Mr. Gleeson and Officer Dulley as possible. "Now say all that again, would you?"

For the next few hours there were dealings at the adult level that Peter couldn't quite follow. His father noticed him sitting on the staircase in the dark, listening, and sent him to his room, but he returned not two minutes later and listened more. Mr. Gleeson and his father were in the same precinct again, Peter gathered, like they'd been for a few years when they were rookies, but now their precinct was in Manhattan, the Two-Six, near Columbia University. He remembered now. Mr. Gleeson had a brogue that was different from his mother's but they both said "Brian" like "Brine"—blending the syllables into one.

"Brian," Mr. Gleeson said, "no one wants you to get jammed up." Officer Dulley's expression confirmed this was true. His father raised his voice, "I was at home! I was off duty!" Mr. Gleeson pointed out that, in fact, Brian had not been at home. In fact, he was at the auto shop on Sentinel and now he was up a fucking creek. Mr. Gleeson sounded both angry and disgusted, and for the first time Peter wondered if Kate's dad was his dad's boss. He tried to remember how the ranks went. His dad was a patrolman. Mr. Gleeson was a lieutenant.

"Get organized, Brian," Mr. Gleeson said. "You have to *think*," he said, jabbing the side of his own head as he said it. Peter tried to peer around the banister to see his father's face where the weak light from the corner lamp found it.

Once, when Mrs. Duvin told Peter he had to get his act together in front of all the other kids, he felt his face burn and was afraid he would cry. He prayed his father wasn't crying, but he couldn't see his face, only his knee, the leg of his pants. They were quiet in there for a long time. Then, without warning, they seemed to decide something. Officer Dulley handed his father a gun that Peter realized was his father's own gun. His father shoved it into the waistband of his jeans.

His mother slept and slept.

———

Nineteen ninety-one arrived, winter break ended, and Peter went back to school. On that first school day of the new year he made himself a good breakfast. He packed his lunch. He brushed his teeth. His mother came downstairs as he was rinsing his cereal bowl but she didn't speak to him at first. Instead, she opened the window over the sink and closed her eyes to meet the blast of cold air that rushed in. "You're exactly like him," she said after a minute, still with her eyes closed.

"Like who? Like Dad?" Peter said. He knew she didn't mean it as a compliment.

"Like Dad?" she mimicked, exaggerating his expression without looking at him, making her face dopey and stupid, like she was performing for an audience she hoped to make laugh. "Like Daaaad? Like Daaaaaaaaaaaaaad?" He calmly took his backpack from the peg by the door and fitted it over his shoulders. He felt lonely all of a sudden. Everything in their house was lonely: the dark china cabinet filled with fragile things no one ever touched, the fake plant sitting next to the sofa, the crooked window shade, a silence so violent he wanted to clap his hands over his ears. The bus honked outside.

"Bye," he said.

She made a wave in the air like she was swatting a fly.

"Did something happen to your mom?" Kate asked when they'd taken their seats on the bus.

"No," Peter said.

"I thought I heard my parents talking." At school, none of the kids said anything, not even Chris Smith. Peter could tell Kate, he knew, but he didn't know what he'd even say. His mom took pills now. That was new. He could tell Kate that they'd shown up by the kitchen sink on New Year's Day. That there were two big amber bottles and she took one pill from each with a huge glass of water. Then she sort of leaned over the sink for a minute and groaned. Sometimes his father picked up the bottles and held them up to the light, shifted the contents a bit like he was counting how many were inside. "Is Mom sick?" Peter had asked one evening.

"Who? Mom?" his father said. And didn't answer.

———

She returned to work the same week Peter returned to school. She'd taken her leftover vacation days at Christmas, and everything that happened fit neatly into that two-week frame. No one mentioned Food King, or the ambulance, or Mr. Gleeson carrying her inside. But after a few weeks, Peter could feel something new stirring, a shift in air pressure, a tilt in a direction he had to reorient himself toward. Breakfast, school, homework, playing—the days and weeks looked mostly the same as they always had. After Mass on Sundays they still slipped out the side door while the other families stood around and talked out front. Now they bought their groceries at the more expensive store two towns away and whenever they left, his mother would stand by their car for a minute to study the receipt with a downturned mouth. But that wasn't it. Ever since the New Year, it was as if what they were saying to each other—he and his mother and his father—was not really what they were saying to each other.

His mother seemed better. When the amber bottles were near empty, two full ones replaced them. On Valentine's Day she left a heart-shaped chocolate on his dinner plate and one for his father, too. One evening she shared a joke she heard at work—three surgeons walk into a bar— and his father had smiled. Still, he seemed always on the verge of saying something and then at the last moment changing his mind. She sensed it, too. Some nights when he didn't say much, she'd jump up and fill his plate with seconds before he was quite finished with firsts. She'd go to the freezer and get ice for his drink. She'd never been like that before. "I'll do that," she'd say when he started to clear the dishes, and he'd let her do it, retreating to the sofa. Later, when Peter would come down from his bedroom to tell them he'd finished his homework, he was going to bed, he'd find them on opposite ends of the room, his dad staring at the TV, his mother flipping through a magazine, glancing over at him every time she turned the page.

And then one morning while he was getting ready for school and his mother was getting ready for work, Peter ran downstairs to see if there were any clean socks in the dryer and almost slipped on a glossy pamphlet at the bottom of the stairs. The pamphlet seemed to be about a golf course in South Carolina. His father used to golf, Peter knew, or at least he'd purchased a set of clubs in hopes of learning. He'd promised to show Peter one day when he got tall enough. The man on the cover of the pamphlet had just hit a ball and was smiling as he watched it sail away. On the inside there was a picture of a man and a woman on what looked to be a date. There were lists of numbers and prices. Studios. One, two, three bedrooms. Seasonal rentals or year-round. Peter was the one who took in the mail most days, but he didn't remember seeing it. He put it on a table in case it was important, hunted down socks, and returned to his bedroom. When he was fully dressed, he looked out his bedroom window and watched his dad shovel out his car after a surprise March snowstorm. He watched his dad turn the shovel over and tap the icy windshield with the edge of the handle. The ice fractured into shards and he removed a glove to pry them off one by one, flicking them onto the driveway. Every once in a while he'd shade his eyes with his hand and look off down the length of Jefferson.

He doesn't want to be here, Peter thought. He wants to leave. The idea landed lightly and easily, and as soon as Peter noticed it there, everything that hadn't quite made sense made sense again.

He heard his father stomping snow off his boots on the mat outside, and then the squeal of the rubber weather strip on the bottom of the door as he entered the house. When Peter went down for breakfast, the pamphlet was gone.

———

But weeks went by and nothing happened. Spring came. Baseball season began. His father said that it was high time Peter went to a real game.

He'd get the list of home games and decide on a date. The tulips pushed up along the side of the Gleesons' house. The days were warmer and Peter and Kate got off the bus each day with their uniform sweaters tied around their waists. They began practicing for graduation. Kate had been paired with John Dills for the processional. There were more boys than girls in the grade, so Peter and the second tallest boy had to walk down together. They'd be off to high school soon and then things would speed up. A driver's license. A job. College. Freedom. And in the meantime, it would be fine if things stayed exactly as they were. And for a few weeks, things did.

four

THERE WAS A SPOT near the rocks where, if they positioned themselves just right, they could glimpse Peter's mother's car through the Maldonados' arborvitae before it turned onto Jefferson. Peter had a bloom of acne across his forehead, and he knew Kate had noticed. He wore his Mets cap to school that morning and took it off only when the second bell rang. At the end of the day he dug it out of his backpack and held it on his lap, ready to return it to his head the instant they lined up for the buses. Kate's legs were scabbed from a weekend softball game where she'd slid badly into third base. She couldn't seem to stop herself from running her hands over the scabs—as if she wanted to compare the roughness there to the smoothness of the rest of her skin. Peter caught himself following the path of her hands as if in a trance. Kate had recently pointed out how much thicker and stronger Peter's legs were than hers.

"Hey," she'd said, shimmying closer beside him one afternoon, both of them in shorts and sneakers, both of them sitting on the curb waiting to see if any of the other kids would come by. "Look." When her skin brushed his, he startled, moved away. She was quiet after that, and when he spoke to her next—"Did you hear Joey Maldonado bought a car?"—she blushed.

That day, a late May afternoon, their backpacks stuffed with text-books and information on the eighth grade graduation ceremony that was just a few short weeks away, Peter vowed to keep things light, but it was weighing on him, this strange thing that was happening between him and Kate. Sean Barnett had told the boys that he liked Kate, that he was pretty sure she liked him back, and he hadn't even looked at Peter when he said it. "What the hell?" Peter said, not sure why he felt so furious.

"What?" Sean said. "Aren't you guys cousins or something?"

"Uh, no. We're definitely not cousins."

"Well, have you kissed her?"

Every head turned to study him, every boy in the eighth grade who'd gathered to play stickball in the parking lot, every face waiting to hear what he'd say. "What makes you think she likes you back?" Peter had asked, stupidly, and felt in that instant whatever claim he had over Kate evaporate in their eyes.

"I just know," Sean said.

"How do you know?" Peter asked. "Because I really don't think so." He said it in a way that implied privilege, like Kate would have told him if she did, and in doing so hoped to remind everyone that no one knew Kate Gleeson as well as he did. And she really would have told him, he considered. Or at least he thought she would have.

There was nothing Kate appreciated more than information, insight into what the boys said when the girls were not around. But he didn't want to tell her about Sean Barnett in case it gave her an idea to like him back. So with one eye on the Maldonados' arborvitae, he stepped from the shortest rock to the next tallest to the next as he confessed that the boys in their class had all agreed to throw easy pitches to Laura Fumagalli during stickball so that she'd connect and send the ball past Monsignor Repetto's black Mercedes—the only car allowed in the school lot during recess. A home run meant they could watch her boobs move under her uniform shirt as she ran around the bases.

Kate nodded from where she was sprawled on the grass with the same serious expression she wore when she took in their history lesson, or pre-algebra. He could see a tiny flicker of jealousy pass through her, but it was only a flicker, and was immediately drowned out by admiration for their slyness and for the way they stuck together. She nodded as if in complete agreement that this made sense.

"You won't tell her, right?" Peter said.

"Of course not," Kate said, insulted. She stood abruptly, walked over to the middle rock, and executed a perfect standing jump, as if her legs had springs. She looked over to see if Peter was impressed. He shrugged, but he couldn't stop himself from smiling. She poked him in the belly. "Pretty good. Say it." And just as Kate began to tell him that Laura's mother had taken her bra shopping in fifth grade, they both leaped to the tallest boulder at the very same time and Kate slipped, catching her chin on the hard edge of the rock as she fell off.

Peter jumped down beside her. "Kate! Are you okay?" he asked. He put his hand on her face.

"I think I broke a tooth," Kate said, and with one hand in her hair Peter put his thumb against her bottom lip as a signal to open up. He lightly ran his finger along the edges of her teeth. She could taste salt on his fingertip. When he glanced at her, he saw that she was watching him closely, searching for his eyes underneath the brim of his cap.

"There's a ton of blood," he said, withdrawing his hand so fast it was as if she'd bitten him. Kate sat up and leaned over to spit. She wiped her mouth with her forearm and then she spit some more.

"Oh. Hey. Shit. Peter," she said then, the words thick and muffled like she'd just left the dentist after a filling. She nodded at Peter's back door and he looked over. There was his mother, squinting into the yard.

Peter scrambled to his feet. His mother had crossed the yard in an instant, was standing over them before Peter even had a chance to think.

It was as if she'd not only seen what had happened, but she could also see what they were thinking, whatever was beginning in their minds and hearts.

"She just—"

"Inside," his mother said.

"But I only—"

"Now."

"Wait," Kate said, and Peter turned to Kate even as he felt his mother's anger rise.

"He was just helping me," Kate said to Peter's mother as she gradually rose to her feet. "We were just talking and I fell. I hit my jaw. You can see I'm bleeding." Kate put her hand on Peter's arm to stay him.

Shut up, Peter thought. He shook his head as discreetly as he could, and he knew that Kate caught it but chose to ignore it.

"You're a nurse, right?" Kate said. She leaned over and spit more blood. Her point was so clear she might as well have said it. *Thanks for your concern.*

Mrs. Stanhope took two quick steps closer to her. Peter flinched and Kate stepped back. But when she didn't hit her, Peter thought, for a moment, that she was going to help. That as mad as she was she was going to make sure Kate was okay before she dealt with him. But she stopped just short of Kate and didn't seem to have the least interest in discovering where the blood was coming from. She leaned over like she had a secret to whisper in Kate's ear. Kate watched her eyes as they traveled over her hair, down her body, down even to her white Keds, which she'd threaded with blue laces.

"You think you're so smart," Anne said finally. A few mornings earlier she'd taken the usual two pills out of the bottles, but instead of swallowing them, she placed them inside an empty eggshell she'd returned to the carton after breaking the egg over the small frying pan. She reassembled the egg to make it look whole again, and then she placed it in the trash.

"Are you supposed to do that?" Peter had asked.

"Am I supposed to do what?" she asked as she crossed the room toward him, put her hand on his cheek. It felt like a caress at first but she squeezed harder and harder until he pulled away.

"Excuse me?" Kate said now.

"I *said*, you think you're so smart. Don't you?"

Kate looked at Peter as if he might be able to translate.

From Kate's side of the yard came the sound of the Gleesons' screen door squealing open and then slapping shut. Lena came rushing outside. "What happened?" she asked, concern and love and reprimand all tied up into one.

She seemed to take stock of everything so quickly that Peter felt embarrassment well up in his chest. All along, everyone had known exactly what his mother was like, only they hadn't said anything.

"Into the house," Lena said to Kate.

"We weren't even doing anything. Can someone tell me why we're in trouble?"

"Get into the goddamn house."

"This is bullshit," Kate said, and her mother whipped around and slapped her across the face.

"Mom!" Kate choked out as she staggered and tried not to cry.

"Jeez, Mrs. Gleeson, she's already hurt."

"You shut your mouth," his own mother said.

We will leave them all one day, Peter thought, not for the first time. We'll live on our own and we won't have to listen to any of these people.

————

Inside, his mother paced while Peter held the back of a kitchen chair, refusing to sit. When she finally spoke she said it showed what kind of people they were, the Gleesons. Trash. Imagine hitting a person in public, in front of a neighbor.

Peter thought of all the things he could say to her right then. He thought about how much bigger he'd gotten since the year before. He was as tall as his father now. He could tear down every cabinet in the kitchen. He could push his way out the back door, knocking her over if he had to, and go get Kate, and they could get on a bus somewhere right then. People did things like that all the time, Peter was sure of it. He was fourteen already and by the summer Kate would be, too.

"You're not going back there," his mother said, cutting across his thoughts.

"Back where?"

"To that school. For trash girls like Kate Gleeson to try to pin you down."

"Fine! Done! Kate won't be going back, either, you know. Graduation is in three weeks."

"No, I mean you won't be going back, ever. Not tomorrow. Not for graduation. Not for anything."

He stared at her. "What are you talking about?"

"Now you're listening."

"I'm calling Dad."

"No you're not." She rushed across the kitchen and tore the handset from the phone. The late afternoon sun fell as a square across the table. Peter felt its heat on his leg, on his fingertips.

"Okay, Mom." Peter held up his hands. "Let's say I don't go back. Does it bother you that everyone hates you?"

"Go to your room."

"Nope."

She threw the phone across the room but Peter dodged it. He felt wound up enough to sprout wings and fly away.

"Go to your room."

"No."

She opened the drawer where she kept serving spoons, wooden spoons, a whisk, a few spatulas, a heavy cast-iron mallet she used to tenderize meat. She lifted the mallet over her head and rushed at him. He caught her by the wrist and held it.

"Stop it," Peter said. "Stop."

His mother released the mallet and it clattered to the floor. She looked around as if she'd mislaid something, as if something important had gone undelivered. Peter pushed the chairs neatly up to the lip of the table, one by one.

"You are not going to see that girl again," she said.

"I will," said Peter, and then left her.

————

His father always seemed to want to defuse things by agreeing with her. "Okay, Anne," he'd say, and his face would go blank as he stared straight ahead and pushed through to whatever task would bring him out of the scene, away from her. He'd turn on the television, or disappear into the garage, or head over to the Grasshopper Pub for a few hours. "You're right," he'd say, and then he'd move around as if in a fugue state, as if nothing had happened. If he spoke at all, he'd talk about the price of gas, about whether the deer population had exploded in recent years or whether it just seemed that way.

One exception was the previous Thanksgiving, when Peter's uncle—his father's brother, George—made a rare trip to Gillam from Sunnyside with his new wife, Brenda. George Stanhope was ten years younger than Brian, and the brothers didn't even look like relatives. Where Brian was blond and lean, George had a barrel chest and thick arms from lifting iron beams into place all day long. He was short and dark and had a belly that hung a little over his belt. His wife seemed not that much older than Peter. She worked in the union office, handled the insurance claims and workman's comp. Peter had only met George a handful of times: once at a diner in the Bronx, another time at a funeral his father had dragged him along to because it was a Thursday in the summer and his mother was at work. At the diner, George had pretended he just found a brand-new package of baseball cards, and casually asked Peter if he had any interest. At the funeral, while all the adults were standing together in the parking lot of the cemetery, George folded up a twenty-dollar bill and tucked it into the pocket of Peter's shirt. Peter was only about six or seven at the time and had no idea what to do with a twenty-dollar bill. "Bet you'd like to be somewhere else," George had whispered. Another time, Peter came home from school to find George helping his dad take a tree stump out of the ground, and it was like coming home to find a celebrity waiting for him. The three of them ate pizza on the back steps, and though Peter hoped and hoped George would stay longer, that he would stay all night and wake up to have breakfast with them the next morning, he somehow understood that George would leave before Peter's mother came home.

When his father told him that George and Brenda were coming for Thanksgiving, Peter cautiously checked his excitement in case the plan would change. For years Peter had looked over at the cars pulling up at the Gleesons' and the Maldonados' on Thanksgiving and Christmas, but not once had a car ever pulled up to his house on those days. Peter imagined George walking through their front door carrying a tower of bakery boxes like the Gleesons' guests all seemed to do. When George arrived, even before he introduced his wife, he put his hand on Peter's shoulder, and Peter felt as if he knew his uncle much better than just those few times they'd actually spent together.

"You doing good?" George asked him. "Pretty tall now, huh? Your dad, he puts fertilizer in your shoes?"

All went well for a while. The adults discussed the election, poor Michael Dukakis, whether Kitty had really burned a flag in college or if Bush's people had made that up. Peter went out to the driveway for a while to check out the pogo stick George had brought for him—Kate shouted hello from her bedroom window and Peter waved—but when he went back inside the mood had changed. In just fifteen minutes Peter's mother seemed to have taken a strong dislike to George's wife, Brenda. She made a twist of her mouth whenever the younger woman spoke, and Peter saw George noticing. There hadn't been a wedding, Peter had gathered, but he didn't see why that would bother anyone.

George was the first to raise his voice. "Cool it," he said to Anne, raising a hand to indicate he'd had enough. Anne raised her voice back at him and after a few minutes of shouting, Anne went to the closet and got the vacuum cleaner. She lifted it over her head, and George's wife shrieked as Anne swung it at all of them. They all dodged it but three water glasses went flying, along with some cutlery, a dish of mashed potatoes. All of it skidded across the wood floor, onto the carpet. His father yelled at his mother like Peter had never heard before, and his mother, still holding the vacuum, squeezed her eyes shut. Peter took a step back, took another step back until he felt the wall behind him, and watched. When his mother finally went upstairs, slamming the door to her bedroom so hard that the whole house shook, the four people remaining in the dining room looked around at the mess and at each other.

"What the fuck, Brian," George said. "What was she so mad about? Did I miss something?"

"You can't reason with a person who won't be reasoned with," Brian said quietly. A plea that his brother not push. An acknowledgment that there was something going on that he'd lost control of, that he didn't understand, that he'd have to do something about, and soon.

"Didn't I tell you?" George asked. "Didn't I tell you—what?—fifteen years ago?"

"George," Brian said, and glanced quickly at Peter.

But instead of letting it go, of feigning harmony as all adults did, George turned and studied Peter. "You're a cool customer, aren't you?"

Who was the first to start laughing? George probably. His father got a bottle of something from a cabinet, and when George poured a little quarter-inch measure in the bottom of a water glass and handed it to

Peter, his father didn't object. His mother showed no signs of coming back downstairs.

"You okay, sweetie?" Brenda asked Peter after a while. The brothers were getting louder. Brian pounded his fist on the table as he told some story from growing up, and Peter felt as if he were listening to a stranger.

"Yeah, I'm fine. Why?" Peter said breezily, as if he wasn't sure why she was asking. The first sip of alcohol had burned a path down his throat to his belly. His breath felt hotter when he exhaled. He took the rest in one gulp, as he'd seen George and his father do.

"Okay, tough guy. Okay."

The potatoes were still on the floor, the glasses topsy-turvy on the carpet. He could just push the potatoes back into the bowl and dump them into the kitchen garbage can. The glasses he could collect in one pass and stand them up in the sink so that no one would step on them and maybe get a cut on their feet. He looked around to check if everyone was wearing shoes. But cleaning up felt like it might ruin something, so instead he just turned his back to the mess and let it be. He'd never heard his father be loud. He'd never seen him pound a table. He didn't know whether witnessing his father like that made him happy or afraid. George tilted the flimsy chair back on two legs. They'd moved from the dining room to the kitchen, and still, the mess stayed exactly where it had landed. George poured another quarter inch into Peter's glass. Brian Stanhope looked but didn't object.

"I'm just gonna . . . ," Peter said as he grabbed a wad of paper towels and turned back to the spilled food. Brenda followed with a damp sponge.

———

Inside the Gleesons' house, Kate tried to make sense of what had happened while her mother wrapped an ice cube in a gauze-thin kitchen cloth and made Kate suck. Her teeth were fine but she'd bitten her tongue so hard that there were two swollen purple dashes there, and every time she moved her head they let loose a little more blood. It didn't seem like much when Kate went over it, but the sum added up to more than the parts. *You think you're so smart*, Mrs. Stanhope had said. Kate wondered if it bothered her so much because it was true: she did think she was smart. It was as if she'd pried open Kate's secret and stuck her finger in it, stirring it around until the most shameful part emerged.

The whole exchange—only a minute long—already had the quality of a dream. Maybe, Kate thought, being an adult, Mrs. Stanhope saw something in her that Kate, having no perspective, couldn't see, and that her own mother couldn't see because she loved her so much. Kate recalled a morning a few weeks before, dress-down day at school—for a dollar every kid could show up in jeans and sneakers just like the public school kids got to do every day, and the money would go toward new basketball uniforms for the boys. Kate brushed pink powder along her cheekbones that morning and imagined some of the boys might notice. That was the day that Deacon and Mrs. Gallagher came to teach the monthly sex-ed class. They had nine children—their youngest had been in Sara's class—and seeing them together, arranging the dittos at the front of the classroom before the deacon led the boys across the hall, she couldn't stop thinking that these two—she short and husky, like a fire hydrant on legs, he tall and angular and not a single hair on the top of his head—had done what Kate knew people had to do to get nine children.

That night, late, long after her sisters and parents were asleep, long after the throbbing in her tongue had finally dulled, Kate noticed a light shining on her bedroom wall. As soon as she noticed it—a circle in the dead center of the wall opposite the window—it blinked out. Then it returned. Then it blinked out again. When it returned, she went to the window. There, across the immense night, was Peter, standing at his bedroom window. He turned the flashlight to himself and then to something he was holding in his hand. He raised the window screen and launched what looked to be a paper airplane into the darkness. He tried to follow it with the light, but the bright white of the paper and the circle of light kept chasing and passing each other, making something spectacular and frantic against the perfect stillness of the night. The plane landed on the grass, on Kate's side of the lawn. Peter found it and held the light steady for a second, then back up at Kate, who nodded and waved so he'd know she'd seen it, that she knew it was meant for her.

five

AS THE BUS LUMBERED around the streets of Gillam, and all day at school that Thursday, Kate's plan to meet Peter was like a warm stone she cupped in her hands. The paper airplane had been saturated with dew but he'd anticipated that, writing the message in pencil so the words wouldn't run. She'd raced out the back door to get it before breakfast, before the rest of them had a chance to glance out the window and spot it there beside the holly bush.

"Were you outside already?" her mother asked when Kate came back in, blades of wet grass stuck to her bare feet.

"I thought I left a book out there," Kate said, and her mother shuffled on, bleary-eyed without her first cup of coffee.

Midnight, the note said. He had to talk to her. He probably wouldn't be at school. He hoped her mouth was okay. Meet him by the hedges.

At breakfast, Natalie and Sara wanted to know what had happened, exactly. They'd had a track meet the previous afternoon, came home late and had to finish their homework. They only pieced together the clues that something was up when Kate refused to leave her room for dinner and their mother banned them from the kitchen so she could talk to their father in private.

"It was the craziest thing," Kate began, keeping her voice low.

"Yeah?" Natalie said, grabbing an apple from the fruit bowl.

"I fell off the rock and bit my tongue. Blood everywhere. Mrs. Stanhope came out and she was so mad. She asked me if I thought I was smart. Then Mom came out and smacked me so hard. . . ." But Kate felt their blank stares. She couldn't explain it. She couldn't boil the whole encounter down to one riveting sentence.

"What's with you and Peter?" Natalie asked. "Are you two fooling around?"

"No!" Kate cried as she felt a ball of light gather under her breastbone.

The simple fact that Kate was still at St. Bart's and Nat and Sara were a senior and a sophomore at Gillam High meant that her stories could never be as interesting as theirs. Nothing rated until high school.

Sara leaned over her bowl to get closer to Kate. "Nat's going out with Damien Reed."

"Sara!" Natalie said.

"She won't tell," Sara said.

"Oh," Kate said as she felt her own story get shouldered aside. She didn't know who Damien Reed was.

Sara continued. "She said that if she ever gets pregnant, she'll rent a car, drive to Texas, get an abortion, and tell Mom and Dad she's at a track meet."

"Sara!" Natalie said again, this time with more feeling. "I'll kill you."

"Why Texas?" Kate asked.

Nat sighed. "It doesn't have to be Texas. Somewhere far."

"Wouldn't you want someone to go with you?" If they'd expected her to be prudish about it, she hadn't given them the satisfaction.

"Sara would come," Natalie said, looking at Sara to confirm this was true. She turned to Kate. "You could come if you wanted to. Not now, but in a couple of years. Not that I expect it to ever happen."

Kate considered this.

"And if you guys ever need one, you can say you're visiting me at school," Nat said, closing the subject. She was heading to Syracuse in the fall.

Their mother came in and began taking everything she'd need out of the fridge and the bread box to make their lunches. "Whisper, whisper, whisper," she said as she counted out six slices of bread, three black plums, three bottles of Snapple. She opened a tub of tuna salad. "You'd all better be ready for the bus. I don't feel like driving anyone this morning."

———

Mrs. O'Connor looked up from her attendance sheet and said his name twice before moving on. At gym Mr. Schiavone announced that it was Peter Stanhope's turn to be captain and then looked around at everyone before naming another boy instead. Kate felt a hum of fear and joy rush through her every time his absence was noted, as if the shape of him were there beside her. Idly, throughout the day, she'd touch her hand to her jaw where he'd touched her less than twenty-four hours before.

"Where's Peter?" some of the kids asked on the bus ride home.

"Not feeling well I guess," Kate said, swallowing back a smile.

When she got off the bus, she was careful not to look too long at Peter's house in case anyone would catch on. His mother's car was in the driveway. Their front door was closed. Lena Gleeson was standing on the porch with an armful of mail. She waved to Kate's bus driver as he drove on.

"Peter didn't go today?" she said once they were inside.

"Nope." Kate shrugged.

"Hmm," her mother said.

Homework, dinner, dishes: Kate did all of it meekly, hoping not to draw attention to herself. "Are you feeling okay? Let me see your tongue," her mother said when Kate announced she was going upstairs to read before bed. Kate opened wide and stretched out her tongue as far as it would go.

"Looks fine," Lena said, smoothing Kate's hair away from her face. She brought her forehead to Kate's, like she used to do when Kate was small. "Are you upset about your friend?"

"What do you mean?"

"He probably won't be allowed to play with you anymore, Katie."

"We don't *play*, Mom. God. I'm almost fourteen."

"Okay, well, whatever it is you do, I'm sure she'll stop him doing it. But you steer clear, Kate, okay? Peter's a nice boy but the family is trouble."

———

That night, Kate lay on top of her quilt and waited for the minutes to pass. Natalie and Sara had been sharing a bedroom since Kate was born, her days and nights reversed. They'd stayed in those rooms ever since, and only that night did Kate wonder if it meant something, if it had been preordained, if she'd ended up with a room to herself only so she could sneak out so many years later to meet Peter at midnight.

Her father was working a four to twelve tour that night, but that meant he wouldn't be home until at least one o'clock. When her sisters filed upstairs sometime around ten, she felt her nerves begin to electrify. At eleven the laugh track of her mother's show abruptly stopped as the TV shut off and the house settled down into silence. Kate considered that less than fifty feet away Peter was doing the same thing: lying in the dark, waiting. If their bedroom walls fell away, they could have walked straight out of their rooms toward each other and been next to each other almost instantly. Kate's childhood would end soon and that would be fine because that meant no one could tell her what she could and couldn't do, and no one could tell Peter either. One day, she and Peter would sit in restaurants, they'd order dinner from a menu, they'd chat easily about what happened to them that day. Sometimes adulthood seemed far away, but that night, as the clock finally showed eleven fifty-eight and Kate pulled a cardigan over her pajamas, it felt very near. And she felt ready for it. That readiness coursed through her as she tiptoed down the stairs to the back door, as she put her hand to the knob and pushed. Once outside she jogged to the side yard, where Peter was already waiting.

"Let's go," he whispered, grabbing Kate's hand. Side by side they ran north on Jefferson—Kate's cardigan flapping, Peter's laces untied—and turned onto Madison, where there was an empty house, a cockeyed For Sale sign in the front yard. They went around back to an old swing set. This had been the Teagues' house, their kids older than Natalie. They'd moved somewhere south when their youngest went to college, and the house had been sitting empty ever since. There was a lofted section on the play set that they had to climb a rusty ladder to reach. Peter pushed aside empty soda cans. Kate felt her pulse beating in her injured tongue.

"I have to pee," Kate said.

"You're just nervous," Peter said. Everything about him seemed male to Kate now: the breadth of his hands, the particular set of his mouth, even the shade of blue of his eyes. They'd been comparing bodies since they were little, and now it struck Kate how much harder his body must have worked to get so much bigger than hers, cells multiplying at twice the rate hers did, muscles growing longer, stronger. Standing, the top of Kate's head came only to his chin.

"Aren't you?" Kate asked. She wasn't sure what she was supposed to do. Where was she supposed to look? Peter inched closer, took her hand again, slid his hand to her wrist and circled it with his fingers, took the other wrist as well. He moved his hands up to her elbows, and Kate rested her forearms on top of his. Together, they looked braced to jump. Neither of them said anything, and then their silence stretched so long that they got past wanting to fill it. He was wearing the Mets T-shirt he'd worn at least twice a week for going on two years. It was getting too small for him—the material pulling a little across his shoulders.

"I guess," he said.

Kate noticed that there was something different about talking with him now, aside from the circumstances, aside from him holding on to her as if he wanted to confirm that she was really there.

"Are you sure your parents were asleep?" she asked. "I'd better be back before twelve thirty."

"Kate," he said, and shifted a little so that now he was examining her fingers, measuring them against his own like they had when they were kids. Then he bent and kissed her knuckles. He turned her hand over and kissed her palm. Kate thought: Everything in my life has been lived only to get to this, his warm mouth in my hand. There were two pencil-eraser-sized holes at the seam of his T-shirt. He leaned forward and kissed her lips.

They parted for air and Kate shivered, though she felt calmer now that it had happened. She wiped her mouth with the back of her hand and then noticed him looking at her with mock pain.

"Oh, sorry," she laughed. A car passed on Monroe and they followed the direction of its headlights as the beams traveled through the trees. It turned onto Central.

"My dad's leaving," Peter said. "He's going to live in Queens with my uncle."

"You guys are moving?"

"Just my dad."

"Are you serious? Peter. When did he tell you?"

"Yesterday after dinner. My mom—she went berserk after, you know, when she saw you and me outside. So she called him at work and he came home and then, I don't know. She said a bunch of stuff and I guess that's when he decided."

"Did he ask you to go with him and you didn't want to, or did he not ask you?"

Peter picked at a splinter that was rising up from a plank of wood. "I think I'm better with her than he is."

"Well what did she say?"

He picked at another splinter.

"Hey, Peter? Are you sure you don't want to try to talk your dad into bringing you with him? I know I'd miss you, but—"

"Thing is though, Kate, I don't think she'd be okay if I went. You know?"

"But." Kate thought about how to phrase it and didn't do any better than when she was little. "What's wrong with her? Maybe there's been a misunderstanding and if we just—"

Peter shook his head. He told her what had happened at Food King over the winter. That explained why the Stanhopes had Evergood grocery bags in their garbage can now. Evergood didn't even sell nuts and raisins in sealed packages; customers had to scoop them out of bins. That it had been almost five months and she hadn't heard about it at school meant that it probably wasn't as big a deal as Peter was making it out to be, but then she considered the opposite: that it was such a big deal that the adults had been that careful not to talk about it in front of the kids.

"Peter—"

"I just wanted you to know things might be different for a while." He kissed her again, this time for longer. She could feel his hands clutching her, moving between her rib cage and her waist. She rested her hands lightly on his shoulders and then circled them tight around him. If his mother had gone berserk after the previous afternoon when Peter had merely checked that Kate was okay, what would she do if she looked in on him tonight and found him not in his room? Kate pulled away.

"You can tell me anything, you know. I would never tell anyone."

"I know." He sat back on his heels. "When we were little it was different, but now—I don't know. I think of how I want to tell you everything and sometimes when things aren't so great at home I think about something funny you said. And the way you are with your sisters and your parents. I used to think what my life would be like if I were your brother instead of your neighbor but then a while back I realized I don't want to be your brother because then we couldn't get married one day."

"Married!" Kate nearly shouted before she burst out laughing.

"I mean it."

The porch light went on in the house next door and they jumped apart. "We better go," Peter whispered. Kate scrambled back to the ladder while Peter took the slide. They sprinted to the sidewalk—Kate slapped the For Sale sign as she passed by—ran down Madison, and turned onto the far end of Jefferson, where Peter stopped, scooped her up in his arms, swung her around, and then set her back down. Stumbling, giddy, they resumed their run until their houses appeared. When they got close they crouched for a moment in the shadow of the Nagles' boxwoods.

"I'm sorry about what happened yesterday," Peter said. Kate studied his face in the uneven moonlight and glimpsed what he would look like when he was grown. She reached up and put her hand on his neck. He closed his eyes.

"It's okay." None of that mattered. They were tied now by what he'd said, by the kiss, by knowing each other their entire lives. Silently, they shot out from the boxwoods like a pair of foxes—Peter to his house, Kate to hers.

———

They would have gotten away with it, too, if Lena Gleeson hadn't remembered that she'd left the garden hose to a trickle after dinner. She'd just planted that hydrangea, and now she might have drowned it. She'd been asleep but something in her dreams had reminded her, jolting her awake. She arrived in the kitchen to find the back door slightly ajar. She stared at it, looked quickly to the living room to see if Francis had come home, and then wondered if she'd really forgotten to lock up. She went outside into the chilly night and turned off the water. The ground under her slippers was sopping. She returned to the kitchen and fingered the little twist lock on the doorknob. When she went back upstairs to check Kate's room, it felt almost good to be right.

"Where were you?" she asked when Kate finally came creeping around the holly bush to the back door. Lena was sitting on the back step. Kate gasped, put a hand over her heart.

"Mom!"

"I asked you a question. Where were you?"

Her voice sounded so calm that Kate thought, at first, she might not be in too much trouble. Behind her, Peter's shadow cut across the lawn to his own back door.

"Hold on a second," Lena called out, striding across the soggy lawn in her bright white bedroom slippers. "Just hold on." She passed right by Peter and pounded on the Stanhopes' back door.

"What are you doing? Mom! Wait. Please," Kate said, pulling on her mother's sleeve like a toddler. "You don't understand. Why do you have to tell them?" A lamp on the first floor of Peter's house was switched on. Then the kitchen light. Kate looked to Peter to chime in, to help, but Peter just sighed.

"You know," Lena said when Brian opened the door and the light boxed them in together. She drew her robe more tightly around her body. "You can tell your wife that her son is no angel either. This was his idea, them sneaking out." From the depths of her robe pocket she removed the paper airplane. A car pulled into the Gleesons' driveway. A door slammed. Everyone listened to Francis walk up the path, fumble at the door for his keys. He flicked on the living room light and walked straight through the house to the back door, which was standing wide open.

"What's going on?" he asked as he approached, though Kate could tell he'd already figured it out.

"She'll tell you," Lena said as she gripped Kate by the most tender part of her elbow and pulled her back toward their house. Brian held the door open for Peter, who stepped past his father with his head bowed.

"Ow," Kate said as she tried to maneuver out of her mother's grip.

"Am I hurting you?" Lena asked as she gripped harder.

———

In all the years they'd lived next door to one another, the Gleesons had never heard the Stanhopes yelling. Hearing them argue now—a woman's voice, yes, they could all hear it, and a man's, and Peter's—made all of them stop to listen. Kate felt the attention deflected from her just a little. Sara appeared at the bottom of the stairs. "There's something going on next door."

Then she saw Kate and said, "Oh boy." She plopped down on the couch and looked around with naked interest in whatever might happen next.

"He's leaving them," Kate offered, desperate to keep their focus on the Stanhopes. "Mr. Stanhope. He's moving in with his brother. Peter just wanted to tell me."

"It has nothing to do with you, Kate," Francis yelled, pounding his fist on the table so hard even Lena jumped. "Make a new friend, for God's sake. Stay away from those people." It was his fault, he knew. Even as he was yelling he knew it was on him. Anne Stanhope rang an alarm in him the first moment he met her, and yet he'd done nothing. Because he liked Brian. Because he thought, they're little kids, what harm? But what does a little kid care except to have another kid to play with? There was a window there somewhere when they could have replaced Peter with any other child and Kate wouldn't have even noticed. Nat and Sara were a pair, but he and Lena could have let Kate invite friends home from school. That's what some of Kate's classmates did, according to Lena. It seemed so American, inviting a kid from across town when there were so many walking distance from home, but they should have done it. They should have encouraged her to go over to the Maldonados' more often. Susannah was maybe a little dumb and that older brother always seemed up to something, but at least their parents were normal. But Lena always said it was sweet, how Kate and Peter sought each other out. She'd stand at the kitchen window and look at them out there in the yard, always talking, talking, talking. She said it was important to have a good friend, and anyway, they'd grow out of it. One would get tired of the other and move on.

"How do you know?" Francis asked after the incident at Food King, when there was no sign of them growing apart. Brian was markedly less friendly to Francis after the New Year's drama, and a few times he seemed outright hostile. People get funny when they know they're in the wrong.

"It's called adolescence," Lena had said. "It's called life."

Kate looked so scrawny in her thin pajamas, her narrow little body the same as it was when she was in kindergarten, only stretched out. She was his girl, Francis thought, though he was always careful to not play favorites. His heart would swell sometimes to see her tearing around from the back of the house in any type of weather while her sisters painted their nails inside. She was the only one who might tag along with him to the hardware store on a Saturday morning, even though she knew as well as he did that they'd spend half their time there standing around with the other cops who'd been tasked by their wives to fix something, install something. Together in their black dress socks pulled up to mid-calf and their plaid shorts—all of them with their off-duty weapons holstered under their short-sleeved button-down shirts—they scrutinized every manner of bit, nail, and screw without having the first idea what to do with any of it because they'd all moved up from the city where they'd just badgered their supers until things got fixed. Having grown up in Ireland didn't make it any different for Francis; where he came from they didn't have ambitions of cedar decks out back. "What did you have?" Kate asked him once. "A patio?" He'd laughed. Once, when she was barely out of diapers, she gathered her stuffed animals on the stairs and told him she'd called them for muster.

But now she was thirteen and he watched her wipe her nose roughly with her open palm. Lena was always after her to stop doing that.

"Listen to me, Kate. There's enough trouble in the world without going out and looking for more."

Lena itemized all the things she could not do. Wasn't there a big graduation party coming up? Well, she could count that out. Also: no phone, no television. Kate smirked and folded her arms. She didn't use the phone anyway. She barely watched TV.

"No going outside after school," Francis added, and Kate's heart dropped. She felt her smirk falter. "And no more bus. Mom or I will drive you."

Natalie appeared, rubbing her eyes. "What the heck?" she said, and then looked past her mother, past her father, and squinted at the front door. "Is that Peter? What's he doing?" Kate jumped up and spun around. There was Peter, standing under the extinguished porch light as if deciding whether or not to knock. When he saw all of them looking at him, he raised his hands like a half-hearted surrender.

It was Francis who opened the door. "What now?" he asked, looking past Peter into the dark.

Lena said, "I think we've had enough for one night."

Peter nodded, taking the comments in. His Adam's apple tumbled up and down the chute of his skinny neck as he swallowed, grew more nervous, swallowed again. He glanced over at his house, and then, taking a breath as if he were about to dive into a body of water, he stepped inside. "Will you guys call the police please?" he asked, looking only at Kate. But instead of waiting for an answer, he simply walked past the entire Gleeson family, through the family room, through the dining room, to the kitchen, where their phone was on the wall in the very same spot as it was in his own house. They all stayed exactly where they were for a moment, listening to the hollow plastic sound of the handset being removed from the cradle.

Lena began to speak, but Francis held up his hand. "What's happening?" he demanded, following the boy into the kitchen.

Peter looked directly at him as he spoke into the phone. "Yes. Hello. Can you send someone to seventeen eleven Jefferson Street? Yes. Please hurry. My mother has my father's gun."

Lena clapped her hand over her mouth as Sara and Natalie flew to the window. Kate looked only at Peter. Francis shook his head. It wasn't possible. The boy had misunderstood. This was why bystanders made terrible witnesses. Peter's mother had taken his father's gun in the past, so the boy only thought she'd done it again. They thought—he and Brian—that they could keep that one detail from the kids just as they'd kept it from the rest of Gillam, but these kids knew everything. They watched and listened and knew too much.

"I'm going over there," Francis said.

"Wait," Peter said. "Just wait a second." As Peter held the curved blue handset like a supplicant offering alms, Kate could see that he was thinking of a way to minimize the drama, a way to keep them out of it despite having to use their phone. It struck Kate how much he looked like his father as he struggled to articulate what he wanted to say. They had the same way of holding themselves, that same way of appearing to wear their trouble lightly.

But just like that Peter's second was up. Francis moved past Lena and in what seemed like a single instant, he was standing on the Stanhopes' faded welcome mat, pounding on their door with his legs set apart in a stance Kate had never seen him strike before. "Brian!" he shouted, "Anne!" He tried the handle. Pounded again. He'd given the gun lock to Brian himself, back in January. It was New Year's Day, the hardware store was closed, but Francis had an extra combination lock still in the packaging sitting in his shed. He'd walked back there with Brian, and when he opened the door they were hit with the smell of old grass and gasoline. He found it right away, a miracle, and he'd watched as Brian ripped it open. As Francis was pulling the shed door closed behind them, he told Brian not to write the code down anyplace. Brian had looked at him as if to ask if Francis really thought he was that much of an idiot, and

Francis had shrugged, angry all of a sudden, very tempted to point out that Brian was the asshole who'd lost track of a loaded gun.

So the boy had to be wrong. Maybe she'd made a threat. It had been almost five months since the incident at Food King, since he gave Brian that lock. Almost five months of making a habit stick. As Francis considered what to do, he leaned over and ran his hand over his calf as if the gun Peter had seen might have somehow been his own. He unsnapped the holster, but then snapped it closed again. It was completely impossible. He remembered a story from home, from just before he left for America. A family up the lane had lost two children, drowned in their well, three years apart. First the one died, and then three years later another, in nearly the exact same way, at nearly the exact same age. "God love them," his mother had whispered to his father in their kitchen, overcome with grief. "Couldn't it have happened to any one of us?" Now, nearly thirty years on, Francis wanted to return to the scene, wanted to raise his mother and father from the dead just to say, no, now that he'd time to think about it, he just did not agree. It could not have happened to any one of them.

"Francis!" Lena yelled across the yard. A light inside the Maldonados' house went on. The Nagles, too, had woken up. The 911 operator had instructed Peter to remain on the line so he had, and now he looked to Kate to relay to him what was going on outside. He should hang up, he thought. It was probably fine. He'd gotten nervous and had overreacted and now everything would be worse. His father had planned on leaving that weekend. He'd said it might be for just a little while and Peter decided right then not to call him on anything, to let him say whatever ridiculous thing he wanted to say, and Peter would just do what he liked. That's when he'd sent the paper plane out the window. That's when he decided he didn't really care if he got caught. The operator on the other line was asking him what happened, what kind of gun, whether it was loaded, but Peter ignored her. "Just tell them to come quickly," he said. "As quickly as they can."

From inside the Stanhope home came footsteps. "Coming!" called Anne Stanhope, as brightly as if it were three o'clock in the afternoon. Francis looked across to Lena and waved in a way that would let her know it was all fine.

Anne threw open the door and staggered back several steps. She was empty-handed, Francis noticed first. She was wearing a paisley nightshirt, little colorful teardrops hanging loosely over slim legs. She looked like she was in pain, and Francis wondered for a moment if the boy had only gotten half mixed up. If in fact it was Brian who'd had enough and reached for the closest thing.

"Are you hurt?" he asked, taking one tentative step inside. Anne dropped slowly to her knees, sat back on her heels. Francis looked quickly around the room, to the stairs, to the shadowed place behind the open door. In the distance, sirens.

"Where's Brian?" He took another few steps farther into the house.

"I'm very sorry about all this," Anne said, and when Francis glanced at her, she seemed sorry. Her face was ashen and she looked exhausted, brokenhearted. Then she reached under the couch cushion next to her and, moving faster than Francis thought possible, removed a gun, pointed, and fired.

QUEENS

six

IN GEORGE'S APARTMENT, THEY ate on paper plates. Peter tagged along when his uncle headed to the wholesalers in Long Island City every few months to buy a six-pack of the white undershirts George wore every day and a package of two thousand premium, heavy-duty paper plates, which he kept stacked on the counter in two equally sized towers. He didn't have a kitchen table so they ate in front of the TV, their dinner on their knees. For utensils, they used the silverware that Brenda left behind when she moved back in with her parents, and the sink always had a scatter of forks, knives, and spoons across the bottom. In the bathroom, Brenda left a jar of face cream that George shoved to the corner of the counter, where it slowly became crowded out with cans of shaving cream, Old Spice, Clearasil, mouthwash, toothbrushes left in scummy puddles here and there. Once in a while, after a shower, Peter would open that tub of cream and inhale. Cucumbers. Dryer sheets. The bright silver cap of the jar never seemed to gather dust, and Peter wondered if his father and George did the same.

Brian got moved to modified duty after everything happened, and then to Traffic once the case settled. The house sold quickly, to a young family from Rockaway, and the realtor arranged for an estate sales-person to go in and tag all their furniture. Their dishes, even. Linens. Tupperware. The umbrella stand and the three umbrellas that sat inside. Peter's bike went, his old Lincoln Logs. Every dollar had to go to legal fees, medical fees, all in and straight out again as if through a swing-ing door. Brian made the mistake of telling Peter, and Peter, who had been stoic through everything, who had remained unflappable through his mother's detention—the county jail, an indictment, most of a trial, a settlement, a state hospital—was rattled, finally, by this: the thought that there were strangers moving through their house in Gillam, looking at his sticker collection and trying out his creaky desk chair, while he and his father sat on George's couch in Queens, watching *Jeopardy!* Brian watched him take it in. They were nearly the same height now. Their hands the same breadth. Peter flushed a deep red and Brian looked away. It was easy to forget how young he was.

"What about my stuff?" Peter asked. "The stuff that's not worth money. My notebooks. Other things."

"We'll get it, Pete. Don't worry. The lady will set that stuff aside and we'll pick it all up."

"My tapes?"

"Yeah, I told her to leave them aside, too."

"They're in a shoebox in my closet. You told her that?"

"No, but I'll tell her today. I'll call her."

"My books, too." He had a beautiful hardcover copy of *The Hobbit* that had a thick gold page across from the title page and another at the end. He'd won it in the fire prevention poster contest in sixth grade, and the moment he held it he decided he'd never crack the binding. When he became too curious about the story inside, he'd gotten a library copy to read and leave winged open on his pillow all day. Kate had won second place and got a copy of *Anne of Green Gables*.

"Yeah, your books, too. All that. We're going to go back and get it."

"When?"

"I don't know, buddy. Pretty soon."

Peter nodded, and then carefully placed his fork on top of the torn-off paper towel that was his napkin. He plucked his jacket from where it was strewn across the back of the TV, and walked out of the apartment. The deli downstairs had two video games in the back, and Peter often went down to play *Duck Hunt* or *Pac-Man* in the afternoons. He also liked to sit outside the noodle shop on Queens Boulevard and watch the 7 train rattle by overhead.

"What did I say?" Brian asked when he'd left, leaning back into the deep cushions of the couch.

"He just wants his things," George said. "Are you really going to go back there? Like you said?"

"Of course. Why wouldn't I?"

George shrugged and glanced over at the closed apartment door before turning back to his show.

————

There were some, Brian knew, who thought he should have been fired, who thought he was incompetent, who thought he was a d-bag who couldn't control his wife. But he hadn't committed a crime; she had. He'd been a witness. A victim, even. Francis Gleeson's face looked better, Brian had heard. Not normal, exactly, but you might not need to look away. He could speak and eat. He was walking now. They'd known almost right away that he would live. Once he made it through the first twelve hours, there was hope. Once he made it twenty-four hours, it was clear that he was stronger than anyone expected, but then what? He'd live but in what capacity? In the stack of paperwork that came months after it happened, just before the criminal suit was settled, Brian read that as they were rolling him into surgery that first night, a nurse had told Lena Gleeson that he'd already gotten a round of blood transfusions, and asked if they should give him another if he needed it. Lena had not understood the question at first, the question behind the question, but once it clicked she became ferocious and told them to use their own blood if they had to; she told them to wring themselves dry as long as they saved him. And then she waited outside the door for six, seven, eight hours, just to see him for ten minutes. She was there the next day and night, and the next, for the next three months, until he got moved to a rehab hospital upstate. Some of the nurses were annoyed by her doggedness, by her suspicious regard of every move they made, but others said it was her will that saved him. He was strong, yes, and had gotten lucky, but those things alone wouldn't have been enough.

The stack of paperwork was six inches deep, but the details about Lena were what Brian returned to again and again. He heard on the job that as soon as Francis was strong enough, she'd drive upstate to the rehab hospital only to drive him all the way back down again to Gillam and over to the lake. He was still in a wheelchair then, so she'd fix him up beside a bench with a broad straw sun hat and a blanket on his knees. She'd talk away to him there, and coming up behind them, Brian imagined, seeing only their silhouettes against the sun, they looked like any couple out enjoying the day. People would pass them on their morning walks and say hello, ask how he was doing. Lena would turn and smile at Francis to include him, as if his face were not a blasted-out shell, as if he were a well man who might add something: lovely weather today. When he was well enough to go to Mass and could walk short lengths on his own, she'd led him by the hand down the side aisle. Now she didn't need to hold his hand, Brian had heard. He could walk the whole circumference of the lake on his own. Last time Brian saw him was across a courtroom. His hair was buzzed very short. He wore an eye patch over his left eye. His skin looked raw and stretched tight. On one side of his face, his cheek gave way to his neck without the interruption of a jaw, or so it seemed.

Foolishly, Brian thought it might all go away once Francis stabilized. That Francis would wake up and tell the world it was partly his fault, really. It was Francis, after all, who used his influence—everyone knew him, everyone liked him—to keep the whole incident at Food King a private matter. And why? Francis should have let them charge her right then. He should have let them take her in. She would have done a month at the hospital and then come home better.

For over a year now Brian spent his days directing the cars and trucks on the Manhattan side of the Queensboro Bridge. "Oh, fine," he'd always say whenever Peter or George asked how his day had been. Or, "Good except for the damn rain." Or the damn cold. Or the damn heat. But he said it pleasantly, or tried to, and pretty much everyone in the world complained about the rain and the cold and the heat. It was just a thing to say. Peter said that he noticed the weather more now that they were in Queens (he never said that they'd *moved* to Queens, only that they were *in* Queens now) because there was so much more time spent standing in it, waiting for buses, walking to the train, walking home from the grocery store with the plastic handles of heavy bags cutting into the palms of his hands. One day, Brian took the Q32 into the city as always, but instead of getting off at Second Avenue he stayed on, swaying along with the rest of the passengers as the bus barreled across Third, Lex, Park. He got off at Thirty-Second, bought a hot dog, ate it, then took the bus right back to Sunnyside, where he lay down in the honeyed rectangle of light that shone onto George's worn parquet floors. He didn't even know what he was thinking about. The next day he pretended he'd gotten his schedule mixed up. He called the pension fund administrator and double-checked his tier, his eligibility. He was young, still. It would be better to wait until twenty years, but when he pictured another whole year of standing on Fifty-Ninth Street and inhaling exhaust fumes, he felt something inside him lie down and die. Then one day, a few weeks later, without discussing it with Peter, without discussing it with his brother, whose pullout couch he and Peter had been sharing since they left Gillam, Brian handed in his shield. He always imagined he'd wait until a Friday, but he couldn't wait even one more day, so he did it on a Thursday, then took the bus back to Sunnyside, got in his car (even though it was a prime spot, good on the street until Saturday), and drove out to Shea, where he sat idling by the right field gate and had a clear view of the bleachers along the third base line.

That night, while Peter was doing homework, Brian stood in front of the TV and said that he had something pretty exciting to tell them. When Peter looked up he noticed once again that his father had grown thinner. Every pair of pants he owned was too big for him, and cinching his belt tighter only made them look worse. He was jittery, quick to smile, but his grin had a manic quality that made Peter nervous. Now, watching his father clear his throat as if he were addressing a large audience, Peter saw a spark of joy in his father's eyes for the first time since the night his mother shot Mr. Gleeson.

As they knew, Brian began, he'd always wanted to live down south—George and Peter glanced at each other—and after making some calls and talking to some people, he had a good lead on a condo in South Carolina. He also knew a person who could connect him with a security guard position down there. The guy was retired NYPD himself and it was all but guaranteed. He'd collect his pension, and living was cheaper down there. Peter was welcome to come with him if he wanted to.

Peter could see that his uncle was just as surprised as he was. Peter was fifteen years old. He'd been reading about the capture of Fort Ticonderoga because his teacher had hinted there might be a pop quiz the next day. He'd just started his sophomore year at Dutch Kills Preparatory High School for Boys, which still felt like a placeholder. Mrs. Quirk, his science teacher from St. Bart's, had met him in the city and brought him to meet a bunch of people he understood were evaluating him, somehow. It was summer. He assumed teachers went into hiding in the summer, and yet here was Mrs. Quirk, stepping down from the commuter bus and onto a sidewalk grate in the heat of late July. "Come along, Peter," she said, and he did. The adults spoke in private. All he could focus on was how odd it was to see Mrs. Quirk making her way across a city street with the same helmet hair and thick stockings she wore in Gillam, and his first thought was that he couldn't wait to tell Kate. Then, as always when he thought of Kate, he felt a clenching in his belly as if he were bracing for a punch. His father was so busy that summer—lawyers and doctors every day—so it was George who took him where he needed to go, George who got the phone numbers and addresses and the deadlines from Mrs. Quirk. It was George who told Peter he had Mrs. Quirk to thank when he got into Dutch Kills. "What's that?" Peter had asked. And when they told him it was a specialized high school, sort of like a private school except there was no tuition, that it was one of the best schools in the city, public or private, he still couldn't quite understand what they meant. Staying in Queens for a while was one thing. Going to school there was another. When he pictured high school, he still pictured the fieldstone façade of Gillam High.

That was over a year ago. He'd made a few friends at school since then, none who knew about his mother or what had happened in Gillam. None of whom he'd ever met up with on a weekend or after school. They went places together, each other's apartments or to hang out in the park. They referred to things that Peter understood had happened after school, after practice. A few of his cross-country teammates had witnessed a dog walker get tangled up in several leashes and dragged along the bridle path in Central Park. They talked about it for weeks, Rohan imitating the way the man had hopped and stumbled, Drew and Matt howling and yipping like dogs. "You would have laughed, Peter," they said to him, so he knew they weren't excluding him, he knew they liked him, and that was enough. It felt like too much to enter their homes and see their bedrooms and eat snacks with their brothers and sisters like they all seemed to do with each other. He could tell that they assumed he did other things on the weekends, that he went back to "the country," perhaps, where they knew he was from. Once, in his first few weeks there, back when they still peppered him with questions that he mostly deflected, he told them that he had a girlfriend back home whom he tried to see on the weekends. He said sometimes he took the bus out to see her and other times she came to see him. They asked what she looked like not because they were curious, he knew, but because they were deciding whether to believe him. He told them the truth: dark blond hair that fell to the middle of her back, hazel eyes, average height.

"Big tits?" a boy named Kevin asked, and they all laughed as they stretched their hamstrings. Peter grinned along with them but he felt something cold pass through him, and for a terrifying moment he thought he might cry.

Now, in the fall of his sophomore year at Dutch Kills, he was the second best runner on the cross-country team, and when Barry Dillon graduated, he'd be the best. Coach wanted to move him from the mile to the 1,200 meter for winter track, and down to the half for spring. Barry Dillon hadn't been running his times at fifteen, Coach told him over the summer, and added that if he worked his ass off, he could end up being the best middle-distance runner in the city. Peter had been thinking maybe if he just sent Kate the meet schedule, she'd understand what he wanted to ask. If he sent it by mail with a different return address, they might just leave it out for her to open and never even bother to wonder about it. Then she could figure a way to come to the city and they'd finally get to see each other. Despite what his friends at school believed, he hadn't seen Kate since the night he'd used the Gleesons' phone to call 911.

———

What Peter understood was that his father was going either way, that he'd retired from the police department, that he'd signed a lease for a place in either North Carolina or South; Peter kept getting them mixed up. If there was any debating whether or not he should go, that debate had already happened, privately, inside Brian's head. He was inviting Peter, but he was also inviting him to stay behind. Peter's impression was that he'd made the offer as a mere courtesy, a nod to the fact that their lives had intersected up to this point. If it was an inconvenience to George for Peter to stay, then, in his father's view, that was for Peter and George to work out.

"How will you see Mom?" Peter asked.

"How will I see Mom?" Brian repeated in a tone that implied the answer was obvious. He ran his hand through his hair, seemed to search for something in the hidden thicket of his own thoughts. "Average temps down there run about twelve degrees warmer than here. The community I found has a pool for residents. Also a fitness room."

"Also a fitness room," George repeated. He turned to Peter. "You're welcome here as long as you want, kiddo." George spent many of his workdays straddling a four-inch steel beam, several hundred feet above the sidewalk; over time he'd developed a sixth sense for danger that came from always looking around for hazards. "I'll run you up to Westchester whenever you want."

"I'll stay then," Peter said. "At least for a while. See how it goes." He watched his father closely.

"Okay!" Brian said. "It's a plan."

Thirty minutes later, George walked the two blocks up to the boulevard and joined Peter on the stoop of the noodle shop. "I'm glad you're staying, kiddo. We'll have a good time, me and you." Then he put a heavy hand on Peter's head. "You good?"

"Me? Yeah. I'm fine."

"I don't know from golfing, but I know it's not for me, down there. Not for you neither. And you're in this good school. You know there's kids dying to get into that school? And look at you kicking ass there with your running and everything."

"Thanks for the heart-to-heart, George. Nice."

George belted a laugh that turned heads on the city-bound platform. "Now you're a wise guy. They don't have wise guys down south, I don't think."

Brian left a few weeks later, on the morning of the biggest cross-country meet of the season. Peter hated the feeling he got whenever he came home to find his father packing, organizing. One day there was a brand-new duffel bag. Another day a pile of golf shirts in bright colors spilling out the top of a plastic Marshalls bag. It didn't annoy him, exactly; he just preferred to drink a Coke on the front stoop of George's building and watch people hurry home from work, walk their dogs. One afternoon while his father was on the phone, he went down to the street and watched a woman parallel park her station wagon in just three moves, with maybe two inches to spare on either side. He wanted to applaud. A kid he recognized from school walked by, but that kid wasn't a runner, wasn't in any of his classes, so Peter just gave him a quick "Hey" and looked away.

When the morning arrived, Brian threw two bags in the back of his car and slammed the door. "I gave George some money," he said to Peter, who had walked down to the street with him. "So don't worry about that part." Peter hadn't worried about that part. He worried only about having enough time to digest a bagel before the starting gun went off. Now it occurred to him that George had bought those bagels. He'd have to chip in from time to time. He had no idea how much money an ironworker made.

"Be safe," Peter said. He'd heard George say the same thing earlier that morning before he went out. Peter felt in a big rush all of a sudden. He couldn't miss the team van. He needed to stretch. He needed to go to the bathroom. The morning was cool and smelled like apples. He was wasting it standing on the sidewalk.

"Be good," Brian said. "I'll see you soon, okay, Pete?"

"Yeah. I know. That's what you said."

Peter remained on the sidewalk as his father shimmied the car out of the tight parking spot, headed toward Woodside Avenue, and turned right. Before the light had even turned red again, a car pulled up and took the vacant spot.

Two hours later, after a nerve-filled journey to Van Cortlandt Park with the rest of his team, Peter dropped out of the race after only a mile. He'd gotten off to a strong start, had been in the lead as usual, but as the pack headed into the woods, he fell back. He couldn't find his wind. His quads felt heavy. The JV kids started passing him. He slowed to a stop, stepped to the side of the path to let the others get by. "Cramp?" Coach wanted to know as he jogged up. It wasn't like him. Back in the van after the meet was over, heading back to Queens, Coach asked him to sit up front. "You okay?" he asked. "What happened?"

Peter shrugged. "Not feeling too good I guess."

"Want me to call your dad?"

"No, I'll tell him later. I'll tell him when he picks me up." Peter felt pressure on his chest, felt short of breath. He stretched but it didn't seem to help. He rolled down the window and closed his eyes as the rushing air washed over him. "Close that!" one of his teammates called from the backseat, so Peter did. A little while later, the van returned to its spot by the gym doors, and Peter was standing beside the cemetery with his track bag, waiting for the bus.

———

He saw his mother on Sundays. Not every Sunday, but most. His father used to drive him, but after a few months Peter started taking the train instead. He liked going alone. He usually took the 7 to Grand Central, and then transferred to Metro-North for the seventy-minute ride up the Hudson. He wore his Walkman so that no one would start a conversation with him as he stared out the window, watching the towns of Westchester slide by, one after the other so quickly that they bled together, and then less so as the landscape opened and became farmland, stone walls tracing shapes in the distance. Houses gave way to horse paddocks, paved driveways gave way to loose gravel and packed dirt. None of the towns the train went through reminded him of Gillam, but he found himself comparing them to Gillam anyway. Occasionally he spotted a cow. When he got off the train, it was a near two-mile walk to the hospital along a two-lane road. Once, when it was raining, he took a cab from the train and when the driver, a woman, asked him who he was visiting at the hospital, he told her the truth. When she pulled up out front, she said she was very sorry but she still had to charge him the five bucks because she'd already called it in to her dispatcher and things weren't so great for her either.

There had been a period of months when he hadn't been able to see his mother at all. His father saw her a few times when she was being held in the hospital in the Bronx, but both the lawyers and the doctors thought Peter shouldn't see her yet, not until things were settled. Seeing Peter, his father said, would upset what little balance she had, and they didn't want to risk that. They framed it as their decision, all the men involved in her fate, and Peter worried about what she'd think about him not coming to see her. One night, not long after the trial was settled and she was transferred to the state hospital in Westchester, when his father finally got back to Queens, he put his hand on top of Peter's head and told him she'd come around soon.

Then he said, "I mean—"

"You mean it's her who doesn't want to see me?"

"She doesn't know what she wants, Peter. Honestly. I only meant . . . I don't know what I meant."

Peter mulled this over. It was as if he'd been looking out at the world from one window, and now he walked across the room to look at the same world from a different window. "If I show up there, she'll see me. I know she will."

"Okay, bud," his father said. "Next time. Let's give it a try."

And Peter was right. She didn't turn away when she saw him waiting there in the family room next to his dad. She was wearing a loose dress with bright flowers printed on the fabric, a black cardigan, slippers. She looked tired. She'd put on a lot of weight. She smelled like soup.

"That's the medicine," his father told him later. "Puffs her right up. Changes her coloring, even. That's one reason she hates it. It's hard-core stuff. They have to take her blood every other day to make sure it doesn't poison her." She didn't ask Peter any questions about himself, so he just began talking. He told her about his new school. He told her about Sunnyside. She stared blankly past him for a few minutes and then she held up a finger and shushed him. His father looked at his watch, used his smiling voice to say they'd better hit the road, there'd probably be traffic. He smiled harder to smooth their way out the door. "Go to that workshop Dr. Evans was talking about last week," he said to his wife. "You'll enjoy it! Anne, isn't it great Peter came? He wanted to see you so bad."

"Get out of here," Anne said. "I regret the day I met you." Then she wrapped her cardigan tight around her body, and something in the regal sweep of the gesture soothed Peter, confirmed that the mother he knew was still in there, somewhere.

Brian smiled like she didn't mean it, smiled for Peter, and for himself, and then for the nurse who was sitting not six feet away.

"But you," she said to Peter, and her eyes welled up. She held her breath. "You." She pressed hard on his shoulders and then withdrew her hands. "Don't come here again," she said.

"Time to go," the nurse said, coming up behind her and steering her down the hall. "That's all for today."

"Another idiot," Anne said.

———

Brian went to the hospital less and less. He said he had to work. He claimed to have gone to see her while Peter was at school. He was the one who told Peter it would be a cinch to take the train if he wanted to go on his own. George didn't drink like he used to—he allowed himself two beers during Mets games, and so as not to tempt himself, he bought

Budweiser singles from the bodega—and he asked Brian to head up to the Banner if he wanted a whiskey. Peter knew this because his father told him. "He fucked it all up, you know," Brian said to Peter a few weeks after they moved in. "Brenda." He wanted to warn Peter, he said, of what could happen if you lose control over your drink. What happens is your wife ends up leaving and you end up too scared to go to Shea, or to even watch a game at the same pub you were raised in.

"I feel sorry for him," Brian added.

And where did you end up? Peter wanted to ask. If George was such a loser, what did that say about the older brother sleeping on his pullout? Now, instead of driving Peter to the hospital on Sundays, he went up to the Banner and made small talk with the bartender.

The hospital staff didn't like when Peter, a minor, showed up alone, but after conferring by the Xerox machine behind reception, they let him in anyway. The same nurses were always there on Sundays, so he got to know some of them by name, and they got to know him. A few times, he was only allowed to glimpse her through a glass panel in the door. On those occasions she was usually seated on the floor of a padded room. The first time he saw her like that, the nurse seemed to realize what she'd done, seemed to worry all of a sudden that she shouldn't have let him see, and offered Peter a soda from the nurses' fridge, which was normally off-limits to visitors. "You're so tall," she said to him. "What are you, a senior?" she asked. When he told her he was a freshman, she went pale. Once, his mother had an abrasion on her forehead, and though he normally tried to make himself as inconspicuous as possible, he couldn't stop worrying about how she'd gotten it. Shaking, he'd walked up to the desk and asked what had happened, why her family hadn't been called. He felt very grown up. "I'm sure someone spoke to your dad," the nurse called Sal said. And then, leaning forward with a conspiratorial expression: "Peter, she probably did it to herself."

One time he arrived to find they'd cut her hair. Another time she refused to come out of her room, so he walked the two miles back to the train station wishing he'd left her a note to say it was okay, he'd see her next week. Sometimes she shuffled down the hall and sat with him but refused to speak.

And now he had news that would upset her. He wouldn't blurt it out. He'd wait until she asked for him. But that Sunday, twenty-four hours after his father left for a condo in South Carolina or North, she was waiting for Peter to arrive. Her hair was combed nicely. She looked neat and clean, somehow less swollen than she'd been.

"So he left," she said. He hadn't even sat down.

"Yeah, I guess so," Peter said. "How'd you know?"

"He came by here and I couldn't tell what he was going on about at first and then I put it together. And you're still with George?" She was lucid. Crystal clear. Like some series of adjustments had been made and here was his real mother, back again.

"Yeah."

"And going to school? Your grades are good?"

"Yeah."

"Good. Okay, Peter, listen. It'll be fine. What's going to happen is I'm going to get out of here. They're going to let me go soon. I was thinking we could start a shop, you and me. Not in New York. Maybe in Chicago. Or London. A specialty shop. A place people can buy things that are hard to find. We'll have to live in public housing for a while and then we'll get our own flat. We'll meet loads of people going in and out and they'll be a high-quality people. If George is good to you—is he good to you?—we'll let him come on as an investor."

Peter didn't know what to say, so he said nothing. The seconds ticked by. She went and stood by a bookcase that was stacked with board games.

"I don't think you're getting out soon, though, Mom," he said finally. It was his job to tell her the truth now. Better tell her that truth than to say that her plan worried him, that it didn't seem sound, that he had no interest in getting involved in a specialty shop, that he didn't know what that even meant. Nurses and people on the administrative staff passed back and forth through the family meeting room, which was arranged with fake intimacy, a set of love seats and armchairs like they might pretend they were sitting in their own living room at home.

Anne hugged herself and squinted up at a corner of the ceiling like she'd spotted a cobweb there.

"Have you talked to that girl?" she asked after a while.

"What girl?" Peter asked, though he knew. And then, "No."

"And her father? Good as new?"

"I don't know, Mom. I know he's at home because I heard Dad and George talking about it once. I don't think he works anymore. I don't know."

His mother was quiet for a long time.

"I knew girls like that. My sister was one. It's witchcraft or something, the way they operate. But you're strong, Peter, and you're smart. Use your head. Picture her. She's average in every way. You see that now, don't you? A plain Jane. A nothing."

Peter told himself it was not cowardice that kept him from sticking up for Kate. What would be the point? Just then he remembered the way Kate used to fix her eyes on him when she knew something was troubling him. He thought of the way she'd tuck and retuck her hair behind her ears when she was excited about something. She probably hated him now.

"I didn't know you had a sister."

"Are you paying attention? Say it. Say, 'I'm strong.' Say, 'I'm smart.'"

"Where's your sister now? What's her name?" He knew his mother came from Ireland, that she'd had a family there, but she'd never, ever spoken of it.

"Are you listening to me?" she asked sharply. One of the nurses glanced up, began walking over.

"I'm strong. I'm smart," he whispered. She seemed satisfied. She sent him over to the refreshment corner to get a cup of water and a stale cookie with a gummy piece of candied cherry in the middle.

"Now," she said when he returned. "Tell me about the race yesterday." The nurse who had walked over returned to the sidelines.

He didn't know she kept track of his races, that she even remembered from visit to visit that he was on a team. He had a flashback of himself throwing his arm around the trunk of a tree after dropping out, Jim Bertolini's thin blue-white legs passing by so closely that Peter could see the gooseflesh on his thighs. Dutch Kills had ended up placing third. They'd been favored to win.

"It was good. It was fine. I did well."

"You see?" she said. "You're strong. You're smart. I told you."

———

Back in Queens that afternoon, Peter opened the door to the apartment to find it had been totally rearranged, George standing in the middle of the room like he was surveying his kingdom. There was a small, unfinished table with two dining chairs facing each other. The couch was on the opposite wall, the TV moved to the corner. The recliner was gone. The enormous stereo was gone. The room looked twice as big. The plastic bins Peter had been using as a dresser were gone, and in their place stood a small wicker chest of drawers. A pan of meat sauce sputtered on the stove.

Peter felt his whole heart well up and he was afraid to say anything. He dropped his backpack, curled his hands into tight fists, and held his breath.

"It's good, right? Looks awesome, huh?" George stepped toward him, and when he saw that Peter was struggling, he bear-hugged him, lifted him clear off the ground, swung him around a bit until Peter laughed.

"Jesus," George said, handing him a napkin. "Look, I bought napkins."

When dinner was ready George bustled around and eventually set down two plates of pasta, two ginger ales. They sat at the table, which was so small their knees touched. They angled the chairs a little. George prattled on about the Mets, about the construction on the FDR, about a girl he met years ago that he wished he'd dated back then, about whether it would be a cold winter or a mild one. Peter hoped he'd never stop talking.

"So, you didn't say anything," George said when they'd finished eating and it was time to clean up. "You didn't notice."

"What?" Peter asked, alarmed.

"Take it easy, kiddo," George said softly. "I only meant you didn't notice these."

He opened a cabinet to reveal a stack of six white porcelain plates sitting there, gleaming.

seven

THE DOCTORS RELEASED FRANCIS to home care once he could manage a full lap of the fourth floor corridor without stopping. He'd come to think of his brain as a delicate jewel set within a hard crown. It had to be protected because it controlled everything. He knew it before but now he really knew it. Thoughts, feelings, all those things people spoke of as coming from the heart, the gut, they were all physical processes, no more abstract than a bone or a tendon. One of the consulting neurosurgeons told him that he'd once put his finger in the place thoughts are made, and Francis wondered how a person empties the dishwasher after that, how he balances his checkbook and does his laundry. Francis's own brain was damaged, but the good news was that the bullet had not crossed hemispheres. He and Lena learned quickly that the good news was always called good news. The bad news was called something else.

The bullet had entered somewhere behind the left side of his jaw and exited through his left eye, destroying the medial wall and most of the lateral wall of orbit. He could now diagram the anatomy of an eye socket and brow ridge as easily as he could draw directions to Food King from his house. The doctors explained to him the next steps in photos and 3-D models, and he'd gotten into the habit of letting his fingers play across his face to make sense of what they were saying, and of the new topography there. There were days when the pain drew a map all on its own, sharp lines stretching from his nose to his ear, like red-hot razor blades moving under his skin.

The therapists told him to break everything he did into a series of small movements. Bend right knee, lean forward, step. Swing left arm. And rest. Walking, turning in bed, raising the phone to his ear—any movement at all sent waves of electric shocks through the fragile architecture of his face. They'd taken skin from other parts and stretched it across his cheek, where it would never grow a five-o'clock shadow. He could only compare their explanations to construction work he'd done around the house—repairing drywall with wire mesh, spackle, sandpaper, paint. When he got a staph infection in his new cheekbone, they had to take it apart and do it again. The left side of his body didn't need any coaching and most days his right side mimicked the left, but on days when his gait was too out of whack to make it very far, he imagined a little drawbridge that connected the two halves of his brain had been lifted, and no cars were allowed to pass. Sometimes, when he was in bed, he might glance toward the yellow den of light the nurses stepped through when they came to tend to him, and see shapes and patterns slide by, tumbling over one another as if afraid to be seen. Almost every afternoon, for a period of minutes, the shape of a currach hung on the wall across from his bed, but when he looked away and turned back to it slowly, it was never there. Occasionally, human figures stood outside the window, no matter that his room was on the fourth floor. They wore dark hats and mostly kept their backs to him. He thought they might be playing cards. Once, feeling good, he bent over to tug up one of his slipper socks that had fallen down around his ankle, and the blood rushed straight to the seams of his face and he passed out from the pain. When he came to he was on the cold linoleum floor and one nurse was telling the other that smelling salts wouldn't work because his olfactory nerve had been so damaged. No one had said that to him yet. It explained why the heavy gravy-laden dinners they served most nights tasted like nothing, and the only difference between each meal was the texture of the food inside his mouth, but sometimes the smell of a campfire wafted into his room without cause or explanation.

He told the doctors and Lena only a portion of what he experienced, what he noticed. He'd lost his left eye and the right had gone rogue, seeing things that weren't there. They knew that. Why go into the details of what it meant? They told him he was lucky. The bullet had missed the high-value real estate of his brain stem and thalamus. That he could speak so soon after they took him off the vent meant that his language and verbal cognition were unharmed. They'd removed a section of his skull in the beginning, and replaced it when the swelling went down, but then removed it again when he got an infection, and replaced it again when it healed. Things that would have once struck him as horrifying now seemed matter-of-fact. The girls used to pull dandelions from the grass and sing, "Mama had a baby and its head popped off." Then they'd use their little thumbs to pop the flower off the stem.

He wouldn't be ready for a prosthetic eye until he'd done more healing, so they fitted him for a pressure patch and told him that was so his right eye would get stronger, start doing the job for both eyes, but once he saw his face, he wondered if it was also to be merciful to his family and his friends, who had to look at him.

There was no mirror in the bathroom of his room. At night, with the light on, he could look to the window and see himself, but the reflection was too bright at the top because of the fluorescent overhead light. When he actually saw his face—Lena sat next to him on the bed and drew out a hand mirror from her bag—it reminded him of a clay model of a head that was handled too roughly before it had set. The top of his forehead to his jaw was a shallow concave bowl, like a dented fender. It

117

was discolored, full of blues and yellows and grays. They'd been repairing him bit by bit, and he understood that what he was seeing had once been a lot worse, that he'd already come a long way toward looking like a normal person again. Lena said softly, "Not that bad, right? Nothing that can't be fixed." He hadn't seen her cry almost at all since everything happened, but she cried that day. "Say something," she said, but he didn't know what. It wasn't that he'd ever considered himself handsome. It wasn't as if he'd ever taken much notice of that sort of thing. But when he'd last looked in a mirror, he recognized himself.

A week before he was released, they brought him to the stairwell and had him summit ten steps. He still felt every step in his face. Lena held his elbow while the therapist stayed close behind, hands out and feet braced should he come tumbling down. The social worker looked on, asking questions about their house that had been asked and answered already, how many stairs out front, how many stairs inside, handrails, did the interior doors swing inward or out. When he got to the top of the stairs, he rested, tried to stave off dizziness by fixing his good eye on a single spot. He clutched the banister. Lena, he knew, wanted him to stay at the hospital longer. He was safe there, she said. The hospital had all the equipment he needed. His room had a walk-in shower. They took his temperature and kept track of his painkillers, his antibiotics, as well as his input and his output, and nothing went unnoticed. Early on, before the cranial swelling went completely down, he was still too numb to feel a urinary tract infection boiling his insides. A nurse caught it when she checked his catheter and noticed the smallest thread of blood.

"What would have happened if you were at home?" Lena asked.

"Is insurance covering this?" he asked almost as soon as he could speak. "All of it?"

And the way Lena busied herself told him that she had no idea, didn't really care. Bills were something they could worry about when he recovered.

———

He went to a rehab hospital for three weeks and when he truly came home, he had daily visits from a nurse and a physical therapist and an occupational therapist and a speech therapist, but they came at different times so it usually fell to Lena to get him upstairs to the bedroom or the bathroom. They didn't have a bathroom on the main floor, and Lena joked that that was one way to get the renovation she'd been wanting for a decade. Until then she took his arm and wrapped it around her shoulder and skirted her arm around his waist, and together they took the steps one at a time. The shower was another problem, the lip of the tub too high to lift his leg over on his own so she helped him there, too, holding him tight, her face pressed to his naked chest as she leaned over and lifted first his right knee, and then, when he was ready, his left, just as the therapist had taught her. The water had to be aimed at his chest or lower because if he felt water pressure any stronger than a fine mist on his face, he couldn't stop himself from crying out, especially if his last painkiller was wearing off but he wasn't yet due for another. For a few weeks Lena was so afraid that she stood in the shower with him and helped him wash. For this, she wore her underwear and a camisole. "Your clothes are getting wet," he said.

"That's okay," she said.

"Why are you wearing them?"

"I don't know," she said.

After a few weeks she let him wash himself but she stayed in the shower with him. He felt more naked since she wasn't. After a while she began sitting on the closed toilet lid while he washed himself alone. Eventually, she trusted him to move around the house without her and she began leaving him for errands—the grocery story, mostly. The pharmacy. The bank. And it was only when she was on line at one of those places, sweating under her coat, anxious to get back to him, did she allow herself to wonder if she'd ever in her life go anywhere else again. She drove by the hair salon she used to go to, and it seemed like a relic from another lifetime.

The girls had trouble looking at him. Nat and Sara each had a way of talking at him without really looking, their eyes skittering around his general presence without landing anywhere, without focusing. Kate was more brave. Pale, solemn, she seemed to make a point of looking not only at his one eye that was not bandaged, but at the rest of his injuries, her glance slowly traversing the top of his head, the side of his face, his neck. For a long time it was like that whenever they visited the hospital, the visits bleeding into the same interactions every time. Nat and Sara reliably filled the quiet with talk about school and neighbors, a determined cheeriness they copied from Lena, while Kate studied him, not listening to a thing her sisters said.

Once, out of nowhere, when he was still in the hospital, Sara in the middle of a story about auditions for the school play, around the time the doctors were beginning to talk about sending him home, Kate said, "You can figure out where she was standing based on the angle."

"What?" Lena asked.

Kate stood up and crouched closer to Francis, looking at the entry point behind his jaw. "You turned your head to the right, I bet, and that exposed the left side of your head. Maybe you tried to move out of the way. She was probably about . . ." Kate walked across the small room and stood under the television. "Here."

"Jeez, Kate," Nat said. Sara looked nervous.

"What?" Kate said. "We're not supposed to talk about it? I don't see why."

Silence.

"Also, where was Mr. Stanhope? No one has said."

"That's enough, Kate," Lena said.

Everyone looked at Francis.

"It's okay," he said. Why did it make her feel better to know? he wondered. Of all of them, she was the one who would never accept a story in broad strokes. He was shot. Anne Stanhope was arrested. But what about all the in between? Kate had wanted to know from day one. What had Anne done next? Had she tried to stop the bleeding? Where was Brian Stanhope? Where was Anne now? They'd tried to protect the kids, they kept them away from the lawyers and the investigation, kept the newspapers out of the house, but maybe that had been wrong.

"Yeah, that's about right," Francis said that evening. "Give or take a foot." And he could see that just having that little part of the story acknowledged and confirmed helped settle her. She seemed calmer. She listened to the rest of Sara's story and then like the rest of them watched the TV.

———

The new people who'd moved into the Stanhopes' house may not have known much about what had happened before they closed, but after, they couldn't leave the house without hearing it from one direction or another. They had a ten-year-old girl named Dana whom Kate didn't have much time for until she realized the girl might know where Peter was. So she played sidewalk chalk with her a few afternoons in a row. Dana would only let her use white because it was the most boring and green because it was her least favorite. When Kate made her own name in bubble letters, Dana demanded that Kate do her name, too, over and over again until the word "Dana" was repeated all over her driveway. After they'd gotten to know each other sufficiently, Kate asked if she'd ever met the boy who used to live there, if he'd been there when the keys were passed from one family to the other.

"No," Dana said. And then: "But I think I found stuff that's his."

"What stuff?" Kate demanded.

"All different stuff. Baseball cards. Army guys. Some race cars. Junk, mostly. It's in a big shoebox."

"Where was it?"

"In the closet in my bedroom."

Kate pointed up to Peter's window. "Is that your room?"

The girl nodded.

"Can I see that box?"

The girl shrugged. "Sure."

As they made their way up to the porch, Kate felt as nervous as she would have if Mrs. Stanhope were still inside. Dana pulled open the storm door, kicked off her sneakers. Kate glimpsed a row of large black-and-white photos framed on the wall, a leather couch with buttons sewn in two neat rows along the back. The house smelled like vanilla, and Dana's mother peeked her head out from the kitchen as she wiped her hands on a kitchen towel. "Oh, hello. It's Kate, right? Come on in."

Kate stood just inside the front door as if stuck to the mat. She no longer wanted to go upstairs. She didn't want to take a single step further.

"Dana says she has stuff that might be Peter's."

"She does? The boy who used to live here?" Dana's mother said, while Dana scowled at Kate.

"Just a box of junk," Dana said.

"I'm going to take it for him," Kate said.

"No you're not," Dana said, alarmed. "It's mine. It came with the room."

"It's Peter's," Kate said. "And you know it." She leaned over to get closer to the smaller girl's face. "Hand it over."

"Dana, honey, get the box," her mother said.

"What the heck!" Dana shouted.

"Dana!"

When Dana stomped upstairs, her mother turned to Kate. "I know you were close with their son."

Kate wiped her face blank.

"Poor kid," she said and looked at Kate with soft eyes, inviting her to say more. When Kate didn't say anything, Dana's mom laughed lightly,

"Of course the realtor didn't mention much about what happened. Just that there'd been a domestic incident and a hasty exit." Kate could see that the new people knew less about the Stanhopes than she did. It was pointless.

"Here," Dana said, shoving the box at her when she returned.

"Dana, please," her mother said. "Be sensitive."

Kate tucked the box tightly under her arm, leaned over, and said, "You're super annoying, Dana, you know that?" Then she banged out the door.

———

Once everyone was certain that Francis would recover—with time, with physical therapy—the Gleeson girls went back to school to finish out the year. Kate couldn't recall having a single conversation with anyone at school in that month. Later, she couldn't remember if she'd ever made up the work she missed, or if her teachers had just let it go. Graduation was a blur. Nat graduated, too. No one thought to take photos. No one bought a cake. They'd once talked about having a joint graduation party but that, of course, didn't happen.

Lena Gleeson had left Francis for the day to attend Nat's graduation and take them out to dinner after, but high school was more important than grammar school, so on the morning of Kate's graduation, which was just one day after Nat's, Lena kissed Kate and congratulated her and then headed to the hospital. Kate's aunt and uncle came to take Lena's place, and they stood out from the crowd in their city clothes and the way they didn't mingle with the other parents. Sister Michael hummed softly as she removed the two brown bobby pins Kate had used to secure her mortarboard, and replaced them with white ones she held in her mouth until she'd fixed the cap just so. There was no valedictorian named that year. Everyone knew Peter had had the spot cinched since sixth grade, and since no kid in the history of St. Bart's had stopped coming to school with only one month left to go, no one knew what to do. Maybe Mr. Basker left the option open in case Peter strolled into the building on graduation morning, and Kate spent most of the ceremony wondering if he would. In Peter's absence Vincent O'Grady was asked to say a few words. Vincent's grades were so-so but he was an altar boy and a Boy Scout and he'd had a solo in the Christmas musical and the teachers loved him. Though no teacher or anyone on staff ever addressed what had happened in any specific way except to lead them all in prayers for the Gleeson family, prayers for the Stanhope family, Vincent went up there and said a bunch of stuff about the cards they were all dealt in life, how growing up is learning how to cope, and with God as their guide and St. Bartholomew's as their foundation, they would all go forward and honor God's gift of life. Only when Melissa Romano leaned sideways and whispered, "Are you okay?" did Kate realize how furious she was to be getting advice from Vincent O'Grady, a boy whose mother still peeled and sectioned the orange she packed with his sandwich.

That summer broke heat records. Nat got a job at the ice cream parlor. Sara babysat for some kids on the next block, but most days, from late afternoon until bedtime, they were home alone together. Instead of running wild as they'd always fantasized, or inviting all their friends over for a party, they made easy dinners for themselves, watched TV on the couch until they fell asleep or their mother came home from the hospital and sent them up to bed.

On the Saturday Natalie was to leave for college, Mr. Maldonado backed his station wagon across the street into their driveway and packed the trunk full of Nat's stuff. He drove her up to Syracuse because that was the weekend Francis was being moved to the rehab hospital, and Mr. Maldonado said he had a whole weekend of nothing to do. When Nat realized neither of the Maldonado kids would be tagging along, she begged Sara and Kate to come for the ride because it would be way too awkward to sit in a car with him for four hours, but since the car was so full that meant Kate had to sit up front between Nat and Mr. Maldo-

nado, while Sara sat in the back, buried under a garbage bag that held
Nat's bedding, towels, and pillows. It was only when they were already
on their way that Kate and Sara registered the fact that they'd have to
do the same journey back without Nat, and that he'd keep asking them
if they had to "wee." Just a few minutes into the return trip, Kate knew
that if he asked one more time and if she made even the briefest eye
contact with her sister, she'd either dissolve into a fit of giggles or start
sobbing. When he pulled up at a rest stop to buy them McDonald's, he
made them eat outside while he did calisthenics on the stretch of grass
beside the parking lot. Sara waited politely for him to finish while Kate
peppered him with questions about his routine, if he'd crafted it himself,
if he'd been an athlete when he was young, if he had any favorite videos,
if Mrs. Maldonado exercised, too, if they enjoyed exercising together.

Then, when she couldn't think of any more questions, she said, "I
can't wait until my dad comes home," and Sara shot her a look that told
her not to be so rude.

Francis came home that October, and with him came a battery of
therapists, one after another. All day long, Sara and Kate would try to
retreat to other parts of the house to give them privacy, but sometimes
they would find themselves in the kitchen together, making a snack and
listening. "Big one," they'd hear the one therapist say to their father in an
encouraging voice. "Okay, another big one," and though they knew their
father was just taking a big breath, reaching for the ceiling, touching his
toes, it would occur to Kate that they should be making fun of the therapist a little, with his tight sweatpants and his butt that looked like two
little fists held next to each other. But the new Gleesons were a family
that pretended they didn't find things funny.

———

Through all of this, Kate thought Peter might call one day. Her sisters
never mentioned him, and the fact that they didn't bring up his name

felt to Kate like she shouldn't either. She wasn't sure what would happen if he did call and she wasn't the one who answered, so she tried to answer the ringing phone as often as she could. Once in a while, when she was lunging for it, she'd catch Sara and Nat glancing at each other. On her birthday, she felt the frisson of expectation when she approached the mailbox, hooked her finger on the latch. But she found only a Caldor flier and something from St. Bart's.

She missed him all the time. She missed even the expectation of seeing him. She missed looking for him and the thrill she'd feel through her whole body when she'd spot him stepping out onto his porch. She imagined him playing with the zipper of his green hoodie as he walked around Queens, where she imagined he must be because that's where his father was going to go when he planned on leaving. But Queens was big. She'd looked at a map. He hadn't mentioned a neighborhood. And maybe, when she really thought of it, maybe he'd said Brooklyn. Maybe the Bronx. Sometimes she felt sure he didn't go to his uncle's place at all, and so she imagined him somewhere else. Did he tell her once that he had family in Paterson? She tried to imagine Paterson, where she'd never been, and then Peter against this imagined backdrop to see if it fit. She was certain that if she lit upon the right answer, she'd know it; her body and mind would feel stilled and she'd be able to read a book, finally. But even in those first seconds after waking up in the morning, before even her first conscious thought, she'd find her body oriented toward the window, already listening. Once, before Dana and her family moved in, she thought she heard the scrape of the Stanhopes' garbage can being pulled to the curb. She leaped from her bed to look but found nothing, and didn't hear the sound again. Some days, whenever the phone rang and it wasn't him, she felt sure that he was out there somewhere with his finger poised over the dial pad but wouldn't press the buttons.

She went out to the rocks sometimes, always bringing a book along in case her mother or sisters looked outside. Once, she thought she saw the corner of an envelope poking up between the third and fourth tallest of the boulders. She reached as far as she could between them, tearing up her knuckles as she drove her hand again and again into the rough crevice. When she finally got smart and found a stick thin enough to wedge in and push the paper out, she discovered it was not an envelope at all but a folded receipt from May that listed one Coke and one Big League Chew.

One evening—Nat away at school, Sara reading, her father asleep, finally, in his own bed—her mother sat beside Kate on the couch. "You miss your friend," she said.

The tears pressed forth before she could stop them. It was the week before Thanksgiving. She hadn't seen Peter in six months. It was so good to have her father home and yet it wasn't how she imagined it. Sometimes when he entered a room she felt a sudden, jumbled rush to tell him all the things that were on her mind. Then she'd draw up just as suddenly and feel so unaccountably sad. There he was, after all, alive. Making himself a snack. Scratching his shoulder. Reading the paper. It wasn't his face; she hardly noticed that anymore.

"Is it my fault what happened? Mine and Peter's?"

"Oh, honey, no."

"But we snuck out. And she really hated me. Hated that Peter liked me."

"You snuck out because you were a pair of eighth graders. One day a hundred years from now I'll tell you what I got up to in eighth grade." They were both quiet for a long time. Then Lena said, "But she did hate you. I think you should know what she said at the hearing. Your father doesn't, but I do."

"What Mrs. Stanhope said?"

"Yes."

"What?"

Lena stroked Kate's hair, gathered it up in her hands and draped it over her daughter's shoulder. "You're such a pretty girl, you know that, right?"

Kate shrugged.

"And smart. And, I don't know, 'tough' is the wrong word. You're more like your dad than you are like me."

Again, something inside Kate wobbled for a second. He was tough. And yet there didn't seem to be any future on the horizon. They were all waiting for this period to end, but maybe this was just the way it was going to be from now on, all of them watching him and reminding him to take his hands out of his pockets when he walked.

Lena pulled Kate close. "She said she'd kill you if you went near her son. She said she shot Dad because if he died, that meant we'd have to move away, and you wouldn't be near Peter anymore."

Lena let that sink in. "Before you go feeling guilty I'll tell you the rest. She also said that she knew the Nagles had painted their house a similar shade of blue to her house just to prove that the shade they chose looked better. She said she was sick of Monsignor Repetto singling her out at Mass. She was also sick of everyone thinking she was responsible for the *Challenger* explosion. She mentioned an estranged sister who tried to sabotage something or other back when they were kids, and a person she worked with who was plotting to have her fired. And so on."

They were quiet for a few minutes.

"She mentioned so many people and so many grievances that it sort of diluted the mention of you. But she kept coming back to you, harping on you, like you were plotting to steal her son from her. It was so nuts it sort of felt like a joke. The *Challenger* explosion for God's sake. Until you consider what she did."

Kate remembered running down Jefferson holding Peter's hand.

"The point is she's sick, Kate."

Kate nodded, though she wasn't entirely sure why.

"I'm saying that what happened is no one's fault, really. Not even hers when you think about it. We came to a plea agreement this week. Instead of going to prison we all agreed that she should stay in the hospital for a long time. Dad agreed to that for me. Otherwise it would have gone on and on and on. I don't want to see them anymore. I don't want to talk about them anymore. Your poor father. Can you imagine if . . ."

"Do you know where Peter is?" Kate asked.

"Honey . . ."

"I just want to know. I promise I won't contact him."

"I don't know. That's the truth. I really don't."

"Does anyone?"

"Well, sure. Their lawyers do. His mother's doctors know, I'd imagine. She probably has a social worker, too. I'm sure they know on the job. Brian is still working, I think."

Kate looked at her and hoped she wouldn't make her say it. After a moment Lena just shook her head slowly. "Forget it," she said, but with tenderness, like she understood that she had to ask.

"But they're probably still in New York," Kate said. "Since she is."

Lena's face was as blank as stone. "Kate. I've known Peter since the day he was born. He's a good boy. No one thinks he isn't. But you have to forget about him. He was your friend but now he's gone. You might not believe this now, but one day you'll have a friend you love as much as you love Peter. All of this is too much for a little girl to handle. Your whole life is ahead of you."

Kate was silent.

"For your father, Kate. Don't you go looking for trouble. Okay?"

The telephone rang. Natalie. The long-distance rates dropped after 9:00 p.m.

"Okay?"

"Okay."

eight

A ND SHE DIDN'T GO looking for trouble. Sometimes she felt she deserved more credit for how completely and truly she did not go looking for trouble, or at least the trouble her mother meant.

She made friends easily, without trying, and didn't understand how there could be people who didn't. All you had to say was one pretty funny thing and you made a friend. There was a crew of girls from St. Bart's that stuck together now that they were mixed in with the public school kids, and they all went out for soccer. Kate made JV as a freshman even though there was a freshman team. She wore her uniform to school on game days and sat with a group of seven other girls for lunch and took all honors classes. She raised her hand when she felt like talking and didn't think that was notable until Mr. Behan told her parents in the parent-teacher conference that he was glad to see a girl raising her hand. Kate's friends agreed they'd go together to the holiday formal in December, and they all went to Marie Halladay's house beforehand to get ready. "How fun," her mother kept saying when she drove her over, her dress folded carefully inside a Macy's bag. The more details Kate gave her mother the happier her mother seemed to be, so she started making them up:

"We'll probably trade jewelry," she said.

"Jeannie made a mix tape to listen to while we get ready."

"Marie is going to do everyone's makeup."

"Makeup?" her father asked from the passenger seat. "Are you allowed to wear makeup?" He'd just had another surgery, this time to build out his jaw, and half his face was wrapped in bandages. He took pills to blur the pain but they wore off quickly, it seemed, and the doctors had warned him not to overlap doses. His words were a little muffled but Kate could still tell he was teasing by the tone of his voice. He was as delighted as her mother.

"Kate," her mother said, "we are so proud of you."

———

Afternoons felt long and aimless without Peter, but a routine settled over her days. School, soccer, homework, TV, bed. Sara was the editor of the school paper, and on the weeks an issue was due, Kate walked home alone. The sky seemed bigger, emptier, since high school started, and for the first time she saw Gillam as a small place, set among other small places, and she craved to know what it would be like to walk beyond it, walk beyond the next town over, too, and the one after that, until the craving had been satisfied. She imagined a camera overhead pulling back and back like it did in movies sometimes, and Gillam lost among the twinkling lights of so many other places until it was just a speck, and then New York was just a speck, and then the United States, North America, the entire globe.

Sometimes, she'd try to conjure up the feeling of Peter walking beside her—the shape of him, the smell. Once in a while, usually on a Friday, one of her friends would come home with her after school and they'd chatter the whole walk to Jefferson. Then at her house they'd gobble the cookies and sodas Kate's mother put out for them and keep chattering up until the moment their mothers came to pick them up and they'd go bounding across the Gleesons' lawn crying out that they'd see Kate on Monday. "Did you have fun?" her mother always asked, looking at her closely, and she'd assure her that she had. But as she waved and yelled her goodbyes across the twilit lawn, she always felt relieved, completely exhausted, like these departures could not have come too soon.

When freshman year ended, Kate got a job as a camp counselor. Monday through Friday she woke up already running late, so she'd pull a bra on under whatever T-shirt she'd worn to bed, brush her teeth, and grab an apple or a banana before sprinting the ten blocks to the Central Avenue fields, where camp was held. There were bonus nights when the kids stayed nearly until dark, and Kate volunteered for those shifts, too. "Keeping busy!" her mother commented when she came in after one of these extra-long days, and her father watched her move around the kitchen. Toward the end of the summer, one of Kate's friends who also worked at the camp, a girl named Amy who was also on Kate's soccer team and had been over to Kate's house plenty of times, said in front of the other counselors that Kate was like a sister to her, and looked over at Kate with a bright smile. Kate had been filling water bottles at the water station when she heard her say it, and she felt her stomach drop. She coughed. Her face went red when she realized everyone was looking at her, waiting for her to say something.

"But you have sisters," Kate said, finally, the only thing she could think of.

"It's an expression, Kate," Amy said, rolling her eyes. The others, embarrassed, looked away.

"No, I know it is. I just mean you have two sisters. So do I. This isn't what it's like."

Amy's face fell and some anger passed there. "What's with you today?"

Later, Kate had to say that she hadn't really been listening, hadn't really known what they were talking about. She'd misunderstood. "You're one of my closest friends," she assured Amy. "I only meant that my sisters can be so annoying." Amy agreed that was certainly true, and for the whole walk home Kate tried to remember if Amy's oldest sister was named Kelly or Callie.

In the fall of sophomore year two interesting things happened at once. She made the varsity soccer team and she heard that Eddie Marik liked her. The girls were in a tizzy over it, because Eddie was a senior, and was good-looking, and had two good-looking older brothers that somehow made him even better looking than he would have been if they were just considering him alone. There was no debate about whether or not Kate should like him back. Kate thought at first that he meant Sara, who was his year, and had gotten their names confused. They didn't look alike, but even people who didn't know them sometimes told them that they could tell they were sisters by the way they walked. Word came down that he did not mean Sara; he meant Kate. Every day at lunch the girls leaned across the cafeteria table until their heads were almost touching, and reported on the details they'd heard: Eddie had said to Joe Cummings that Kate Gleeson was pretty. He thought she was an awesome soccer player. He was thinking of asking her out.

"What are you going to do?" they asked her one day when this had been going on for a few weeks.

"Nothing," Kate said. "See what happens, I guess."

Eddie was one of those eighteen-year-olds who looked like he could be twenty-five. He was nice, as far as Kate knew, though she'd never spoken to him and couldn't imagine why out of all the girls at Gillam High he'd set his sights on her. Sara, too, seemed puzzled by the whole thing. She told Kate that based on the few interactions they'd had he seemed neither smart nor dumb. He was just there. He was neither funny nor serious. He'd worked on the paper for a while but then he quit. He'd joined the yearbook but he might have quit that, too. Girls liked him, Sara granted. It was just another fact about him, same as the fact that his hair was brown.

He waited for her after practice one day, and when her teammates saw him they fell back and urged Kate forward. Kate pretended not to see him and instead walked around the back of the school and snuck into the girls' locker room through the custodial door. The next morning he was waiting by her locker, and the whole thing felt way too much like a movie she'd seen once.

"Hey," he said.

"Hey," she said.

By lunch, the whole school knew they were together.

———

Eddie didn't have a car but when they went out, he was usually able to borrow his mother's. They went to the movies a few times, always with other kids from school, and which movie they saw didn't matter because they spent the whole time kissing and feeling each other in the dark back row while the kids who were uncoupled chucked popcorn at them. He had to circle back to his house once after picking her up because he forgot his wallet, and when she assumed she'd just wait outside, he'd looked at her like she was crazy and insisted she come in. "Hello," she said, tugging down the hem of her skirt when Mrs. Marik came down to the kitchen to meet her. "It's nice to meet you. I was just—"

"Sit down, sit down," Mrs. Marik said. "Are you hungry? You're Francis Gleeson's daughter, right?" When Kate nodded, she knew that Mrs. Marik knew every single thing that had happened on Jefferson just a year and a half earlier, and wondered for the first time if Eddie did, too.

Their game schedules mostly conflicted, but he managed to come to a few of her home games and brought friends along with him, which made the girls on her team happy. They went to the Gillam Diner one night, just the two of them, and instead of driving her straight home, he drove his mother's hatchback to the most shadowed corner of the lot behind the post office and took her hand and slid it into his pants. "You're so serious," he whispered as she raised her hand up and down like he showed her. In the moonlight—full and luminous that night—she saw how handsome he was, how much he liked her, and yet sometimes, after being with him for a few hours, she felt lonelier than she had before. He reached up and pulled out her hair tie so her hair came tumbling down. He closed his eyes and inhaled.

The only fight they had was not a real fight, just a very tense few hours. They were at Pies-on-Pizza, the Giants game blaring over their heads. Eddie kept sucking on his straw though his cup was empty. He rattled the ice inside, looked at her, and out of nowhere asked about Peter and everything that had happened at the end of eighth grade. "When you first got to school last year it was like you were famous. Everyone knew you were Sara and Natalie's little sister, and that your dad had been shot. So that guy was really into you, I guess?" Eddie put his elbows on the table. "Made his mom crazy?"

Kate felt something in her close up. She couldn't account for how angry she felt that he'd asked, that he presumed to know a thing about what had happened.

She put down her slice and pushed her plate away.

"I heard different stories at school but I figured I'd ask you."

"It's really no one's business."

Eddie smirked. "Well, that's true. But your ex-boyfriend's mom shot your dad. Something like that will get mileage, Kate. Look at your dad's face. You think people aren't going to talk about that?"

"Don't talk about my dad," she said, and stood up from the table.

"I can talk about whatever I want." He sat back and folded his arms. "Why are you acting like this?"

"And he wasn't my boyfriend."

She walked out of the pizza place. She turned onto Central Ave. and with her head down walked quickly past the dance studio, the tobacco shop, the firehouse.

Eddie jogged up beside her. "Okay, okay, I'm sorry. The newspaper said he was your boyfriend."

It had never occurred to her that the whole thing had been in the newspaper. She walked faster. Her mother must have stopped the papers from coming to their house. She must have hidden them away.

"He was my best friend."

"So then—"

"I want to go home."

"Kate, come on."

"I'm walking. You can go."

But he couldn't go, of course, because he'd been raised to see a girl home when he took her out. So he followed her from a few paces behind until they arrived at Jefferson. Then he jogged back to town to retrieve his mother's car.

At home Kate told Sara that she would never speak to him again. She told her mother that she didn't feel well, and went to bed early. She heard the phone ringing, her mother asking Sara to see if she was awake, so she closed her eyes and pulled the covers over her head. The next morning, a Sunday, as Kate and her parents were headed out to Mass—Sara claimed she went the night before but Kate knew she spent the hour browsing lipsticks at CVS—they opened the door to find a pot of mums on their welcome mat, and a note from Eddie. "From who?" her father said as her mother elbowed him. "John Marik's kid? Wouldn't he be older than Kate?"

"What am I supposed to do with a pot of mums?" Kate asked.

"You should invite him over some night for dinner," Lena said.

"Oh, that would be wonderful," Sara said.

They made up because it was the easiest thing to do. Paul Benjamin asked Sara to the holiday formal, and for a second it looked like they'd be at the same table as Eddie and Kate. Kate looked forward to sitting with Sara, but Sara seemed annoyed by the idea, so it was for the best when the table got too big and had to be split in two. At the dance, once Sara went out back to smoke, Kate let Eddie kiss her on the dance floor, in full view of their teachers and chaperones. Eddie drew her close, his hand pressing the hard cage of her dress's bodice, the reflected light from the disco ball dancing across his face and the white tuxedo shirt he'd rented, the purple cummerbund selected after his mother called Lena to ask the color of Kate's dress. He'd left his tuxedo jacket at his seat, but he'd already sweat through the back of his shirt and kept asking Kate if she wanted something to drink. He was nervous, Kate realized, and felt a swell of real affection for him. After the dance, he told the rest of the people who'd been at their table to go ahead without them. Sara looked over her shoulder at her sister as she and Paul exited through the gym doors as if to ask if all was well. Kate waved her on.

Alone in the parking lot, Eddie asked if Kate wanted to check out his older brother's apartment, so Kate went. His brother had graduated from college, was commuting in to the city every morning, had renovated the garage by himself so he'd have his own space. The Mariks lived just two blocks from school so they walked, and when Kate complained that her feet hurt from the stupid heels she was wearing, he offered her a piggyback ride. "Giddyup," he said when she climbed aboard. She swatted his butt while he galloped along the sidewalk, her dress dragging along the ground.

When they got to the brother's apartment, the brother was not there, and Kate understood immediately. "He's in Boston until Sunday," Eddie offered casually. "Visiting some of his college friends." The lights of the main house were off and she wondered if it was only the parents of girls who waited up or just Kate's parents in particular. Eddie unzipped her dress and she thought, Okay, this is fine. When he guided her to the pullout couch that had already been pulled out and made up, she felt a tiny bit scared. She was wearing new underwear. She'd spritzed perfume on her stomach. A person who did these things, she knew, could not then pretend to be taken by surprise. "Be careful," her mother had said when he picked her up, another couple, a pair of seniors, in the front seat of an unfamiliar car. She'd looked at Kate as if there was something urgent she wanted to tell her but had forgotten, and now there wasn't enough time. And though Kate didn't mind what was happening, didn't object, she found herself thinking of home, and how she would have been just as happy staying in that night. As Eddie reared away from her to open a condom—no doubt his brother's—and tug it on with a look of total concentration, she thought of a mug of hot tea with honey and Sara on the couch next to her with a pile of cookies lined up on her lap and Natalie on the phone at the stroke of nine o'clock to ask what were they doing, put her on speaker, let her listen to the house for a minute.

After, Eddie propped himself up on his elbows and studied her. He wanted to know if it hurt. When she said it did, he wanted to know if it mostly hurt or if it hurt just a little. Did it also feel good? Kate said it did, though it did not. He seemed very sober despite all the sips from the flask the boys had been passing around back at school.

"I love you, Kate," he said.

"Get outta here, Eddie. Cut it out." She wondered what they were going to do about the sheets. Did the brother have his own washer and dryer, or would Eddie have to sneak them into the house?

"I'm serious," he said. "Don't say it back if you don't mean it, but I think you love me, too."

Kate rose up to kiss him.

———

She told no one. Not Sara or Nat. None of the friends she sat with at lunch. It didn't seem that important, not nearly as important as people would make it. It was just a thing that happened, same as all other things that happened. The main difference was that Eddie stopped by all the time now, and no longer called first. She'd see the shape of him in the glass before he rang the bell and feel tired, wish she had five minutes of warning so she might hide. At Christmas he bought her a pair of earrings, and when she popped open the box and saw them, she knew she'd learned at least a little something because she didn't blurt out right away that she didn't have pierced ears. Sara and Nat had warned her that he'd probably get her a present, so she'd gotten him a book about football because football was his favorite sport and it was on display at the end of the aisle at the bookstore.

"You like him?" her father asked one night. He was sitting in his recliner, a drink in one hand, the remote in the other, and for a minute Kate could pretend he was just home from work. There had been talk about him going back in a few months, an inside job he'd called it when she overheard him telling Lena, a desk jockey, they'd drum something up for him. But his eyesight was a problem, even with the prosthetic eye. He'd get his pension, and while he hadn't been on duty when he got injured, they'd found a way that he could go out on the higher tier of disability so he'd get more. Sometimes men came to see him in pairs or groups of three, and Kate recognized them as cops from the moment they stepped out of their cars and looked around. Now, he muted the television before swiveling around to look at her.

"Yeah, he's fine," Kate said.

The room was silent. In the kitchen, Lena was mashing bananas for bread and watching an episode of *Days* she'd taped.

"Kate," Francis said simply, an admonishment and a question all wrapped into one.

———

And then her busha died. She had a cough, which turned out to be the flu, and then that turned into pneumonia. Kate's lab partner had had pneumonia that fall but she'd returned to school after only a week, so it never crossed Kate's mind that Busha wouldn't return to her little kitchen, to the leftover bits and pieces of food she kept Saran-wrapped in her fridge for far too long. Lena went to stay in Bay Ridge for a night to help sort her things and figure out what to do about Nonno. As they planned the funeral and made decisions, Kate's parents talked about money bluntly and openly, something that had never happened before, and for the first time Kate worried that they might not have enough.

The price of a mahogany coffin. The price of food for the reception after, whether they could get away with cold sandwiches or if people would expect hot food, whether they needed a full bar or just beer and wine. Lena said she didn't want her father to feel ashamed, and at that Francis had sighed. How much could Karol kick in on his bartender's salary? And Natusia? "There can't be any surprises now," Francis said to Lena as they sat at the dining room table and calculated, recalculated. But how could a person head off what they don't know is coming? Kate wondered. She remembered the expression on her mother's face when she told her that she'd grown out of her cleats.

If Kate could chart on a graph when she thought of Peter and when she didn't, the week of Busha's wake and funeral would have shown a seven-day-long peak. New York City was a big place, and Bay Ridge was only a small part, but still, she kept imagining him showing up at the church for the funeral Mass. She fantasized about turning around in the pew and spotting him standing at the back by the holy water font, but when the day came and she did turn around, the back half of the church was completely empty, the front half populated mostly by childhood friends of her mother, aunt, and uncle. After the funeral, Kate and Sara spent two nights at the apartment keeping their nonno company while Lena and Natusia completed paperwork at Busha's little kitchen table. Whenever she had a chance to be alone—one day she walked down to the diner for an egg cream, the next day over to the water to look at the bridge and the birds—she thought, it will be a time like this. It will be an ordinary, overcast day, and he'll just walk by. "Kate?" he'll say, doubling back.

———

Eddie was waiting for her when she arrived home. His family had sent flowers to the funeral home, but now he was on their porch with a tray of eggplant rollatini from his mother. He hugged Lena. "Hey, Eddie," Sara said and kept going past him to the front door.

"Are you mad that I didn't go?" he asked Kate when the rest of the Gleesons were out of earshot. "I wanted to go but my mother needed her car, and the bus and then the subway would've taken hours."

"Go where?" Kate said.

"To the funeral."

"No, of course not. I was busy with my family anyway."

"Okay good." He took a breath. "Guess what? I got off the wait list at Holy Cross." He had the letter in his pocket. "Who knows, I might get a single. Maybe you'll go there, too." He took her hand and pulled her gently toward his car, no doubt so he could drive her over to his brother's place. It was a weekend and Jack seemed to spend most weekends out of town.

"Yeah, who knows," Kate said, and for the first time in weeks felt a cool wave of relief wash over her. In a few short months he'd disappear to Massachusetts and once that happened, if she made sure to lie low over school breaks and holidays, she might never see him again.

"Kate," came her father's voice from the door, which they'd left open except for the screen. Kate blushed and wondered how long he'd been standing there. "Your mother needs you."

Eddie, startled, dropped her hand.

"I have to go," Kate said to him as she slid past her father.

Francis stayed put, and because Francis stayed put, so did Eddie, unsure of whether he'd been dismissed or not.

"She's great," Eddie said finally. "Kate, I mean. We were just talking about—"

"She's the best," Francis said, and continued to stand there, looking at the boy as if he were waiting for something. "She's the best one."

Dana rode by on her bike, ringing the handlebar bell as she passed.

"She's been through a lot," Francis said. "She's still going through it even though it doesn't seem that way."

"Yeah, I know," Eddie said, a little impatiently. There was no need to tell him, of all people.

nine

NEITHER GEORGE NOR PETER ever answered the phone at the apartment because George said it was always people looking for money and if anyone really needed him they'd find him at work. Anne had never called, not one single time, though once every few months the social worker from the hospital left a message to let them know that Anne needed a sweater, or a pair of slippers, or a particular kind of soap because the hospital soap gave her a rash. They hadn't filled out any official paperwork to let Dutch Kills know Brian had moved, to say that George was acting as Peter's guardian, so when Peter needed a parent's signature, George just went ahead and signed Brian's name. The secretary at school had the number of both the Local 40 office and the business office of whatever job site George was at for a particular stretch of months. They played the answering machine tape maybe once a week, and would delete each message before the person had finished speaking. "Blah, blah, blah," George would mutter at the machine, and lean against the wall next to the phone like he couldn't possibly stand there listening for one more second. Once in a very long while there'd be a message from Brian, shouting into the machine as if he were calling from

Beirut with a bad connection, saying that he was sorry to have missed them, that he'd try back another day soon. George would let his brother's messages play all the way out and then ask with an impassive expression if Peter wanted to play it again or save it. When Peter told him it was fine to delete, George would punch the button just like he had with all the others. The time stamp was always an hour when Peter had been in school, and for a long time he thought it careless of his father to have forgotten that he would never be home to answer on a school day.

About a year after Brian left, the answering machine tape broke. It was rewinding so fast one evening that it snapped and jumped right off the spool. "Oh for the love of God," George said, and threw the whole tangled mess into the garbage. Every few days George said he had to go buy a new tape, but never did. "Who are we expecting to hear from?" he'd ask, and shrug.

In the fall of Peter's junior year, Coach Bell began pointing out college recruiters at the big invitational meets: usually skinny men, former runners themselves, wearing sneakers with their khakis and dress shirts, standing a little away from the crowd with a stopwatch and a notebook.

"I don't want you to turn into a head case," Coach Bell said after one meet, "but you're having a strong season. They'll notice." But they didn't approach him, so Peter figured Coach had read them wrong. Then, in the spring, Peter got a handwritten letter from the coach of a Division I school in Pennsylvania—just after he ran a personal best in the half and beat Bobby Obonyo, whose father had been an Olympic middle-distance runner, and who himself had run the fastest mile in the city that year. A week later he got another letter from a different coach along with a questionnaire about what he was looking for in college, what he hoped to achieve both athletically and academically. A week after that the coach who'd written to him from the school in Pennsylvania introduced himself at sectionals, told him he was impressed with his race, asked if he'd started thinking of college yet.

"Are your folks here?" the coach asked, glancing over Peter's shoulder at the stands, where other kids' parents stood dazed and hungry, waiting around all day for their child to run a race that might last only thirty seconds.

"Couldn't make it today," Peter said. "But we've been talking about college, sure." Just that week Peter's guidance counselor had asked him to make a list of jobs he might like to have when he grew up, and then they could begin to strategize where to apply. Her hands had flown like little birds around the wall of pamphlets displayed in the hall. She plucked from here and there until she had a neat stack to give to him.

Once the season ended and summer came, the calls began. First among them was Coach Bell, telling Peter to fix his goddamn machine, that he'd tried Peter at home twenty times already, that he did not consider himself Peter's personal answering service. George had gotten Peter an apprenticeship with the iron men that summer—he had to say he was eighteen even though he was only seventeen—and when Coach said practices would start in mid-July, Peter said he'd try to be there but it all depended on the shift he landed in a given week. He was making $9.20 an hour, way more than any of his friends were making at their summer jobs, and he planned on giving all of it to George. Coach was silent for what felt to Peter like a long time.

"Okay, I'll schedule practice around your shifts," he said finally. "But, Peter, I beg you. Do not get injured. I'm not sure you understand what's going on here."

"What's going on here?" Peter asked.

"What's going on is you're going to go to a pretty good college. I don't want to get your hopes up, but there's money in these programs. You play this right and you might not have to pay much more than you would for City College."

"How much is City College?"

"I don't know. Three thousand maybe?"

Peter divided three thousand by nine twenty.

"Jeez. How much is a private college?"

"Doesn't your guidance counselor talk to you about this stuff?"

"Ms. Carcara always asks for my father," he said, and then because he'd already said that much, and because he was beginning to sense that he'd need help, he continued. "My uncle went to the parent-teacher conferences this year and everyone assumed he was my dad, so he didn't say anything. When the coaches send those questionnaires, I leave the family stuff blank. I don't know what to put."

"I'll take care of it," Coach said. "But where is your dad, Pete? I know your mom is . . . not available to talk. But I've met your dad, haven't I?"

"Maybe freshman year."

"Does he work long hours?"

"He went away for a while. So if these recruiters need to talk to someone, they need to talk to my uncle."

At work, no one was interested in his half-mile time or his training schedule. They only shouted at him to do things—to get on the other end of that beam or get the fuck out of the way, to hold this, brace that, make a pot of coffee, run down to the deli and get a flat of Gatorades. They told him not to go too many stories up because he was so skinny the first stiff wind would blow him over. They asked him about girls, about what kind of girl wanted a guy without meat on his bones, and then someone reminded the gang that he went to a boys' school, and they went on a tear about that. There were two guys on the job who were only a year older than Peter and were working full-time. One had a beard and a barrel chest just like George, and Peter would sneak looks at him to decide if they could really be just one year apart. These eighteen-year-olds had dropped out of high school and had a relative—a father, an uncle—get them into the union. They made double what Peter made and each one was saving for something big. They spent lunch breaks asking Peter what he thought college would get him, if he thought he'd end up in a mansion just because he went to college, and then no matter what Peter said, they'd look at each other like he was an idiot. They claimed the kids graduating from college now could only dream of making what they made per year, and on top of that they had to sit in offices all day, and on top of that they couldn't hope to start making real money until they were done with school at twenty-two. "A waste of time," they said as they tore into their chicken Parm heros and made plans for the evening. They each had serious girlfriends. After a few weeks Peter began to wonder if they were right.

The men at work knew he was George's nephew, and George, Peter noticed, was well liked. He was grumpy, maybe, but fair. They invited George out after work, but George always declined. He had no time for bars anymore, he told Peter, not since Brenda left, not since he had *that* lesson taught to him, as he put it.

"Maybe it's dumb to go to college," Peter said one afternoon as they were getting into George's car to drive off the job site. "I could go full-time with you after graduation and then I could get a place of my own and get out of your hair. That guy Jimmy was telling me—"

They had not quite passed the boundary of the job site, when George slammed on the brakes so hard that Peter pitched forward, caught himself on the dash. "Jimmy McGree can't add two and two with a calculator, Pete."

"He seems okay to me. He said he almost has enough saved to buy a Camaro."

George studied him. "Who gives a shit. You want a Camaro?"

Peter let that sit with him, and agreed, mostly, that he didn't care about cars. But maybe that was only because he'd never considered them before.

"Okay, well, John says he almost has enough for a house he looked at on Staten Island. He said he's going to ask his girlfriend to marry him."

George sighed. "John Salvatore should have gone to college. He might go, still. I hope he does. I'd hold a job for a kid like that. But, Peter, don't make me regret getting you on here. Maybe you should be making funnel cakes on Coney Island like I used to when I was your age."

George began driving again. "Don't get me wrong. This is a great career. A good union. And it does something to you, seeing a building go up that you made. Picking that building out of the skyline and thinking you're one of the reasons it's standing there. You still want to do this after college, then I'll do what I can."

"But what's the point then, if I come back?"

"The point is you'll have gone and educated yourself. You'll have seen a little of what things are like for other people and why they think the way they do. And you'll meet people who have careers that we don't even think of as careers. You know what I was watching the other day? A show about the people who make the sounds on television shows. When doors slam, or when something spills. When one guy punches another guy. Did you know there are people whose job it is to make all that sound real?"

Peter was caught short by the strength of his uncle's response and went quiet as he took it in.

"Plus, you're not like them, Pete. They're assuming you're just like them, and you're not. Except for your age you have zero in common with Jimmy McGree. John Salvatore, on the other hand . . ." George trailed off for a moment. "If he were my kid, I'd make him go to school."

"Why didn't you go?"

"Because I'm a dum-dum."

"That's not true."

"No, I'm not a complete dum-dum maybe, but there are different ways to be dumb and I'm some of those. Or I was."

"Am I like my dad?"

George laughed. "Your dad wasn't like your dad when he was your age, you know? You're like your mom, maybe. I don't know her too well, but I guess she's pretty smart. Nursing school and all that. Coming here so young. I think she managed a bunch of people at Montefiore, but you'd have to ask your dad about that."

Considering this, Peter's thoughts opened wider, pulled in images from Gillam. Sometimes, lying awake on George's pullout, he tried to remember the details of his old bedroom, how big it was, and blue, and if it really had shelves on the wall above his dresser for his books and cards and action figures. He tried to remember what it felt like to close a door and be totally alone in a space that was his. The only times he was alone now were nights George went bowling, or went to a movie "with a friend." Peter remembered how quiet his house in Gillam had been, a quiet that went deeper than silence. George gave him privacy; he retreated to his bedroom around ten o'clock every night and watched the news in there instead of the living room. When he was alone, Peter tried to remember what it was like to see Kate every day, to look out his bedroom window at any given time and almost always see her out there in the yard, her cheeks flushed from the cold or from running. In the beginning, when he was a freshman and even a sophomore, he thought of Kate whenever he could. He'd close his eyes and send her messages with his mind. He'd see girls from other schools at track meets and scan them to find one that reminded him of her, but none did. For a long while he thought of calling her house whenever he looked at a phone, but it was impossible to know what to say, and if she hated him, he didn't want to know that. As time passed he thought of her less often. Lately, when she crossed his mind, he understood that she'd be different now, older, that if they met, they might not even like each other; that's how much people change. When he thought about that—that Kate was basically a stranger to him now—a feeling like fear would shiver through him.

"What were my parents like before I was born?"

George shook his head. "I don't know, Pete. It's all ancient history now anyway. They had that stillborn baby a couple of years before you were born. Sometimes I forget about that. I was at the hospital when it came. They knew the baby was dead but for some reason the doctor made your mom deliver it. It was healthier for her or something, and being a nurse she understood that. I remember that she held the baby after. Your dad—no way. He didn't go near the room. He called me to come up and wait with him, and then when it was over we had a drink. But what did I know? I'd come straight from baseball practice, I remember that much. Our mother was still alive but she didn't know nothing about it. She didn't like your mom too much. Anyway, Brian had this little flask he used to keep in his boot. He couldn't see how your mom would want to hold a dead child and she couldn't see how he didn't want to. I was so young that I didn't think about any of this until a lot later, you know? I was only . . ." George calculated back. "Fourteen, maybe? God, younger than you are now. I remember feeling like he was way, way older than me. When we sipped from the flask, we didn't hide it away or anything. That felt grown up to me."

After it was quiet in the car for a while, he added, "That baby dying made everything worse, but things were bad between them before that."

They approached a traffic light.

"You didn't know that? About the baby?" George asked, taking quick glances at Peter as the light turned yellow, and then red.

"No," Peter said. He thought of the single baby picture he'd seen of himself, and then imagined himself dead, his skin ashy and cold.

"Was it the reason they got married?" Peter asked.

"I think they would have gotten married anyway. They're both totally nuts when I really think about it."

———

Despite the meet schedule, despite his homework, which had gotten more intense over the years of high school, Peter still tried to see his mother at least twice a month. When he saw her, he said nothing about his job with the ironworkers or the recruiters who were calling or really anything that was going on with him. She'd started a new medication that left her in sort of a trance, and she seemed completely indifferent to the things he said. If anything, it appeared to annoy her to see him coming down the hall on a Sunday afternoon with his headphones around his neck and his backpack slung over his shoulder.

"Why are you here?" she asked one Sunday at the end of the summer.

It was Labor Day weekend. Sitting in that family meeting room chair, he felt the heat coming off his skin. He was browner that summer than he'd ever been, and stronger: all the lifting at work had changed his body, he could feel it. He'd let his hair grow longer and the sun had kissed it with gold lights. She sat in an identical chair to his with her cardigan wrapped tightly around her shoulders and her legs crossed at both the knee and the ankle, one twisted around the other like a vine twists around a post. School, his senior year, would start that coming Tuesday. He'd taken one box of questions from the Trivial Pursuit box—she liked to go through the questions but hated actually playing the game—but she refused to play. She only squinted toward the corner of the room and turned her face away from him. "Don't you have things to do? Aren't you busy enough? I asked you why you're here. You don't have an answer?" She loved him, he told himself. This was just the way she acted sometimes. That was the way she acted when she was afraid.

"Because I wanted to see you."

She turned away and pressed her cheek into the chair cushion. If he didn't come to see her, who would? How would she feel if not a single person in the world cared enough about her to go see her for an hour or two? So for fifty minutes he sat there and read the questions out loud that he thought she might be interested in, then, after a few seconds, flipped the card and read the answer. When it was time to go, she stood by the window and refused to say goodbye. "I'm leaving now," he said and waited. He didn't mind, exactly, when she got like this; it was more that he felt embarrassed, like he didn't know what to do with his hands or what to say. He knew it didn't quite have anything to do with him, but some days, often when he least expected it, he removed his sympathy from her and took it back to wrap around himself. Sometimes it all seemed temporary, a thing they had to get through, and sometimes it seemed like this was always the way things would be, that he'd stay silent and do his work and be a good boy all in hopes of a change that would never come.

On his way out that afternoon, a woman with a hospital ID stopped him, told him she was the chief administrator, asked if his father was picking him up. He told her he was taking the train, and the woman asked if he could pass along the message that the director of the hospital needed to speak with him as soon as possible.

"We tried calling, but—"

"Yeah. Sure. I'll tell him," Peter said. He couldn't remember the last time he'd spoken to his dad. It was before George put the air conditioner back in the window. Before summer set in.

That night, when George went out to pick up a few slices of pizza, Peter found the little phonebook in the drawer nearest the phone and flipped through pages of his uncle's scrawl to find his father's name and an 843 number beside it. He dialed. He let it ring and ring. He hung up and tried again. And again. Panic rose in his gut, followed by fury. He returned the phone to the cradle, then picked it up and tried again.

"What's up?" George said when he returned, two grease-spotted bags in his hand. But Peter could only hang up the phone and pick it up again and start the cycle over.

"Peter. What are you doing?"

"I have to talk to my dad," Peter said, and turned all his fury on himself when he realized that no matter how hard he clenched his teeth he was still crying. "We have to fix this fucking machine, George," Peter said in a voice thickened with tears. "He's probably calling all the time. He's probably worried about me."

George nodded, placed the bags on the counter. "You're right. I'm going to do that tomorrow. Okay? You're right about that. I'm sorry. I'm terrible for putting things off."

And the next day, Peter's first day of school, he woke to find both the phone and the answering machine had been disconnected, were thrown in the garbage. He pulled on the new pants and the new button-down he'd bought the week before with his summer money—George had insisted he keep his earnings and promised he'd ask him for money if he ever got caught up short—and slung his old backpack on his shoulder.

George was already long gone. At school, he met his new teachers for the year. He got his new locker in the senior wing. He signed out the textbooks he'd need, but it was difficult to concentrate until he figured out why the people at the hospital wanted to talk to his father. At practice, Coach had them run intervals until a couple of kids threw up. Two of the freshmen approached him, blushing, and told him they'd watched him run at states in the spring.

When he stepped into the apartment late that afternoon, he saw a new phone sitting where the old phone had been. Cordless. Updated. It gleamed like a new car, and George explained they wouldn't need a tape anymore because the messages were all stored inside the phone, a thing called voicemail. He'd waited until Peter got home to set up the code so that Peter could pick something he'd remember easily. Peter felt the tension of the day slowly leave his body.

"But, Peter," George said as he scratched his head and shifted his weight from foot to foot. "Your dad, he moved. He's down in Georgia now, I think. I talked to him a while back and I figured I'd wait to tell you until I had his new number. But I never heard back, and that number in South Carolina doesn't reach him."

"But my mom's doctors need to get hold of him. They need to tell him something."

"Yeah, you said that. So I called up there today and they only wanted to tell him that she's being moved to a different hospital upstate. There was a space issue."

"Where upstate?"

"Albany."

"How far is Albany?"

"Two hours."

"Is there a train?"

"I'm sure there is. But I was thinking you could get your driver's license, take my car if you want, you could—"

"When does she leave?"

153

George stepped toward him like he wanted to touch him but didn't know where or how.

"She left today."

Peter felt the information pass over him like a gust of air. "She knew yesterday. She knew she was going."

"I'm not sure," George said.

Peter nodded and nodded and hugged himself hard when he felt his body begin to tremble.

"I should have told you that your dad moved, Peter. I should have—"

"I don't care about my dad." As soon as he said it, it felt true. "I don't care if I never see him again."

Now it was George who was nodding, taking that in. "Okay. I can see that. He did a selfish thing. He was going through something, and he made a move that was all for himself. I've done selfish things. You'll probably do a few selfish things before you're through. But he loves you, Peter. I know he does. When you were little and we didn't get to see each other that much, he used to call and tell me all the funny stuff you did, and how smart you were."

"Why didn't he help my mom? He knew there was something wrong with her. He knew. All this"—Peter gestured toward the couch that was his bed, his schoolbooks stacked on the floor, the little roll-away hang rack that served as Peter's closet—"could have been avoided."

"Well, if he'd known what was going to happen, he might have, Peter. But he didn't know. You didn't know. Even your mom, she didn't know either."

"He could have stopped her from taking the gun. He'd started hiding it after the thing at Food King—the little cabinet over the fridge that we never used. He used to hide the bullets somewhere else but at some point he stopped doing that. And if I figured it out pretty quickly, I'm sure she did, too. That night, after they'd been arguing for hours, he saw her push the chair over to reach the cabinet. And you know what he did? He just turned around and headed upstairs. What did he think she was going to do? As soon as he left her there in the kitchen alone with his gun, I knew he was useless, so I went over to Kate's house to call 911. I didn't want to call from our house because I'd have had to walk right past her to get to the phone. I never thought that Mr. Gleeson would go over there."

Saying to George what he'd never said to anyone brought back his house in Gillam so vividly he could see the old lamp in the corner of the living room, barely casting any light. He could look one by one at his stack of games, his shoes lined up along the bottom of his bedroom closet. He thought of the rocks out back, hopping from peak to peak while Kate looked on. He thought of how warm her hair had felt when he'd had his hand in it, sitting knee to knee on that abandoned swing set on Madison Street.

"I thought you told the police that he'd been upstairs most of the night, that he didn't have any idea she'd gotten his gun."

"That's what I said, yes."

"Did he tell you to say that?"

"No. I just knew that's what I should say."

From the street below came a car alarm, and then, just two seconds later, another. George leaned over and slammed the window shut.

"The thing is, Peter, grown-ups don't know what they're doing any better than kids do. That's the truth."

———

By October of senior year, there were four schools with strong running programs asking to set up an official visit. They were good schools, with tough academic standards. Coach Bell explained the visit would be Peter's chance to check out their facilities, their programs, talk about what each respective coach had in mind. Peter had no idea what he should be looking for in a college, and so he followed Coach Bell around on these visits like he was a kindergartner. Coach made sure to give Peter time alone with the team, so he could ask them any questions he might not like to ask in front of the coaches, but even then, out of earshot of the grown-ups, Peter wasn't quite sure what to say.

"How much will tuition be?" Peter always asked on the way home from these visits, but Coach Bell didn't know. As much as half his tuition might be covered. They had to wait and see. Only half? Peter wanted to say, but he had the sense he was one of the lucky ones, and should keep his mouth shut.

And then, just after Halloween of his senior year, he got a call from a coach at a small school in New Jersey, Division III. The school couldn't even offer athletic scholarships. But this coach knew about Peter's SATs, his AP classes, his class rank. He knew his PRs in the mile, the half mile, the quarter. What this school could offer was a combination of grants and scholarships based on merit and need that would cover his whole tuition, plus room and board. For his walking-around money, as Coach put it, they would set him up with a nice work-study that would be flexible about hours when he had out-of-town meets. Since he was no longer a dependent of his parents, he'd qualify for more. All he had to do was a bunch of paperwork.

Elliott College was not the best school, academically, and when he considered their offer he also thought about the pamphlet from Dartmouth that he'd been carrying around inside his American history textbook for a few months. History was his favorite subject, like a long, riveting story with plot twists and turns, and often, before tests, while the other students were cramming in every last minute to study, Peter would flip to that pamphlet and examine the photos one more time. Ms. Carcara had promised him that Dartmouth was not out of the question, that Coach Bell had already spoken to the coach up there and there was no doubt Peter would qualify for a partial academic scholarship, a need-based grant. They couldn't offer him a full ride, but there were student loans available that would cover the balance. When Peter told Ms. Carcara about Elliott College, she seemed disappointed.

"They have a new president," Ms. Carcara told him when she'd had a chance to do more research. "Trying to become more competitive. So they're willing to put themselves out for a kid like you."

No other school had offered him the chance to come out without a single dollar of debt. When a few weeks went by and he still hadn't responded, they offered him a living stipend on top.

"Sorry?" George said on the night Peter explained it to him, and put down his knife and fork. He was taking a date to a seven fifteen movie and had rushed in from work to the shower and then to heat up the brick of lasagna he'd gotten from the deli for him and Peter to share. Peter was looking forward to being alone in the apartment. This woman was great, George had said hurriedly as he buttoned his shirt, but she was an EMT and her only free nights were Tuesdays and Wednesdays. Peter tried to tell him through the bathroom door, and again while he was getting dressed, but George was distracted, too rushed. Finally they sat down and Peter tried once more.

"Are you telling me that somebody has given you a full scholarship to a college and I'm only hearing about it now?"

Peter shrugged. "I'm really sorry but can you take a day off? They want an adult with me. Coach Bell would come but it's a Division Three school and I know I'd be putting him out. They've set it up so I sleep in a dorm with a guy from the track team, but I can give you some of my summer money for a hotel."

"Peter. I can pay for a hotel room, for God's sake. You worry too much, you know that? So you're that good? I guess I should have gone to one of your meets. When did you take the SATs?"

———

Two days later, as the rest of the kids at Dutch Kills were hustling to homeroom, George and Peter set off in George's fifteen-year-old Ford Fiesta that leaked oil all the way down the New Jersey Turnpike. George had gotten new clothes for the trip, and at McDonald's he made a show of tucking napkins all around his collar and spreading them over his lap. Peter wore one of the collared shirts he always wore to school, but George asked if maybe he shouldn't put a sweater over it, to look more collegiate. Two and a half hours later they came upon a long wooded road that ended at the iron gate that marked the entrance to Elliott College.

Together, George and Peter walked from the parking lot to the admissions office, where a young woman greeted them and offered them refreshments—"Thanks, honey," George said when she brought out a plate of fruit and cookies—and told them all about the school's core requirements, some of which Peter could place out of thanks to AP scores. Peter shot George a brief look of apology but George was rapt and didn't appear the least bit bored. When they finished up in admissions, the same young woman walked them over to the track, where the middle-distance coach was waiting for them.

"George Stanhope," George said, and extended his hand before immediately stepping back behind Peter. "As you can see I don't do much running." Coach invited both of them to his office, but George waved them off. "I'll take a look around," he said, "and leave you to it. Peter, I'll see you tomorrow." He read a plaque about the football team while they walked off. Once they disappeared inside the field house, George headed over to make small talk with a security guard, ask a few questions of his own. Were they nice kids, mostly, from what the man had seen? Were there any regular kids or all silver spoons? The guard said there were a lot of weirdos but they were nice enough, mostly. As for him, the pay was the same as anyplace despite all the college's bragging about fair wages, and if he got his chance, he was going to take a job in Toms River, get closer to the ocean.

———

"How was it?" George asked when Peter got in the car the next morning. George had pulled up to the stadium a bit early, had watched Peter stretching in a circle of kids just that little bit older than he was. He watched them pull off their sweaty clothes in the cold November air and root through their bags to find dry ones that looked exactly the same, which they pulled over their heads as they talked. Peter was alabaster white, George could see, but stronger looking than he seemed with his shirt on. Finally, Peter broke away from the circle and jogged over to George's car looking entirely like himself—warm-up pants, his old turtleneck, his cheeks apple red. George wondered for the first time if Peter had had any fun in high school. It had all sped by so quickly. Never once had he come in late, or come home drunk, or brought a girl home. Didn't kids smoke anymore? Didn't they cut class? When Peter used a dish, he washed it. When he used the last of the toilet paper, he went down to the store and bought more. Sometimes he let his heap of dirty clothes get too big—and Jesus did they stink sometimes—but the one time George teased him about it Peter looked so embarrassed and George felt terrible. He went up to the Laundromat that very night with his drawstring laundry bag and a book, insisting that had been his plan all along. He hadn't known a thing about laundry when he first moved in, but George had shown him, and the women at the Laundromat had shown him, and now he could treat and soak and press and fold like a 1950s housewife. George wondered if he still felt like a guest in the apartment or if he'd come to think of it as his home. He'd never even asked to put up a poster or a picture. It struck George now that he should have told him it was okay anyway, just in case.

"It was fun," Peter said, tossing his bag on the back seat. He'd stayed with a group of sophomore runners, and he'd gotten the same impression he'd gotten at all the schools he visited, that the students were performing for him a little. These particular students spent part of the night talking about a time the year before when they'd all gotten drunk and shaved their heads. They'd asked Peter his best times, about where he'd placed in sectionals, at states. When they heard his times, they grew quiet. One asked why the hell he was thinking about running for Elliott.

"But," Peter said as George merged into traffic, "I think maybe I should stay in New York. It was fun for a night, but I was thinking I might take a year or two off before college. Figure out all the financial stuff."

He thought—though he'd not mentioned it to anyone yet, not Coach Bell, not Ms. Carcara—that he could work with the ironworkers for a year or two, bank the money, and then go to a top school without having to take on so many loans.

George was quiet for a long time. He wondered if it was about the boy's mother. Peter hadn't seen her since she was moved upstate. Anne didn't want to see him, but George could tell that the boy didn't know she'd made it official, that she'd refused to put her son's name down on the list of visitors. In fact, she didn't put a single name on the list. George didn't know whether he should just tell him now or wait until he made plans to go, and then either talk him out of going or drive him up there so he'd be with him when he got turned away. The Capital District Psychiatric Center had stricter protocols, was run much more like a prison than the hospital in Westchester had been. Maybe it comforted Peter in some way to live in the same state as she did, even if he didn't see her. Then George wondered if it was him Peter worried about, that he'd be lonely or something. He tried to think about how he'd see this decision from where Peter was standing, that maybe to a kid who'd been dealt the cards Peter had it was more important to stay put in a place—who knew? At eighteen a boy can only see forward, and can't imagine looking back. Then George thought of his brother and felt rage settle in his body. For years now he'd been scrolling through his memories to find evidence that Brian was capable of this titanic degree of selfishness. At the exact moment the boy needed him most, he'd looked at a picture of a golf course and taken off.

The cornfields and peach orchards of central New Jersey rolled out behind them in the rearview mirror. Peter, who hadn't been expecting an answer anyway, stared out the window with his chin on his fist.

By the time George spoke, they'd wound through all the local roads and were merging onto the parkway. "Hey, Peter, I'm not your father. I know that. But in my humble opinion, you don't take a chance like this, then you're a real dummy." George had just started worrying about college, believing all that didn't get decided until the end of senior year. Here it was only fall. He'd been meaning to tell Peter that he'd help him however he could, but when he talked to the accountant the union used to organize retirement benefits, just for a little advice, it seemed like the only practical help he could give Peter was to cosign for a loan. And, privately, George knew that probably wouldn't be possible, not with his credit. He'd been chipping away at it, doing all the things he should have done years earlier so that Brenda would have stayed, but it wouldn't happen soon enough to help Peter.

Peter felt the blood rush to his cheeks.

"What?"

"Are you a smart kid, Pete? Like all these people say you are? Or are you dum-dum?"

"Are you really asking?"

"Which are you?"

"I'm a smart kid?"

"Yeah you are. Now use the brain God gave you."

ten

IT WAS FRANCIS WHO decided they should have a party. All in one week the cold ended and the heat began and they talked as they did every year about how that's not the way the seasons used to work. The day he thought of a party they'd opened the windows of the house to let the air in and ended up keeping them open while they slept. Kate went to school in a sweatshirt on a Monday and by Friday she was wearing some thin thing with straps as narrow as shoelaces, and he asked her if it was meant for under another shirt, like a—but he got caught up on the word *bra* and she knew it, cracked a wide, delighted grin.

"It's a tank top, Dad," she said. "It's fine."

"It doesn't seem like enough," he said, but she was still laughing and didn't listen. He was too busy to notice these things with Natalie and Sara, but now he was not busy. It was like he'd stepped through a hinged door, and on one side his life was made up of rushing, rushing, rushing: to get in the shower, to run a razor down his cheeks, to get a cup of coffee, through traffic, through paperwork, to a meeting, to another meeting, looking for a parking spot, arguing down the telephone, back into the car, out to find a perp, out to make an arrest, back into the car, back to the coffeepot, over and over and over. And now there was mostly silence, the flap of a bird going by in the morning, the rumble of the garbage truck making rounds, the tulips he'd planted as bulbs before Halloween now pushing through the hard earth like a row of green blades.

The party would be for Lena, really, though he suggested it for Kate's graduation. "You?" Lena said. "You, Francis Gleeson, are suggesting a party?" She seemed astonished, like he'd suggested a walk on the moon, and he wondered if all along he'd been a grumpier person than he realized. They could invite everyone, he said, all the girls' friends, all of Jefferson Street, the people they knew from St. Bart's, the people at the small, local insurance company where Lena had been working full-time since the start of Kate's senior year. They could get a tent if weather was too much of a worry. They'd invite far more people than could fit in the house, and that would be half the fun of it. Something about sending Kate off to college felt to him like the beginning of a new time—better or worse was still to be seen—but it would also be like a big thank-you, he said, for the meals people brought and the help they gave and all the well wishes that had come his way over recent years.

"We have thanked them," Lena said, studying him as was her habit now. "I would never have left it this long." She didn't often ask if he was feeling okay anymore, but the question was always there. "But I'd love to have a party. You're sure? It'll be expensive."

"I'm sure. Invite everyone."

They hadn't slept together in going on two years, and before that had been before he was hurt: another two years. He was home enough now to know this was the sort of thing discussed with an air of tragedy on daytime talk shows, but he couldn't find a way to bring it up to her unless he blurted it out over dinner or while they were watching the news, and that would only make everything worse. And anyway, the time for bringing it up had passed. Once, he'd gotten up out of his chair and walked over to the couch where she was reading, and pulled the book out of her hands. Before, that's all it would have taken. But now, she'd looked up at him in confusion. "Are you okay?" she'd asked, reaching up for him to hand the book back to her. So he gave it back. Two years was a bewildering length of time to think about in total, but it had slipped by day by day, week by week, month by month, until the time piled up and they got used to it. He'd never been a man who kept track of these things. They'd always just fallen into sex before, sometimes a few days in a row, sometimes not for a whole week, but it never mattered because they were always searching for ways back to each other. That last time, they'd been in their bedroom, morning, the girls at school, Francis sitting on the edge of the bed, Lena crouched at his feet. She'd been helping him with his socks because two years ago he still got spells of dizziness whenever he bent over—it was most likely the drugs, the doctors said, not something about his brain that hadn't recovered. She'd put her hand on his thigh to steady herself and he'd drawn her up, drawn her closer. He put one hand on her warm neck, the other on the sliver of skin between the top of her skirt and the hem of her sweater. The longer he kept his hand on her bare skin, the more he remembered his old life, and for a few minutes it felt as if he could will himself back to that life, stroke by stroke, push by push. She made herself do it, he could feel it, but he didn't care. She didn't kiss him like she used to. She didn't touch his face. She just reached under her skirt, pulled down her underwear, and carefully, gingerly crawled forward so that she was on top of him. There was nothing to be afraid of, he told her then, but she'd gotten so used to caring for him and worrying about him that it reminded him of what she'd been like when the girls were toddlers, when she spent her days clearing paths, following them up the stairs.

He hadn't seen her fully naked since before he was shot. She'd begun changing in the bathroom. In the cooler months, she climbed into bed each night in head-to-toe plaid, her face scrubbed clean. In the summer she wore a T-shirt that came nearly to her knees. She was considerate, more considerate than she used to be. Now, she'd never ask for the light to read by if she thought he might be drifting off to sleep.

That one time, the last time, once he'd finished, she leaned forward and pressed her forehead to his. She didn't try to coax him to keep going, and that's when he knew she'd done it only for him and not at all for herself. "Lena, love," he'd said when he realized she was crying, and tried to catch hold of her hands. But she stood up, shimmied her underwear back on, went into the bathroom, and ran the water for a few minutes. And then she went downstairs.

Since then he'd waited for a sign that something would flare between them again, and sometimes when she bobbed her hips along with the music coming from the kitchen radio, or curled the phone cord around her finger while she talked, a longing opened up in his chest like a blossom. Everyone told him how lucky he was, and he knew they weren't wrong. She'd tended to him from the very first moment the shot rang out, and refused to leave his side. In those early weeks, before he could walk, she never let him be; she was always taking a limb in her hands and massaging him so that he wouldn't get a clot. She fed him and kept him warm and smeared Vaseline on his lips and checked his IV and his wound site, and when she didn't like what a nurse or doctor told them, she asked to speak to another. "You'll be fine," she repeated to him over and over and over, and because of her, he never doubted it. But now, he could see, she'd gotten too used to being the caretaker and him the patient. She no longer went pale every time he made for the stairs, but she'd placed him in a category alongside the girls, the mortgage—another thing to worry about.

In most ways, he was back to himself. It had taken a full four years but he'd finally arrived more or less where he began—minus an eye and with some paralysis in the muscles of his face. One side of his body grew tired more quickly than the other. A run-of-the-mill head cold always felt to him like an infection. But he began taking up the odd jobs he'd done before. He began mowing the lawn again. He trimmed their trees and bushes and hauled the dead brush to the curb. When he worked hard he sweat, and when a drop of sweat dripped from his brow down his face, it felt completely different on the left side than it did on the right. He shoveled the snow when it fell, and seeded the lawn in the spring and fall, and he soldered the basement pipe that had been weeping for years. When he hung the Christmas lights along the roofline, Lena held the ladder and scolded him the whole time, that he shouldn't be up there, that it wasn't worth it, what if he got dizzy, that he'd better come down that instant. But he'd done it and it was all fine.

And still, they couldn't seem to fight their way back to each other. Not once since he came home from the hospital did she roll up against him in her sleep, not once did she slide her hand across his chest like she used to and settle there. When he thought about it too much, he felt like a child for letting it bother him. "Hug me!" Kate had shouted at Lena once as a little girl. Someone's German shepherd had gotten loose and had chased the kids around the block, trying hard to nip their heels through his muzzle. Terrified, Kate had run inside. "Hug me!" she'd demanded of Lena, opening her little arms. Lena, smiling, had hugged her tight.

Once in a while, at night, he tested himself against her boundary to see what might happen, but it was getting more difficult all the time. Just the other night he'd run his fingertip along the ends of her hair, which was hanging in a sheet over the edge of her pillow. A whisper-light touch in the dark. All she had to do was not move and he might have tried something bolder. "Sorry," she said, her back to him, and quickly flicked her hair out of his way. "Are you okay?" she asked over her shoulder.

But now Kate was leaving, and the house would be theirs again. He could barely believe how quickly it had happened. For twenty years they'd been talking about putting on an addition, maybe, like so many neighbors had done, but then they'd looked up and discovered they didn't need it anymore. Used to be he'd come home from work and shout at everyone to pick up their markers, their papers, their sweatshirts, their backpacks, and then one day he'd looked around and there were no backpacks thrown anywhere. And during the day now there wasn't even Lena. She worked at the insurance company from nine to five and when she came home, she went straight to the kitchen, started chopping and boiling something for dinner. As a young man, as a young father, he'd never imagined there'd be a time when he'd be alone in his house every day. He thought about Ireland more and more, tried to remember if there was ever a day in his life when his own father didn't have something to do. Sometimes he kept the TV on for company, and one day as he was flipping through, he came upon a scene where a woman and a man were kissing in what looked to be a hotel room. He stayed on the channel. Next thing, just as the man began to undress the woman, he turned her around, pushed her onto the bed, and entered her from behind. Francis was never one for porn, but this was different. It was cable. He couldn't actually see anything, just the suggestion of something. Watching, he slid his hand inside his pants and touched himself until he came, and that started a stretch of months that reminded him of being fourteen again, disappearing to a remote field where he could curl up and slip his hand inside his pants in privacy because there was no place to be alone in the crowded house.

He still took a painkiller every day, and when his doctor said that one pill likely did very little for him at this point, he understood that as permission to take two. Sometimes two in the morning and another two in the afternoon. Nothing seemed to happen except that he felt quiet in his center, at peace. He took an antidepressant, which didn't work nearly as well as two painkillers, and which felt a little embarrassing but which his doctor said was standard.

Sometimes, still, when he was standing at the kitchen sink looking out the window, he would hear the buzz and slap of a grass edger and expect to see Brian Stanhope's head moving along the other side of the rocks. Then he'd remember and feel astonished all over again. He tried to recall what he used to think of Anne Stanhope. He'd mostly wanted to stay out of her way. Otherwise he hadn't thought much about her. She was an odd bird, that was all. A person they'd have to encounter for a little while but could one day, when the kids were gone, ignore. He'd been kind to her. He'd been kinder than anyone else would have been. And still. Sometimes he let his imagination wander and he placed Kate on their front porch instead of himself. What if she'd killed his child?

He knew she'd been moved to a different hospital. It was generous of him to have agreed to the plea deal that removed her from prison, and sometimes he felt that generosity warranted more acknowledgment. If he were a different person, a vengeful person, he would have insisted on prison, and he knew what happened to crazy people in prison. He was worried when their lawyer called that he was going to tell them she'd been released to a halfway house or some nonsense, but it sounded as if the new hospital was not as nice as the first, and Francis was pleased. He tried to examine his pleasure—what did it mean about him? As Lena had asked many times, what did it matter, really, where she was, as long as she wasn't near them?—but at the end of these examinations, he always concluded he was within his rights to wish ill upon her. He would have been captain by then. He would have been captain or better, and if things had gone as they should have when he walked into his house at the end of a day, his wife would look at him in a way she hadn't looked at him in four years now. Once a cop always a cop, the guys said when they visited. But the more they said it the less it rang true.

————

It occurred to Lena as she began to gather the bottles of soda, the cases of beer, the chips, the dips, the pounds of ground beef for burgers, box after box of macaroni for salad, the gas for the grill—that this was how she'd once pictured living in Gillam. She'd seen herself hosting parties, throwing open their doors, and inviting in anyone who wanted to come. She'd pictured music playing, bottles uncorking. She'd pictured sitting outside with friends and neighbors while the kids raced around the house. She'd selected a dining table with double leaves instead of the usual single because she imagined she'd need seating for twelve, one day, even if that meant the table would extend right out of the dining room and into the living room. But when she brought the dining table leaves down from the attic, she noticed they were a slightly different color now than the table. The dowels were still covered in manufacturer's plastic. She'd called for Francis to take one end of each—they were too heavy to move on her own—and as he shuffled backward he staggered for a moment. "Pick up your feet!" she cried, and then insisted on switching sides.

———

Graduation was on a Saturday. Kate had won the science prize and had to cross the stage to accept a certificate and shake the principal's hand. Natalie had graduated from Syracuse the previous week, and Sara was halfway through SUNY Binghamton. With Francis's pension and Lena's job and a few loans, there would be enough to cover Kate's first year of tuition. Lena had assumed she would go to a state school like Sara, but Francis was the one who noticed the brochures and envelopes from NYU coming in. "You want to go here?" he asked her one night after taking in the mail. She was eating a bowl of cereal before bed; Lena had already gone upstairs. He thought of the Ninth Precinct, and of Brian Stanhope, of all people—a field mouse of a thought that shot through his brain and disappeared. Kate shrugged and it broke his heart a little to see she'd become a girl who wouldn't say what she wanted.

"If you had your pick of any school, which would it be?" He was determined to make her say it.

"Well, we can't do private, right?"

"This is a dream scenario, Kate, which is it?"

Finally, she'd nodded to the envelope in his hands.

"You can get in?" he asked.

"I think so."

"So apply, and then we'll see."

170

The party started at three and most of the guests arrived at exactly the same time. Some rang the doorbell before walking around the side of the house. Others just followed the sound of the stereo and trudged through the side yard bearing flowers, wine, platters of cookies and pies. He couldn't remember how people used to greet him before he was hurt, but now they seemed to make a special point of it, and he wondered if talking with him made them feel virtuous, like they'd done a good deed. He could tell that most people had trouble looking at his mismatched pupils—their own perfectly synchronized eyes would dart back and forth between his as they decided which one to settle on. Most people had presents for Kate, and when Francis saw that he felt guilty—he hadn't pictured people going out to buy presents on top of everything else they'd done for them. But Kate accepted everything gladly, and when he looked at her across the patio, he was reminded of what she'd been like as a little girl, running a private inventory of her gifts as they came in. Her friends greeted her with hugs, and the boys in the class hung around the girls in a loose circle, long armed and mostly shy.

He fired up the grill at four and began lining the grate with burgers, hot dogs, foil-wrapped corn on the cob. He had a beer. Two beers. Four beers. He refilled the coolers. A few men kept him company, while the women mostly clustered around the appetizer table. At one point Lena led a group of women upstairs to look at their bedroom closet and get advice on what could be done. She was delighted to be hosting, and when her voice carried over to him, it sounded giddy and girlish. She'd made pitchers of margaritas and when they went in the first hour, she brought out all the bottles that had gone into them and a pile of limes and mixed up more. They ate, ate more, drank more, and still, people kept arriving, Francis kept grilling. There were other graduation parties that day, and some of their guests hopped from one to the next to the next until it felt like all of Gillam was one big party.

A woman came up and asked Francis if she could get a burger without cheese, and while she waited, she asked him how he was doing, if he still got those sharp pains around his orbital wall. He turned to her quickly and she smiled, put her hand on his arm. "You don't remember me. I'd just started at Broxton around the time you were moved there. I wasn't on your floor but I came in to see you because our girls were in school together."

"I do remember. Yes, of course."

She laughed. "You don't. But you're very polite. You were getting a lot of visitors then. I remember a stream of cops in and out. Some of the young nurses used to put on lipstick in case any of them were single. They were sad when you were discharged."

"Ah. That would have been pertinent information at the time, I'm sure."

Francis took another look at her. She was petite, with long, auburn hair and a pretty dress with flowers printed on it.

"You have a daughter in the high school? You look so young," he said, and blushed. He hadn't meant to sound like he was flirting. But she did look young.

"I did until yesterday. Casey. Do you know Casey? She's . . ." She turned and tried to find her. "Well, she's here somewhere."

He put the burger on her plate, and she put her hand on his arm once more and squeezed. He felt a charge on his skin where she touched him. "Good to see you looking so healthy," she said, and then she slipped off into a crowd of women talking by the shed.

———

It was nearly dusk when he finally turned off the grill, and after dusk when he finally sat down. There were still more people arriving, and now, in the near dark, they snuck up on the crowd in the backyard like a jolt of new life. A local cop named Dowd was just telling him about a case when Kate came up behind Francis's chair and whispered that someone was puking by the rhododendron. They'd told the girls to be careful, to watch their friends, but it was inevitable, he supposed. They should have been more strategic about where they put the coolers, but they figured it would be okay. Lena had pointed out that when they were eighteen it was legal to drink, the law was arbitrary, and at their age Francis had been on his way to America, for God's sake. Plus most of the teenagers at the party had a parent there, too.

He excused himself and as he crossed the yard, he looked around for Lena, who must have gone inside. Someone had found a pack of cards and as he passed the kitchen window, he saw a group of men sitting around his table as Oscar Maldonado dealt. Some of the wood chairs from inside had somehow gotten outside, and the chaise lounge from outside was now in the middle of the kitchen. Kate had an urgent expression on her face, and walked quickly ahead of him. When he turned the corner he expected a crowd of people, but it was the dark side of the house, the side that didn't lead to the driveway, and once he arrived at the bush where Kate stopped walking, it felt like the party was far away.

"How much did she have?" he asked Kate.

"I don't know. I just saw her going around this side of the house so I followed her."

He had to squint into the shadows to spot the figure on all fours, her hair hanging around her face. "Okay, I'll take care of it," he said, feeling mostly sober all of a sudden. "And, Kate? That's it for all of you. Unless a kid is with his or her own parent, not a single person under the age of twenty-five leaves this house without me getting a look at them. Got it?"

"Got it," Kate said, but then gave him a look before she jogged away.

He went down on one knee and gathered the person's hair in his fist. She retched for several seconds, the volume and drama of which didn't match what little came out.

"Okay, okay," he said, and patted her on the back. "Let's get you cleaned up." He took firm hold of her upper arms and helped pull her to standing. "Oh!" he said when he saw who it was.

"I'm so embarrassed," she said as she swayed back and forth. She was barefoot, and one strap of her dress had fallen down around her elbow. She leaned for a moment against his chest and closed her eyes. When he felt the steady rhythm of her breathing, he knew that she'd fallen asleep. Her hair smelled like tea. Her frame was smaller than Lena's. He pushed her away, gently.

"Sorry, you said your name is? I forgot to ask before."

But she slid her hands up his arms, clutched his shoulders, and he couldn't understand what she said.

"Oh, poor thing! That's Joan Kavanagh," Lena said when she came looking for Francis and saw whom he was leading around the side of the house. The card game was still going strong around the kitchen table, but Lena squeezed by the men to bring out a glass of water and two aspirin, which Francis dropped into Joan's mouth one at a time. Lena was in bad shape herself, and after asking twice if he could handle it, she went upstairs to lie on their bed with all her clothes on, including her sandals. Joan's daughter had already left, thank God. She'd walked to another party with a group of half a dozen other kids.

"Is she all right?" Kate asked, and Francis realized that she'd hung back and let all her friends go on without her. Sara was upstairs. Who knew where Natalie had gone off to, but she was an adult now, a college graduate.

"She drank too much," Kate said.

It was so obvious that Joan Kavanagh had drank too much that Kate's statement, framed with cautious certainty, betrayed her innocence. He could see that up until that hour she thought drinking too much was just for kids.

"She might have eaten something bad. Who knows?"

Kate looked at the woman for a long time, as if deciding.

"She can sleep here, can't she? You won't make her go home?"

"No, I won't make her go home, but she might like to wake up in her own house." But then he thought of the next problem. "Do you know where the Kavanaghs live?"

Kate shook her head. "One of those blocks by the playground, I think?" She glanced down at her friend's mother as if to make sure she wasn't listening. "I think it's just her and Casey who live there. I'm not sure. I think the dad doesn't live there anymore."

Francis contemplated the sleeping stranger, curled up now with a beach towel over her shoulders for warmth. She was snoring softly with her mouth open. "I'll sort it out, Katie. Okay? You go on up to bed." How long had they been out there? One by one, without his noticing, every guest had left. The kitchen was dark except for the light above the stove. Francis went in and pulled the throw blankets from the couch and arm-chair. He turned off the TV, which was blaring music videos. When he came back outside, he pushed two armchairs together until they faced each other, and used one to sit in and the other to put up his feet. He draped one blanket over Joan and wrapped the other around himself.

He was drunk, he realized as he stared at a group of moths darting and swooping under the porch light. He was drunk and he was exhausted. He tried to remember meeting Joan at Broxton, but it was too tiring to recall, and he decided he'd do the work of remembering tomorrow.

———

When he woke into the blue chill of morning, she was looking at him over the edge of her blanket. In the space between their chairs were a few stained napkins, a sea of crushed potato chips. "I'm mortified," she whispered. It was not quite dawn, and his neck felt stiff and frozen. The inside of his mouth felt like fur. She stood and neatly draped the blanket he'd given her over the back of the chair where she'd slept. "I'm leaving," she whispered. "I'm walking home. You should go inside."

She took a moment to look around for her shoes, and when she found them she just hooked them on her first two fingers. As she passed by he reached out and grabbed her free hand, held tight. Twisting around in his chair, he moved his hands to her hips, then up to the narrowing at her waist, and for a second, for only half a second, perhaps, he felt her move closer to him, her muscles tensing under his palms. The morning felt thin and breakable and if he asked her a question, he knew it would lead to another. And that one to another. And so on.

"I'm going," she said, and then she was gone.

eleven

GEORGE WENT DOWN TO Skillman to play basketball while Peter packed. He'd planned on helping, but that morning when they were standing at the couch shoulder to shoulder, folding Peter's few clothes into piles, they realized it wasn't a job for two. In early August, George took him to a Sears on Long Island where he bought Peter a set of bath towels and new, extra-long, blue and red plaid sheets for his dorm room bed. George asked what else he needed, and Peter knew some kids were getting small refrigerators, thirteen-inch televisions, but he said nothing, all his meals were included, what else could there be? On the way home they stopped at their usual diner and George cleared his throat and said that since his dad wasn't there it was up to him to tell Peter a few things before he headed into the world on his own, and Peter felt his stomach drop, sure George was going to say something about sex that Peter already knew but didn't want to know that George knew, too. Once, Peter had a bad head cold and left practice. He arrived home two hours early and believed, at first, that George wasn't home. Then he heard sounds coming from the bedroom, small movements, a quick, hushed conversation. He froze, his keys still in his hand, and then he left again. He walked down Queens Boulevard towards Manhattan's skyline. When he got as far as the movie theater, he turned around. When he returned home a second time, there was no one in the apartment and George's bedroom door stood wide open.

Instead, George said that he knew there was a lot of drinking that went on in college, and that might be okay for the other kids but not for Peter. "I mean, a little, sure, a few beers here and there, but you've probably got the gene, Peter. Some people have it and some people don't. If you're like the Stanhopes, then you have it."

George had been making references to the gene for a few years now but Peter didn't know if he meant a real gene, as in a distinct sequence of nucleotides that formed part of a chromosome, or if it was just a notion invented by people who needed to understand themselves.

"Did my dad have a problem? In that way, I mean?"

George gaped at him. "Oh, Peter. Buddy. Yes."

"I never noticed."

"Well," George said. "You were a kid."

"I don't think so. I would have noticed. And I didn't."

"Okay."

Peter removed his napkin from his lap and refolded it along the seams. He went to the bathroom, washed his hands without looking at his reflection in the mirror, and when he got back to his seat, he made himself eat two-thirds of the burger so that George wouldn't ask why he wasn't hungry.

Instead of packing his suitcase with his running T-shirts and thermals, Peter put his books in there because they were the heaviest and the suitcase had wheels, and George said that was the sort of thinking that got him the big bucks. He stuffed his clothes into his old track duffel. Since he'd worn a uniform through high school, he only had one pair of jeans, a few sweaters, two pairs of khaki shorts. He went through his running clothes, and anything with yellowed armpits he stuffed in a giant Hefty bag and then carried down to the trashcan on the curb. Already, the space he'd taken up for four years was emptying of his presence, and he could begin to see how the place would close up around any memory of him, like the walling up of a door.

His classmates' graduation parties were spread across the summer, and Peter had gone to most of them, though at each of these parties, he always wondered why he'd come. Every one of them was an incongruous mingling of friends and elderly aunts and oddball neighbors, all of whom had different ideas of what to expect from such gatherings. Peter grinned for group photos but he knew when the pictures were developed that the reluctance would be clear on his face, and that made him never want to see them. At one party, Henry Finley's parents had gotten a keg they told Henry was full of Budweiser, but it turned out to be full of O'Doul's, and the adults laughed at the kids who pretended to have gotten drunk. At the same party, his friend Rohan asked him if he ever saw that old girlfriend of his anymore.

"Once in a while," Peter said. "Not often."

"But you're still into her," Rohan said. "That explains why you never came to hang out with the girls from Higgins."

Did that explain it? Peter wondered.

He had to report to Elliott for cross-country practice, which began a week before freshman orientation, then classes would start. At graduation he had thought, maybe, you never knew, maybe he'd look over and see his father at the back of the gym, or his mother with two orderlies next to her, a van running outside at the curb, and three months later, on the day he lifted his suitcase and his duffel into the trunk of George's car, he had the same feeling, like his parents might come walking quickly down the street, afraid they would miss the chance to say goodbye. Sometimes it seemed like a lifetime since he'd seen either of them. On the night before he left, George took him to eat at an Italian restaurant in the city, and over dinner he told a story about a man he knew a long time ago who couldn't do the thing that was right, and the longer he waited to do it the more difficult it became, but it didn't mean the man didn't want to do it.

It was a parable, Peter realized, and gave up trying to follow.

"It's okay, George," Peter said. "I know what you're trying to tell me."

The next afternoon, after checking out Peter's room and walking around campus for a while, George handed Peter an envelope and said it was time for him to take off.

Peter clapped his uncle on the shoulder, shook his hand. "Well, thanks for everything," he said. His chest hurt.

"Hey, hey," George said, pulling Peter in for a tight hug. "Don't look so worried. Okay? You always look so goddamn worried, Peter. It's all good stuff. Okay? I'll see you at Thanksgiving. That's no time at all."

Several hours later Peter remembered the envelope, which he'd shoved into the pocket of his shorts. Inside were five stiff hundred-dollar bills.

———

Practices weren't much different than those under Coach Bell, and Peter saw immediately that he was the best on the team. He wasn't used to practicing with girls—with the *women*'s team—as Coach called it. Not that the men and the women saw much of each other once they finished warm-ups. He liked that no one knew anything about him except that his name was Peter Stanhope, that he came from Queens, that he ran the fastest eight hundred meter in the city the previous spring. No, he didn't have a girlfriend. No, he didn't know his major yet. His parents? Yeah, they split a few years back. His mom lived in Albany now. Yeah, he saw her when he could.

On the third day of practice, one of the seniors on the girls' team said something about having been home for the summer, back to her hometown of Riverside, which bordered Gillam. Peter calculated: she would have been a junior at Riverside High when everything happened. For the rest of the week he made sure to stretch on the opposite side of the circle, to drop his head in case she might turn to look at him when Coach called out his name. But when she didn't seem to recognize him or his name, he felt the heavy cloak of worry he'd been wearing grow lighter, until it was as if he'd simply shrugged it off his shoulders and let it fall to the ground. Little by little, he felt the shiver of a new idea forming, a new space opening up wide enough for him to stand in.

Friday was move-in day for the rest of the freshmen, and Peter left a note for his roommate to say that although he'd already chosen a bed, a dresser, he didn't mind switching. The first note he wrote seemed too formal so he tore it up. The second draft seemed too brusque. So in his third draft he added a few exclamation points and only a few minutes later, when he was crossing the quad, did he worry that exclamation points might seem kind of gay. All week he'd been looking at the proximity of the two beds in his room, trying not to think about the fact that he'd never—not even in George's apartment—lived in such close quarters with another human being. He didn't know if his habits were normal, if he was too neat or too messy, if he was too quiet or too loud, when a person should ignore one's roommate in order to grant a sort of false privacy, or if it was better and less weird to always acknowledge the other person and try to keep up light conversation. And would that be possible if they were to sleep and study and hang out all in the same ten-by-twelve-foot space? Wouldn't conversation run out by Halloween? He'd known for a long time now that his tendency to be careful was part of what kept him apart. The guys on the team showered after practice and walked around in their underwear and laughed at each other's privates and then went on to eat together, play video games.

That night, not long after the last of the parents had kissed their darlings goodbye, a ritual Peter had been observing all around him, all day long, there was a late-summer storm that brought down branches, pried power lines from the sides of buildings. When his dorm lost power, his roommate, Andrew, a husky guy from Connecticut whose first words to Peter were, "What are you listening to right now? Hip hop? Metal? Don't say country," kept saying that his mother should have packed candles, his mother should have packed a flashlight, he couldn't understand why she hadn't. So Peter told him to come on, and they gathered in the common area with the other freshmen who'd just moved in. Peter suggested they have a scavenger hunt in the dark and for the first time in a while he thought of Kate, thought about how much she'd have loved that idea. He wondered where she was at that moment. He tried to imagine what he'd do or say if he showed up to his first class and there she was, sitting with her notebook open. Would he even recognize her? Would she be glad to see him, or would she blame him for what happened, for his long silence.

At orientation, Peter groaned along with the others at the corny icebreakers, the forced fun meant to bond them. He was grouped with three other freshmen for a trust exercise, and the leader had barely finished explaining the instructions when the blond girl in his group was literally falling into his arms.

"You almost dropped me!" she said.

"I wasn't ready," he said, defensive.

After, the other boy in their group said, "Dude, she was flirting."

When orientation was over, all that was left to do was buy books, register for classes. Peter headed to the main campus bookstore one morning and had to stop in the crosswalk for a bus to pass by, the words "41st Street Terminal" lit up above the front windshield. He stopped walking and stared at it until he realized a car was waiting for him to cross.

The next day, the bus was there again. The driver pulled into the wide cul-de-sac outside the bookstore just before nine. What started as a stray thought began to take shape. The upperclassmen were arriving now in droves, taking up all the picnic tables and grassy spaces of the quad, and on the day before classes were set to begin, Peter climbed the steps of the bus and confirmed the destination was Manhattan. It was an express, the driver said. He stopped at another college in New Jersey, then two park and rides along the turnpike, and then the Port Authority Bus Terminal. Peter patted his back pocket and felt for his wallet, and then he climbed aboard. He didn't bring a book or a magazine. He didn't tell his roommate or his coach or his RA. He refused to ask himself what he was doing.

It was a Tuesday morning in September 1995, the day after Labor Day, and the roads were empty. From the Port Authority he took the subway one stop to Penn Station. He approached the first Amtrak teller he found. The train he wanted was departing in fourteen minutes.

It was mid-afternoon by the time he got to Albany. From the Rensselaer station he took a taxi to the hospital, but he was too anxious to go in right away so he walked a lap around the entire complex, and then he sat on a bench and tried to calm down. All day, all week, all summer, he'd felt in himself a weather vane swinging around wildly to face one direction, and then another, whenever the wind blew. Now, here, he'd settle things, face the chill he'd felt between his shoulder blades for four years, tell his mother he loved her no matter what and find out if she loved him, too. When he felt more ready, he told the man at reception who he was, whom he wanted to see. He'd gotten a Coke out of a vending machine at the train station and had clutched it all through the taxi ride and as he walked across the hospital grounds. He was afraid if he opened it now it would explode, so he set it on the narrow ledge that ran along the bottom of the reception window while the man squinted at his computer screen.

"First time visiting?" the man asked. Before Peter could answer he said, "No cameras, recording devices, tobacco products, drugs, drug paraphernalia—that includes prescription medication, insulin pens, syringes. No weapons, chemicals, personal property including keys or identification. No tapes or DVDs, no Walkmen or headphones. No electric toothbrushes or electric razors. No metal cutlery, any beverage that has caffeine." At this he glanced at Peter's Coke. "No solid-colored clothing, or clothing with solid-colored patches. No paint, pens, highlighters, scissors, knitting needles, weights, magnetic devices."

He let that sink in. "So," he said. "What do you have?"

"Nothing," Peter said. He dropped the unopened soda into the trash bin next to the desk, and it landed with a heavy thud. He was sweating so much that he was afraid to lift his arms in case there were rings there.

"Can you repeat the patient's name?" The man leaned closer to his computer monitor.

Peter did, and tried to read what it meant when the man pinched the bridge of his nose, closed his eyes tight, told Peter to take a seat because he had to call upstairs.

"Is there a problem?"

"Just take a seat."

A woman who was older than his mother was also waiting, and on her lap were two enormous bags of cookies. She had another clear Ziploc that held toothpaste, floss, plastic razor blades. He worried the razor blades would be taken from her. Peter was wearing a polo shirt, shorts. After a few minutes of waiting he went into the grim men's room and used a wad of paper towels to wipe his forehead, his neck, under his arms. On his way back to his seat he asked at the desk if they'd called his name while he was in the restroom. He waited another forty minutes and watched other visitors get escorted through the double security doors. He watched through the murky windows as security guards lifted their bags to the light, went through them, and every once in a while plucked items out, set them aside. He went back up to the desk, and the man told him he had to wait longer. It was late afternoon already. Soon it would be dinnertime. Would a patient be allowed to see a visitor during dinner? He listened to everything and tried to feel her presence in the building, some distant sound that he would know came from her. Whenever he pictured his mother, he always saw her alone in a room somewhere. He remembered a time years ago when she sat on the edge of his bed and told him about a rooster she once knew that crowed all day long, and how she thought it so strange until she found out that almost all roosters crow through the day. It's only the sunrise crowing people notice, because the world is so quiet at sunrise.

"But you noticed the other crowing, too," he had said. "You're the only one?"

"I'm the only one," she said.

Eventually, a buzzer sounded and a sunken-eyed man with a hospital ID hanging around his neck stepped through the double doors and said Peter's name.

The man put his hand on Peter's shoulder and led him over to a potted tree, an attempt at privacy. "I'm afraid your mother won't see you today," he said, and Peter nodded vigorously as if this were what he'd been expecting all along. They were willing to bend the rules a bit—Peter hadn't applied to be a visitor, hadn't gone through the requisite waiting period—but his mother simply wasn't up to it.

"She isn't up to it or she doesn't want to see me?"

"You might try again in a few weeks," the man said. "You could arrange a particular date, give her some advance notice. That way she might prepare."

"Is she doing well, though? What can you tell me?"

"Just try again. Register first. Go through the protocols. By then . . ."

But Peter tuned him out. He knew he would not be trying again in a few weeks. Something had carried him onto the bus that morning, and it wasn't a feeling that would come over him twice. Already, the journey back to his dorm room seemed impossibly long, and the return bus didn't even go all the way to Elliott. He'd have to disembark in the little town nearest to the college and then take a taxi. He thanked the man and as he left the hospital, he hurried across the wide lawn. He walked as the crow flies—cutting through residential blocks, strip malls, parking lot after parking lot, keeping the skyline of the city center in front of him. He walked over a footbridge and passed a bar where people were sitting quietly, watching something on television. Baseball. The strike had just ended. When Peter approached another bar, he decided to go in. Except for a bag of M&M's on the train, he hadn't eaten since that morning. He sat at the end of the bar and ordered a soda and a plate of fries. Then, as soon as the bartender stepped away, Peter called him back and told him to make it a beer. He looked at the row of tap handles and picked one, though he didn't know one from another. The bartender didn't ask for ID, so when he finished that beer he ordered another. Then one more after that. Three pints of some kind of dark beer, heavy for a summer day, but once he made a choice he thought he'd better stick with it. The only time the bartender seemed to be appraising him was when he handed over one of George's hundred-dollar bills. He held the bill up to the light.

Peter got to the train station with twenty minutes to spare. He felt warm, easy in his body, realized he might be a tiny bit drunk. He didn't know it would feel so cozy.

"I know what I'm going to do," he said aloud, and made for the bank of telephones. He picked up a phone and pushed random coins through the slot until the dial tone went steady. Then, his finger poised over the pad, he realized he'd never called her, not once, and didn't know her number. Why memorize her number when he could just stand outside and look up at her window?

But he did know her address, just one digit different from his own. He returned to the newsstand, bought a small spiral notebook, a box of envelopes, a pen. They didn't sell stamps, but an elderly woman over-heard his query and told him she'd sell him one for a quarter.

He didn't want to think too much about what to write or what not to write, so he bent his head over the page and filled it with his scrawl, a list

186

of stray thoughts, maybe, but ones that she would understand. He wrote about Queens, about George, about running, about the trouble he had making close friends. He wrote that he missed her and had tried sending her telepathic messages a few times, years ago, and also how sometimes a week or two might go by without thinking of her. He told her that there were times when he was certain that she hated him and other times when he was certain she'd forgive him for everything that happened. He asked if she thought it was weird that he felt like he still knew her very well, and that she knew him, even though they hadn't seen each other in more than four years. He wrote that he'd like to see her. When he was finished he tore out the pages and left the ripped bits along the side. He folded and stuffed them inside one of the envelopes, wrote her name and address on the outside. He'd passed a blue USPS mailbox on the sidewalk, two or three blocks from the station. He looked at the departures board and knew he'd make it. He ran like someone had a clock on him, pushing out the swinging doors and dodging commuters hustling toward him. He sprinted two blocks, crossed a street, and dropped the envelope into the mailbox. He was back on his train's platform in less than three minutes.

For the whole journey home, the long two-hour ride to Manhattan, and then another two hours back to Elliott, the bus's air conditioner blasting despite the mild evening, Peter thought of his letter to Kate sitting in the dark belly of that mailbox. He flipped through the spiral notebook where he'd torn the pages out, running his fingers over the blank top page as if it might help him recall what he'd written. He felt a few misgivings but was still glad he'd done it, and he looked forward to what might happen next. By the third hour he was having trouble tamping down his panic. It had seemed like such a great idea in the moment and he'd let that enthusiasm carry him. Now, he only felt ill. He tried to imagine George's voice in his ear, saying, Peter, buddy, you worry too much.

When he got off the bus it was after midnight, and he stood alone on the lighted sidewalk, listening to the crickets of central New Jersey. The air smelled like peaches, and along the main road there were signs for orchards everywhere, as many peaches as a person could pick. The houses lining the wide avenue were modest but sweet looking, and Peter imagined the kids inside sleeping among their toys and their books, their ceilings dotted with glow-in-the-dark stars. In the distance, from the direction of the college, came the sound of car horns beeping—a call and an answer.

He toed the edge of the circle of lamplight and fought the urge to howl, to wake all the people in all the houses. Instead, he crossed his arms tight across his chest and began the long walk back to campus. He should have been wilder, he thought. He should have been out roaming the streets of the city at night, no parents to tell him not to; he'd have had a ready excuse for any trouble he might have gotten into. He should have broken things, stolen things, listened to music so loud that the neighbors pounded on the door. He should have tried smoking pot when the other kids did. He should have tried coke that time Rohan had gotten hold of some; he should have followed the other boys when they filed into the bathroom of a Pizza Hut in Kew Gardens to see what it was like. He should not have hung back at the table, worried that their waiter would think they were skipping out on the bill. He should have found a girlfriend, multiple girlfriends, one from one school and one from another like some of the other boys did, and then he should have smirked about it in homeroom. He should have been so wild that George would have had to hunt his father down and make him come back, so wild he would have had to get his mother's lawyer involved to figure out what could be done. But instead, he'd been so very good.

He should have gotten on the commuter bus back to Gillam and gone to Kate. He should have broken down her door if they wouldn't let him see her. He should have at least stood on her front lawn and shouted her name.

He stayed to the road's narrow shoulder, and when he saw car lights approaching he stepped off into the shadows of trees until the car was safely past.

Reaching his dorm room, he slid his key into the lock and turned the doorknob slowly, slowly, just in case Andrew was asleep.

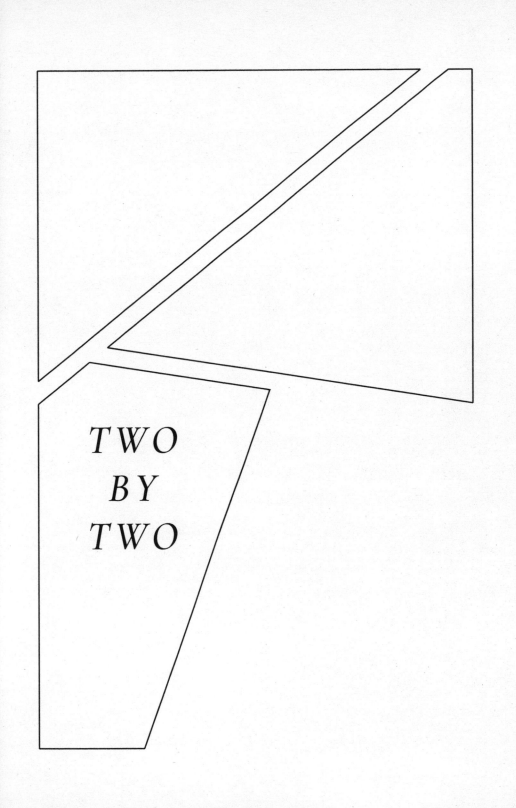

TWO
BY
TWO

twelve

DR. ABBASI PUT ANNE'S name in for case review at the end of her fourth year at Capital District Psychiatric Hospital.

"What does that mean?" she asked, and heard a harsh edge in her voice that she hadn't intended. Dr. Abbasi was dark. Indian, maybe. Or Pakistani. He started at CDPH during Anne's second year there. He had a posh British accent, hooded eyes, and a deadpan wit that surprised Anne the first few times she encountered it. He didn't seem as tired as the other doctors did. She wondered what he was like at home when he changed into his weekend clothes. What he did for fun. She had never, not once, wondered that about any of her other doctors. None of the other doctors ever made her feel hopeful about herself, about what might happen. He said, once, early on, "When this time in your life is behind you, Anne . . . ," and she lost track of what he was talking about because no one had ever referenced a time when *all this* might be behind her. It was as if a wall had been built between her real life and her life in the hospital and that wall just kept growing taller and taller. And then Dr. Abbasi arrived with a catapult to help her over.

"It means we're going to go over your case, your progress, and talk about whether you might be ready for the next step."

"Which would be?"

"An environment with more independence, but with support if needed. A residential reentry center seems right to me. To start."

"A halfway house," Anne said, and remembered with a pang a petition she'd signed years ago that sought to block the opening of a halfway house in Gillam.

"We're going to discuss several options."

"But chances are good that I won't pass the review." Right then, she ticked off in her head all the people who had been up for review since her arrival, and were still there stirring powdered eggs around their breakfast plates each morning.

"I wouldn't say that. I only mention it because I don't want you to be taken by surprise if you do pass."

"But I probably won't. There are people who've been here twenty years. More."

"True, but I have a different perspective than some of my predecessors, and the thinking is changing surrounding this."

"This?"

"This." Dr. Abbasi gestured to the walls, the windows, widened his arms to take in the world. "You committed a crime, yes, but you were found not responsible due to your mental state at that time. You weren't taking your meds consistently, and what you were taking wasn't right for you. That's changed, Anne. You're doing very well. You'd still see a doctor as an outpatient, and your medications would have to be recalibrated from time to time, but it doesn't make sense that you be here longer than you would have spent in prison if you were found responsible for your actions. You're a good candidate. Start thinking about it."

Dr. Abbasi's arrival coincided with Peter's visit to the hospital. By the time Dr. Abbasi inherited her case from a doctor who was scaling back, Anne been removed from all group therapy. She'd been moved to the fifth floor. The first time she met Dr. Abbasi, he entered her room tentatively, politely, as if it were up to her to ask him to stay or go.

"I hear you've been having some trouble," he said. He didn't carry a notebook or a clipboard. His hands were clasped behind his back.

"My son," Anne said, her voice cracking. She knew they were watching her. She knew she must remain composed. That day, when a social worker came in and told her that her son was downstairs, that she would be allowed to see him if she wished, she felt Peter's energy move through the pipes that snaked secretly through the floors, made them hum and glow. The air immediately took on glints of silver and gold. She was certain she knew he was there several seconds before she was told.

She hadn't been brave enough to see him that day, so she'd sent him away. Immediately after, she felt her internal clock speed up, a central agitation that always foretold a bad time. She tried to hide it by keeping her face placid and putting food in her mouth at meals and sitting rigidly in the common space and not saying a single word lest she give herself away, but she knew they were studying her, and the quieter she made herself the closer they looked. It was exhausting work to keep up. So after a few days of this, when a nurse came to escort her to group—always group, endless group, everyone nattering on about every little thing while the planet spun and wars were won and lost and Anne's own child was out there somewhere, an adult, hoping to see his mother—Anne saw lights, like fireflies, over the nurse's head. She began swatting at them. The nurse called for backup, claiming to have been attacked. Her history of violence was referenced. But what Anne hated more than being lifted, physically, what she hated more than feeling a stranger's hot breath near her ear, what she hated more than being drugged or locked in a room, were the smirks on the faces of the other patients.

While every other doctor at the hospital would have asked, Why do you believe they were smirking at you? Dr. Abbasi asked instead: "Why does their smirking bother you? Considering the other things you must know you have to face when they carry you away."

"So you agree that they were smirking?"

Dr. Abbasi paused to consider his answer. "I agree that human nature allows for that strong possibility, yes."

———

The day Anne learned she passed the review was a Tuesday, more than two years since Peter's visit, and by Friday morning she was in a van heading to a house on the edge of Saratoga County. She sat ramrod straight on the bench seat behind the driver, swallowing hard against the acid rising in her throat. She didn't say goodbye to anyone, didn't have anyone she'd call a friend, except a woman she sometimes sat near at meals.

"Nice day," the driver said kindly, and glanced at her in the rearview mirror several times in quick succession. The sky was a dazzling blue, but the oily puddles that dotted the shoulder of the highway told her there'd been recent rain. Dr. Abbasi had shaken her hand and when she didn't let go, he put his other hand over hers, too. He wouldn't be getting into the van with her. He wouldn't be showing her around her new home.

Rounding a back road in Malta, she glimpsed a white sail moving among the trees. The ocean was at least two hundred miles away.

"What's that?" she asked, squinting.

"What's what?" the driver asked.

"It looks like a sail."

"Day like today boats are on the water by dawn."

"What water?"

"Lake Saratoga," the driver said. "Don't they tell you anything about where you're headed?"

———

Since addiction had never been part of Anne's pathology, she was free to look for nursing work again, and if she found a job quickly, she could enter immediately into Phase Two, which meant she could come and go freely, and also get out of mandatory vocational training. Eirene House was just thirty miles north of the hospital, and the driver told her that made her lucky. Some people ended up in Buffalo or all the way down-state. Anne had heard terrible things about halfway houses. Several pa-tients at CDPH had been in and out and told her to watch herself, watch her stuff, the experience was more dehumanizing than the hospital. And arriving at Eirene seemed to match what she'd been warned about. The house itself was a depressed-looking three-story box that sat too close to the sidewalk. The house director, a woman named Margaret, had shown her to her bedroom, which Anne would share with another resident, and when Margaret opened the door, Anne expected to glimpse a family of cockroaches scurrying every which way. Instead, the room was sim-ple but clean, small but surprisingly bright, despite wall-to-wall carpet the color of moss. Margaret told her to go ahead and freshen up if she liked, her roommate likely wouldn't be home until dinnertime, and she handed Anne a key before stepping out and closing the door behind her-self. A moment later, alone, Anne pushed the button lock on the door and then turned the knob so that it popped open again. Over and over. Every time she pushed the button, she felt a thrill.

She'd been there for only a few days when she got a job offer from an assisted living home for the elderly in Ballston. It was really a job for an aide, she wouldn't provide any medical care, but when she told her social worker, a wraith-thin woman named Nancy who had hair the color of shoe polish, that she'd decided to take it, Nancy had given her a look over the top of her glasses that told her she was lucky to have gotten it and should never imagine she could do better. She would help the elderly residents get bathed and dressed, bring them plastic cups of water with straws. Nancy said to be on guard for housemates who would figure out she had access to pills, and to immediately tell her or Margaret if any of the other residents of Eirene tried to strike a deal with her. The warning reminded Anne that she had to be careful about what she told people about both her present and her past. It was best not to say anything at all.

Dr. Abbasi had told her that she might feel disoriented when she noticed different things that had changed since 1991, despite only six years having passed, despite having done all the field trips. Twice a year, the patients who were stable enough were brought in small groups to a mall or to a farmers' market or a beauty salon with an assignment to purchase a dozen tomatoes, or ask for change of a twenty. Even if Anne had been paying close attention on those trips, her doctor warned, she might feel differently once she was really out and had to participate.

———

A few days before Anne started at the nursing home, she walked into a bank for the first time in more than six years and faced what little was left after the sale of the house in Gillam.

"There hasn't been activity on this account since 1991," said the teller. Brian had long ago sold the house and her car to pay the legal fees, to pay the medical bills, and when it was all over he split the remainder of their assets down the middle and deposited hers in her individual account. If he'd stuck by Peter, it would have been his right to take it, to pay for the things that Peter would need, but he hadn't stuck by Peter. Still, so many years later, when she stopped for a moment and tried to comprehend that he'd left her child, her boy, in an apartment in Queens with his idiot, alcoholic brother, she felt a physical weight on her rib cage, a striking pain where she knew her heart must be. They'd gotten him into that good high school, at least, and by the time she got to Eirene House he'd have finished at least a few years of college. She knew he was applying because the financial aid office of some college in New Jersey needed all sorts of paperwork to prove that Peter was no longer her dependent, to sever his financial ties to her. An assistant in her lawyer's office brought it all upstate for her to sign.

After that, Anne liked to daydream about what he'd become one day. President of the United States was not out of the question. CEO of an international company. Brain surgeon. University professor. She'd been told that her thoughts ran grandiose when she was entering a manic cycle, and so she tried to examine each prospect for him honestly, with the evidence at hand. But everything checked out. He was a smart boy. He was going to college.

Brian was still her husband, as far as she knew, though he seemed more like an idea than a person, as removed from her as the family she'd left behind in Ireland so many years before she ever married him. The idea of him still living in the world and doing all the things he used to do—showering, shaving, snaking his belt through the loops of his pants—felt to Anne like a ripple in the space-time continuum. Five thousand two hundred thirty-one dollars was all that remained of their life together. All those years of commuting to Montefiore and rushing to deposit her check on Friday afternoons. All those years of sweeping the front porch, keeping the hedges straight and trim and presentable. She withdrew four thousand to buy a used car. She knew better than to complain. With this, she had a ride to work without having to wait for a bus. She had a place to be by herself. And she'd made her own bed, as her lawyer once said to her. He'd had it with her by then.

———

Eirene House was meant to be a one-year arrangement but when the year passed and no one asked her to leave, she'd stayed on. But now, Margaret told her that her bed was needed. They'd taken a look at Anne's file and said she was more than capable of living on her own.

She'd not had any sort of alarming episode in her time at Eirene, and at least part of that was because she no longer had to count out daily pills and tablets that she might choose to take or to push through one of the little holes in the drain of the women's showers, depending on her mood. Instead, she got a monthly injection, and ever since that change she'd felt steadier, less haunted by the feeling that something bad was always about to happen.

Anne had never lived alone in her life, and when she returned to her room after their meeting, she sat on the edge of her bed, the corners neatly tucked in the military style, and tried to catch hold of the fear she felt rising in her belly. It was all right, it was okay, it was all part of what was supposed to happen. It was all right, it was okay, it was all part of what was supposed to happen. She repeated it to herself fifty times.

The studio apartment she found was small, and the two single-paned windows were no doubt drafty, and the rent would eat sixty percent of her income, but she didn't need much. A yogurt for breakfast, an apple for lunch. Often, she was able to take food from the nursing home. The cook was always giving away the stale bread, the milk that had reached its date but was perfectly fine. Fruit cups full of sweet syrup that would have to be thrown away after they reached a resident's tray, even if the resident hadn't so much as touched the tinfoil tab of the seal. The studio was walking distance to her doctor's office, though it meant a longer commute to the nursing home. A long commute seemed like something other people would mind, but Anne really didn't. The drive to and from work gave her something to do, and it was a way of filling more of the day. A television would help but it seemed extravagant. She would wait.

Dr. Oliver was no Dr. Abbasi, but Anne liked him okay, and he said she was doing very well. Since arriving at Eirene she'd been going for a blood draw every week to make sure she wasn't toxic, and only one single time since being discharged from the hospital, after a brutal stomach virus that left her dehydrated and weak, did she feel the familiar agitation bearing down on her. Margaret found her in the common room at three o'clock in the morning. She'd been watching a game show on TV, and when the players buzzed, Anne slapped the particleboard coffee table and shouted the answers. When Margaret appeared, Anne commanded her to watch closely and tell her if it seemed as if one of the contestants was cheating. Margaret led Anne to her room and said good night, but the next morning, bright and early, she was knocking on Anne's bedroom door. "Get up," she said. "Get dressed. You're going to see the doc."

Once Anne and Dr. Oliver were alone, something told Anne to keep her lips sealed until she was out of there, to refuse to say a single word. They stared each other down, and then Dr. Oliver told her gently that she'd be admitted to the local hospital for just a few days until the adjustment he was about to make leveled out.

Anne thrust her wrists out to be cuffed.

"No, no cuffs, Anne," he said. "You haven't done anything wrong." She'd keep her job, he promised. She'd be okay. There was no reason they shouldn't keep this one challenging week private. She'd been doing remarkably well.

———

It occurred to her as she jiggled the lock of her new home that somewhere not terribly far away Peter was likely graduating from college. She hadn't taken comfort in the idea of him living with George, but at least she knew where he was. When he went to college he felt farther away because he was in a different state, but again, at least she knew where he was. But now that he was graduating—it was May, cherry blossoms coated the sidewalks of Saratoga and felt like velvet underfoot—she imagined him like a top spun loose across a board, zigging and zagging wildly across the contiguous United States, Canada, Mexico. She studied the college students on the streets of town, walking billboards for Colgate and Bucknell and Syracuse, home on break for summer. She studied the boys in particular and tried to make herself understand that Peter was now as old as these boys, these young men. He was the same age as his father had been when Anne met him.

By September 1999, not knowing where he lived felt like an itch she couldn't scratch. Maybe he'd gone to Dubai or Russia or China. She'd read that a lot of businessmen had to be willing to travel and put in their time in foreign countries these days. Maybe he was somewhere on the other side of the world, speaking Japanese. She could call George. He'd tell her anything she wanted to know.

"Why don't you?" Dr. Oliver asked.

Because it would be one more thing, she wanted to shout. One more goddamn thing! All this weekly talking and it was as if he'd never heard a single word she said.

"I miss Dr. Abbasi," she said instead of answering his question, hoping to stir some professional jealousy.

—

In mid-October of that year, the doorsteps of Saratoga County made festive with pots of mums and jack-o'-lanterns, Anne stopped at the same gas station she always used, but on this day, hanging in the window of the small storefront catty-corner to where she was standing, was a sign: "Private Detective, Discretion Guaranteed." At different times that same storefront had housed a psychic, a therapist, a tax preparer. Now this. She jogged across the road while her car was filling and just walked by, at first, taking one quick glance at what was within. She turned and passed again. By her third pass a man had opened the door. He barely came up to her nose and had a paper napkin tucked into the collar of his shirt. She just wanted to know, was all. She wasn't ready to hire anyone or anything. How much did it cost, anyway? Just an address would be fine, she said, in case there were different prices for different levels of information. If she were handy with the internet like the young nurses at the home, this might be something she could find herself. One of these days Anne planned on asking the nice one, the fat one named Christine, how to open an email account.

Anne told the little man everything except the reason she didn't know where her son was. She wrote him a check for one hundred dollars because it seemed safe enough; the balance wouldn't be due until he got her the information she wanted, but almost as soon as she was back in her car, driving off to work, she began to feel like a prize idiot. He'd probably collect one hundred dollars from one hundred idiot women that week, and then he'd pack it in and take off for a new location. But she didn't call the bank to stop payment on the check.

It took him only two days to get back to her, and the price was far cheaper than she'd braced herself for. He told her that if there was anything else she needed, anything else she wanted to know, to just be in touch. But what she wanted to know was whether he was doing okay, whether he was happy. If he wasn't happy, if he wasn't doing okay, what would she be able to do about it? Take him back to her three-hundred-square-foot apartment to live with her? These were things the man couldn't answer. He handed over a manila folder, and she took it home and left it in the middle of her bed and avoided looking at it as she heated soup for dinner.

Finally, when there was nothing left to do, she opened it. On top, a typed address. Info about the building, how much his apartment cost to rent. The name and phone number of the management company.

After that, a photo of the building.

After that, a photo of him, walking. Something in his hand. A backpack on one shoulder. The photo showed Peter from a distance of maybe fifty feet. Zoomed from an even greater distance. Anne brought her nose to the photo, tried to see him more closely, tried to breathe him in, this young man who was the baby she'd pushed out nearly twenty-two years ago. He was silent, too, at first, like his brother, and after one second of silence, two seconds, three seconds—the nurses huddled over him, their faces screwed tight as they handled him with alarming bluntness—four seconds, five seconds, six seconds—she let her head drop back to the pillow and accepted what she felt sure they were going to tell her, that this one would end like the last, only more cruelly because last time they'd been warned, at least, had time to prepare.

But then he'd arched his back and cried, his face purpling with the strength of his howls, and they placed him on her chest, pale from whatever viscous material was inside her, whatever he'd lived on those forty long weeks. When she touched him, his body tensed against her hand.

"You see that?" the delivery nurse said. "He's already trying to lift his head."

"A strong baby," Anne said, and realized the vibrations she was feeling weren't coming through the bed but from her own body, which was sobbing, heaving. She gritted her teeth to stop from shivering.

"A very strong baby," the nurse said.

———

She thought she'd be able to make it until that Friday, when she had off, but just an hour into her shift she knew there was no way she could wait that long, so instead she started feigning illness. It was a plan that took shape as she was making it happen. She coughed into her fist a few times. Third and fourth graders from local schools had been trickling in all morning to make small Halloween parades for the residents. They answered questions about their costumes and held out their bags for candy, which they realized quickly came from the nurses' station and not from any of the ailing souls who seemed perplexed by the small ghosts and skeletons, the witches and vampires. Anne put her palm to her own forehead when she felt sure people were looking. Eventually, she got noticed, and the charge nurse sent her home. She raced to the apartment to change, to brush her hair, and then she made straight for the thruway. It took three and a half hours to get there, Amsterdam at

103rd Street. A yellow brick building. Six steps up to the door. A broken light outside.

What did she expect to see? Him, she supposed, more clearly than in the photo, perhaps sitting on the stoop just as she pulled up. Perhaps he'd come walking down the street at the perfect moment, from the perfect angle, and she'd know by the set of his shoulders how he was. When he was a boy—nine, ten—that age when boys are dying to be older than they are, he suddenly stopped crying when he was upset and instead would set his shoulders like he was pushing them apart to make them seem broader than they were. He'd put one foot after another in a way that scared her, that determination to keep going, that determination to not cry, no matter what. And while she knew his intention was to seem older, he always, always, seemed younger instead. It should have been enough to draw her out of herself, seeing the extraordinary effort a boy made to be okay, but it wasn't enough. Some days she could put her hands on those small shoulders and steer him around to look at her, to make him understand that she was his mother and she loved him, even if she didn't always say the words. But other times, times when he'd all but press his face against hers to get her attention, times when he'd kneel on the floor beside her bed and hold his grubby finger beneath her nose to check for breathing, it was impossible for her to even so much as open her eyes. But the worst times of all were when she punctured his strength on purpose just so she could see whether it was possible for those shoulders to wilt, to see if there was a limit to what he could handle.

"I regret having a child," she said to him once, for no reason at all, as he was doing his homework. "Greatest regret of my life." It was quiet in the kitchen, just the two of them, Brian on an overnight tour. There were two potatoes baking in the oven, the house full with the earthy scent of roasting skins. Peter was about ten at the time, maybe eleven, and still, a decade later, she could see the way the white oval of his face had snapped up in surprise. He'd looked right back down at his homework page as if it hadn't happened, but she could see in his posture that she'd thrown him, that where before he was concentrating in earnest, now he was just pretending. The tips of his fingers were white where he was gripping the pencil. The lead point hovered above the page.

It had taken her a long time to tell Dr. Abbasi about that moment, her absolute worst, worse even than the times she smacked him, worse than shooting Francis Gleeson in the face.

And whenever she glimpsed that moment—it came to her at any time, without warning, and always felt like a punch in the mouth—she wondered if it was possible that she had none of these things the doctors said she had, paranoid personality disorder, schizophrenia, schizoid personality disorder, borderline personality disorder, bipolar disorder, the diagnosis changed and morphed every year, new names for the same symptoms, but whether, in fact, she'd tricked them all, in a way, by going along, by taking the meds, by going to the sessions, tricked them the way Brian used to say she'd tricked him into getting married, into having a second baby, having Peter, when he'd never gotten over losing the first. She wondered if she was simply very, very mean.

———

"I'll clean up," Peter said that long, terrible night, May 1991, looking around at the mess she'd made of the house. He was fourteen already. Who could have predicted how that night would turn out? Five more minutes and she would have been too deeply asleep to hear the racket of Lena Gleeson pounding on the back door. She'd taken a sleeping pill, a half dose. She'd cracked the pill in two by pressing it hard into the palm of her hand. It would have been Brian's problem to deal with and they probably wouldn't have even told her about it. But when she walked to the window and looked down, there was Francis and Lena Gleeson and their daughter standing in the light of the Stanhopes' back step. There was Brian's long arm, holding the screen door open. By the time she got downstairs the Gleesons were gone, and Brian was telling Peter that he shouldn't have snuck out like that, but he was so half-hearted about it, so damn soft about it like he always was, and so Anne had walked up and belted Peter across the face.

"That's for hanging around with that brazen girl in the first place," she said. "And that's for sneaking out." She tried hitting him a second time but he dodged her, held his cheek, half turned to the wall like a child sent to the corner for punishment.

And then she caught a look on Brian's face. Disgust, yes, but also a confirmation of the thing he'd announced already, but was maybe still unsure about. So although her head was splitting and she felt so unbelievably tired, she turned to him and started up once again with the argument they'd been having for weeks. He wanted to take a break. He wanted to do some thinking, alone. She thought of the morning she told him that the baby was dead. She hadn't seen the doctor yet. She just knew. No movement at all for more than twenty-four hours. A dull ache across her back. She knew in the shower. She knew as she sipped her tea. She knew as the wind stirred the odors of the sidewalk below their first floor window—they were still in the city then—and blew them into the room where they were standing, getting ready to head out to work. So she told him what she knew, told him how she knew it. But Brian poured cereal into a bowl, told her she didn't really know, no, not really, only the doctor could tell them. And then, a few hours later, when the doctor did tell them, Brian had looked at her like he was looking at her now, like she'd done it, she'd made it happen, by just saying the words out loud.

The night she shot Francis Gleeson, she hadn't been feeling well for a long time, but she only realized that later. For months, conversations were drowned out by static, and she found herself having to speak louder, listen harder. She lost track of what people were saying. She lost track of what she was saying and sometimes heard herself speaking as if from across a room. Physical movements were becoming more and more difficult, like trying to swim through a vat of wet cement. But these were symptoms she only noticed after the static quieted, after the cement drained away.

"It's mostly like that for everyone," Dr. Abbasi said. Everyone like her, he meant. It was impossible to have sufficient detachment at the most dangerous times. This was his way of saying she had to forgive herself.

But there were other times, rare times, but still, they happened, when the fact that she didn't feel well settled in her thoughts easily, clearly, like a sentence typed on a piece of paper, slipped under her door.

"Brian," she'd said one morning, not long before everything happened. It was a typed-sentence morning, perfect clarity. She could see herself in vivid color, high definition. They were still in bed. It was raining hard outside, and every time a car passed on Jefferson she could hear the water whipping under its wheels. What was she going to say? That she knew she made things hard? That she'd try that doctor again, the one who'd given her the prescription after she went into Food King with a gun? But before she could say anything, she saw him wince. She put her hand on his arm, she said his name, and he winced, kept his eyes closed even though she knew he was awake. Kept his eyes closed even though he was terrible at pretending, and as she watched his eyelids flutter, she had to fight the strong desire to poke him hard in each one, to blind him.

Peter wanted to take care of everything, all the time. That terrible night, as she and Brian argued, Peter bent to pick up the lamp she'd knocked over. He crawled around on his hands and knees picking up magazines and mail and the little wicker basket that had held them and the figurines that had been lined up on the mantel before she flung them. The lights were on at the Gleesons'. The lights were on at the Maldonados'. She imagined all of Jefferson Street crouched outside in the dark, listening. She called Brian every name she could think of, and then she turned to Peter and used all the names again. She used words she couldn't stand to hear other people say. Faggot. Fairy. Cunt. Why? She didn't know. Still, no matter what name she called him, Peter kept that blank expression plastered to his face. Why was he so sure she didn't mean it?

It was hazy then, what happened next. Even in the privacy of her own mind, not remembering felt cheap, easy, and she tried to look closer, look more deeply, to discover whether she was being totally honest with herself and with the other people for whom it mattered. She did remember some things, but those memories were of a poor quality, like someone had smeared Vaseline on the lens. She remembered pressing the heels of her hands to her mouth and biting down. She remembered tasting blood on the tender inner part of her lower lip. The police said there was a kitchen chair pushed up to the fridge, no doubt so she could step up and reach the cabinet above. She couldn't remember pushing a chair across the room. She couldn't remember climbing on top. But she was the one who'd ended up with the gun, so it must have been her.

"What *do* you remember?" The district attorney and another lawyer had asked her, their faces full of skepticism. She remembered the girlish giggle she used to feel rising up in her whenever Brian disappeared into the kitchen after his tours. As if she didn't know exactly where his new spot was almost as soon as he picked it. He always emerged from the kitchen with a beer, as if that's what he'd been in there doing, finding and opening a beer. As if that would ever take him more than two seconds.

"What *do* you remember, Anne?" they asked her, two men, both in brown suits; it was impossible to keep track of them except that one was a little less ugly than the other.

She remembered what Brian did. She remembered so well that she could play the scene, stop it, rewind it, play it again like a video. She had the gun centered on the flat of her palm, like on a plate or a tray. In her memory it looked like someone else's hand, but she could feel the weight of the gun there when she really thought about it, so she knew it was her own. She wasn't pointing it. She was simply holding it, observing it. It was dead, inanimate, but firing it would make it come alive. Peter put his hands to his hair when he saw it, and she wondered if that movement was written into his genetic code or whether he'd learned the gesture from being around Brian his whole life.

"Mom," Peter said, calmly, bravely, and looked to his father for help. But Brian said not one single word. Instead, he turned around and walked upstairs. That's the part she could play for herself, for a lawyer, for a doctor, at any hour of the day or night, no matter what medication she was taking, no matter what sort of week she was having, if only they could hook up a cord to her brain and see it for themselves. Anne knew what he was hoping for, she knew exactly what he was hoping for, and he didn't even have the basic decency to take Peter upstairs with him. So Peter went charging out the door to the Gleesons', to get help.

———

After two hours of waiting in the chilly dusk, she could no longer deny that she had to use the bathroom. There was a Dunkin' Donuts on the corner. Murphy's Law was that he'd pass by just as she closed the rest-room door, but she had to go and it couldn't be helped. After her long vigil she was stiff getting out of the car, but she walked briskly to the corner, entered the store, bought a small black coffee just so the woman behind the counter would hand over the key, which was attached to a Ping-Pong paddle.

The small place filled in just the short length of time Anne was in the bathroom. At the counter was an NYPD patrolman with his back to her, and next to him, a young woman dressed like a schoolboy of some kind—a dark wig cut short under a red beret, glasses with thick black frames. Behind them was a person dressed as a cookie, and just after that person, milk. Bacon and eggs. Wonder Woman. Bill and Hillary Clinton. The falling evening had an edge to it, the temperature dropping quickly. Outside on the sidewalk Pippi Longstocking walked hand in hand with the Cat in the Hat.

The girl schoolboy had one tendril of dark blond hair dangling from the back of the wig, and when she and the patrolman turned, Anne stepped back to let them pass in the tight space. The young woman passed Anne first, and then the patrolman, and as they passed, the coarse fabric of the young man's uniform jacket brushed Anne's hand, and she felt a shiver. She held the Ping-Pong paddle before her, like a shield.

At the door, the girl dressed as a boy turned around to say something to the cop, and as she was speaking she looked at Anne, briefly, without really seeing. But then she turned slowly back. The cop was holding the door for her, but still, she stopped, took off her costume glasses, and held Anne's gaze across a room full of people, the leaves skittering along the pavement outside. Kate Gleeson, Anne thought, the syllables of the girl's name banging around inside her head like a gong. "Jesus Christ," she said aloud, and then she looked hard at the patrolman next to Kate. It was like looking at Brian Stanhope in the year 1973.

"You okay, lady?" Bill Clinton asked, tugging up the bottom half of his mask. "You good?"

Anne nodded, stepped around him so that she wouldn't lose track of Kate and Peter. This wasn't what she'd pictured. Maybe they only ran into each other an hour earlier. Maybe it was all one great coincidence. Maybe there was a St. Bart's reunion in the city and they'd included Peter. But behind these thin possibilities, she felt a great turbine moving. Anne waited for him to turn and see her, too, and when he did and despite Kate, she'd make herself say what she wanted to say and he could take it or leave it, but the point was to have come and if he wanted to see her again or not was totally up to him, but she hoped he'd want to, that was the point, after all, not just to check on him but to talk with him, to be in his life again, no matter what, she was so much better now, and they had time to make up, yes, but it wasn't impossible, nothing was impossible. If she had to she'd apologize to the girl, too, for hurting her father like that. It was an accident. He'd accidentally come to their door at the worst possible time.

But when Kate turned her gaze away she didn't signal Peter, like Anne expected her to. She just stepped through the door behind him and together they walked off into the falling night.

———

Two hours later, going eighty miles per hour, almost back in Saratoga after having made a series of blind turns and somehow finding the highway, she realized two things: first, that Peter's costume might not have been a costume, and second, that she was clutching between her thighs a filthy Ping-Pong paddle, a bathroom key.

thirteen

HERE WAS THE THING he couldn't say to Lena but that he knew was true, that thing leading men say to their long-suffering women while the audience sits in a dark theater, thinking, This asshole, don't you fall for that bullshit, honey. You're too good for him.

But it was true, Francis thought now. Whatever happened between him and Joan had nothing to do with Lena, and it meant nothing to him. He'd started it, he knew, if he was really being honest. There'd been that morning after Kate's party, holding her sandals like a teenager, a moment like a live wire he'd touched and then couldn't let go. He thought about it for weeks after, almost nonstop, the surprise of it coming then of all times in his life, after the wreck of his face, the certainty of what had been exchanged between them without either of them saying a word. But he didn't see her for months and months and months, and there was no harm in thinking about a thing as long as he didn't act.

Once, around Halloween that same year, Joan's name was listed along with several others as one of the women who'd collected signatures for a new candidate running for county executive, and seeing her name had given him a charge like she was standing in the room.

And then he saw her at the Christmas carnival. Lena was working a baked goods booth to raise money for St. Bart's and had asked him twice if he was okay to wander, if he was okay with a late supper since she'd probably need to help pack up the booth at the end, if he was okay without his walking stick. He'd spotted his stick leaning by the door when they left the house, but he hadn't had any dizzy spells in several months so he ignored it. He knew she was dying to suggest he take it, just in case, dark would come quickly, after all, and the leaves on the ground were slick, but she was sensitive to everything he felt and knew he didn't like using it, didn't even like when she suggested he needed it. Once Lena was settled in her booth, he walked up the road and watched for a few minutes as the Dance Academy students filed out of the studio to do a routine on the street, the little ones with tummies pushing out their leotards, their baby skin goosefleshed in the cold, and he thought they should have jackets on. He sampled four Dixie cups of chili and then wrote his vote on an index card and dropped it in a box. He stopped by one of the contractor booths, chatted with a retired cop who sold and installed vinyl siding now and was there trying to drum up new business. Francis got caught up on every shared acquaintance from the Four-One, the Two-Six.

"You don't see anybody?" the other cop asked Francis tentatively. "I thought, with everything, wasn't there a group from the Four-One who visited regular?"

There were three guys who came to the hospital a few times, and then a few times after he came home. Lena had set him up on the couch for these visits because he didn't want them in his bedroom. They stood around in their sport coats having no idea what to do or say.

"Yeah, they do, of course, they're great about that. Everyone's busy, you know?"

The other man told a long story about his kids, varsity baseball, a controversy about who got picked to start. "You have girls!" the other man concluded. "You're lucky you don't have to deal with this stuff."

Francis agreed because it was easy, but thought: My Kate is a better athlete than all of your boys combined.

Close to the firehouse, where Santa was giving out coloring books on fire safety, he saw her. She was sipping a drink she was holding between mittened hands. She saw him just a second later and glanced over her shoulder as if looking for a place to hide.

When he got closer, instead of saying hello, she just began talking. "Right now, you're thinking, there's a woman who should not be drinking."

"I'm not!" he said, hearing once again that thing in his voice that had made him self-conscious at Kate's party. Warm. Full of fun. He wasn't always.

He blew into his cupped hands, said it was good to see her, and then could think of absolutely nothing else to say, so he blew into his hands again.

"You're freezing," she said. "You want to go in?" They were in front of a new bar, two bartenders outside ladling mulled wine out of a Crock-Pot and selling it for three dollars per Styrofoam cup.

Inside, no one took notice of Francis Gleeson taking a barstool with a woman who was not his wife because that was the sort of day it was, and people knew him, they knew Joan, if there were anything amiss, they wouldn't be having a drink in the middle of town with Lena Gleeson just a hundred yards up the road. It was very crowded inside thanks to the unexpected cold of the day, but there were two barstools near the back, as if waiting for them.

Later, Francis thought of all the things that would have stopped him, would have been too much. If he'd seen Oscar Maldonado, who mentioned several days later that he'd seen him there, asked what he thought of the place. Or, if Joan had told him that her ex-husband had finally signed the divorce papers earlier that week, that the warmed wine she'd been sipping outside was the first chance she'd had to celebrate. But she didn't tell him that until later. If Lena had told him before they parted ways that she didn't feel great, thought she might have a low-grade fever, had taken an aspirin before walking with him into town, that it just didn't seem to be working. It was unlike Lena to not feel well and had he known before the festival instead of after, he probably would have stayed with her at her booth, to help.

What did they talk about for that hour and a half? They were so warmed up after just a few minutes that they had to take off their coats and scarves, pile them on their laps because the stools didn't have backs. Lena would never let him sit on a stool without a back. What if he lost his balance? Francis noticed how close Joan's knee was to his, the line of her clavicle where her blouse was a little askew. He asked about her work, and when he asked the same question twice, she laughed, dipping her chin to her chest like she was trying to hide it from him, and when she looked at him again it was as if she knew every thought he'd ever had.

It was easy, and that surprised him. He felt young and strong and completely unconnected to the person Lena had been fussing over for so many years. Joan was frank about it, which helped, at first. Later, it was her frankness that made him most disgusted with himself.

"I live in the Hilltop apartments now," she said. "Renting until my settlement."

She touched his elbow. She tapped her index finger on his forearm, just once, so quickly he thought he might have imagined it except that he could feel his pulse beating there. But then she was gathering her coat, her mittens. A short walk. A turn. Another short walk. His heart was beating so loudly he thought surely she would hear. The noise of the festival disguised the direction of their footsteps. Mid-December, the gloaming came early, the sky going orange and then a bruised purple and then dark gray. She pushed through the front door to the lobby, and they stood side by side without looking at each other, without speaking, until the elevator arrived.

"What are we doing?" he asked, once they were inside, but Joan only looked at him and smiled, opened her cabinets to find glasses. She switched on the TV and turned the volume low. No point pretending now, though he was shaking like a schoolboy. His hand passed over his eye—he had a new prosthetic as of that month, hand painted by a ludicrously expensive ocular artist in Connecticut, and the girls were floored by how good, how real, it looked. Worth every penny, Lena had said, though they hadn't paid all the pennies yet; the day they paid off this one single eyeball would be the day he decided whether it had been worth it. But he did like talking to people again like he once had, not having to pretend he didn't notice them studying his face, their eyes darting back and forth as they tried not to stare at his old prosthesis, which had been so uncomfortable and so false in appearance that Kate told him the patch looked better. He'd gotten so used to the patch that his face felt naked now.

She put her hands on either side of his neck, cold despite the mittens, running them in perfect symmetry across his shoulders, down his arms. He shivered and fitted his hands on either side of her waist like he had early that morning in May, seven months before.

———

It had nothing to do with Lena, whom he loved as much as he did the day they married. It only had to do with him, and the things he wanted, and the things he missed about himself, the things he missed feeling. Whatever had happened with Joan, whatever would happen, again, he hoped, could exist entirely apart from his life with Lena, couldn't it? And yet, just an hour after stepping over the threshold to Joan's apartment, when he hurried back down to the sidewalk and approached the festival from the southern end, as if he'd only taken a little walk over to the duck pond, and saw Lena waiting for him on the double yellow, the detritus of the festival scattered around her, the naked fear on her face, he wondered if, in fact, it did have something to do with her. He'd been a good cop, a good husband, a good father. He'd been great, actually, at all of those things, and it didn't feel immodest for him to think so. But then, through no fault of his own, because he was good, because he was responsible and dependable, he'd gone to his neighbors' front door and been blasted into a new reality, one where he wasn't a cop at all, wasn't a good husband, apparently. Was he still a good father? He hoped so, but as of the last hour he had his doubts.

"People said there's black ice near the firehouse," Lena said. "They said someone slipped and fell." She delivered her worry like an accusation.

"I'm fine," he said, taking her bags from her. Her tablecloth, the trays she'd taken from home for the displays.

"People spill drinks, they don't realize how quickly it freezes up, weather like this."

And then, "Are you okay?"

"Lena, for the love of God, please stop asking me if I'm okay. Just stop." He sounded angrier than he felt. "I went to the new bar. I ran into a lot of people."

"Sorry," Lena said, chastened. She touched her fingertips to her temples. "I just don't feel very well. I thought it was a cold but maybe it's the flu."

———

Francis met Joan twice more after that. Twice more over the course of ten days. They met at her apartment again. And the last time was at a park a little upstate where Lena didn't like to bring him because she thought the walking path wasn't even enough, that he risked tripping on a cracked paver or a root. He took the bus to a strip mall in Riverside and from there Joan picked him up. He pressed her slim body against the concrete wall of the park's restroom, closed for the season. She suggested they go to the Holiday Inn on Route 12, stay for a couple of hours, and then she made fun of him for seeming shocked. "What?" she laughed. "My treat. It's not the Plaza."

But at the front desk he waved her money away, mortified. He put down his credit card.

"Do you want me to drive?" he asked later, when they got back to her car, and just like that she handed over the keys. He drove to her place, and from there he walked to Jefferson. At that point, he hadn't driven a car in over four years. Just sliding behind the wheel made him feel younger, more like himself than he'd been since the accident. And Joan didn't seem the least bit worried about being his passenger. Merging onto the thruway, glancing left over his shoulder, he got disoriented for a second, but almost as soon as he looked straight ahead again it was fine.

On the day he was planning to see Joan for a fourth time, Lena stayed home from work because she couldn't shake that same cold she'd felt coming on the day of the fair, made a doctor's appointment, asked Francis if he wanted to come along. She didn't need him in the room with her, nothing like that, it was just that the doctor's office was near the hardware store, and maybe he wanted to browse. They hadn't been down that way in a little while. There was no opportunity to call Joan, so he hoped when he didn't show up that she'd figure it out.

That day, just after Lena's appointment, they were sitting at a window booth at the Gillam Diner when Lena asked if it was possible a person could give herself cancer. The doctor took a chest X-ray, diagnosed bronchitis, said she needed rest. "Can a person give herself cancer just from worrying about things? Stress?" She looked off toward some distant point out the window. She'd read a book about it, she said.

Francis couldn't remember how he'd responded, but when he thought back on that moment, the sun on the window, the film of oil floating on top of their coffee cups, the bustle of the waitstaff and customers all around them, he imagined a small, dry seed falling through Lena's body and landing somewhere near her left lung. He imagined the seed growing fat on Lena's warm center, a sprout pushing through soft tissue, wrapping itself around and around. He imagined all of this happening while he stared at his plate and thought about Joan Kavanagh, the way her long red hair looked against the white of her narrow back.

"You knew already," he said when she finally told him. "You knew and you didn't tell me." He was angry with her. He was angry with himself. He wanted to comfort her but instead he crossed his arms and stepped away. The doctor had diagnosed bronchitis, yes, but he'd also noticed something else, and had ordered more tests.

She apologized when she gave him the news, and he couldn't get himself to say what he was supposed to say, which was of course it wasn't her fault, and they'd get through it, and it would all be okay. But was it her fault? When had she first had an odd feeling in her chest? According to the doctor it could have been several months earlier. When she said she had no symptoms, the doctor said it was just that she hadn't noticed them. Some people are more tuned into their bodies than others. When Francis caught her coughing on her way to their bedroom, her hand on the wall to steady herself, he stood at the bottom of the stairs and told her he thought she was smarter than that, why in the world had she waited so long to go to the doctor? And even when she sat down on the step and cried, he found he could not go to her or say any of the things that would make her feel better.

"You're going to be fine, Lena," he said eventually, her at the top of the stairs, him at the bottom. It was an order. He once had a dozen men in his command.

The girls came home the night before her surgery, to help her get ready. "Lena," he whispered into her hair that morning, the house still sound asleep. She'd set her alarm for 6:00 a.m. but it hadn't gone off, and now they'd need to rush. "Lena, love," he said, and drew her closer to him, told her he was sorry about the way he'd been acting, he was just so shocked, and he couldn't lose her, it was something that absolutely could not happen. She reached behind and found his hip, squeezed, told him she knew all that, of course, that it was all going to be okay, that he would see.

He got dressed quickly, and while the girls bustled around—Sara and Natalie cross-checked the contents of Lena's bag with the list the doctor's assistant had provided them; Kate offered to go into the shower with her, to help wash her with the special surgical soap (Lena had laughed. "Oh, honey," she'd said)—he realized he had a little time to kill before they had to leave for the hospital. Without telling any of them that he was stepping out, he walked down to the deli like he did most mornings for his coffee and a paper. Something about sticking to his routine was soothing, and as he watched his breath in the cold air, he began to feel for the first time that all would be well. His face hurt. His body was not in synchrony. But it felt temporary. The doctors would do their mysterious work and she'd suffer, no doubt, but she was strong and in the end it would be fine.

And when he turned the corner onto Main Street, there was Joan Kavanagh in her blue coat, her long hair brassy in the sunlight, looking at him coming like she'd known him long enough for him to hurt her. But she hadn't known him long enough to earn that look, and he hadn't known her long enough to feel anything other than shame. He thought of his mother for the first time in a very long time. He thought of his father. The two of them dead and buried, gone twenty-five years. Neither of them able to fathom America beyond the little bit of it they'd seen together, when Francis was an infant. Neither of them capable even of half-baked promises to visit, one day, like other old-timers sometimes said to make it all easier. Neither of them capable of lying in any way, not even when a lie would be merciful. "Sure I'll be back to visit in no time," Francis had said that day when they clutched him in the threshold of the cottage, and his mother pressed her dry cheek to his over and over again.

"Arrah, why would you?" his father had said.

His father told him that in New York City there were bakeries galore and he'd have to take care not to get fat. It was his single piece of advice. They'd not warned him about money or women or drinking or fighting because Francis was a good boy, a sound young man, with a good head on his shoulders. If they were looking down on him now, from heaven, they might not even recognize him. Francis had not seen Joan since that afternoon at the Holiday Inn. He hadn't returned her calls since Lena's diagnosis.

It was a Monday morning. Surgery was scheduled for eleven, but Lena had to report to the hospital by nine. It was early still, just after seven, and construction workers passed Joan by, rushing in and out the door that jangled with every swing. She kept her eyes on Francis as he approached. Local cops left their cruisers in the No Parking zone, ran in for coffee. 'Scuse me, 'scuse me, g'morning, they said as they passed, one, two three. He remembered being a cop once, jogging up stairs, steering his vehicle down city streets, the heady pleasure of knowing he was about to stop a bad thing from happening, the crushing disappointment when he arrived just a few minutes too late. On that particular morning, a frigid cold day in late January, Lena whispering her prayers at home, Kate on break from her first year of college, far too young to lose her mother, Francis remembered settling a ten fifty-two in the Two-Six by calling each party into the fifth floor hall of their building one at a time and asking each one if they loved the other, and if so could they please stop throwing things at each other. To please stop waking the neighbors. After that the guys called him Lieutenant Love for a while.

Once, Joan called the house when she thought Lena was at work, but Lena answered. Francis stood outside their bedroom door listening to their conversation with his fists clenched so tight he got a cramp in his forearms.

"Joan Kavanagh," Lena said when she hung up, a question mark in her tone. "Casey wants Kate's address at school for something, a reunion of some kind." And then: "I think she was drunk, to be honest."

Francis had murmured signs of interest and then stepped into the bathroom. He studied his face in the mirror and saw that the old scar tissue was livid and sore looking.

"I heard about Lena," Joan said outside the deli that morning when he was close enough to hear her. Hearing Lena's name in her mouth would be part of his punishment, too, he supposed. She didn't have the right to say her name, but it was his fault she didn't see it that way.

"What happens now?" she asked, and looked at him like she deserved an answer.

How to say what he needed to say without making everything worse? So he said nothing at all. He brushed by her like the construction workers had, like the cops had, and he got his cup of coffee, tucked his paper under his arm.

She drove by him, slowly, just a minute or so later and called him all the things he already knew he was: a coward, a cheat, a prick. He could have crossed to the other side of the street, where he wouldn't be able to hear her as well, but he stayed where he was. Every name she called him was true. She followed him and shouted the words until he turned onto Madison.

———

In the hospital, Sara and Natalie wandered in and out of the waiting room. They fetched coffees and sandwiches that none of them ate. They took walks down the long hallways to stretch their legs. Kate stood rooted to her spot next to Francis.

The surgery seemed to go on forever, and different surgeons were coming out to the waiting room to reassure other families.

"Katie," Francis said, pulling her toward his chest like he hadn't done since she was little. Kate assured him it was all normal. The surgeon had explained to them what had to be done, and had given them a time frame they were still within. She said his own surgery, which of course he didn't remember, had gone several hours longer than they'd been told it would, and just like that he saw Lena in his place, himself on the table in the OR, and understood why she'd never managed to let go of that baseline worry.

"Dad," Kate said. "It's not the right time, maybe, but I have to tell you something."

Francis was grateful for the distraction despite a pang of dread. He was relieved to look away from the clock for a moment. If she was about to tell him she was pregnant, he'd be disappointed but he wouldn't tell her what to do. If she'd flunked out of school, he'd be surprised but it would be okay to have her home again for a little while until she figured herself out. Whatever it was wasn't the end of the world, and he'd tell her so. All that mattered was getting Lena healthy again.

He studied her, his lovely girl, her hair so shiny under the fluorescent lights.

"I got a letter from Peter," she said. "It was mailed home. Mom kinda figured who it was from, but she forwarded it to me at school. She said I should tell you but I never found the right moment."

He removed his arm from around her shoulder. "You got a letter from Peter Stanhope," he repeated. "Saying what?"

Kate looked off, shrugged. "Just stuff we used to talk about. So I wrote back. Now we email sometimes. He wants to see me. I told Mom already and she said I had to tell you." Kate hesitated. "He's doing very well. He got a full scholarship to a college in New Jersey."

Francis had been standing but now he sat. Sara and Nat would be back any moment.

"I'd like to meet up with him once Mom feels better. We were best friends for so long. I'd just like to see him, see how he is. We'd meet in the city. Just for closure. I promise. You have to understand. Everything happened at once and then all of a sudden he was gone."

Closure. That was a word she'd learned in college, no doubt. Did he have closure when he left Ireland at her age and never returned?

"Are you going to say something?"

It had been some time by then since he heard from his lawyer that Anne Stanhope had been moved upstate. No one had heard a thing about Brian in a very long time, not even on the job, though he supposed the pension checks must be mailed somewhere. What did Peter want with Kate?

"It's harmless," Kate ventured.

"Look at me," Francis said. "You know what I'd be right now? If Anne Stanhope hadn't shot me? I'd be a captain. Higher, maybe. No doubt about it. I had a bad feeling about her from the get-go, and I have a bad feeling about him. I should have listened to your mother. I should have let the local cops arrive and I should have let them handle it. I should have sent Peter home to wait on his own porch."

"Last you saw him he was only fourteen. That's not fair."

"Life isn't fair, Kate. I don't want you seeing him. Period."

"You can't treat me like a kid anymore, Dad."

It was so absurd that Francis had to laugh, despite the circumstances. "Oh, Kate," he said.

———

Lena made it through surgery. She made it through chemo and radiation. He cooked for them, and when she was weak he spoon-fed her like he used to feed the girls if Lena was too busy. A few times when she fell asleep on the couch downstairs he lifted her in his arms, her body so light it felt hollow, and brought her up to their room. He didn't get dizzy. He didn't wobble. Hour to hour, day to day, he kept his head down and thought about what she might need next. The first time he packed her into the passenger seat of their car and settled in behind the wheel, she'd glanced at him like she might protest but then just decided to let it happen.

She lost every hair on her body, and when it began to grow back she looked like a baby bird. She didn't bother with a wig or with scarves. When she was chilly she pulled one of the girls' old hats over her head.

When she felt strong enough to walk outside she leaned on him, and once she had to sit on the curb and wait while he hurried back home to get the car and then drove around the block to pick her up.

———

Finally spring came, Lena on the mend, both of them sure they were through the worst, that all that was left was recovery. Kate would soon be finished with her first year of college.

Francis said to Lena across the silence of the kitchen, "We could go to the nursery today, if you want, see about getting some annuals? We could plant them this weekend?"

Lena was sipping tea at the table. The kettle poured steam from its spout.

"Francis?" Lena said. "Did something happen between you and Joan Kavanagh? Over the winter?" Her expression was so calm, so peaceful, it was as if she were merely curious, as if the answer didn't matter to her either way. She wore a half smile, as if to reassure him, as if she knew this would be hard for him.

He gripped the counter, closed his eyes. All the blood in his body rushed to his face.

"I thought so," Lena said.

When he had the courage to look at her, he saw that she was crying with her hand clapped over her mouth.

"The thing is," she said plainly, matter-of-factly, "in a million years, no matter what, I never ever would have done that to you."

And Francis knew that was the truth.

———

It took him a while to figure it out, and every time he realized he was trying to figure it out, he chastised himself, as if it mattered. The credit card bill, maybe. Maybe they'd been seen. It was reckless to drive Joan's car through town with her in it, to drive right up to her building.

But it was Casey Kavanagh who told Kate, who told her sisters, who told their mother. Casey had called Kate in a rage, angry on her mother's behalf, angry at Kate's perfect little family that the whole town adored just because her busybody father had stuck his nose in where it didn't belong and got shot.

The word "busybody" attached to her father struck Kate as funny, and it took her a second to comprehend what Casey was yelling into the phone. A busybody was a woman, for a start. A certain type of highly strung advanced-middle-aged woman. Not her near-silent father, who'd only gone next door that night because he was brave, and he was trained, and it was the right thing to do. What was Casey going on about?

Kate didn't believe it until, at Natalie's insistence, they spoke to their mother about it, how crazy it was, that this was some strange rumor she might encounter around town and they didn't want her to be caught up short. Instead of being horrified, instead of being shocked, Lena remembered the odd phone call that one night. And there was that afternoon when she'd called the house from work and let it ring and ring and ring—hoping to tell him to turn on the Crock-Pot, which was filled with ingredients but which she was almost certain she'd forgotten to turn on. Later, when she asked what he'd gotten up to that day, he said he hadn't done a thing.

"Mom," Sara said, "you have to kick him out. Don't stand for it." Natalie said the same. Kate was angry at the three of them for believing it all so readily. Surely there was an explanation.

"Girls," Lena said. "It's between me and your father."

———

The girls came home for Mother's Day, and Francis planted the flowers before they arrived. Sara and Natalie mostly avoided him, but Kate kept her eyes on him, followed him out to the shed later that afternoon to confront him.

"Did you really do what Casey said?"

227

He could have lied to her then, and she would have believed it. She was desperate to believe anything that might take the place of the truth.

He hung the hedge clippers on the hook. He threw the little hand rake in the gardening bin.

"It's between me and Mom," he said, without looking at her.

"It's so disgusting it makes me want to throw up," she said, and took a step toward him like she might shove him.

"How could you? Do you know how she took care of you? How could you hurt her like that?"

"I don't know." It was the truth.

"You don't know?" Her voice was thick with fury. "You don't know?" she repeated. She turned back to the house and seemed about to walk off, but all of a sudden she turned back.

"I'm seeing Peter. We visited each other at school. I love him. I felt bad about that but now I don't."

She studied him to see how that went over. "He would never do that to me. What you did to Mom."

And suddenly Francis was the one who was furious. He had never hit any of his girls but his hand itched to smack her face.

"Kate. Please. Grow up, will you?"

"And guess what else? Mom knows. Mom doesn't mind."

"Sure."

"It's true. Ask her. Oh, what's that? Are you hurt that she kept something from you? That she did something behind your back?"

———

The next afternoon, when the girls finally boarded the bus to the city, Francis went up to Kate's bedroom, where Lena was resting. He didn't know if she wanted him to come into the room, so he stood awkwardly at the door and told her what Kate had said, and asked whether it was true that she knew.

"It won't come to anything, probably," Lena said, not looking at him, running her fingers along the pattern of Kate's childhood quilt.

"She said she loves him."

"I warned her. I told her love only helps up to a point. But the more we object the more determined she'll be."

Francis felt a shiver of fear pass through him.

"But after all I went through. How could she be so dumb? This kid? Why? She won't listen to me, so you have to tell her. We never made her feel bad about sneaking out that night."

Lena looked directly at him then for the first time in several days. "You blame her?"

"No, of course not."

They were so young still. Maybe it would fizzle out. Lena, he saw, was happy that Kate had someone to love, and that it was Peter was somewhat beside the point. She loved so easily, and so fully, maybe Kate was the same. Lena had told him that she loved him before he said it to her. In those days, that was unusual and had shocked Francis. They were walking along the sidewalk in Bay Ridge and he'd stopped to kiss her, their cold noses brushing up against one another. She wasn't looking for him to say it back, she was just letting him know that her love was his to keep or to fritter away.

"Lena," Francis said. He walked up to the edge of the bed having no idea what he wanted to say. "I—"

But Lena was like a fist that could not be pried open. She gathered the covers and drew them up to her throat. She shrank back against the wall. "It'll all be okay soon, Francis. But not yet."

fourteen

BY PETER'S SENIOR YEAR at Elliott, the guys on the team came to him instead of going to Coach. Coach was angling for a Division I job in Pennsylvania and was often distracted, so it was Peter who told them where they should be pacing, what distances they should be covering in practice. Peter moved runners around, switching lifelong two-milers to the fifteen hundred meter, holding brief but pointed meetings with them on the bleachers that overlooked the track as if that were his private office. They were awkward kids, mostly, who'd walked onto their high school cross-country or track teams because they'd failed at other sports. Running was straightforward. Going fast for a long time was the hard part, and most of them left that to Peter and the handful of other kids who'd been recruited. One guy who was a middle-distance walk-on took a hurdle for fun after practice one day, and Peter saw that he'd be perfect for steeplechase. He mentioned all these changes to Coach as if they were mere suggestions, and then told Coach to watch, see if he didn't see what Peter saw. Next meet, the changes would be in the books. The team got better. After every solid race the runner would pick his head up and search the crowd for Peter.

Coach said Peter could spend less time analyzing his teammates, and more time analyzing himself. How could Peter improve if every chance he got he was on the bus to New York to see his girlfriend?

"And another thing, Pete," Coach said. "Your sweat smells eighty proof, at least. Cool it, maybe, okay?"

————

Kate was exactly the same and also completely different. When she walked into the bar that night, the first time they met up, she raised her eyebrows just like she did the day their seventh grade teacher announced the first pop quiz of the year, and the floodwaters of their long history together rose quickly around him. Later, she confessed that she'd almost not come. Her mother was about to start chemotherapy, her father had outright forbidden it, plus she was so nervous. She'd changed clothes at least ten times, and in the end borrowed an outfit from her roommate. He was mostly through a pint of beer by the time she got to the bar, and when he stood from the table and walked around to hug her, neither of them had any idea what to say. He'd gotten there a full hour early and after circling the block to kill time, he stopped into a different bar and had two shots of Jameson, one after another, snapping his head back like he used to see his father do, followed by a Jack and Coke he sipped slowly. It didn't help, at first—his nerves felt like spiders crawling under his skin—but then, back on the sidewalk, heading to their meeting point, he gradually felt steadier, calmer, less worried.

"Peter," Kate said, standing back from him a little and looking at his face. "I can't believe it." The ends of her hair were dyed purple. Her nail polish was black and mostly bitten away. Her long, slender fingers were covered in thick silver rings and she was wearing Doc Martens that laced to her knees. But her face was the same, bright eyes, that impish smirk. He studied her mouth when she spoke.

"I'm glad you wrote," Kate said once they sat, as if she hadn't already said that very thing in the dozen letters and emails that had been exchanged between them. It was nearly spring break for both of them. Peter had already taken two midterms and had only two papers to hand in before he headed back to Queens for the week. Kate had her first midterm coming up.

"So." She grinned. "How was high school?"

————

They visited each other often, and spoke on the phone almost every day. They tended not to discuss Gillam, or their parents, or anything that might brush up against what had happened between their families in May of eighth grade.

Although each of them had looked different back in eighth grade, there was a feeling of returning to the familiar, to what had always been theirs. Peter had always had a pair of freckles on his neck that looked like a vampire bite. The freckles were the same but the neck was different, thicker, stronger, rough with stubble. Each had long, lean torsos, though Kate's dipped in at the waist while Peter's was as straight and solid as the trunk of an oak. Kate had a splatter of freckles across her nose and her shoulders, but beneath her clothes she was milky white. Peter's neck, face, and forearms were dark brown from running outside in a T-shirt. When she discovered he had chest hair under his shirt, and a soft, dark trail that ran down the center of his belly, she pulled back for a moment, embarrassed.

And then there were the things that surprised her in how moved she felt just by seeing them: the sight of his yogurt next to her orange juice in her mini-fridge. His boxers on the floor next to her bra. Once, she began to pull on his jeans because she thought they were hers, and when she realized, she wondered if she'd ever been so happy in her entire life.

They had only one disagreement that spring. Kate was talking about her father, how he'd hurt her mother by having an affair, how it was the biggest mistake of his life, including the night he went up to the Stanhopes' door. But Peter had no reaction.

"I hope you don't feel guilty," Kate asked, trying to account for his blankness.

"Guilty? No. I was just thinking that there were so many victims that night. Your father, your mother, my mother—"

Kate drew back to look at him sharply. "Your mother was a victim?"

"Well, yes," Peter said slowly, deliberately.

"Are you serious?"

"Yes, of course I'm serious."

"Explain that to me," Kate said, arms akimbo.

"She was obviously sick, Kate. As far as I know she's still in the hospital. If she'd just gotten the right medicine from the beginning—"

Kate held up her hand like a stop sign. "Actually, don't explain it to me. I think we're going to have to be at peace with disagreeing about this." But then, "She's definitely still in the hospital. My father's lawyer would have called us if she'd been released."

"Oh," Peter said, the information as sudden as a slap.

"Because of what she did to him, they're responsible for letting him know if there's a change in her status."

"Yeah, I got that. Thanks." He paused. "But it's not like she did it to him. In the sense that she had a thing against him, in particular. He was just the person who came to the door. Why would they notify him of a change in her status? Like she might go after him again?"

"She shot him because she hated me. My mother told me that."

"Ahh." Peter was so incredulous he had to swallow back a laugh. "It's quite a bit more complicated than that, Kate."

"Do you want to see her? Is that it? I thought when you said you weren't in touch that meant your relationship was over."

"She's my mother."

"And?"

"No, I don't want to see her." He checked himself as he said it, but it

234

seemed true. Just thinking about walking into a room where she was felt like inviting chaos back into his life.

"Peter," Kate said, bringing her fingers to her temples as if trying to block out static. "Can you imagine what it was like for us? When my father was in the hospital? When we worried about his brain? My mother cut up his food for him. She washed him and dressed him."

"I'm sure it was awful. What are we arguing about?"

"And no word from you. Not a single word. I chose a college in New York City partly because that's where I figured you'd gone. You mentioned Queens, that night, do you remember? But you could have found me whenever you wanted to. I was exactly where I'd always been. Why didn't you?"

"But I did," he said meekly.

"You scribbled a letter on a whim and mailed it to me four and a half years later."

But Peter could no better explain that than he could explain his feelings for Kate to guys on the Dutch Kills track team. It made sense in his heart and in his gut, but to his brain the logic was incoherent. They were walking along Broadway and Kate had sped up, was standing with her arms around herself in front of a display window. Broadway Chocolatier. Tuesday night wine pairings. Thursday night truffle-making classes.

Her profile was made of stone.

"You're right. I should have contacted you earlier. It's like I said in my first letter. I kept thinking I would and then time passed and I was afraid you hated me. I thought about you all the time. I don't know why I didn't write sooner. I think . . ."

"What?"

"It was a lot. I was worried about my mom, then my dad left. Then I worried I was imposing on my uncle. I took each day as it came and didn't look forward or back too often because it would have been too much. I kept thinking I'd write to you once I got settled but then I never got settled."

She stood still, without looking at him, for a long time.

"I don't want to talk about it anymore," she said finally.

"Okay," he said.

———

Neither of them felt like a normal college couple, or even like normal college students, but they acted the part.

Kate said, late one night, after smoking half a pack of cigarettes and vomiting all over the steps of Peter's dorm, that they'd already gone through all the heavy stuff couples go through so why not enjoy the light stuff now? Peter agreed. It was time to have fun. And he'd figured out that the fun was often not the thing itself—the party, the keg stand, the naked running into the duck pond—but the endless talking about it after, the reliving and describing, and laughing about it in front of people who wished they'd been there. Used to be he was one of the kids listening, one of the kids who missed everything, but now, since college, since Kate, he was in the stories.

One day, he'd have to work. One day, he'd have to decide whether he ever wanted to see his parents again, but until college was over, he copied what everyone else did. When a central worry rose up in him—it was impossible to smother his nature entirely—he called up some friends and asked who was free, who wanted to meet up. They headed to football games and tailgates and dorm parties when Kate visited Elliott. When Peter went to NYU they went to bars and clubs with groups of other college students and ended every night out at the diner on St. Mark's. Peter thought about how different high school would have been if he'd been able to look across a room and find her there. If he had her walking alongside him, everywhere he went. They drank like they were getting paid, as Kate always put it, everything from Bud Lights, to Zimas, to boxed wine, to whiskey, to vodka, to rum.

"I hate rum," Peter observed one night as he was pouring some into his cup. Everyone laughed.

To anyone who asked where he and Kate met, they said only that they grew up together. High school sweethearts, people said, and they issued no corrections.

———

And then, almost no sooner than he felt he'd gotten the hang of college, had gotten the hang of navigating the lower intestines of the Port Authority bus tunnel to the subway that would bring him closest to Kate's dorm, no sooner, or so it felt, than he had really started to like his life and feel like he was not living for the future or the past, people started asking him what he was going to do next, what he was going to be. He majored in history, and his advisor was the first to bring it up. Then George, who told Peter he was welcome to come back and live with him for as long as he needed. He'd gotten a new apartment with his girlfriend, Rosaleen, but it was a two bedroom, and there was plenty of room for Peter if he needed time to get on his feet. It was just around the corner from George's old apartment. Peter had stayed there for several weeks over the summer before senior year. It was clean and beige and had knickknacks and potted plants and bore absolutely no traces of George, unless Peter counted the bits of stubble coating the sink every morning. George's girlfriend called Peter separately one night to reiterate the offer, in case Peter thought it was just George being overly generous.

"You've been through a lot," Rosaleen said, and Peter felt the slow burn of embarrassment push up from his throat to his cheeks. Of course George would have told her everything. Of course. He didn't mind, it had just caught him up short.

"Oh, and, Peter?" Rosaleen said. "I'm throwing a birthday party for George. Would be fun if you could come. He said he thinks you might be seeing someone? That you're being shy about it? Bring her, too, if you like. He's turning thirty-seven and he's depressed about it. We're just going to have a little dinner at the Thai place he likes."

"Sorry. Did you say thirty-seven?" Peter did a quick calculation. But that meant George had only been twenty-nine when he and his father moved in so suddenly. He knew George was a decade younger than his father, but Coach was forty and seemed younger than George. When Peter thought about it, most of his professors were probably older than forty, and all seemed younger than George.

"I know, right? He's been through a lot, too."

———

Peter majored in history, but majors didn't seem to matter as much as he expected them to when it came to getting a job. English majors were going to law school. Philosophy majors were also pre-med. Going to med school was out for Peter because he hadn't taken the prerequisites. Finance didn't interest him, plus there was a towel-snapping vibe in any econ seminar he'd taken that reminded him of the locker room at Dutch Kills. Accounting was too boring. What else could a person be? A teacher, maybe. There was a job fair in December of senior year and Peter ambled through, looking at booths. Marketing, advertising, consulting, health care, hospitality, insurance, childcare, Department of Corrections, Department of Transportation. Starbucks had a booth. Sears. The local utility company. The Adventure Aquarium in Camden. They all had shiny posters and bowls of candy and smiling representatives. Every job was located in either New Jersey or New York and made him feel like a butterfly pinned to a board. There was a whole country to explore. He'd just finished a biography of Steve Prefontaine and had been wondering about Oregon. Also, Colorado. California.

Sometimes, in his dreams, he asked his mother questions that she refused to answer. Sometimes, also in his dreams, he brought her his college transcript, like a kindergartner eager to show off his gold stars, and she let it slide to the cold linoleum floor without even looking. Recently, in his waking life, on his way to a track meet in Syracuse, the van had pulled off in Albany so the team could eat and pee and stretch, and Peter felt himself looking around, furtively, as if he might be spotted in the area. While the team finished eating, he went to the rest stop lobby to stare at a map of the city, all the broken lines that indicated routes in and out.

———

He didn't tell Kate about George's birthday party, and he told himself that was because he could only barely make it himself. He'd mentioned Kate to George, just once, telling him only that he'd met up with her for drinks, and George looked completely confounded, asked why in the world Peter had seen her, that it seemed like opening a whole can of worms. "Is she the type who stirs up old drama? Or maybe, do you think her father put her up to it? Maybe thinking of a civil suit?" George asked. He was still in the old apartment at the time and they were trying to fix the air conditioner. The condensation had leaked inside and warped the parquet floor. George was lying on his back, staring at the unit from underneath.

"No, she's not a dramatic type," Peter said, and let it go.

———

Kate cut off the dip-dyed ends of her hair, removed the polish from her nails, and interviewed for a criminalist position with the NYPD. She got an offer on the spot. She'd considered engineering. She thought about biochemistry. She even considered something in agriculture for a week or two before she realized how few of those jobs were in New York. The day she walked into the crime lab in Jamaica for her interview, wearing an ugly brown suit that had been handed down from Natalie, to Sara, and then to Kate, she told Peter it had felt like home. "It can be a culture shock," Dr. Lehrer said when he invited her to sit down among the microscopes and Bunsen burners. But she'd grown up in the culture; she spoke the language.

Peter felt a twinge of envy that she could be so sure. Even the choices she struggled with were in the same category. She knew what she wanted and had homed in on it. One day Peter thought he'd like to be a track coach, and the next day he thought he should go to graduate school and become a college professor.

"And I accepted. I start June first."

"In New York."

"Yes, the lab in Queens."

"You already accepted?"

"Yes. Why? You don't sound happy for me."

"No, I am. But that means we'll be staying in New York."

"Well, yes. Were you thinking somewhere else?" They'd never discussed what would happen once college was over. They both assumed, correctly, that the other wanted to be nearer, that they would see each other more often.

"I don't know. I was thinking of maybe you and me together in a place where we don't know anyone."

"Oh," Kate said, confusion plain in her voice. "Why would we want to be in a place where we don't know anyone?"

But Peter couldn't say why, because he didn't know. Sometimes he thought of himself hiking in unfamiliar terrain, reaching a summit and not recognizing any of the landmarks below. The feeling was exhilarating.

———

Their graduations fell on the same day, and both were relieved that they could put off facing each other's families for just a little longer. George and Rosaleen came to see Peter graduate, and after the ceremony, when his friends and teammates were going out for one last round of parties, Peter told them all that he'd made plans with his uncle and would catch them soon. He told George and Rosaleen that he was going out with his friends so they could have a nice lunch on their own. Instead, he walked two miles along the county road to a townie bar, where he planned on sitting alone all afternoon and watching the Yankee game. On the way there he passed an abandoned lemonade stand—a Fisher-Price register toppled over in the grass, one dollar bill still in the drawer.

———

Peter moved in with George and Rosaleen for the summer, and shaped for shifts with the ironworkers while he figured out what he should do. "It's just temporary," he must have said a dozen times around the apartment that first weekend, because eventually Rosaleen put her cool hand on his arm and told him to please not worry about it. His bedroom there smelled like potpourri and gave him a headache, even after he covered the bowl with a towel and placed it at the bottom of the narrow closet. George seemed more confused than disappointed that Peter had graduated without a plan. He said he liked the company when they hurried to his truck every morning, their lunch boxes in hand, but he would ask Peter to talk about the business classes he'd taken in college, as if to remind him of where his head should be.

On his first day back with the iron men, Peter looked around for his old friends. After a few days went by, he asked for them. The guy he asked seemed surprised that Peter didn't already know that John Salvatore had gotten badly injured and probably wouldn't work again. Peter wondered if he ever bought that house he'd had his eye on, if he'd ever married his girl. Turned out Jimmy McGree was there working beside Peter all week, only Peter hadn't recognized him. He'd put on a lot of weight and his face was weather-beaten, haggard. He looked ten years older than Peter. Peter reintroduced himself one morning, reminded Jimmy that last time they spoke he was saving for a Camaro.

"Yeah, I remember you," Jimmy said. "The boss's son."

"No, not his son. His nephew."

"Let me ask you this, nephew. How many days did you have to shape before they let you on? I got a cousin, he's been out there for weeks. He has a newborn at home. My brother shaped for a month before he got a day."

Peter had done exactly what George told him to do. He'd lined up at the gate and when they called his name he'd stepped forward.

"Sorry," Peter said, though he wasn't sure what he was apologizing for. He'd make over three hundred bucks that day, before taxes, and he needed the money badly. He couldn't stay in George's potpourri-infused room forever. Jimmy snickered but there was no joy in it. His teeth were sharp and stripped with brown and reminded Peter of a jackal.

———

George finally met Kate on the last day of August 1999, on the day she moved off campus, where she'd gotten free summer housing thanks to a tutoring job, and into an apartment she'd share with a few girlfriends. Peter had hoped they'd be living together by the fall, but he still didn't know what he wanted to do, and a few of his teammates from Elliott were going in on a shitty apartment on Amsterdam and 103rd, so he agreed to live with them. It was Kate who told him to stay with his friends, have fun, between all of them the rent would be pretty cheap, but Peter suspected she also wanted him to get a place without her because she didn't have the courage to face her parents. She'd told her father they were seeing each other years earlier, in a fit of fury, but as far as Peter could tell they'd never discussed it again. And Francis must not have told Kate's sisters because, once, when Peter and Kate were juniors, he was staying with her at NYU for the weekend when Sara stopped by unannounced. "I brought you a burrito," she said when Kate opened the door, and then she looked past Kate and saw Peter, who was sitting at Kate's desk in mesh shorts and T-shirt. It was early November, and

Sara had just started a job on Bleecker Street, not far from Kate's dorm. "Holy shit," she said, visibly pale as she handed the takeout bag to Kate, and without another word she turned and left. Natalie called within the hour. Kate recognized her number on the caller ID and shrugged. "Better face the music," she said to Peter, and picked up. She ushered him out of her room. "Get lost for an hour, will you?" she said, and leaned up to kiss him.

When he returned it was obvious she'd been crying but she assured him it was fine, they were fine, it would all be fine. After that, listening to Kate's end of phone conversations with her sisters, he could tell that they asked about him, but Kate always kept it light.

Peter, for his part, was not all that eager to see Natalie and Sara, but if Kate wanted him to spend time with them then he would, and it would be okay. The person he most dreaded seeing was Francis Gleeson, and he'd surely have to if they moved in together.

When he discovered that Kate was looking into renting a U-Haul van, Peter offered up George's truck, which he was sure he could borrow for a few hours on a Saturday. George didn't mind Peter borrowing the truck, but he did mind Peter driving it. Peter had gotten his driver's license in his senior year of college, and only then because his buddy on the track team had a little hatchback he kept at school and said Peter could borrow once in a while if he wanted to see Kate in New York without dealing with the bus.

"For who, did you say? You need the truck to help who?" George asked. He'd promised Rosaleen a set of shelves above the television and he'd just returned from the hardware store with two long pieces of oak, a pair of brackets. When Peter said Kate's name, he could see the astonishment in George's face.

"Of all the fish in the sea, Peter? Weren't there pretty girls at that college?" He put the wood down, dropped the plastic hardware store bag on top. He screwed up his face like it was a physical process, a painful process, making sense of something that came as a surprise.

"Yes," Peter said simply.

George nodded, gave the information a moment to breathe. He walked to the kitchen sink, and keeping his back to Peter, he poured a glass of water, drank it.

"I don't like it. Something about it."

"I know."

"It's just trouble. For no reason, you know?"

"I know."

"This girl, that girl, literally any other girl, and it wouldn't matter. There's just one girl in the world who seems like a bad idea and it's this one."

"But why is it a bad idea?" There, he said it. His father had left. His mother was gone. And so, who would object? Her parents, probably, but that was for her to handle. And if he had a chance to speak to them, he felt certain he could convince them to come around. And if they didn't come around, well, that was their problem. He and Kate had never done anything wrong. He was very sorry about what his mother had done, but surely Mr. Gleeson couldn't really think any of it was Peter's fault.

"Because . . ." George struggled but was determined. "Because it means that all that stuff, from years ago, it didn't end back then. It's still happening."

Well, no, Peter thought, but he didn't want to argue. Everything that happened had happened to their parents. Or at least, their parents were the agents of all that had happened. Or at least, their parents were the ones who could have stopped it from happening. Or . . . He got that choked-off feeling he always got whenever he thought about that night. If he'd never suggested to Kate that they should sneak out. If they hadn't been caught. One thing leads to another which leads to another, yes, but who could have predicted that last fallen domino would skid so far from the neatly toppled row? Not the pair of teenagers, that was for sure. When he and Kate started seeing each other again, they decided that they'd leave all that baggage behind and start fresh. He was old enough now to know what sustained him, and so was Kate. They were apart long enough to know the shape of each other's absence.

"Well, all I know is this is the girl. I love her."

George flipped the faucet on again with a flick of his wrist, refilled his glass. He gulped the water down like he'd been in the desert for weeks.

"You're stubborn, Peter. You're a great kid, but you're stubborn."

"I'm not a kid," Peter said, though saying so made him feel like a kid.

"You love her. Okay. It's a strong feeling, but think about it all the way through. What's next? You're going to marry this girl? Have kids with her? Your mother and Francis Gleeson are going to have the same grandbabies? They're going to sit at the same table at the christening?"

"Huh?" Peter said. No one had said anything about babies, for God's sake. He dreamed of sharing an apartment with Kate someday, coming home to her each evening and telling her about his day, hearing about hers, going to bed naked with the covers pulled up to their chins, feeling her warm skin next to his when he woke up every morning. But that could only happen after he decided what to do with his life.

George sighed. "I'll drive," he said. "I'm sure she could use another set of hands. And I guess I should meet her, right?"

———

Peter was nervous when they pulled up to Kate's dorm, jittery all the way down to his bones, like he was in the track van, heading to states. Kate was wearing cutoffs, sneakers, clothes to lift and haul in. Her hair was piled at the top of her head, but he could see that she'd already sweat through the back of her T-shirt, a straight line down her spine. It was hot, and she'd schlepped a dozen boxes down from her dorm room even though he told her to wait until he got there.

"That her?" George said as they pulled up.

"Remember, she's not expecting you," Peter said. He could tell she hadn't spotted him yet, didn't know what kind of truck to look for.

George was wearing black shorts, a tight black tank top that pulled at his belly, bright white sneakers. He checked his teeth in the mirror and then winked at Peter. "How does my hair look?" he asked.

Peter watched Kate notice the man walking beside him. "George!" she said when they got close enough. "I'm so glad to meet you," she said. She thanked him for coming, for lending both his truck and his muscle. George took her thanks in stride, and was more reserved than usual, though Kate wouldn't know that. She asked if Peter had told him the details of the move they were about to embark on.

George glanced at Peter. "East Seventy-Ninth, right? At Second?"

"Did he mention anything else? No? Great. Let's get going."

It was a sixth floor walk-up, was the thing neither of them had mentioned to George. "Jesus H. Christ," George said after the very first trip up the stairs, setting the first box down inside the apartment. "You couldn't find a twelfth floor walk-up?"

"You're fine," Kate said. "Think of the powerful quads you'll have when we're through."

George grinned and Peter felt the low-grade dread he'd been feeling since that morning begin to melt away.

Every trip they made up those stairs, the closer George and Kate seemed to get. Up and down they went, and the stairwell rang out with Kate's voice chattering away, asking George questions about himself, what he thought about things: Monica Lewinsky, the Catholic Church, the euro. They took a break when they were more than halfway through, and George told Kate the meaning of each of his tattoos. He told her about Rosaleen, that he'd liked her for a long time before he asked her out.

When they were finally finished moving up all the stuff, the three of them sprawled across Kate's new kitchen floor in exhausted silence. The apartment air felt stale. Already, Peter hated the idea of visiting Kate's life and having her visit his.

"Who wants a beer?" Kate asked, without making a move to stand up. George said he'd pass, he had sodas in his truck. Peter got up, opened the door of the fridge, and let the cold air wrap around him for a moment before removing the six-pack Kate's roommates had left for them. He took one and downed it in two long sips before offering one to the others.

"Jeez," Kate said, "leave some for the rest of us."

"Yeah, really," George said.

———

When Peter and George returned to the truck, they found a cop hassling a delivery boy who had someone's takeout order dangling from the handlebar of his bike. The cop was huge, with arms so thick they strained the material of his uniform shirt. "Excuse us," George said, stepping around them. He'd double-parked, left the hazards on, and the cop looked over at George as if to let him know that he'd noticed and could do something about it if he wanted to.

Once they were driving, George said that the problem with the cops today was that the job attracted a different kind of person than it used to. They still had great guys signing on—"and women," he added—and one thing they did better than the old days was now they got people of every stripe and color, but there were too many young cops nowadays who were just after the power trip, carrying a gun. Maybe that's why they didn't get as much respect as they used to. In a just world, becoming a cop would be as prestigious a pursuit as becoming an investment banker. Or a doctor, even. Was there anything more important than keeping people safe? Being the one people turn to at their most desperate? And yet.

"You know what I saw the other day? On Broadway, by the Bowling Green station? There were like thirty City College students protesting. One girl had a sign that said 'Fuck the Police.' Did you see that? It was the Monday of the week we were down at the Standard and Poor's building for that job. A white girl. A woman, I mean. Probably came from New Canaan on the train that morning. Now you tell me what beef she might have with the police. You tell me who she's going to call if some man pulls out his junk on the crosstown bus."

Peter had seen the protesters, but hadn't really thought about them. He wasn't paying close enough attention, but George's point seemed both solid and completely flawed.

"But the history of policing is also a history of protest," Peter said. "I'm sure they were reacting to that cop who roughed up the kid in Bed-Stuy over the weekend. What was he? Thirteen? They could have killed him."

"Thirteen. But he looked older."

"And if he were older? He wasn't doing anything wrong."

"Peter." George looked at him. "I'm not denying that some cops are racist assholes. I'm saying now that girl from New Canaan decides that every cop is a racist asshole. Just because some meathead in the Seven-Nine beat up a kid. He never should have gotten near a shield and a gun, that guy."

Peter laughed. "Isn't that what every minority in this city has to deal with every single day? Whole groups being judged based on the actions of a few?" But Peter was only half debating since he was still thinking about Kate, and the overcrowded apartment he was about to move into. The thought of four guys sharing the same small bathroom made him wonder why he'd agreed.

George said he was willing to bet most of those protesters had never personally met and spoken to a cop.

"A big problem is the job doesn't pay enough," George said. "You listening? Not for the danger. And then another problem is first chance a good city cop gets, he or she heads to the suburbs. I read an article about it."

"About what?"

"About the police. Hello? Earth to Peter. Young people have to see it as a place where they can use their brains."

In the passenger seat, Peter sat up straight, felt a tug of such force it seemed impossible that it had come from within.

"It's an important job."

George glanced at him. "That's what I'm saying."

———

That night, Kate no doubt long asleep in her new apartment, Peter lay awake and felt a world older than he had when he imagined college as a road that would bring him somewhere far away. Around midnight he gave up on sleep, slid his feet into his weathered sneakers, slipped out of the apartment and then outside into the drizzly dark.

At the Banner he acted as if he were new to the neighborhood. After his second drink he asked the bartender if he remembered a guy from a few years ago, a tall guy, wavy hair. A cop. Used to be a regular, before he moved down south.

"You're describing everyone," the bartender said. "Narrow it down."

"Nah, it's nothing," Peter said, and waved him off.

An hour later, when Peter set his glass down on the bar and reached for his wallet to fish out a few bills, he felt his hands tremble. Outside again, the drizzle now a downpour, he felt himself swimming toward the lure of the familiar, a path he could make his own and make right. He wondered if recruits got paid through academy. He wondered if the health insurance started immediately or only after several months' delay.

———

He'd tell Kate as soon as he took the written exam. Then he told himself he'd tell her as soon as he found out whether he passed. He kept shaping for the ironworkers, kept getting per diem work. He tried to go for a run every day, after work, because it made him feel like he was still a student and it kept him out of the apartment for an extra hour. Autumn came and went. Christmas. The evening news was in a lather over Y2K. The world had just a few more months to organize itself before the century changed and all files were lost. The subways would stop running. Planes would drop from the sky. All because programmers in the 1960s had not prepared for an existence beyond 1999.

The new millennium arrived, and the world kept turning.

In February, he heard from the Applicant Processing Division that he passed the written test and that there was additional paperwork to be filled out. Among this paperwork was a form that consented to a background check. An investigator was assigned to his application. He sat for a character screening, a psychological screening, an oral test, the medical test. They checked his vision, hearing, blood pressure, his heart. When the doctor took his resting pulse, he said either Peter was a runner or he was dead.

After all that came the formal interview, scheduled with the same investigator who had completed his background check.

George figured it out when he saw the envelopes arriving. He told Peter it didn't feel like all that long ago that he'd brought in the mail and noticed similar envelopes for Brian. He asked Peter if he was sure, how far along he was in the process, how he'd done on the formal interview. If he'd met with anyone since the background check.

"That's the last step. Next week."

"Ah. Okay," George said, but seemed concerned.

"What?"

"Nothing."

———

The investigator introduced himself as a member of the detective bureau. He seemed jolly enough and Peter could tell he was trying to put him at ease. He told Peter about the car trouble he'd had that morning, how his wife was a nag but was always right. Peter had shaved carefully, was wearing a sport coat and tie. All the other tests had taken place in LeFrak City, but this one was held on East Twentieth Street in Manhattan. Peter had a folder with him that contained every document they'd asked for, from his social security card to his transcript from Elliott. His backpack was too scuffed for him to use and he didn't have a briefcase, so he clutched the folder in his hand on the subway, and all morning he was paranoid that something had slipped out and fluttered away without his noticing. He checked and rechecked.

When he got to the building, a young woman directed him to the interview room and brought him a glass of water. When the investigator came in, he sat across from Peter at a beat-up wood table. The older man began with the questions Peter expected, the ones he'd practiced answering in his head on his evening runs: why Peter wanted to join and how he envisioned the job. He framed everything like a casual chat, like they were simply getting to know each other at a barbeque or a baseball game, though Peter could tell he was ticking through the items on his list. Finally, he asked about Peter's parents, and Peter gave the answer he'd rehearsed, the answer he'd been giving for years. His mother lived upstate. His father lived down south. They'd separated a decade ago and Peter didn't have a relationship with either of them. He nodded quickly to indicate that was the extent of his answer, but the investigator tilted his head, leaned forward.

"Your father. He was on the job, no?"

"Yes. Yes he was."

"Nineteen years. Did he get injured? Something happen?" He flipped through his notes, and Peter felt his pulse firing in the palms of his hands. He knew it was possible that the man knew everything already, but he also knew it was possible the department was so vast, with so many moving parts, that it might have gotten missed. Nothing that happened in Gillam had happened on the job for Brian.

"There was a personal matter that prompted an early retirement."

"Oh? What was that?"

He'd been warned that there was no limit to the scope of their questions. In the psychological exam they asked him if he was seeing anyone, if that person was a man or a woman, how he would feel if his eventual partner were a woman. How about a gay man or a gay woman? How about Black, Hispanic, Asian? He'd assumed those questions were illegal.

"We're not close. We don't have a relationship."

"That wasn't the question."

"He retired early, because he wanted a change. At least I believe that's why. But you'd have to ask him, honestly. He moved down south when I was fifteen. I lived with my uncle after he left."

"Your uncle George Stanhope," the investigator said, and Peter felt his stomach drop.

"Yes."

"And your mother, she lives on Sixth Street in Saratoga now?"

"I don't know," Peter said. This, at least, was the truth.

"She was arrested in 1991 and charged with attempted murder. The man she shot was a neighbor, an NYPD lieutenant, off duty. She pleaded not guilty by reason of mental disease or defect. The case settled. Correct?"

Peter remained silent while his heart pounded.

"I was fourteen. I wasn't privy to most of the details."

"It was your father's off-duty weapon that she used, correct?"

"Yes, I believe so."

"You believe so." The investigator pushed his notes aside. "You aced the written test. You aced the physical. Your college transcript is solid."

Peter waited for the other shoe to drop.

"But the psych exam raised a flag. I'm talking about your psych exam, Peter. Not your mother's. Not your father's. Yours."

Peter knew he might be testing him. The psych exam consisted of a thousand questions over the course of six hours. At one point he was asked to draw a house, a tree, himself. After, he remembered he'd forgotten to draw a doorknob on the front door of the house. How would he get in through a door without a knob? As for the self-portrait, he'd drawn himself in shorts and a racing singlet and afterward thought he should have drawn a suit and tie.

"And your father's record with us is troubling. He has a citation for drinking on the job. January 1989."

"I'm not my father. I don't even know him anymore."

"And Uncle George has a sheet. Minor stuff but worth mentioning."

Peter looked toward the narrow window and tried to gather his scattering thoughts.

"I've never done a single thing wrong. I'm the one who's applying. Not my mother. Not my father. Not my uncle. So their histories don't matter, only mine matters."

"Maybe," the investigator said. "That might be true. Depends."

———

He waited two weeks. A month. Six weeks. He'd heard there was a new academy class starting up soon and if his name didn't get added to the list of eligible recruits, he wouldn't be able to join. Kate was enjoying her job despite the odd hours, despite the things she had to see when she was called out to crime scenes, down on her hands and knees with her black light, searching for fluid and blood.

"What's with you?" Kate asked. They'd gone to see a movie but the few times Kate looked over at him in the flickering dark, Peter wasn't looking at the screen. The movie wasn't even halfway through when he took her hand and pulled her down the aisle, out to the lobby, and then to the frigid air of the sidewalk outside.

"When are we going to live together, Kate? When are we going to get married? When are our lives going to be the way we agreed they were going to be instead of just getting together two or three nights a week? I don't like it."

Kate laughed. They were standing six feet apart on a gum-flocked sidewalk. The woman sitting in the ticket booth was behind glass, reading a book.

"I'm serious, don't you want to get married?"

"Well, I think you're supposed to ask me if I'm up for it."

"I did, didn't I? About ten years ago?"

"No, you told me it was going to happen. I don't think you asked. Plus I was thirteen."

"Well? Are you up for it?"

"Of course I am," she said, "but I hope you know this doesn't count as a proposal." And then, "Peter, what in the world is wrong with you?"

He paced back and forth as he told her everything, starting with the night he decided to become a cop, all the way up to the formal interview and the long weeks he'd been waiting, wondering if he was going to get in. He was sorry he didn't tell her, but he wanted it to be a surprise. Kate watched and listened as she shivered and hugged herself tight.

Because what would he do otherwise, was the question he kept coming back to. Now that he knew what he wanted to be, he was sure of it. There were so many different ways to be a cop, so many different trajectories, no two careers looked alike, it was insane that they could hold against him something that had happened so long ago, something that truly had nothing to do with him. He thought of calling up that investigator and asking for another interview. What did Kate think of that idea?

"Did he say anything more about whatever flags were raised in the psych exam? Did he give you details?"

"No. He probably made that up."

Kate nodded and Peter could almost see all the information he'd just given her get sorted into compartments in her brain.

"If I don't get in I was thinking we could move. I could try Boston or somewhere in Connecticut. Hartford. Stamford. They probably don't have so many applicants. Plus . . ."

"Peter," Kate said, unwrapping her arms from around herself and approaching him. He felt her body's warmth through her thick down coat. "You're sure?" she asked. "You're certain this is what you want?"

"Yes," he said. He'd be a better cop than his father had been. He'd be more like Francis Gleeson, before he got shot. He'd get to the place Francis would have landed, had his career not been derailed. He'd be respectful and he'd follow the rules and he'd climb the ranks. He could see it already.

"Let me try one thing. Can you hang on a little while longer? What's the guy's name? The investigator, I mean."

———

Kate took the early bus to Gillam that Sunday, and walked home without calling for a pickup. She stopped walking when she was halfway down Jefferson and saw the windows of her childhood home were decorated with her and her sisters' old heart cutouts for Valentine's Day. The thought of her mother unfolding the stairs to the attic and getting down the old decorations while her father held the stairs steady and said, as he always did, "Be careful up there, Lena," made Kate want to drop to her knees and cry. She remembered her father coming home from a midnight tour one Valentine's Day and presenting each of them with heart-shaped erasers for their pencils. For Lena he had a dozen roses, and as she trimmed the ends and fussed about finding a vase, she said he should have waited until late February, when the markup wasn't so steep, she wasn't the kind of wife who would mind.

Kate knocked softly at the front door, and when no one answered, she went around the side of the house, the frost-stiffened grass crunching under her sneakers, and got the hide-a-key from under the false rock. When she pushed open the back door, her father was already opening the cabinet to remove a second mug.

"I saw you coming," he said.

"Where's Mom?"

"Sleeping." It was not quite eight o'clock. Lena's hair had grown back, curls as full as ever, only she didn't bother coloring it anymore, so it was threaded with steel and white. Her cancer had been in remission for several years. She never discussed what had happened between Francis and Joan Kavanagh, but Kate was with her once, about a year after her surgery, her hair still impish and short, when they were walking through the parking lot of an Italian restaurant back to Lena's car, and Lena stopped all of a sudden, turned back to the restaurant. "I forgot something," she called over her shoulder. Kate almost laughed at the abruptness of it until she saw Joan Kavanagh walking through the parking lot across the street. Only when Joan had entered a shop on the other side did Lena reemerge.

"Mom," Kate had said, once they were seated in the car.

"I just don't like seeing her," Lena said. "I feel embarrassed for some reason."

"You have no reason to feel embarrassed. She should be embarrassed."

"Still." She shrugged.

"Mom sleeps later than she did when you girls were young," Francis said now. All of Kate's life, he seemed to always know when there was something on her mind. She put her bag down by the door and took the mug he offered. He passed the milk in silence.

"Just felt like a visit?" he said. He folded his newspaper into quarters. He was already dressed, had been to the deli. He had an empty sheet of wax paper in front of him, another wrapped around a buttered roll on the counter, waiting for Lena.

"Yeah, haven't been home in a little while."

"Well, you're busy. How's work?"

He knew, she realized. She didn't know how, but he did. She listened for her mother's footsteps on the stairs but the house was silent. The space heater hummed lightly in the corner by the stove.

"I need to ask you a favor," she said.

"Oh?"

"Peter is applying to the police academy."

Francis was silent for a beat. "Peter Stanhope."

"Yes. That Peter."

Francis studied her with a blank expression.

"Anyway. He hasn't heard whether he's eligible yet, but it's been longer than usual, and a few things came up in his interview."

"And in his psych exam," Francis said.

Kate felt every part of her body go still.

"Did he tell you that?"

"Yes, of course he told me, but they may have only said that to rattle him."

"No, it's true. A few little things. Minor. But combined with his family history it's troubling."

"How do you know all this?"

"I have a friend. He called to let me know, asked what I thought."

Kate stared at him over her tea.

"What did you say?"

"Is that the favor? To put a good word in for him?"

"Yes."

"Why?"

"Because he wants to be a police officer and he'd be a very good one. And because I love him and one day probably pretty soon we're going to get married."

Finally, Francis sighed, pushed back from the table. "You're throwing your life away," he said.

She put down her mug just as neatly as he had, and pointed out that it was her life. Besides, was he in a position to lecture about throwing one's life away? It was only because of Lena's forgiving nature that he was even sitting there right now, in front of her.

Francis let that pass over him.

"You think a person comes out of a house like that undamaged? You don't see it now, Kate, but it's there. I promise you. Marriage is long. All the seams get tested."

"Well, you would know, right?" Kate said,

Francis gave her a warning look. She looked right back.

"Why him?"

"Because I love him."

"Love isn't enough. Not even close."

"It is for me. Him, too."

Francis smiled but there was no light in it. "You don't have the first clue what you're talking about."

Kate stayed exactly where she was and tried not to react. How dare he of all people tell her what love was. Along the windowsill was a row of jam jars stuffed with dirt and seedlings. Francis stood and Kate saw that his jeans hung from his hips. Even his shoulders seemed narrower than they used to. He had crumbs down the front of his shirt. She wondered, as she did once in a great while, why he'd never returned to Ireland, why he'd never brought them there, how it was possible he'd lived a whole life before she was even born. She'd always felt sort of sad for him, leaving his parents forever when he was still so young, but now she saw how much freedom that had given him, with no one hovering on the sidelines telling him what to do.

"You can be against it, Dad, but it's happening. I love him. You can be a part of our lives or not, it's up to you. He can stay on with the iron-workers, or he can go to law school, or he can do something else. He wants to be a cop, but the truth is that I don't care if he ends up digging ditches."

Francis sighed. He got the ice tray out of the fridge and cracked it by twisting. One by one he removed cubes and dropped them into the jam jars. When he finished he remained facing the window.

"I told them to go ahead and put him on the list for the next class. I told them he was a good boy, a good student, though his parents were trouble. I told them I had no problem with it."

Kate stood so quickly that her chair tipped backward and clattered to the floor.

"I told them none of it was his fault, what happened that night. I told them that he'd gone on to do well in school and all that. What you told me that time, when Mom was in surgery. Running and getting a scholarship. They already knew that, of course."

"So you forgive him then? You don't blame him?" She wanted to throw her arms around him like she was ten again. "You don't blame me?"

Francis turned. "I never blamed him. He was fourteen years old. Why would I blame him? And why in the world would I blame you? You're not understanding the problem here. You're not even near understanding it."

But it was he who wasn't understanding, Kate knew. All would be well now. They had gone through a bad time—the Gleesons, the Stanhopes—but now look at them. Look at the funny way life could go. Immediately, Kate pictured Peter on Jefferson Street for Thanksgiving, Christmas, all the holidays, sitting between her sisters on the couch, getting up to make them another pot of coffee, pulling gifts from under the tree and calling out the names. George, too, maybe. Rosaleen. Look at the happy ending that could come out of a terrible thing. Theirs was a story for the ages, star-crossed, but without the tragic ending, without the fatalities.

"I still worry about her," Francis said. "Your mother does, too. Now that she's living on her own we don't get updates."

"You mean Peter's mother? He doesn't even see her. He never talks about her. She doesn't matter anymore."

"Doesn't matter? Katie. Love. She's the person who made him. She's always going to matter."

At that, Kate turned away from the memory of the woman framed in the door of the Dunkin' Donuts restroom on Halloween, her face pale and gaunt, the expression in her eyes wild. She turned away from the other glimpses she'd had since then—Anne Stanhope sitting in a car on 103rd Street, engine off, a cup of pistachio shells on her lap. Kate had pulled up her hood as she passed, and walked quickly by Peter's building, calling instead from the Thai restaurant two blocks away, asking him to meet her there. Another time in Riverside Park, where Peter liked to run, standing next to a tree in a bulky coat that was far too broad in the shoulders for her. Kate had noticed her just before Peter arrived at their appointed spot, his sweaty skin steaming lightly in the cold air. "You okay?" he'd asked that day.

"I'm fine," Kate had said, glancing over her shoulder and then taking hold of his arm, leading him down to the river to point out the faint Christmas lights all the way over in New Jersey. Here was a woman who'd wanted to hurt her, a woman who had hurt her father so badly that the father Kate remembered from when she was a little girl had disappeared, and in his place came a new father, a man she often struggled to recognize. And he'd never returned, that first father. She waited and waited but he never came back after that, not completely, and that was Anne Stanhope's fault. Kate should be afraid of the woman. She knew she should be, and yet she wasn't, at least not the way her father meant.

And the most recent time, near Kate's apartment, Peter all the way across town. Anne was sitting on a bench outside the Hungarian bakery, scowling at the passersby. Her eyes lifted when Kate arrived at the opposite corner, as if sensing her there. Kate was beginning to turn back, beginning to flee, but she decided, No, I will not flee, and instead felt something like rage rise up in her throat. Four lanes of traffic divided them—two northbound, two south—and Kate began to cross before the light turned. She held up her arms to stop traffic and knew what Moses felt like when he stopped the waves from crashing over him.

When Anne stood from her bench, Kate felt her courage falter but she jutted out her jaw and kept moving. She stretched her body as tall as she could to make herself seem bigger, just like her father had done that night when he strode up to their door. The sunshine was bitter cold, and trapped in the gutter ice were cigarette butts, candy wrappers, a pen.

"What do you want?" Kate asked when she was close enough for Anne to hear. The subway entrance was just a few paces away. Whenever she needed to she could disappear down there, reemerge somewhere far downtown, pretend to herself and to Peter that this encounter had never taken place. She'd take a cab back home and she'd avoid this corner for a week.

"I want to talk with Peter," Anne said. "I thought you could help me."

"Me? You want me to help you?" Kate laughed, but it came out clotted and choked. "You have some nerve. You know that?" Kate took a step closer to Anne.

"Stay away from him," Kate said, her voice a low growl. "And stay away from me. He doesn't want to see you."

Anne took a breath as if to speak, but Kate was already gone, crossing traffic against the light once again.

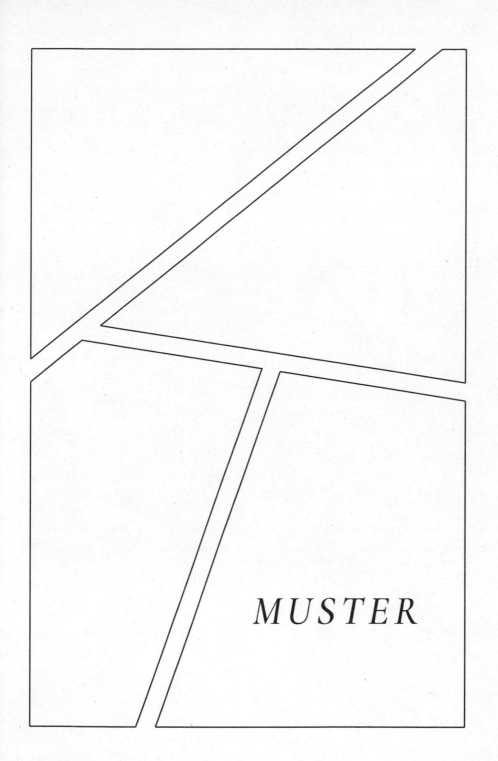

MUSTER

fifteen

WHAT HAD BEEN DONE to Anne at twelve by their neighbor, Mr. Kilcoyne, kept being done until she turned sixteen
and left for England. He'd show up with a fistful of ribbons, or a dress
that needed mending, and ask if she could come help with the little
girls. He was hopeless with bows and plaits, he said. Mrs. Kilcoyne
had died of a stomach ailment the same year Anne's own mother had
walked into the rough water at Killiney Beach with all her clothes
on, her shoes, three days before Christmas in the year 1964. She left
a mother-of-pearl brooch and a few pound notes on the mantel. That
first time Mr. Kilcoyne came for her, once they got just past the stone
that marked Kilcoyne land, Mr. Kilcoyne said, "Wait there just a minute, Anne," and then clutched her by the shoulder and by the hip, pulling her up against him, hard. It was a bit like a hug except Anne didn't
hug back and he was trembling, clutching her tighter and tighter as
the trembling became more violent. Something was happening to him
under his clothes.

"The girls will be waiting for us," Anne said when he finally let her
go, and in her bewilderment—she felt dazed, light-headed, though what

had happened? Maybe nothing—she strode through a thicket of nettles and her shins went afire.

When she got to England she made a friend called Bridget and after a while told her about Mr. Kilcoyne, how it had begun and how he'd graduated from clutching her over her clothes to asking her to follow him into the hayshed.

"But, Anne, why'd you go? Could you not think of any reason not to?" Bridget asked. "There was a man had a shop at home who was like your Mr. Kilcoyne, and I always told him my mother was expecting me. That she'd come round looking for me any minute. And then I'd run off." They were sitting on a low wall in a schoolyard on the outskirts of London, both assistants at the hospital, both Irish and living with a group of other Irish girls they found through an ad in the newspaper.

Why did I go? Anne wondered. It was a good question, and one, even more than forty years on, she couldn't answer. Once, she almost sent her sister, younger than Anne by one year but older seeming than Anne in some ways, and Anne had heard in the schoolyard that she had a fella. Mr. Kilcoyne had come to the door as always, but instead of pulling on her cardigan right away she said she wasn't feeling well. "Bernadette can go," she said. Her father turned the radio down and rubbed his wiry brows. Bernadette looked up from picking her fingernails in surprise. Like a school pantomime, everything stopped for a beat of one or two breaths. But then, before Bernadette or Mr. Kilcoyne could even respond, Anne continued. "But the girls are used to me now," she said. Always, when she returned home, her father would ask after the Kilcoyne daughters, two of them still in nappies when it all began. Bernadette would have made the tea and would be sitting in the corner, hopping her foot, waiting for time to pass. She almost told them once, the first time Mr. Kilcoyne put his hand under her clothes, his cold hand that had delivered a calf that morning, but her father was taking his tea and listening to the radio and next thing she knew he was packing his pipe and heading out again. Watching him cross the small yard to the path by the cowshed, she knew that even if she told him, nothing would change except then it would be in the air between them, undiscussed, just like her mother's death. Bernadette went flying outside to visit with her schoolmate, who was passing on the low road.

Anne regretted telling Bridget almost immediately. Telling her, bringing that story to England, spoiled England for her. When she left for America two years later, she knew she would be smarter. She'd bring none of Ireland with her. She'd start the training program in New York City and she'd buy a few new blouses and she'd get her hair cut like Jackie Kennedy and she'd never even think about Ireland again.

But she'd learned a thing or two from all those years of being made to sit in rooms with doctors, first in the nice hospital and then in the one that was less nice. She'd learned that the beginning of one's life mattered the most, that life was top-heavy in that way. Why else would the doctors keep asking about it, when the events that had gotten her locked in a hospital had happened so much more recently? She'd turned her back on Ireland the day she left but it was still there, behind her, like a shadow that followed her from place to place to place. The body that had driven several hours south along the New York State Thruway to see a son she hadn't spoken to in so many years was the same body that cut through the tall grass of St. Dymphna's in 1967. It was the same body that pushed out two baby boys, the same body that made itself stiff as a plank when Mr. Kilcoyne breathed too close to her ear.

The beginning mattered for Peter, too, whether he knew that yet or not. All those years of moving carefully around the house in Gillam had made an imprint on him, somewhere.

———

There were some months when Anne would drive the four hours downstate to check up on Peter as many as three times, staying six or eight or even twelve hours at a stretch. She'd turn on the radio while she waited to glimpse him, listen to a celebrity interview or instructions on how to brine a turkey or how to save herself if she were to ever find her car submerged in water. On those trips, if the weather was especially nice, she'd stop at the lookout on the Palisades and sit on a bench, gazing at the broad Hudson. Often, when her mind was so full of Peter that she needed a break from thinking about him, she'd force herself to change the subject, like an engine releasing a bit of steam, and instead she'd imagine the wilderness on either side of the river as it had once been. She'd imagine what it must have been like for Henry Hudson, how terrifying and how thrilling and, ultimately, how frustrating. The thing was, sometimes four hundred years seemed like an impossibly huge amount of time to fathom, and sometimes it seemed like nothing at all. A patient at the nursing home, a man who used to work at the college, once told her about humanity's common ancestor, a woman named Lucy who lived over three million years ago. Compared to Lucy, Henry Hudson had navigated the north river for the first time only yesterday. Compared to Henry Hudson's first voyage upriver, Anne had last lived in a house with Peter only a second ago. Less.

There were some months when she didn't go to see him at all, and instead told herself that she'd seen what she'd wanted to see—he was healthy, he was happy—and now it was time to leave him alone. She told herself that just knowing where he was would have to be enough for her, but whenever a few months went by, the same aimless impatience welled up that she'd felt all those years ago in Gillam. Kate Gleeson had been nothing but a regular suburban girl, like a million others. Was she especially beautiful? No. Was she particularly smart? Anne doubted it. So what was it then? When she dwelled on the question too much, her internal gears began turning more quickly. He could have gone to a better college. He could have become a doctor or a senator and then she'd point to him and look back to her life in Ireland and she'd be able to measure a great distance. But to come all the way here and raise a child who became a cop (how Irish, how typical) and fall in love with any old girl—what was the point? When she thought too much about all of this, she wouldn't be able to sleep for staring at the ceiling.

Used to be, at the very least, she could make Peter stay inside their house if she didn't want him seeing Kate. And now here was Kate, arms crossed, always standing between them.

She tried to let it go, to breathe in and out and let the information go still inside her brain, but there was a twist in Kate that Peter didn't see—her face, livid and red outside the Hungarian bakery on Lexington that morning, was like the shedding of a mask, and Anne thought, Yes, exactly, *this* is what you're really like—but that was the story with men and women since the beginning of time. They never saw each other clearly until it was too late. And yet, even as she thought those things, she also thought there was something to admire in the way Kate had come striding directly at her, the way she'd looked right into her face and told her to stay away. She loves him, Anne saw that day. She loves him more than whatever else she has in her life. And she's fierce. There might be more to her than Anne had credited.

If she didn't have the courage to approach Peter, to try to connect with him again, then what was the point of watching him like a stalker? She knew that was the question, and she didn't need Dr. Oliver to be the one to ask. The crazy thing was that Kate almost always saw her. It was as if she knew when Anne was out there, and looked around for her as soon as she stepped through the door. Of course, it was possible that she went through every day with the same hunted expression she wore when Anne was watching, but it always felt to Anne like she knew.

———

They moved in together. To a dingy ground floor apartment in Alphabet City. She lost track of them for a few months, but then the detective found them. Anne looked in the barred window one afternoon when neither of them were home and saw dishes in the sink, a pile of empty bottles in a bin by the door, a pair of cereal boxes on the counter.

She hadn't been down in several weeks when September 11, 2001, arrived. According to the news there was no point in driving down right away because she wouldn't be able to get near him, not by car, not by public transportation, so instead she watched the television she'd finally purchased, and searched for his face in the footage of police officers trying to make sense of the chaos. He wasn't dead. If he were dead, she was certain she'd know. Still, she wanted to hear his voice. So, every few hours, she went down to the payphone on Perry Street and using a prepaid card she dialed his number, a landline, but it just kept ringing. Finally, on September 13, he answered.

"Peter?" she said, when he said hello.

"Yes?" he said, after the slightest hesitation. He sounded tired. He waited and waited and waited. Don't go down there, she wanted to say. Leave it for other people. There were stories of rubble sliding, of objects falling from great heights.

She could hear him breathing on the other end of the line when she hung up.

———

About a year after they moved in together, Anne saw Kate coming around the corner with dry cleaning slung over her shoulder when she ran into a woman she seemed to know, showed that woman her hand. Where a moment before she'd seemed so serious, now she looked radiant, and nodded to accept whatever the other woman was saying to her while the dry cleaning bags brushed the filthy sidewalk. She was still smiling into the collar of her coat as she fished out the keys to her building. Next thing Peter jogged up, began to move more stealthily when he realized Kate hadn't seen him. He crept up behind her and grabbed her by the waist. Anne's heart clutched inside her chest.

Married, Anne knew. She tried to get a good look at him, at his left hand, as if looking closely might give her the details she craved. Had the Gleesons all been there? George? Had they had a big party? In the early morning, Peter came outside alone. She could always tell when he hadn't worked in a few days because his beard came in thick and sudden, just like Brian's used to. She followed him to the park, where he did a few half-hearted pull-ups and then quit, sat on the cold tarmac, then lay flat, arms and legs thrown wide. He'd grown a little thicker in the years that had passed since she first saw him, that Halloween night. He squinted at the sky and after a while closed his eyes as his breath rose straight up from his mouth in plumes. She hadn't seen him coming back from a run in a long time.

Kate worked odd hours, whatever she did—she used to commute to Queens, but now she took the subway to Twenty-Sixth Street. Peter's hours shifted weekly, too, and sometimes he was just coming home as Kate was leaving and they'd pause at the security door of their building to hug each other, talk about things that Anne couldn't hear.

They moved out of that apartment in 2004. She sensed something was brewing, something about the way they rushed around and conferred outside the building, and then the next several times she came down she didn't see them at all. Finally, she worked up the courage to peek in their window once again, but drew back quickly when she met eyes with a stout middle-aged man cooking something in a pan, not wearing a shirt.

The man came to the window. "See something you like?"

Anne stood her ground. "Wasn't there someone else who used to live here?"

He laughed. "There probably was, yes, but now I live here." He looked her up and down. "You want to come in?"

Anne hurried away.

———

The private detective she'd enlisted all those years before was no longer in business, so she had to find another. He got her the address in Floral Park and a photo of a little Tudor that looked like a gingerbread house. He also confirmed they were married. They'd only put ten percent down on the house.

"What's the block like? The neighborhood?" It had come as a shock, this change, though she supposed when she thought about it that she hadn't expected them to live in that grim apartment forever.

The detective shrugged. "What do you want to know?"

"I don't know," Anne said.

She stayed away for months and months but studied Floral Park on a map, memorized the route she'd have to take. The year 2005 arrived, and she was still trying and failing to imagine him in a house that was not their house in Gillam. Finally, she drove three hours down to the city, over a bridge, and then out to Long Island. As she read the signs, she remembered that she'd once been to a beach on Long Island, years earlier, with Brian, before they were married, maybe their second or third date. She'd forgotten all about it, and then all of a sudden she could see Brian sitting on the sand and telling her to go swim, he'd stay with their stuff so no one would take it. In America, in New York, he said, someone always has to hang back and stand guard.

It was a very small but sweet house, snow on the eaves and the tops of all the bushes, warm yellow light inside. The driveway was pitted and cracked. She looked around at all the things her son must look at when he stepped out the door in the mornings. Anne turned off the engine and watched for signs of Peter, as if she might spot his old bike outside. After not very long she saw Kate pass by a ground floor window, the blinds open, the lights inside illuminating her as clearly as if she were on a stage. Tidying up, it seemed, laundry in her arms. She passed by the window again and Anne realized that what Kate was holding in her arms, pressing to her chest, was not a pile of laundry, but a baby.

It took a beat to put it together: Peter's baby, too.

She got out of the car and stood in a place where she was well shadowed. There they were again. Kate Gleeson and Anne's own baby grandchild. A brand-new person, made out of nothing. Anne remembered Peter as a baby, how quickly he transformed. For so long he could barely move at all, and then one day he pulled himself up to standing. Another day he walked. Another day he seemed to already know all the words he'd ever need to know in a life.

A few cars passed, and with each one Anne leaned away from the sweep of the headlights and vowed that if Peter came home right then, she would approach him. It was even more important now. She thought of her father for the first time in years. He'd been dead and gone since before Peter was born, but this small person living in a place called Long Island, United States of America, wouldn't exist if Anne hadn't existed, and her parents before her, so on and so forth until the beginning of time. She thought of her father's muck-caked boots, him spitting outside in the yard. She thought of the small threads of tobacco that used to rain down around him at the table, how they'd stain the floor if she didn't sweep them up quickly enough. She thought about how lonely he and Bernadette must have been when Anne left for England, announcing her plan on a Thursday and gone by Saturday morning.

She thought of her mother, about how much of her, too, might be contained within that small body. Suddenly, she went cold with worry.

But none of the cars were Peter's, and no one came outside, and eventually the sky became streaked with morning.

———

When she left Floral Park after finding out about the baby, it was with a plan to return in no time at all. She was no longer required to see

Dr. Oliver. She could get a job somewhere near them. She could stop by and mind the child for an hour if Kate wanted to get to the store. She thought about how little was in her apartment, how she could pack it up in a single hour if she wanted to. And yet, as soon as she parked her car, walked up the stairs to her apartment, opened the door and sat down on the edge of her bed, she knew that Kate would never let her mind that baby, her grandchild. And in a moment of perfect stillness, Anne couldn't blame her. Where an hour earlier she had a mind to stop by her apartment only long enough to pack up and drive right back down to them, now she saw that the baby would make it more difficult. She knew time was passing, of course she did, but she thought at some point when the moment was perfect she'd eventually step back into his life and pick up where they left off. He was married, yes, but only to Kate Gleeson. But now there was a baby, which meant he was further along in his life than she'd understood. She calculated. He was twenty-eight already. There'd be more children after this one, probably. What was painful before would now be unbearable.

She drove down to Floral Park every few months, but only once did she glimpse Peter, and that glimpse was so brief it barely counted. Their garage door opened and he appeared. He grabbed hold of the garbage can and carried it down the driveway to the curb. He seemed tired, worried. He looked up at the roofline of the house. He rubbed his eyes. Then he plunged his hand into his pocket, fished out a set of keys, slipped into his car, and drove away, leaving the garage door wide open. Her child, in this grown man's body. She clutched the steering wheel so tightly that her fingers hurt when she let go.

Otherwise, it was only Kate she glimpsed. Kate with that baby who turned into a toddler. A boy. Brown curls. Wriggly in her arms. Then, not terribly long after that boy began taking steps, there was Kate rushing to the car with another baby in her arms. Even when there were two cars in the driveway and Anne thought, surely, he was in there somewhere, all Anne glimpsed time after time after time was Kate moving through lighted rooms, saying things that Anne couldn't hear. "Those babies are my grandchildren," she'd say aloud over and over. Where before she used to leave feeling sad but somewhat reassured—he was doing okay, after all, he had a job, even if he was a cop; he had a partner, even if that partner was Kate Gleeson—since that first baby was born she felt unsettled.

Twice, she spotted George, though he looked different, and it wasn't until the second time that she figured out who he was. He appeared taller than he used to and younger than he should be, though that wasn't possible, was it? The way he carried himself down their front path told Anne he'd been there more times than he could count.

———

It was too much to think about, and so she found things to do up in Saratoga to keep herself away. She volunteered at the food bank every week. She walked dogs around town for people who were on vacation. She tried reading stories to kids at the library but they all seemed so needy, more interested in telling her stories about themselves and their pets and their brothers and grandpas than listening to the story she read. She kept track of the ages of her grandchildren, though she didn't know their birthdays. Whenever she saw them for the first time after not seeing them for several months, it was as if they'd transformed. A few times she felt too tired to drive all the way back upstate, so she stayed at a motor lodge on Jericho Turnpike. She glimpsed Peter driving toward her one morning as she was heading toward his house. The sun was in his eyes.

Who did the children look like? Not Peter, really. Not Kate. The older one looked to be about eight already, the girl maybe six. In the spring they shed their layers like skins, leaving jackets and sweatshirts thrown over bushes and on the steps. In the warm months they turned on the sprinkler in the side yard and played in their bathing suits with some kids Anne recognized from up the street. Had they met their other grandparents? she wondered. Of course they had. What word did they use for Lena Gleeson? She wondered if Peter and Kate ever mentioned her. She could already imagine the story they might tell about that one terrible night. Or maybe they would take the easy route and simply tell them she was dead. Each time she pulled up to the curb and turned off the car, she decided the moment had come, that finally, after so many years, she was going to walk up and ring the doorbell and say she was sorry for everything and it was time to know each other again. She'd think and debate with herself about the best way to do it and then she'd decide: next time. Again and again and again: next time.

———

And then, late June 2016, the smell of a thunderstorm followed her all the way to their street. She parked several houses past theirs, as usual, nearly hidden by the weeping branches of their neighbor's tree, the rearview mirror tilted to show their front door. It was dusk. She did a quick calculation, as she always did when she first pulled up. Peter was thirty-nine, Kate was still thirty-eight for several more weeks. Anne turned the radio on low and unwrapped her sandwich and settled in to watch the house while she still had the light. When it was fully dark she took a short walk to stretch her legs and get closer, pulling up the hood of her light summer sweater in case they should come outside. She looked at their cars and their flower bed and their beach towels slung over the railing of their deck to dry. He was in there. His car was parked in the driveway, Kate's behind it. Lights approached from the main road and Anne picked up her pace, dropped her chin to her chest, and turned away. The car slowed outside Peter's house, and Anne waited until she was well out of sight before crouching to pretend to tie her shoelace. It could be him, maybe, someone dropping him off.

But when she looked over her shoulder, it was not Peter she spotted but another familiar person, a man, though it took her a few seconds to place him.

"Francis Gleeson," she whispered to the cicadas, to the automated sprinklers that were beginning to rise and whir. She watched Francis cross the lawn, how he ignored the walking path. She tried to get a good look at his face, to see what damage she'd caused there, but it was impossible in such low light. She watched him knock on their door three times before simply pushing it open. Something was happening.

When she returned to the car, she didn't bother with the rearview mirror and instead turned fully around in her seat, her back to the steering wheel. She just watched the house, to see if Francis would come out again, or Peter or Kate, to see if she might be able to tell what was going on and who was in trouble. He had the same expression on his face as he had all those nights ago. Not one of the little ones, she prayed.

She waited and waited and waited, but the house betrayed nothing and the front door stayed closed. So he could drive then. His posture was good, his gait was just that tiny bit off, something about the way he swung his arm on one side, but a person might not notice it if they weren't searching for it. She remembered that he'd once carried her in his arms all the way across her front yard and up the stairs to her bedroom. How had he gotten the door open without setting her down?

———

She must have dozed off because when she woke up, the neighborhood was steeped in a middle-of-the-night kind of silence except for the sound of a sharp knock—one, two—on the roof of her car.

She opened her eyes to see, first, that Francis Gleeson's car was gone. Then she turned just slightly to find Kate Gleeson's face framed in the driver's side window, which she'd rolled down to let the air circulate. The night was hot.

"Jesus Christ," Anne said, hand to heart.

"I didn't mean to scare you," Kate said.

Anne wondered if she'd always known when she was out there, every single time.

"We have to talk," Kate said.

sixteen

I T DIDN'T MEAN SHE'D forgiven her, Kate told herself. It didn't mean that history didn't matter. It only meant she'd try anything that might help.

And there were things she wanted to know—about Peter, about Peter's father, about Anne, about Ireland, about all the people connected to Peter by blood so that she'd know for sure what she was dealing with. George could help, maybe, but whenever he sensed questions pushing up from her, he was suddenly in a hurry to get to the restroom, the fridge, his car. Peter, though, Peter he stopped for, tried to make listen. She'd seen them conferring on side-by-side recliners. She'd seen him sidle up to Peter at the grill. "It's the job," George always said, before Kate even got a whole sentence out. It was the weather. The mortgage. Being a man. But he frowned when he watched Peter navigate around their kitchen, offering drinks and things to eat. Peter drank O'Doul's when George was over, one after another, like the next one might quench his thirst.

"Have a real one," George said once, last summer. They were out on the patio, the kids trying to catch fireflies.

"Nah, this is fine," Peter said.

"But you did already, right? Before we came? And you'll have more once we leave?"

"George," Rosaleen said.

"Brian used to do that."

Peter just looked over at him, and George held his gaze for so long that even Kate got uncomfortable and had to look away.

When did it begin? If she had all the information, then maybe she'd be able to figure this thing out, find that critical moment in time when things could have gone in one direction but instead they went another. She was a scientist. She solved problems. Since moving in together they'd always ended their days with a drink or two. If he was on a midnight tour, he came home, slept, and then maybe had a drink after lunch, to tide him over until Kate got home from work. They were always too broke to afford more than one or two drinks at bars in Manhattan, so they mostly drank at home. When he was on a day tour they'd have a glass of wine while they made dinner, and then another with dinner. As they got older they became a little pickier, learned about body, legs, tannins. Peter learned about tequila and gin. They remembered the cheap booze they'd been happy with in college, and laughed. When Kate was in her late twenties, something about a glass of red wine with dinner on a Monday or Tuesday felt sophisticated, and Kate often thought of her own mother, who had a Diet Coke with almost every meal.

Kate was capable of rigorous study, of drawing complex, defensible conclusions. Since her undergrad organic chemistry class she'd imagined the world as a ceaseless machine: churning, grinding, turning matter into other matter. On the day she realized she might be pregnant—a quick calculation of days, the fact that her breasts were spilling out of her bra—she sat on the crackled plastic of her favorite lab stool and swabbed her arm, held the tourniquet with her teeth. She did a qualitative test first: positive for hCG. The quantitative test told her she was about seven weeks. Then she disposed of everything neatly, rolled her sleeve down, and did every single thing she had to do that day except with the feeling that she'd been hit by a shooting star.

Her job, most days, was to find the contours of an invisible universe and then map it for others to see. She performed forensic analyses on hair, fibers, body fluids, fingerprints, gunshot residue, fire accelerants, documents, soil, metals, polymers, glass. On her best day, she found a whole story contained in the pull tab of a hoodie. Another day, she unlocked a riddle with one single strand of hair. So why couldn't she solve this problem, too?

———

When Frankie was born, Kate began noticing how quickly Peter poured that first drink after coming home from work, how eager he was to get to it, but she thought maybe she was just jealous that he could stick to the old routine when she was always worried about nursing, pumping, getting a decent night's sleep. There was nothing wrong with a man having a drink at the end of a long day. Her father had always had two whiskeys while he watched the evening news, and the sight of his glass sweating rings on the *TV Guide* where he set it down was always comforting, a sign that he was home safe.

So when, exactly, did the sound of a bottle clinking against the kitchen counter and the second clink of a glass set down beside it begin to annoy her as the years went by? In her most reflective moments—alone in the car on her way to work, or in the shower before the rest of them woke up for the day—it didn't seem fair that she should feel angry with him for having a drink when it so rarely showed on him. He's bigger than I am, she told herself, seventy pounds heavier. He can handle a lot more. He always cleaned up after dinner, helped bathe the children, read them their books. When they were infants he did his best to soothe them when they cried in the middle of the night. He'd put a hand on Kate's hip and tell her to keep sleeping, and then he'd pick up Frankie or, two years later, Molly, and rock them or offer a bottle or a song hummed low. It wasn't his fault that neither of the kids ever settled until Kate had them in her arms.

Once when Molly was about a year old, she started wailing in the middle of the night, which wasn't unusual. Kate was so exhausted that she rolled over to ask Peter to please go pick her up, but Peter wasn't there. So Kate went to Molly, tried to get her to breastfeed, and when she refused, using her angry little fists to push Kate's breast away, Kate went downstairs to warm a bottle. When she got to the bottom step, she thought she saw something dark on the living room rug, and when she flicked on the light, she gasped. A bottle of wine had tipped over, staining the cream carpet a deep blood red. "Peter," she said, trying to nudge him awake. She thought back to earlier in the day: two vodka sodas when he came home from work; they'd split a bottle of wine with dinner but actually Kate had had only one glass, and he'd had the rest; a few beers after dinner, she didn't know how many; and this, a different bottle of wine. Not an extraordinary amount, but it was a lot when she added it up, a lot for a Tuesday night, a lot considering he'd had the same the night before and would have the same the next night. How much did other people drink when they were at home doing nothing? she wondered.

The thing was, he didn't really drink that much when they went out, met up with friends. A few, yes, but at the same pace as everyone else. If she told him ahead of time that she wanted him to drive home, then that was never a problem. It was at home that he kept going and going. But he always got up and off to work the next day. He always showed up exactly when and where he was supposed to show up. He was patient with the kids, and listened to their endless stories, and he made funny faces while he plunged spoonfuls of mashed food into their mouths. Surely a person with a problem would have to call in sick sometimes. Surely a person with a problem would not be able to play rodeo with a toddler for a solid hour almost every day. That night, as she pressed mounds of paper towels into the carpet to soak up as much wine as she could, she thought back on a recent autopsy at work. A man had been found dead by a piling near Pier 57, and the death was deemed suspicious, though there were no signs of trauma on the body. Friends reported he was not a drug user. He drank a lot of craft beer, considered himself something of a connoisseur, but no wine, no hard alcohol. In the autopsy report, the pathologist had identified fatty liver with cholestasis, and acute portal fibrosis.

"An alcoholic," Kate said, looking up from the paperwork. "But his friends and family reported only beer. Do you think he was drinking in secret?"

"Not necessarily," the pathologist had said, looking at Kate with a curious expression. "His ex said he drank as many as eight or ten beers a day, every day."

"But no alcohol."

"Beer is alcohol, Kate."

"No, I know. I'm just—" But she didn't know, exactly, why she felt confused.

As she blotted and scrubbed the stain on the carpet, as she blocked out the pitch of Molly's impatient howls, as Peter snored on the couch and the television blared, she wondered if, in fact, she had no idea what a problem looked like.

The next morning, at breakfast, she found she couldn't think of a way to begin. As he waited at the counter for the coffee to brew, she asked lightly if he was feeling hung over. She told him about coming downstairs to find that stain, that for a second she thought it was blood.

"Hung over?" he repeated, folding his arms across his chest. She could sense his hackles rising.

"You had kind of a lot to drink."

Again, he looked puzzled. And privately, she understood. He'd not had any more than any other night, really, and so, for him, this conversation was coming out of the blue. It was only for her that something had changed. It happened while she was scrubbing the carpet, her heart racing like something terrible had happened. It was as if some blurry thing that had been hovering in the margins before finally stepped into view.

"Did the stain come out?" he asked. "I'll get at it with vinegar later." It was the sort of practical information he knew: for red wine try warm water and vinegar, plus a little dish soap.

"Might be too late for vinegar," Kate said. "But, Peter—"

He looked at her as if he already knew what she was going to say.

"You've been going pretty hard lately. Did you really have to open that second bottle of wine? The kids need to get to the sitter early this morning. I have to be at the lab by eight."

"And I'm up, right? I said I'd drop them and I'll drop them." He moved his broad body around her as he reached for his favorite mug, as he grabbed the handle of the coffeepot. And it was true: She knew she'd never have to worry. He'd get them where they were supposed to be exactly on time.

After that, Kate watched more closely, and all that did was make him cagier. He drank less when she was awake, and more after she went to bed. The number of drinks he'd had in a given day was always hanging over them, a tally kept by Kate. She never used to look in their recycling bin, but she started looking, and every Thursday morning when she peeked under the lid, it was full to the brim.

He saw her doing it once. He watched from the garage, probably curious why she'd gotten out of her car.

She gestured toward the bin and from the end of the driveway she called to him. "It's too much, Peter. I know you know that it's too much."

———

There'd been a simple arithmetic to life, two and two equaled four. But slowly, as years went by and the kids got older, started school, she often couldn't make things compute. He was still sleeping beside her at night, unless he was on a midnight tour. They were still doing steak on Sundays, pizza on Fridays. They still walked the same routes around the house, doing the same things they'd always done, more or less, but lately she felt a poverty of something—happiness, she supposed—deep inside her ribs, the place were she used to feel her joy spill over. What they'd told each other when they got married was still true, at least for her. She wanted to work, come home to him, discuss their days, eat meals together, go to bed. She wanted to watch a movie on the weekend, maybe go for a long walk, maybe go out to dinner, maybe see friends. She wanted to be able to tell him anything and have him tell her everything. And there were some weeks, still, when they did just that. If they could do all those things and pay their bills and not dread going to work each morning, coming home each night, then that was a life. That was a great life, in Kate's view. What else could there be? If they reminded themselves that these small things were enough, she believed, then they'd always be okay. So that was part of their vows, all those years ago when they climbed the steps of city hall on a Tuesday morning, the first appointment of the day. They vowed to live simply and honestly and to always be kind to each other. To be partners.

But ever since the math stopped adding up, Kate was constantly puzzling over a problem that was so abstract that it was like trying to pin down a fog.

If she were at work and having this much trouble knowing the right thing to do, she would simply hand all the data to a colleague and ask for another opinion. But asking for an opinion on his particular problem meant betraying Peter, telling people things about him, about them. She couldn't tell her sisters, her mother. She certainly couldn't tell her father. Whenever she seemed even vaguely critical of Peter, he reminded her that she could always leave him, come back home, her bedroom was there waiting for her. The kids could sleep in Nat and Sara's old room.

"Are you happy?" her mother had asked her just a few months ago. Kate had taken the kids to Gillam for a visit. Peter tried not to go to Gillam if he could help it, and that morning said what he always said, that he wanted to get things done around their house. He insisted it didn't bother him to be there, didn't bother him to see his old house decked out in beige when it used to be blue. Didn't bother him that the cement steps his father had poured had been replaced with flagstones. And Kate could believe that it didn't bother him because everything he said made sense: The house looked so different he felt no attachment to it. And it was all such a long time ago. Yet it took something out of him, each time they went, whether he realized it or not. People recognized him there. They stopped him on the street and said it was so good to see him, asked how he'd been, said what a great kid he was and how nice it was now to see him grown, happy, a family man. Kate would think about how lovely it was to be welcomed home despite everything, that a native son is always a native son, but she'd turn to Peter and see that he was struggling to nod and smile and accept their greetings. No one ever asked for his mother or his father, and one time, when he pointed that out to Kate as the reason he found the encounters so exhausting, everyone dancing around what was there in front of them, Kate said that was out of respect for him, that they didn't want Peter to think they'd lumped him with those people.

Some of the retired cops knew he was on the job, and when they heard he was a captain, they said immediately how lucky Peter was to have come up at Francis Gleeson's feet. They were happy for him, Kate always pointed out. They didn't mean anything by it. "I know that," Peter always said, and denied that it bothered him, though for hours after he didn't pay much attention to anything anyone said. He and Francis were often in the same room together, but rarely alone. They would either sit in silence or else talk about the mayor, or football, or whether composite decking was worth the money. What was wrong with real wood?

Most visits, Peter avoided leaving the Gleesons' house at all. Lena once asked him to run up to Food King for something she forgot for their dinner—Kate and her sisters were occupied chopping and stirring and basting—and he went pale, stock-still. "I'll go," Kate said, grabbing the keys off the counter and giving him a quick kiss on the cheek. After leaving Gillam, he'd be near silent for days. Gradually, she began visiting on her own. On holidays they either hosted in Floral Park or went to one of Kate's sisters' houses.

"Your father and I—we don't think you seem that happy lately," Lena said to Kate.

"Of course I'm happy," Kate had snapped.

———

The first time he came home drunk in the middle of the day, a Saturday, she was so surprised that she'd laughed, despite her growing worry. Later, she was haunted by that laugh, what it said about her. Molly was around four years old, Frankie was six. He'd walked to the hardware store, claiming he needed something for the Christmas lights, and he stayed out for four hours. When he came home he was chatty, smiley, said he'd run into someone there. He'd grabbed her around the waist and pressed his face to her neck.

"Are you drunk?" she blurted. What harm? He'd run into someone. It was almost Christmas. It felt at least a little healthier that he'd gone out, that he'd been with people. Any setting was better than their dark house in the middle of the night.

It didn't happen again for several weeks. But then it started happening more often, and she began heading him off at the door when he came home from errands just so she could check him, see if he would be strange around the kids. One time she made him go up to bed and stay there though it was only five o'clock in the afternoon because her sisters were coming, and she wouldn't know how to explain it to them, so instead she told them he was sick. He once told her a cop could spot the drunk drivers not by how reckless they were but by how careful. Both hands on the wheel, never breaking the speed limit, until—oops—the car strayed over the double yellow for just an instant. She thought of that on the nights when he set out plates for supper—how careful, how deliberate. Or when he asked about her day, the way he neatly lined one word after another and made the right shapes with his mouth.

———

And then, on a random Thursday, Peter was a full ten hours late getting home, and Kate figured that he'd taken a double and forgotten to call. He usually ate his dinner at breakfast when he came home in the morning, so after feeding the kids she'd taken a pork chop out of the freezer. He still wasn't home by the time she had to leave for work, so she left and forgot about him, but when she got home in the late afternoon and saw the meat still sitting on a plate on the counter, long defrosted, she worried. When he finally came home, his shirt untucked, his face haggard and older than it was twenty-four hours earlier, she knew something had happened.

"Katie," he said, nearly stumbling into the house. He clutched his hair with both hands and then reached for her.

"What happened?" she said. "Tell me quick."

———

Her father showed up that night without invitation. Kate was on the love seat with the kids, looking at an animal encyclopedia Frankie had brought home from school, pretending that the three of them were home alone, that Daddy was still at work. Kate kept her voice light so that they wouldn't know how violently her heart was beating, that her hands were clammy, that she felt short of breath. She looked up from the book and saw her father's crooked stance silhouetted in the doorway. She must have sighed or made some other kind of sound because both kids looked at her, curious, and she had to clench her whole body to stop from crying when he opened her door. What meddlesome old-timer had given his former lieutenant a call, knowing the connection? Or maybe they were always calling him, giving him weekly reports. She could imagine the fight at home when he told Lena he'd be taking the car and driving all the way to Long Island. And in the dark, no less. When he stepped inside her house, he looked around so calmly that Kate wondered for a split second whether he'd come for some other reason.

"This is a surprise," she said, working hard to make her voice steady. He couldn't solve this problem any more than she could, and yet she felt all the blood inside her body heave with relief when he went down on one knee, held his arms out for the children.

"Pop Pop!" Frankie and Molly cried out, running to him.

———

Later, once she was sure the kids were asleep, she made him a cup of tea, but he refused to sit.

"We'll figure it out," she said, sipping her tea as if it were any evening of her life.

"Where is he, anyway?"

"I don't understand why you came all this way. It was a rough day. He's exhausted. Yes, he discharged his weapon in the line of duty. He's a wreck about it, but no one got hurt."

"By the grace of God. Or by dumb luck. One or the other."

Kate agreed, but silently. All evening long she'd been picturing the alternate universe where he'd injured someone, or worse.

"What's going on with him, Kate?"

"Nothing." Kate busied herself by brushing crumbs from the table into her cupped hand. "I don't know what you're making such a fuss about."

Francis looked stricken. "What if he'd killed someone? What the hell was he doing? Do you know if he'd hit someone, his name would be on the front page of every paper tomorrow morning? There'd be protests at city hall. They'd crucify him. And they'd be right. They'd be absolutely right."

"I know that, Dad. But he didn't." Kate sat on her hands so he wouldn't see them trembling.

"Where is he? I want to talk to him." Francis had looked into the bedroom upstairs when he went up to kiss the kids good night. He'd looked into the little den off the living room, where they had a small couch. He'd opened the door to the garage and flipped on the light. Finally, all his glancing around stopped when he considered the basement door.

"Just leave him alone," Kate said. She made a half-hearted attempt to block the door, but Francis pushed by her and leaned heavily on the railing as he made his way down the long, dark staircase.

"Peter," Francis said, standing over him. The air was stale down there, and the television was tuned to the channel that seemed to always be playing the 1986 World Series, the series that, Peter had once told Kate, taught him that anything was possible. He was sound asleep with his mouth open. There was an open bottle tucked between the couch and the chair.

Francis glanced all around the room. "How long has this been going on?"

Kate refused to answer.

"Bobby Gilmartin's son says they've been covering for him."

Peter shifted and kept snoring.

"That's not true. Don't make it worse."

"It is true, Kate." Francis peered at her with his one good eye. "Believe it."

They were like old-time telephone operators, these old cops. They knew everything and discussed everything and never for a moment imagined they weren't still cops, even if, like Francis Gleeson, they'd turned in their shields decades ago. She was furious at her father, at all of them, but a part of her knew that the longer she stayed furious the longer it would take for the shame to set in.

"He'd never drink on the job," Kate said. "It was an accident. He drew his gun, just as they all did, and he thinks he tripped."

Francis pressed the heel of his hand to the closed lid of his prosthetic eye. "What was he like when he left for his tour yesterday?"

Tired, Kate almost said. It was an afternoon tour, and every afternoon that week she'd thought: Today is the day he'll have to call in. But then, just like every day, he got into the shower at the very last minute. He shaved, pulled a fresh shirt out of a dry cleaning bag. He poured twenty ounces of black coffee into his travel mug and headed out. He was annoyed when she asked if he was sure he should go in, and brushed by her to the front door, to the sleek black Explorer that came with his rank, and it was true that he seemed fine. But when she stepped into the steam that lingered after his shower, she lifted her nose like a bloodhound and smelled gin.

"He was fine," Kate said.

"Peter," Francis said sharply. He leaned down, clutched the younger man by the shoulder, and shook hard. It was arrogance, Francis decided. Criminal arrogance. Just like his father. The father more than the mother, even. At least the mother had something wrong with her. A disease, maybe. But this was a crime of the ego, a person believing he could get away with things other people can't.

"I vouched for him," Francis said, looking down. "I said he was trustworthy."

"He is."

"There's more to this. I know it."

The phone rang just then and Kate took the basement steps two at a time to catch it, to get away from the rest of his thought. Lena. She'd figured out where Francis had gone, and begged Kate to make him stay the night. "His vision," she said. "He'll never make it all the way home. The oncoming headlights leave him seeing halos. He admits that himself. I can't believe he could be so reckless."

But when Kate hung up and looked at her father, who had followed her up the stairs, he seemed capable of driving all the way to the moon.

"You didn't tell Mom you were coming here. You didn't tell her what happened."

"No," Francis said. "I'll leave that for you. I'm just so angry. These fucking people."

"What people?"

"Peter. All of them."

"All who? The people on the job? Or his family? The people he was born into through no fault of his own. Are we back on this subject again? Or maybe we never left."

Francis stopped shifting and turned to her. "You see that, Kate? You see what you always do?"

Clutching his keys and glancing over at the basement door one last time, he told her that she and the kids could come back to Gillam anytime. They could come with him that night, if they wanted to. He looked down at the floor, again pressed the heel of his hand to his eye. How easy it would be to gather the kids, Kate thought, to walk out the door with him, to belt them in and sail to Gillam, tuck them into beds there— the sheets always clean and cool, the house always warm and open—and wake up and have Lena make them a pot of oatmeal in the morning. Later, Lena would peel potatoes into a bowl of cold water and have them help her, she'd show them where to place their knuckle on the blade, Francis would read aloud from the paper, and all of this mess could be left exactly where it was. She could take each child by the hand to the place where she began and forget all of this. *The kids.* Her father loved them and had doted on them from the moment Kate's belly began to stretch the limits of her T-shirts, but he also, clearly, didn't really think of them as being Peter's. It was as if he pretended Kate had hatched them entirely on her own. When Lena said, sometimes, that Frankie was like Peter had been as a boy, Francis would study the child as if to ask how in the world that had happened, and what else might be in store.

She knew that if she asked him to stay, he would. He'd settle right in on the couch and stay the night, the whole week. He wouldn't ask for a blanket. He wouldn't ask for a shower. He'd stay exactly where she needed him to be until she told him it was okay to go. Just imagining him there made her feel easier, made her feel as if she'd been thrown a rope, made her feel as if the very room they were standing in was more solidly constructed. She wanted him to stay so badly that she had to sit down, turn away from him a little or else he'd know.

"You're exhausted," he said.

"No, I'm not."

"He'll meet with his union rep tomorrow, I'm sure."

"They met today."

"Do you want me to stay?" he asked.

She felt a thousand pinpricks behind her nose.

"No," she said. "We're fine."

"I could leave before he wakes up. If you want me to."

"No. You go home to Mom." She told him to be careful. To let the phone ring once when he got home so she'd know he'd gotten there safely.

But he didn't move. "Kate," he said.

"Go," she said. "Please. I'll call you tomorrow."

She didn't move a muscle until she heard his car door slam, the sound of the engine fading down the block.

Once he left, she locked the house, turned off all the lights, glanced outside for no reason at all. And that's when she saw the little black sedan parked in its usual spot, where the Harrisons' weeping elm drooped over the sidewalk and into the road. It had been a while since she spotted the car, and seeing it there on that night of all nights seemed to mean something. She watched the car from inside the darkened house for a few minutes, peering through the slats of the blinds like a spy in a novel. When she grew tired of standing, she drew up a chair and sat.

She couldn't go through her routine as usual, not on that night. She couldn't just climb the stairs as if all were well, wash her face, brush her teeth, tell herself it would be better in the morning. He'd explained it to her several times but there was something missing, some crucial thing he wasn't saying. They'd been watching this particular ring for months. They had everything they needed to move in on them, and so they had. It was all planned, organized. Tours had been moved around so that the right people could be in the right positions. They'd already overpowered the room, were making arrests. The drama was over, and yet that's when Peter had fired his gun.

"What else do you want me to say?" he'd said when she asked him to go through it all one more time. "No one got hurt."

The chief had signed off at the scene, yes, but Peter was put on re-stricted duty within a matter of hours. Things happened. Kate knew that as well as any cop. But why restricted duty instead of modified, im-plying that they feared for his safety and, Kate realized only after a few hours, the safety of the people around him? What had he said or done in those hours after the shooting that raised an alarm?

"I'm going to ask you this one time," she'd said to him calmly, and when she asked the question, she braced with all her might for the an-swer. "Were you drunk?"

"No," he said, offended. Disgusted. And that's when he'd gone off to the basement.

I could leave him, she thought now. If they couldn't solve this prob-lem together, then she could solve it alone. She could pack a bag for each child, and go. Or better yet, she could hand him a suitcase and tell him to fill it and be off. She had a good job. The kids were in school. She had a family who would help her if she needed help.

Kate continued to stare out the window at Anne Stanhope's car. In-ternal affairs had interviewed everyone at the scene, and according to Peter they'd all described what happened exactly as Peter had. The room was chaos. He'd tripped on something on the floor. He headed to NYU medical center and his union rep met him there, but that was just rou-tine procedure after discharging a weapon. At the hospital, Kate knew, they would have tested Peter's ears, checked him for trauma. Maybe something that happened there—something he'd said or done—got him flagged.

It had felt for a long time like she was waiting for something, and now something had happened. She looked out the window at the black sedan and knew that across the dark Anne Stanhope might be looking back at her.

———

She never told anyone that Anne was tracking them, watching them all these years. She never even felt tempted to tell. Her mother had once asked her if she felt scared when she thought about Anne, wherever she was now, and Kate realized that her whole family still thought of Anne as a person on the verge of violence, as if until the day she died she'd remain capable of reaching into her bag and withdrawing a gun. Kate wasn't scared anymore, not in that way. She felt angry sometimes, but mostly she felt nervous, like she should apologize for something, like she, too, had done something wrong, though what, exactly, she wouldn't have been able to say. It was illogical. She hadn't done anything wrong— she loved Peter, and so she'd married him. It was George who mentioned to her, not long after she and Peter got married, that Anne Stanhope had lost a baby. She'd lost a baby so far along that he was nearly ready to be born. George told her that she delivered it stillborn, and Kate imagined the eerie silence of that room as other babies roared down the hallway.

Yes, Peter knew, George confirmed. He'd never told her.

Once, seeing the car out there, not long after Molly started walking, Kate sent the kids out front to play. They were at an age when they never played out front, at least not alone, but she'd sent them around front and watched from the garage that Molly didn't run into the road. Let her see them, she thought that day, they were her grandchildren after all. Later, she couldn't decide if she'd done it to be cruel or to be kind.

295

———

She was already outside, walking quickly along the front path with her heart pounding in her throat before she understood what she was doing. If what Peter was struggling with now was anyone's fault, it was his mother's. So then let her know about it, Kate thought. Let her carry some of the blame. Let her know that the consequences of her actions were still reverberating. Why should she, the person who'd damaged him most, be allowed to sit in her quiet car, watching without participating? Kate circled around the driver's side of the car and there she was, Anne Stanhope, twisted around in her seat and sound asleep. The car was littered with peanut shells and gas station receipts and empty coffee cups.

Kate knocked twice on the roof of the car, to wake her, then walked around to the passenger side and opened the door before Anne could object. She swept everything that was on the seat onto the car floor while Anne watched. The night was hot and the car smelled like old banana peels.

"Your son," Kate said. She didn't go out there for small talk or to catch up. She looked off at the neighbors' darkened windows and pretended she was talking to herself. Now that she was out there, sitting next to the woman, elbow to elbow, she had no idea what to say. Not a single part of her life was any of Anne's business. But maybe Anne could shed some light.

"Did something happen?"

"He had a hard day at work."

Anne waited.

"He discharged his weapon. No one got hurt, but still."

Anne rested her hands on the wheel at ten and two. "You talk like a cop. Are you a cop?"

Kate stared into the side-view mirror. "No."

Kate could feel Anne watching her.

"I think . . ."

"Yes?"

"He's been hitting it pretty hard. I think that has something to do with what happened today."

Any normal person would have known what she was saying, but one glance at the look on Anne's face told Kate she'd have to spell it out. She'd have to say to this woman, this stranger, what she'd not said to her own mother or father, her sisters, her friends.

But first: "He's doing great, you know. He's a captain. We have two kids."

"I know."

"He's a great father. He's so good with them. They adore him. It's remarkable." Considering his model, was the thing she wanted to add, but it was there anyway, unspoken.

Kate rested her forehead in her hot hand. "This is insane," she whispered.

"Did something else happen?"

"He's drinking a lot."

"No. Peter looks like Brian, but in that way he's more like me. He doesn't drink."

Kate looked over at the older woman, and when she saw that Anne was serious, she felt a laugh gurgling up from her belly. So she let it come and laughed until she was sobbing, her head hanging between her knees. Anne kept her hands on the steering wheel, white knuckling it, as if she were driving through a storm. Kate didn't care. The moment she'd approached the car, she decided she'd say whatever damn thing she felt like saying.

"I really don't know what to do." It was the thing she hadn't said aloud to anyone. Not to her father. Not to Peter. Not even to herself.

Anne released her grip on the wheel, sank back into her seat.

"Where is he now?"

"Inside. Sleeping."

After a few minutes of silence, Anne asked, "What are the children's names?"

"Frankie. As in Francis," Kate said. "And Molly."

"How old are they?"

"Frankie is ten. Molly is eight."

"Molly is a nickname for Mary?"

"No. She's Molly."

"Is there a Saint Molly?"

Kate looked at her.

"It doesn't matter," Anne said. "It just wouldn't have occurred to me to give a child a name like that. Did your mother mind? That there's no Saint Molly?"

Lena had not liked it, but Kate decided Anne didn't need to know that.

"I don't dislike it. The name Molly."

Kate made a sound that said she didn't care whether Anne liked it or not. The instant she didn't want to be in that car anymore she'd simply open the door and leave. But then what? Peter hadn't seen his mother since he was fifteen, but Kate had to believe that knowing one's child as a child meant always knowing what was most essential about them. Kate knew Peter better than anyone else in the world, but there was one person who knew him first.

Anne fiddled with something on her lap. An old booklet of CDs.

"I don't know how I can help Peter," Anne said. "But I would like to. I'd like to talk with him."

Kate tapped a song on the car door with her fingertips. A pop song that was on the radio every minute that summer. What did she imagine? That she'd march out there and Anne would be able to tell her the words to a magic spell, and then they could part ways again?

She thought of Peter, passed out in the basement, how he cringed lately whenever she tried to talk to him about what worried her.

"Okay," Kate said after a while. "You'll come for lunch. But I need time. I need to warn him, get him used to the idea. He's dealing with this thing at work and it's just too much right now. I can't tell him while all of this is happening. I don't think he could process it yet."

"When?"

"Two weeks from Saturday? What's that date?" Kate counted in her head. "July sixteenth." She took a breath.

"Did you ever tell him . . . that I've been around?"

"No."

"I wondered about that."

"It would have been too confusing for him."

Anne looked over at her son's wife, the mother of his children, and had a similar thought to the one she'd had so many years ago, after their confrontation outside the bakery on Lexington. He doesn't want to see you, she'd said to Anne that day. She loves him, Anne thought, and like most people, she thinks the things she's saying are true.

"Say one o'clock," Kate said as she opened the car door. It would be just the one time, she told herself. There was no reason to tell her father, her mother, her sisters. It had nothing to do with them; it only had to do with Peter. And they'd make too much of it. They wouldn't understand. Somewhere, fireworks were going off. Practice before the Fourth. She realized she was shivering despite the muggy night. Anne Stanhope would be standing inside her home, eating a sandwich, in just two weeks' time. It was incomprehensible. And yet, in those minutes alone together in Anne's car, she hadn't felt unfamiliar to Kate. Her profile. Her jaw set upon her long neck. Anne's was a name she'd been hearing since she was in her mother's womb. Even the way she clutched the wheel seemed familiar, almost like being with a long lost relative. And then, Kate realized with a jolt, that's actually what she was.

seventeen

T HE MEDICAL BOARD SCHEDULED a hearing for September. In the meantime, Peter was ordered to see the shrink twice a week. "Twice?" Kate said when he told her. "Jeez."

He should have told her they'd ordered him once a week, and then he could just go the second time without her knowing. But he didn't like lying to her.

He had his two weeks sick, then his two weeks vacation, and then when he had to go back they'd send him to a different precinct for an inside job. And then it would be just a matter of weeks before the hearing.

"But I don't understand," Kate kept saying. "What's the hearing for? What's the issue? If the duty chief signed off at the scene and no one got hurt, I don't see why there needs to be a hearing."

Day and night, he could see by the expression on her face that she was trying to figure it out. And she was right to be confused. Only Peter knew what she did not: that it was those hours at the hospital that changed things. And he already had an old CD in his file for showing up at Central with liquor on his breath. A Legal Aid attorney had made the complaint to the deputy chief, and Peter got called in the next day.

He told the deputy chief that he'd gone to the Old Town for lunch, had run into a friend, it was just the once, and the deputy chief had said it absolutely could not happen again. He also said that he himself thought he smelled booze off Peter once but he figured it was his imagination, now he wasn't so sure. He could have fought it, maybe, but he just accepted the CD and gave up the vacation days they docked and never told anyone a thing about it. What really happened was that he'd stopped into the Old Town for one because he liked the Old Town, and he'd been passing by. The bartender had given him a second. But two drinks in a two-hundred-pound man was nothing, had no more bearing on his day than having ginger ales.

Leaving that meeting with the deputy chief was one of the first times Peter wondered if he was liked on the job. He'd been promoted, he was respected, but was he liked? He had a reputation for being by the book. He went to the parties and he bought rounds but he kept to himself. He assumed that was a thing they said about him: that he didn't call anybody up on days off, that he didn't have other cops over for barbeques or help organize baseball games. Sometimes, at muster, before everyone settled down, he'd stand at the front of the room and shuffle papers for an extra few seconds so that they'd continue talking. It reminded him of stretching before practice at Dutch Kills, the rise and fall of their voices—then and now—passing around him like a river passes around a shoal. Officer Vargas had helped Officer Fischer put in a new master bathroom, and it wasn't the help that shook Peter but the fact that they so easily let each other into the most intimate parts of each other's homes. Some of them went on vacation together every year, weekends at Lake George or LBI. Their kids knew each other. Their wives spoke on the phone. It was all too close, Peter thought. He went to work and came home. He was a good cop in that he looked after his guys and they would look after him, but that was just being a cop. In a closed room, where no outsiders could hear or see, what would they say about him? He'd never wondered before, but now he did.

His father used to say that the only real difference between Francis Gleeson and him was that for some reason people loved an Irish brogue so they just couldn't get enough of the guy. Even after, when Francis was in a rehab hospital and Brian was directing traffic, he stuck to his story: people just loved Francis Gleeson. And then he'd throw up his hands as if to ask why they didn't love him, too.

Peter told Kate only that he went to the hospital to get checked out as any cop would after firing his weapon. What he didn't mention was that during the ear exam, when the nurse looked to see whether his eardrums were still intact, he could barely bring himself to stop pacing long enough for her to insert her instrument. His whole body was shaking. It was ludicrous that his gun had fired and he couldn't even understand how it had happened. When the nurse stepped out he asked his union rep, a guy named Benny, to go out to First Avenue to a liquor store he knew and pick him up a few of those little fifty milliliter bottles before the doctor came in. They both knew they'd be there for hours. He needed to calm down.

And when Benny kept refusing—actually, he thought Peter was joking—Peter crossed the room and pushed the tips of his fingers hard into the man's chest. He was in a hospital gown, black dress socks, but Peter was a big man, broad, six foot three, and Benny was a slight five foot nine. The doctor came in and saw it happen, and when his face snapped closed like he would not even be willing to hear Peter's explanation, Peter felt his body hum like an engine switching into a higher gear. He picked up the computer keyboard that was on the counter and whipped it across the room like a Frisbee. His eyes felt so dry that every time he blinked they burned.

The doctor stepped backward into the hallway as quickly as he'd stepped in. Next thing there were six people in the room. Benny, loyal no matter what, was telling him not to say a single word.

"Okay, Officer, uh, Stanhope," the doctor said, double-checking his chart. "We don't want to have to restrain you. We appreciate your work for the city and I know you've been through a lot today." Peter saw then that the large young man at the back of the room was holding a pair of padded cuffs in each hand.

He calmed down immediately, like a bucket of cold water had been dashed over his head. Yet another doctor arrived for a psych consult, and all the others left the room. It took so long that a tiny part of Peter hoped that Benny had taken pity and gotten the little bottles for him after all.

———

At first, when he was home, he tinkered in the garage all day long. He decided if he had to be home he'd at least make himself useful. He'd make a set of chairs or something and by the end maybe he would figure out why he'd behaved that way, why he couldn't stop himself. But he only got as far as the braces when he quit, drove over to the liquor store, returned, went down to the basement, and turned on the television. He felt Kate's eyes on him everywhere he went.

The problem started so long before Kate said anything about it that he felt sorry for her, in a way, because he knew she prided herself on being quick, on being observant, the daughter of a cop and all that. She didn't drink much but she was used to drinkers. As far as Peter could tell, Francis Gleeson had no fewer than three whiskeys every night of his life. She liked a glass of wine now and then but a second glass put her straight to sleep. And since the kids were born she couldn't be sleepy unless she was sure they were out for the night, which they never were. "Water!" they cried out long after lights-out, as if they believed she was crouched in the hallway, waiting to tend to their every need. "Light! Blankie! Book!" Every request was a ruse to get her in there to chat with them for ten more minutes.

One night before everything happened, a whole year before, maybe, just after they'd finished up dinner, she'd told the kids to go to the living room and turn on a show, and then she stopped him from heading down to the basement to say that she didn't like it, him holing up down there to drink by himself. For a second, for half a second, just before she spoke, he thought she'd sent them away so that she could kiss him, and his surprised heart skipped with pleasure. She'd been reaching out to him in her sleep lately, clutching him. She'd leaned against the wall of the bathroom that very morning and watched him brush his teeth. Under her gaze he'd stood up taller. Maybe, all day long, all she'd wanted was to get him alone, and the thought made him feel alive, giddy. Once, back when they still had a baby gate blocking the playroom exit, she'd put down the plate she was drying and removed his hands from the sudsy dishwater and placed them on her hips. The tops of her collarbones were just peeking over her blouse, and when he drew his finger along one of them he could see her gooseflesh rise. "Come on," she'd said, no longer grinning but serious, urgent, and leaving the dishes in a heap, they descended just a few steps down into the basement and shut the door. When she cried out he paused, the timbre of her voice sounded different, but she told him to keep going, and only later, when they returned to the kitchen, the kids unmoved from their trance in front of the TV, did she lift the back of her shirt—differently now—to ask if the skin was broken where the wood step had driven into her back.

As soon as he understood her purpose, he felt stupid for thinking she wanted privacy for any other reason. "Kate, please. I'm going down there to watch TV in peace." And it was mostly the truth. They'd banned TV for most hours of the day, but when it was on in the living room it was always a kid's show. If he dared turn it to CNN or ESPN, the kids whined and raged and threw themselves on the ground so that he gave up and turned the channel.

"That's the problem," she always said. "You're the father here. Would I have ever dreamed of telling my father to change the channel?"

But why bother when he could just go downstairs where no one would climb on him, no one would jump on the cushion right next to him, where she wouldn't see him sitting there and poke her head out to ask if he'd gotten a chance to submit those gas receipts, like he promised. Sometimes, from the very instant he turned off the car in their driveway, he felt hemmed in. Sometimes, he could hear the kids fighting before he even opened the door, and he'd stand there on the walkway just listening to them. The hedges needed trimming. Frankie might need glasses. Did they have coverage? The credit card statement listed a bunch of charges Kate couldn't identify, could he? Weeds had taken over the grass. Their taxes were going up. She was after him to take a look at the roof gutter, and the more she offered to simply call someone to come look at it the more he felt accused of something.

"It doesn't bother you? That this is all life is?" he asked her once, years before. She had Molly in her arms and was swaying back and forth, trying to soothe her. "What?" she shouted over the mind-bending pitch of Molly's cries. "Say that again?" He knew better than to say it again. Whenever their sitter canceled in those years, she'd spend a whole day at the lab with Molly strapped to her chest.

But this was different, he saw right away. It felt formal. Like an intervention of one. She'd been rehearsing what she'd say since that morning. "Well, if you want a drink, why not have it here, at the table? Why not with me? I'll have a glass of wine. Why go off by yourself? You stay down there all night sometimes. Why?"

There was no way to answer any of these questions. The truth was that he didn't know why, but she'd never accept that answer, and if he engaged at all, she'd only keep pushing, as if logic were at the center of everything. He could tell all evening there was something on her mind, and that it ended up being this made him want to put on his coat and walk out the door for a few hours. And when she saw that he was annoyed anyway—he knew the way she thought, in for a penny, in for a pound—she decided to go for broke.

"And also, where are those two wine club cases that came last month? It was a bonus month. I hadn't even opened the boxes yet."

"If you already know the answer, why are you asking me?"

"I want you to tell me that you drank two cases of wine in two weeks. I want you to hear yourself say it out loud." And then added, "In addition to whatever else."

"Fuck you, Kate," he said instead, and the blood drained from her face as if he'd slapped her. She dropped to a chair and stared at the wall with a bewildered expression. From the living room came the sounds of the Teenage Mutant Ninja Turtles. He'd never, ever spoken to her that way before. He regretted it immediately. He didn't ever speak that way. Not to women. Not to his wife. Not to Kate, the person he'd loved his entire life.

And as always in the first moments after a fight, he cycled through the same facts: He'd been in charge of himself since he was fourteen years old. He'd gotten himself through school, through academy. He'd flown up the ranks. He'd never done a single thing wrong. He'd never even been late with paperwork. He made a good salary. He took overtime whenever he could. Had she ever taken overtime? Not that he could recall. The kids, she claimed. She had to get the kids, be home for them, drive them to games and birthday parties and the pediatrician and get to class and get her master's degree, which would get her a raise of maybe two percent, all of which had already been spent on the extra childcare they needed for her to attend those classes in the first place.

He apologized for cursing. He apologized on the spot and about a hundred more times in the hours that followed. When after all those apologies she still offered no condolence, he told her that it was unfair of her to yell at him like that when he hadn't done anything wrong.

"Yell?" she said, turning to him finally. "Who was yelling? I wanted to talk to you about something that was bothering me." She sighed. Both of them knew that if they waited it out, it would blow over after a few days. Neither of them could go that long without speaking. "Besides," she said. "We both know you only get mad when you know you're wrong."

She looked at him calmly, with clear eyes. "I hate fighting. I have to tell you something and I want you to listen now, Peter. Listen to what I'm about to say. I won't live like this for much longer."

"Meaning what?"

"Meaning, the kids and I, we have options."

"And what does that mean?"

But she wouldn't say it, and he didn't ask again, and suddenly a door sprang open that he never knew was there, and he saw her walking toward it, a child's hand in each of hers.

———

Sometimes he tried to think of the beginning of their marriage, their years in the apartment and then their first years in the house. The memories seemed almost too sweet to be real. Did they have arguments? They must have, but he couldn't recall any. One time, before Frankie was born, they were afraid they'd be short on the mortgage payment that month, so they hauled the contents of their giant coin jar to the bank to pour it bit by bit into the sorting machine. It was so heavy they'd had to split the load into three backpacks and Peter had to carry two of them. The total came to eight hundred fifty seven dollars, and as the cashier counted out their money in twenties, it felt like a million.

They did all the things they imagined any couple would do: trivia night at a local bar, movies, Saturday morning hikes with sandwiches in their backpacks. Sometimes they'd remember their paper plane date, that night when they'd met up at midnight, when they'd run hand in hand down their street, and somehow, for both of them, that half hour alone on a neighbor's abandoned swing set was separate from what happened later that evening. Over the years the two events moved farther and farther apart in Peter's recollection. Had it really all happened on the same night? One very long night? Kate often spoke of the fantasy she used to have about going out to eat in restaurants with him. About being grown-ups, taking their groceries out of their car and unpacking them together. In the beginning, when she watched him dress, Kate would remind him that when she was fourteen, fifteen, sixteen, when her girl-friends were dreaming of mansions and fairy-tale weddings, this was all she wanted, to know Peter again, for the sight of Peter's naked back to be ordinary, for the clothes he wore yesterday to be tossed over the arm of a chair that was also her chair, under their shared roof, their babies asleep down the hall. For the shape and heat of him next to her to feel familiar. For their stuff and their lives to be mingled so thoroughly that they wouldn't have any idea how to separate them.

He knew exactly what she meant, but it was exhausting to think about it all the time, to drag the weight of their shared history around with them every minute of the day. They won. They were together. Why go over it again and again? Kate thought about their wedding day as a conclusion to something, where he thought about it as a beginning. Rising action versus falling action. They were reading different books.

"Behold," he would say, heading off her thoughts by gesturing toward the mountain of laundry spilling out from the top of the wicker hamper. "All your dreams have come true."

And besides, if their marriage was a conclusion to something, what did that mean for every day that came after?

———

At a few minutes before five o'clock on Saturday morning, just twelve hours after Kate told him that she'd spoken with his mother, Peter awoke from a dream of racing in a cross-country meet.

"Did you say my mother?" Peter had repeated the afternoon be-fore, stupidly. There was a storm coming. He could feel it in his bones, though the summer sky was still blue. Sure enough a slash of lightning cut across the sky, and when the kids came inside, screaming, Kate sent them straight upstairs so she could continue with what she needed to tell him. It wasn't what he was expecting her to say. She was nervous, so nervous that Peter braced for the worst. She pulled a chair to face his so that they were knee to knee. She took his hands in each of hers and he thought, She's going to tell me she's leaving. He felt a cold sweat spring up under his T-shirt, a low-grade nausea through his whole body. But it was like bracing for a punch to the throat only to get hit in the kidney instead. He was still trying to steady himself when Kate plowed forward with the details: that his mother had used a private detective to find their address, and then she'd just shown up at their house one night two weeks earlier. The night after everything happened on the job. Peter was passed out downstairs.

"Oh, fuck this," Peter said, dropping her hands when his mind comprehended what she was saying to him. He stood up, so Kate stood up, too. "What is this? What are you doing?"

"Nothing!" Kate said. "She showed up here! I couldn't let her in given the shape you were in, so I told her she could come back."

Peter walked out of the kitchen, pushed the back door open, crossed the yard despite the pouring rain, but Kate still followed.

When he accepted that he couldn't shake her, he stopped and turned. "We're talking about my mother." Peter looked into her eyes for absolute confirmation. "Anne Stanhope."

The timing was odd, Kate acknowledged, given all that had happened in the last few weeks.

"More than odd," Peter said.

"Okay," Kate agreed. But even before Peter was moved to restricted duty, Kate said, even before Anne showed up, she'd been thinking more and more lately about the fact that Anne had carried Peter in her body just as Kate had carried their children in her body. For so long, Kate had thought of Anne only as the person who shot her father. She'd forgotten that she was also Peter's mother. Not only in title, but in practice, at least in the beginning. Anne had spoon-fed him and soothed him and cleaned him just as Kate had done for their children, and that earned her something, didn't it? Kate asked Peter as she pushed her rain-soaked hair

310

from her forehead. It's not something she ever thought about before she had children, she said. How much work Anne had put in right up until the moment she and Peter parted ways.

"Maybe not having a mother in your life is the reason you . . ."

"The reason . . . what?"

"Come inside, won't you? Let's dry off and talk."

"No. Just say it. The reason what?"

"I don't know. I just try to imagine if I made a terrible mistake and never saw Frankie again. What gets more weight? The good or the bad?"

"Not seeing me was her choice, not mine."

"Now it seems she's making a different choice."

"So I should open my life to her? I'm almost forty years old. It's been twenty-three years since I've seen her. Twenty-three years. And she's had no interest in me or in us in all that time."

"Well . . ." Kate looked back at their house and didn't complete her thought.

"What? Is there something else?"

"No."

"What about your father?" Peter asked.

"I'm not saying I can get over what she did to my father," Kate said, "but for now I can separate that from the fact that she's your mother, same as I'm Frankie and Molly's mother. It's just an hour or so, and then she'll be gone. Because I do think she loved you, Peter. And I think it might help you to see her now."

He listened to every word, and when she finished saying what she wanted to say, he crossed the yard once again. For the first time in years he went to bed before she did.

———

Once in a while, when he awoke suddenly, he carried from his dreams a feeling of total disorientation, and in that half second, less, he understood that the person lying next to him was Kate but she seemed like a stranger, and everything about her—the shape of her profile, the scatter of her hair across the pillow—seemed foreign to him. Not only foreign but terrifying in its presumed familiarity, like one of those movies where a person wakes up in a different family and no one believes he's not who he appears to be.

"Are you awake?" he whispered, and though she didn't answer, he wasn't so sure she really was asleep. As he studied her—genuinely asleep, he could see—he felt a tidal wave of love wash over him. How desperate she must have felt to agree to let his mother come to their home. How he wished she'd just sent his mother away and never mentioned it to him.

"Kate?" he said. "Hey. Kate?"

"Yeah?" Kate whispered, eyes still closed.

"Do you remember the day I climbed the telephone pole?"

Kate was quiet, trying to remember maybe, or maybe had fallen back to sleep.

"It must have been summer because I was wearing shorts. We were nine or ten."

"I don't remember," Kate said. Over the years, whenever Peter remembered something that Kate didn't, her response was always to tell him he had it wrong, that she wasn't there, that he was thinking of someone else. That is, until he eventually coached her back into the place she'd boarded up: you were wearing this or that, it was your Frisbee, it was my Ouija board. They'd both learned that a memory is a fact that's been dyed and trimmed and rinsed so many times that it comes out looking almost unrecognizable to anyone else who was in that room, anyone else who was standing on the grass beneath that telephone pole.

Slowly, Kate's mind went quiet save for one small bell that rang from the way back. She recalled sitting on the curb outside her house, dropping sticks through the sewer grate. After a while, some of the other kids came around, and someone suggested they try climbing the telephone pole.

"Oh, I think I do remember," she said now.

"There's nothing to hold on to," Kate had said then.

"I can do it," he'd said.

It was something Kate might have done, not Peter, and he wondered now if he'd been trying in that moment to be more like her. He began by running at it and taking a flying leap, jumping as high up on the pole as he could get. Then, after clinging to it for a few seconds, he began shimmying up like an inchworm, hugging the pole tight with his arms while he brought his knees up, grasping it with his thighs when he needed to reach higher. She was the one who began chanting for him, he said. "Pe-ter! Pe-ter!" They rooted for him all the way.

And then, two-thirds up, he stopped. His arms were too tired and he was afraid he'd fall. Where Kate would have called down an excuse, a roadblock, a good reason to drop back to safety, Peter said simply that he was afraid to go higher, and no one made fun of him for it. The black wires strung from the top were maybe two arm lengths away.

So he loosened his grip and slid a few feet down the pole. Suddenly, he stopped and cried out, his whole body trembling. "Help!" he gasped, a strangled cry. He sounded like a girl and Kate giggled. Nat and Sara were there. The Maldonados. Who else? Then, before any of the kids could react, Peter dropped all the way to the grass and landed on his back. "Are you okay?" someone said, but he was moaning quietly, had drawn his knees to his chest.

Next thing, Peter's mother came running outside.

"Show me," his mother said as she knelt beside him. Peter parted his legs just a few inches, enough for her to see, and from his knees to his groin all along the most tender skin of his thighs were dozens of splinters. Kate ran her hand up and down the telephone pole and winced. It was smooth on the upward stroke, but rough coming down.

And, lying in a bed fifty miles and thirty years away, Kate felt the roughness of that pole on her palm, a memory so strong she closed her hand into a fist. Like a circle drawn onto the night air with a sparkler, round and round and round as fast as a child's arm can swing, the entire picture hung there for a second and they both glimpsed it: Peter's bony knees, the sun-scorched grass, Kate at the pole's base gaping at him along with four or five other kids. Another circle appeared: Kate's father—five minutes later? A day?—yelling that one touch of those wires would have killed Peter, would have killed Kate if she'd volunteered to go first and had gotten all the way to the top. Kate waited until he was finished yelling, and then she asked calmly how the birds can perch up there if it's so dangerous.

"What about it?" Kate asked.

"I don't know if I ever told you what happened after."

So he told her. Inside his house, always so grave from the outside, so unfriendly, his mother had spread a clean sheet on the couch and told him to lie down. She put a pillow under his head. Before beginning work on a splinter, she dabbed the spot with rubbing alcohol, and as she drew each one out with a tweezers, she said how strong he must be to have gotten even halfway up that pole. She herself, she said, wouldn't have been able to hang on for even a second. It took nearly an hour to get all the splinters, and one, he remembered, was the length of his pinkie finger. She handed it to him for inspection. After, she drew a warm bath, unwrapped a new bar of soap, and told him to wash gently so there wouldn't be any infection. Before he undressed she came back with two butterscotch candies she placed on the lip of the tub.

"You know," he said, "to make it nicer."

Kate listened closely but couldn't make sense of it.

"I already know she loved me," he said.

eighteen

WHEN THE DAY ARRIVED that Anne Stanhope would be coming to their home, eating at their table, neither of them knew quite what to do or how to act or what to wear or how to explain to the kids who this person was who would be visiting later.

"Can you call her and cancel?" he asked at one point, but Kate didn't have her number, had no way of getting in touch.

"Well, when she comes, tell her I'm not here," he said.

"Really?" Kate asked. "Is that what you want me to do?"

He told her to leave him alone, that he needed ten minutes to think. But thinking only made it worse.

"Let's get the kids out of here," Peter said when he understood it was truly happening. Kate picked up her phone to call a friend who had two kids the same ages as Frankie and Molly, but she didn't end up dialing because she couldn't think of what reason she'd give for suddenly needing childcare in the middle of a summer Saturday afternoon. She thought about calling Sara, who'd moved to Westchester a few years before and who wouldn't mind coming to get the kids, but that would mean telling Sara what was happening. In the end, they decided to let the kids stay. After breakfast, Kate put on her brightest expression and told them she had something exciting to tell them, that Daddy's mommy who lived very far away was coming to visit that day, and was looking forward to meeting them, so they had to be very, very good.

Peter, pale and steely at the sink, crossed his arms tight and nodded. He forced a pleasant expression and her heart squeezed for him.

"You have a mommy? I can't believe it!" Molly said, throwing her arms around Peter as if to congratulate him on his good fortune. When the kids left the kitchen, Kate asked for a second time if he might think about calling George. Having another buffer there might make it easier.

"She won't like it," Peter said. "She's never liked him."

"She owes him."

"Exactly. That's why she won't want to see him."

"But you want George here. I can tell."

He did want George there but he didn't want to rattle her, not when she'd be nervous already. It was an old habit, anticipating her moods, and it came back easily. Kate said she'd seemed calm but that didn't mean she'd be the same person when she turned up that afternoon.

"Okay, you call him," Peter said. George had called Peter's cell phone at least a dozen times since the night he fired his gun, and that told Peter he'd already heard what happened. Mrs. Paulino, probably. She lived on the first floor of George and Rosaleen's building and her grandson was in the Fifth Precinct. He pictured the confusion on George's face, like she might have gotten her facts mixed up. For all he knew he'd show up at the house anyway, and at exactly the wrong time.

"No, wait," Peter said. "I'll call him."

———

George whistled down the line when he heard who was coming to lunch. Peter blurted it out so they'd move right past what did or did not or could have happened when he discharged his weapon. But George circled back. "Mrs. Paulino keeps asking me if I've spoken to you," he said. "Something happen?"

Peter told him, quickly.

"But you're on restricted duty? Not modified? A shrink has to clear you?"

There were only a few civilians who knew the difference between modified duty and restricted, but George was one of them.

"Yes."

"Something else happen?"

What else happened, Peter said, steering the ship right back around, was that his mother was coming to lunch in a matter of hours, and Peter would appreciate it if George could be there.

"Me?" George nearly shouted. "You want me to be there while she's there? Oh, God. Rosaleen is going down the shore later. Her friend has a beach house in Avalon. A ladies' weekend or something."

Peter didn't see what that had to do with anything, but if George wanted an out, Peter understood.

"Okay, well, don't worry about it. I'll let you know how it goes and we'll make plans with you guys soon."

"Oh no, I'm coming," George said. "You gotta give a guy a minute to think out loud. I got shook for a second is all. I'm coming. I'll just come by myself."

"Really?" Peter dipped his head and pressed the phone to his ear with both hands.

"You kidding me? Last time I ate a meal with Anne Stanhope she swung a vacuum at me. Can't imagine it'll go worse than that. And by the way, you should think about shipping the kids to a neighbor or something."

Peter laughed, and Kate leaned out from the kitchen as if he'd cried out in pain.

"They're staying. Kate and I already discussed it."

"More bodies if this goes bad."

"George," Peter said, but he laughed again. "Jesus, why am I laughing?"

"What else can you do?"

"Don't joke like that to Kate." Peter glanced toward the kitchen. "She's a wreck though she's pretending she's not."

"I wouldn't. Anyway, what do you want me to bring?"

"Nothing."

"And what about the restricted duty? What's that about? I'm confused."

"Oh," Peter said. The dread that had been lifted for a second or two felt heavier as it settled in again. "That's a mix-up. We're working that out now."

———

Kate cleaned up the breakfast dishes, wiped down the counters. She checked that the London broil in the fridge was covered with marinade, closed the fridge door, opened it again to check that the pasta salad was tightly wrapped. Then she did all of those things a dozen more times. She asked Peter what he wanted, what he envisioned for the afternoon, but he didn't know how to begin to answer the question, so he didn't respond.

Kate followed him around the house to their bedroom and then into the bathroom as he turned on water for a shower. She sat on the closed lid of the toilet while the bathroom filled with steam, and waited for him to talk to her, but he only washed himself, dried himself, got dressed.

"I keep thinking of what my father will say."

"You're the one who was all for this. You're the one who said yes."

"I know."

"So don't tell him."

"He'll hear."

"How?"

Kate shrugged. "He hears everything, eventually."

"Because you'll tell him."

318

Kate sighed. "It's like my mind is splitting into two. One part knows she's your mother and I'm willing to see her because of that. She must have done something right because here you are."

"But?"

"But the other part thinks of her as the crazy neighbor who almost killed my father. If it weren't for her, he'd have put in thirty years. He wouldn't have had an affair. Maybe my mother wouldn't have gotten cancer."

Peter put down the razor he was swiping across his cheeks. "Do you really think that? Even about the cancer?"

"Yes. Maybe. I don't know. There's evidence cancer cells multiply at a faster rate when a patient is stressed."

He continued shaving. "She has a lot to be sorry for already. I'm not sure we have to add all that."

"But those are my things. You have your things. I'm not going to take away mine just because your list is long, too. She's a destructive person. And here we are getting ready to have her over for lunch."

"So why'd you agree to this?"

Kate got up and rubbed a circle in the steamed mirror so she could look at her own face alongside his. She met his eyes, but didn't say a word.

All morning he'd been trying to imagine how he'd feel if his mother didn't show, or if she called and canceled. Would he be disappointed? Relieved? Both? The problem was that he didn't know what he wanted, he didn't know which way to root.

At one point, he thought they should invite more people. Neighbors. The kids' teachers. College friends. They should fill the house with guests so that they wouldn't have to look at each other and talk. But then in the next instant he thought that he should take her over to the beach to sit in the sand, just the two of them. She wouldn't be herself in front of Kate, in front of George. He kept remembering the kid he'd been— looking at the train schedule and trekking all the way to Westchester to see her—and he understood why he'd given up his Sundays. He loved her and he didn't like to think of her alone. But she was no more alone than he was, sleeping on George's pullout. She was no more alone than he'd been the day he walked across the hospital parking lot in Albany, already forgiving her for sending him away.

Thinking so much about his mother that morning also made him think about his father. When Frankie was first born, Peter would spend a whole weekend with him, then get to work on Monday and take out his phone to look at his picture. Would Frankie change so much over the next few years that Peter, too, might be willing to walk away from his son and never see him again? He wondered if Brian Stanhope ever thought about Peter, about Anne, about the life he used to have. He tried to recall his father's face but he couldn't see it. He remembered objects better. His father's car. His father's gun. The nail clipper his father kept hanging from his key chain. Not long ago, Peter had told Frankie to keep his back elbow up when he was at bat, and to always let the first pitch go by. Who had taught him that? His father, he supposed, though he couldn't remember when. He wondered if, standing in whatever southern city he'd settled in, his father ever marveled that there was once a day in March when he'd shoveled four feet of snow from his driveway. And that he'd had a son, who'd helped him. Peter had already brought both of his children to Citi Field, and he wanted his father to know that, somehow. To know that it was not actually all that hard to say you're going to do a thing and then to do it. How many times had he told Peter he'd bring him to Shea? And the craziest part was that Peter believed him every single time.

As soon as the digital clock on the cable box flipped to noon, he went down to the kitchen with Kate close on his heels. Without looking at her or in any way hiding what he was doing, he reached behind the cereal boxes above the fridge and, to Kate's amazement, withdrew a bottle. He reached up again to a different cabinet, to the topmost shelf where they stored a line of shot glasses they'd collected over the years, and he took out one small glass. Then, turning to consider her for a second, he took out another. He poured from the bottle into each, and Kate, realizing what a hypocrite this made her, threw hers down in one go.

"One more," she said, returning her glass to the counter. "For you, too. And then that's it."

———

The shots worked. Kate slowed down, stopped following him, stopped opening and closing the refrigerator door. Peter felt a calm settle over him. He had one more when Kate went upstairs to change her hair again. It was being observed that he hated, and so he decided when his mother arrived he'd listen to whatever it was she wanted to say in private. But then he remembered that Kate said she really wanted to see the kids, and that threw him off. Maybe it was them she wanted to see and not him. And why not? They were great kids. Funny and weird and smart. When one o'clock arrived the kids were outside playing tag with the neighbors. Molly fell trying to keep up with them and got a grass stain all down her dress. Kate brought her upstairs to help her change, to wipe her face, and they were still upstairs when a car slowed down in front of their house.

"Kate?" Peter called from the bottom of the stairs. "Kate? I think she's here. Are you coming?"

He knew she was up there, standing at the top of the stairs, listening. She was going to make him go out there alone. He swallowed, squared his shoulders. What did he care? He had everything. He had Kate and his children. She couldn't hurt him.

"Kate?" he tried, one more time.

———

Upstairs, Kate hugged Molly tight, and buried her face in their child's warm neck. Then, peering through the space between the windowsill and the bottom of the blind, she watched Peter cross the lawn. She watched him run his hands through his hair as he waited for his mother to open the car door. He doesn't know what to do with himself, Kate thought, and was instantly sorry she'd done this to him, forced his mother on him, ambushed him like this. She clutched Molly hard as she watched Anne step out of her car and face him. She'd looked so frail and haggard during their middle-of-the-night conversation two weeks earlier, but now, her face was shining, full of light, and she turned all that light toward Peter. She'd gotten a haircut. Her clothes looked freshly pressed. She reached up and patted him on the back, so he patted her on her back. They didn't embrace. They just kept patting each other, like a person might do to an upset stranger. Kate narrowed her eyes and could see that Peter was fighting like hell not to cry, his chest rising and falling. When he turned he had an expression on his face that she'd never seen before.

"What are we doing?" Molly whispered eventually, and Kate told her to count to thirty, slowly. Then she set her free to clatter down the stairs before her, to say hello to this grandma she'd never met.

———

As if the terms had been decided in advance, they didn't make any reference to the past. Without discussing it aloud, they all agreed they'd wind their way there, as slowly as they needed to go. They spoke of the kids, what each one was good at. Frankie looked like Peter but he also looked like Francis Gleeson, Anne said, and hearing her father's name come out of Anne's mouth gave Kate a jolt. Peter looked over at her. He'd felt it, too. But they recovered, moved on. They talked about the distance from their house to the beach, the quickest routes. Peter said they used to live in Manhattan, when they were first married, and Kate avoided Anne's eyes. They talked about the upcoming presidential election, how what had seemed like such a long shot a year earlier now seemed like a real possibility. They didn't ask Anne about what her life was filled with now, how she passed her days. Peter knew that she didn't like too many questions. Once they sat and had talked long enough—a tray of cheese and crackers on the coffee table, music turned on low so that the room would never get too quiet—Anne told Peter that she heard he was taking some time off, that he'd had a rough patch at work.

Peter looked quickly to Kate.

"Yes," Peter said. "We're working it out." To Kate, he already had that peeled-back look he got when he drank. She thought of the bottle behind the cereal boxes and wondered how many others were stowed around the house. He got up, left the room. Kate heard the rattle of the freezer door swinging open and without seeing she knew the frost on the Stoli bottle would melt where he placed his fingers, four brilliant fingertips and a thumb in the spots where he clutched the bottle in his warm hand and poured. The women met eyes and the problem they'd agreed to face together squatted there between them.

Kate thought about how old Anne had gotten, and wondered how she and Peter looked to Anne. Peter's hair had gone gray at his temples. Kate had been coloring hers for years. She had lines on her chest that used to fade by the time she brushed her teeth each morning but now were still there at lunchtime. Peter had deep grooves radiating out from the corners of his eyes. But they only noticed these things because they were still young and the changes were new to them. They'd be young for a few more years. Anne was so thin that the tunic blouse she was wearing kept sliding off toward one shoulder. Her clavicles looked like the handlebars of Molly's bike. She shifted in the chair she'd chosen, as if she had pain in her hips.

They were still in the living room when they heard George's voice, and Kate looked to the window to find him giving out Popsicles he'd transported in a cooler all the way from Sunnyside. He'd brought enough for the kids next door, for any kid who might show up.

Anne sat up tall and gripped her bony knees.

"Did Peter tell you George was coming?" Kate asked lightly. But when would he have told her?

323

"Anne FitzGerald," George boomed when he came in.

Anne stood up to greet him. "Hello, George," she said, and took a frightened step back as he rushed her, pulled her into a hug. And then, "You sound just the same as Brian. Your voice. For a second I thought . . ."

"That guy?" George said. "How can you even remember?" He greeted Kate as he always did, by hugging her tight and lifting her off her feet. He hugged Peter, too, as if he hadn't seen them only a few weeks before. Then, from deep inside a canvas bag, he pulled out a carefully wrapped bowl of fruit salad, a paper bag of rolls he picked up from a bakery in Queens. Kate could see that he'd decided to play it like a normal get-together, as if they did this once a month, all past grievances wiped from the memory board. "I'm starving."

One by one they made a single-file line through the house and out to the patio, where Kate had already wiped down the chairs and moved them under the shade of the umbrella.

Anne sipped her water, but felt so overwhelmed that she had to hold it in her mouth for a moment before swallowing it. She resented the fact that they'd included George, but now that he was there, it felt urgent that she tell him something. Silently, she practiced what she'd say and considered when she'd say it. Alone would be best, just the two of them. The kids would be upon them soon. Kate was slicing apples. Peter was opening a package of hot dogs and lining them up on the grill grate. My God, he was handsome. He was broader than Brian had been, more like Anne's own father, whose face she wouldn't have been able to recall until she recognized it in Peter's. And he was drunk. She could see it in the big movements he made when he reached for a knife to slice open the plastic packaging. She could see it in the way he planted his legs wide. But he was good at it, well practiced. She never would have known if she hadn't been looking. He kept up with conversation, added his two cents. George plopped down in the seat beside Anne's but jumped right up again when the plastic burned the bare skin below his shorts. He grabbed a beach towel that had been thrown on the grass and folded it up under him.

"Almost burned my arse off," George said to no one in particular.

Anne wondered if George could see what was happening to Peter. But one wrong subject, one wrong comment, and they'd slide right back down to the place where they began. She shouldn't have said Francis Gleeson's name. Another slip and Kate would decide she didn't need her help after all. Another slip like that and she'd be heading back up the thruway to her little studio that seemed so much emptier now. She'd returned home after that middle-of-the-night conversation with Kate and seen it for what it had always been—a place she was meant to stay for just a little while, not a home. But even as she coached herself to stay to safe subjects and to think hard before she spoke, she felt her urgency grow stronger.

"I want to thank you," she said without looking at George. He'd untucked his shirt and now there was a ring of sweat circling his belly. "For everything you did for Peter."

Peter turned from the grill. Kate looked up from the cutting board.

"It was an extraordinary thing you did, taking him in like that. I am very grateful to you." Anne's voice caught and cracked.

There, she said it, and right away she felt dizzy with the weight that had been lifted. Therapist after therapist had promised her that one day, when the time was right, this might be a thing that would be good to say, for herself as much as for anyone else, but she'd never really believed it until he walked through the door that afternoon. Until that hour, she never thought she'd have the chance. "We repeat what we don't repair," Dr. Abbasi had said to her once, and for so many years she'd taken the limited interpretation of that as pertaining only to herself, and figured she was safe since she'd have little chance to repeat her worst errors anyway, having no family left, no one to abandon and no one to drive away. But from the moment Kate's face appeared at her car window that night, she wondered if all that time she'd misunderstood the warning. That the "We" in the doctor's aphorism (one, admittedly, she'd rolled her eyes at when it was first delivered to her) was larger. "We" could include

Peter, could include his children, all the people connected to Anne by invisible thread.

George nodded once, quickly, caught completely off guard.

"It was my pleasure," he said after a moment, and then cleared his throat into his meaty hand.

———

They didn't talk about Gillam, or Kate's parents, or speculate as to what golf course Brian might be standing on at that moment. They talked about the food, and the oppressive heat, and how kids don't seem to feel weather the way adults do. Gently, in a roundabout way, George asked where Anne lived now, and when she told him, he asked whether she liked Saratoga. He said he'd been there a few times to see the races, but not for many, many years.

"I was in a hospital in Albany for several years," she said, as if they didn't already know. "So I was already in the general area." Peter wondered if she even remembered that he'd tried to see her that time.

"You heading all the way back up there tonight?" George asked.

Kate and Peter exchanged panicked glances. If she were any other guest, this would be the moment to invite her to stay. But Anne said no, she'd struck a deal at the motor lodge on Jericho Turnpike to stay for a little while.

"Oh," Kate said, and carefully set down the platter she was holding. "How long is a little while?"

"A week or two, maybe."

"Didn't you say you have a job upstate?" Kate asked. "An apartment?"

"Kate," Peter said.

"I took some time off. I had vacation days saved up." She didn't tell them that she'd never once taken a vacation day before.

Peter could see that Kate was thinking carefully about how to say whatever was coming next. So he spoke first.

"That sounds nice. Time off is good." He signaled Kate to say they'd discuss it later.

This is my fault, Kate thought. I invited her here. How could I have believed she'd see him just once and be on her way? But then she watched Anne cross the patio to the cooler of waters, settle into the seat beside Peter. She was an old woman now. Frail. Bent. Nervous around her son and his family.

"Here," Kate said, getting up to get her a pillow. The chair she'd chosen beside Peter was the least comfortable.

"Thanks," Anne said, and as Kate watched her tuck it behind her, she thought, She has no power over us.

———

Anne stayed until the mosquitoes came out and the kids paraded down in their pj's, their breath minty sweet. One by one they went around the patio, throwing their arms around George, then Peter, then Kate, and then Anne. "Good night," they said, and by turns the boy and the girl pressed their hot faces to hers. Molly extended her hand for an extra shake and wished Anne a nice trip back to wherever she'd come from.

"Molly!" Peter admonished.

Immediately, Anne liked the girl best.

Peter, getting up to light the citronella torches, thought, I can't expect it to be like this if we see her again. I can't assume she's always like this now. I'll take today and enjoy it—so far, so good—but I won't hope for more. She's interested today but maybe won't be tomorrow. He wondered if after all that time she was disappointed when she saw him again. She used to lie on his bed and name all the cities she wanted to visit with him. San Francisco. Shanghai. Brussels. Mumbai. But he'd never seen those places and neither had she. If they unfolded and unfolded the largest map they could find, where he started and where he ended up would be two small dots on that map, side by side.

nineteen

BENNY COULD WAIT WITH Peter up until the last moment, but when they called him, he'd have to go in the room alone. Benny went over once again the things they'd probably cover, and the best an-swers Peter could offer while not saying too much, but Peter was only half paying attention. That morning, twelve weeks after accidentally discharging his weapon, he'd sat on the edge of Kate's side of the bed and told her she might be right, that he might have a problem, but if she could just bear with him for a little longer he was determined to get better. He told her he'd been thinking about it for a while, about a thing she'd said a few weeks back: that not all problems looked the same, but that didn't mean they weren't problems. The things she'd been saying to him, the warnings she'd been giving him, it was possible she was right. It was still possible she was wrong, but it was also possible she was right. Ever since his mother's visit, he'd been trying to go up to bed earlier, and his latest trick was setting an alarm for midnight. The moment it went off he had to march himself upstairs. If he was holding a drink, he had to pour it down the sink. It had worked for a week, and then he kept pressing snooze, and then he just stopped setting it altogether. After that, he made a rule that he could only drink beer, no liquor. That only lasted for three days.

The thing was, he'd promised himself the night before that he'd only have two drinks. But then he'd had another. Then another. It was like running too fast down a steep hill, his legs flying out in front of him. He could not stop. That surprised him. He wasn't sure he'd ever tried before.

She'd looked up at him from her pillow, and for a second he thought she was going to say she was done, that it was too late.

But then she sat up and braced him by the shoulders. She tipped forward until her forehead touched his. "Thank God," she said. "Let's get through today, okay?" she said. "And then talk later? What time do you have to be there?"

———

The hearing was set to begin at nine sharp but at eight fifty-five the clerk came out and said they had to push it to ten. Bathrooms were down the hall. Vending machines were in the lobby.

Benny was going on about the pension hearing, the step after this one, if it turned out that they were going to force him to retire, whether it would be with disability.

"You think that's what'll happen?" Peter asked. "They might see this is all a big mistake and reinstate me at full duty."

"Yeah, they could, they could," Benny said. He'd never seen it happen, personally.

Waiting side by side with Benny on the most uncomfortable bench in five boroughs, Peter tried to think of the most damning things he'd said in therapy. Benny confirmed they'd have his psychologist's notes in front of them, the conclusions he'd drawn. It didn't seem legal. Benny agreed, but it was pointless to think about that because here they were. He wished Peter had told him that he'd signed away his privacy rights, he could have warned Peter to be more guarded during sessions, but Peter hadn't understood that they'd use those notes against him. He stood up and swore and tried to recollect what the psychologist's admin had told him: that they were gathering longitudinal data for the department. Also, if he didn't sign, his commanding officer told him, they'd consider taking his pension. He was a wreck before that first session and didn't even remember reading the papers he'd signed. What could he do? Benny understood both sides. Since Peter was also a commanding officer, they had to protect the people who worked under him. What if it happened again but instead of firing into a cinderblock wall, Peter hit a person?

"Do you think the department could take the storm that would come? They have enough bad cops to deal with," Benny said.

"I'm not a bad cop."

"I know that, Peter. But I don't think they'll risk putting an unstable cop back on the job."

Peter flinched. "I'm not unstable. They don't really think that."

"You know that's just the language, Interim Order Number Nine. That's part of the phrasing." Benny seemed to think carefully about what he'd say next. "There's just that one Command Discipline in your file. My sense is, internally, they think you're smart as hell, but they believe you're hiding something."

Peter remembered once again what he'd said to Kate that morning, how he wished he could climb into bed beside her and stay there until he figured out how he'd gotten there, and how to get out.

"Pete, between us, I haven't said a word to anyone about the favor you asked me to do at the hospital, but it's possible they know about that, too. There were too many people in and out and I know at least one nurse overheard. Had you been drinking that day?"

What was considered that day? Kate had worked overnight in the lab, so she was at home. She'd set herself up at the kitchen table with a pile of textbooks and index cards filled out with different-colored Sharpies. The irony was he remembered thinking life was pretty good in that moment. The weather was perfect, the garage smelled like sawdust, there was a game on the radio, he found a partial growler of IPA at the back of his beer fridge. He reported for duty at four. Technically, he had had a few drinks that day, but Benny should know as well as Peter did that time worked differently for people who work the midnight tour. Anytime Peter drove away from home and to the station house marked for him the end of one day and the beginning of the next. He left his house around three o'clock, and none of that happened until around nine o'clock at night. Agreeing that he'd been drinking that day would be implying something that wasn't true.

"Actually, don't answer that."

———

The doctors on the panel were two orthopedists and one psychiatrist. The orthopedists were there for the patrolmen who'd been on modified duty for broken legs, ruptured discs. The psychiatrist was there for him.

They began pleasantly. One of the orthopedists asked him how he'd been feeling lately, if he was sleeping well, eating right. When his answer came in too short, they asked him to elaborate. Was he still seeing his therapist? Did he feel he was making progress? And how were things at home? Things with his kids? His wife? How was his wife handling everything, in Peter's view? Peter reminded them—it must have been somewhere in their notes—that Kate also worked for the department, that she was second in seniority only to the director of the crime lab. They waited for him to say more. The psychiatrist referred to a note.

"And your drinking. Has it gotten worse since you were moved to restricted duty? We have a statement from a hospital employee that says you tried to get your union rep to bring you alcohol that evening? While you were being evaluated? You couldn't wait until you were cleared? Another hour, maybe? Two hours?"

Peter pressed hard on his thighs to keep his hands steady. He said the words he'd practiced. "It had been a very emotional night and I think I was in shock. But what happened had nothing to do with drinking. Still, if it makes the department feel more comfortable, I'm willing to enter a rehabilitation program if the department sees fit."

"Were you intoxicated when you discharged your weapon, Peter?"

"No."

"Do you believe it's possible to do your job while intoxicated?"

"No. Absolutely not."

They seemed to consider this but said nothing.

"And what about your parents? Your father, he was on the job, correct? You told Dr. Elias that you haven't seen your father in twenty-five years? And that your mother spent over a decade in a state mental institution as part of a plea deal?"

It was annoying to be asked questions that everyone in the room already knew the answers to.

"Can you describe what happened? The incident when you were fourteen?"

Peter had expected the question but now that they'd asked it, he couldn't think of a way to frame his answer. They had all the details in their pile of papers anyway. Why make him say it?

"Twenty-four years. It's been twenty-four years since I last saw my father. Not twenty-five."

"And your mother. It was a violent charge, yes? She shot your neighbor? You told Dr. Elias she had paranoid delusions. At one point she was considered schizophrenic but that might have been a misdiagnosis? How familiar are you with her diagnoses and treatments?"

"Yes," Peter.

"Yes what?" the psychiatrist asked.

"Yes it was a violent charge."

"And are you in touch with her? Is she still in treatment?"

"I saw her recently and she's much better. The medications now are much better than they were back then."

333

"Peter," the psychiatrist said, "you have to answer all of our questions. You can't pick and choose."

Peter sighed. "What happened then, the incident you refer to, it was terrible, yes, but my mother was ill and she wasn't getting sufficient support at home. I was a kid so I didn't know anything but my father, he should have known she needed treatment. But anyway, we've all moved on, even my father-in-law, and if he's moved on I don't see why it's relevant to these proceedings."

"Your father-in-law? What's his connection to that event?"

Peter sat way back. Had he never mentioned that detail? In twelve weeks of struggling to fill those therapy slots with talking, had he never mentioned that part? He figured they already knew. He thought quickly and felt them leaning closer, their ears perked up to receive his answer.

"My wife's father. He was the neighbor. He's the one my mother shot." They all leaned over their notebooks and wrote something down.

———

In the end, they didn't even bother to send him out of the room while they deliberated. He'd retire immediately. They'd continue paying him until the end of the year.

As soon as he stepped out of the room, there was Benny. And sitting on the bench next to him was Francis Gleeson.

"What are you doing here?" Peter asked. Francis had called the house several times to find out how things were going, what was happening. Peter didn't know if Kate called him back.

"I wanted to be here," Francis said. He was wearing his usual tweed flat cap pulled low over his forehead. He was the only man in the building who had not removed his hat when he came indoors. "How'd it go?"

Benny didn't need to ask because he already knew. "You'll appeal," Benny said.

Peter strode past both men to the elevator bank. He punched the button, but then made for the stairs.

"Did you tell them you'd go to the farm?" Benny called into the stairwell. "You said all that?"

———

Outside smelled like autumn, finally. His favorite season. The first sign of cooler weather always made him crave a stack of fresh notebooks, made him want to eat an apple and then run a 10K as fast as he could. Cross-country weather, those glorious perfect weeks between the oppressive heat of summer and the first bitter wind of winter.

Benny hurried to catch up with Peter in the parking lot. Francis wasn't far behind.

"Think about it for a week," Benny said. "If you don't want to appeal, I'll have them schedule a pension hearing." He tilted his head and put a hand on Peter's shoulder. "You good? You okay?"

"I think so, yeah. Actually, I feel fine."

"Peter!" Francis shouted from across the lot. Peter could see he was moving as fast as he could. Peter leaned against the bumper of his car to wait for him.

Benny excused himself, left father- and son-in-law alone.

"You need a lift somewhere, Francis?"

"No. My buddy drove me. I just wanted to say—"

"What?"

Francis held a hand up to shade his eyes, get a better look at Peter.

"Take it easy, okay? I'm on your side."

"You're on Kate's side, you mean."

"Yeah," Francis said. "That's right. I'm on Kate's side. But as far as I understand you two are on the same side."

"Why are you here?"

Francis looked around the parking lot. "I just wanted to tell you it'll be okay. You're a young man. This seems like the end of everything but it's not. I know what it's like to have to stop early."

Peter pulled off his tie and balled it in his fist.

"I'm a good cop."

"I know that."

"It was an accident. It happens pretty often, actually, you'd be surprised. Benny had statistics, specifics from other cases. As long as no one gets hurt, as far as I know, no one gets forced out."

Francis seemed to be considering his responses.

"That may be true but is that why you're out? Because you fired your gun at a wall?"

Peter turned away, fished for his keys in his pants pocket, walked around the car to the driver's side.

"I'm also here because . . ."

"Because?" Peter paused.

"I wanted to say you should still go to the farm. I'll help pay for it if they won't. If you guys can't. You and Kate. Or we can keep it between us. You and me."

"I don't keep things from Kate."

"No?" Francis asked over his shoulder as he shuffled away.

———

Kate had gone off to work that morning but when Peter pulled up to their house, her car was in the driveway. The kids were at school. When he went inside she was sitting at the kitchen table with a mug of tea clasped between her hands. Silently, he sat down across from her. She searched his face.

"They'll pay me through December," he said. "Someone will come around tomorrow for the car. Benny is going to work on the pension stuff."

She let out a slow exhalation. "Okay," she said. "At least it's over." She put her hand on top of his, warm from the hot mug.

"There are lots of things I can't do. Part of me thought I might pivot to security somewhere. But no security firm would ever hire a cop whose guns got taken."

He could see that Kate hadn't thought about that, that some paths would be barred now.

"I don't think you have to worry about that today, do you?" she said. "That can wait until tomorrow. In the meantime, I got you something." She went to the fridge and brought out a mini key lime pie from his favorite bakery. She placed it in front of him. As she stood beside him, he circled his hands around her waist, rested his head against her ribs.

"I trashed the hospital room," he whispered. "I got so frustrated. I just, I don't know. They cleared the room and gave me a psych exam. They brought in restraints."

Instantly, Kate felt a latch lifting, an edge of light spread across the whole night. It finally made sense. She remembered his missing boat from so many years ago, how he'd told her, later, that his mother had smashed it to smithereens, and a feeling had come over him that made him want to smash things, too.

"Did they use them? The restraints?"

"No," Peter said, and held her tighter.

"Good. Okay. That's good."

"I could still go away for a while," he said, and immediately felt her body tense up. "For a little while until I get a hold of this thing."

"Rehab," she said, just to make completely certain they were talking about the same thing. She put her hands in his hair.

"I've been so worried you didn't mean what you said this morning. I drove all the way to work and then I turned around."

Did he mean it? His thoughts on the subject changed every hour. Neither of them had said the word. An alcoholic was a person who stumbled and ranted. If he could just stick to a few rules. If he didn't drink at home, only at parties or if they went out to a restaurant. Only on Saturdays and Sundays. If he set limits. Only beer, no liquor.

Only during Mets games, like George used to until he gave it up completely. He was retired now and that meant his routine would change, and part of the problem had been the old routine. Maybe if they sold their house and moved to a new house he could leave all bad habits behind. Maybe if they moved to another state where no one knew them.

Then he thought about the kids, how they'd soon sense his life was oriented around these rules. He thought of Kate, telling him gently but clearly that she would leave him if he didn't stop.

———

Kate made all the calls. Once he said he was willing to go, she didn't want to waste one single second. By the time he changed out of his suit, she had information. Their insurance was decent but they hadn't paid into the optional rider and so most of what they'd pay would be out of pocket. She checked their bank balance, their retirement accounts. They almost never went on vacation and now they never would. But it was fine. Kate smiled, waving his worries away with a flick of her wrist. She didn't want him to stop and think about it because then he might change his mind. The customer service rep from their insurance carrier directed her to a designated department, and that person was warm and patient where Kate had expected hostility, judgment. When it was all arranged Kate said thank you, thank you so much, he'll leave right away. She felt euphoric. She had not been this happy in months. Now, finally, things were going to be better. The bills wouldn't arrive until he was healthy. They'd solved the problem together, as they always had, as they always would.

"Oh, Mrs. Stanhope, no, he can't drive himself. He needs to have a loved one drop him off and pick him up."

"He has a valid driver's license. He's never gotten a DUI or anything." Kate almost said that that was one thing he'd always been careful about.

338

"It's just policy. Should we schedule for a different date then, if that's a problem? He'll lose this bed but I can see if a spot is opening up somewhere else in the next week or two?"

"No, we'll keep it," Kate insisted. "He'll be there. It's no problem."

It was after one o'clock already. When Kate came home from work early, she'd canceled the teenager from up the street who normally got the kids off the bus. She called the girl's mother back to say she needed her after all, but the mother told Kate that in the meantime she'd made an orthodontist appointment, she was very sorry. The facility they'd arranged with was in central New Jersey, two and a half hours away, five hours round trip. She began calling around to see who might manage the kids for the few hours. There would be paperwork, no doubt. All in, she had to figure she'd be gone for at least six hours. "Stuck at work," Kate explained to the friends who lived across town and wouldn't see that both Kate's car and Peter's were in the driveway. She knocked on their neighbor's door, but there was no answer. She called the daycare where they used to send Molly to see if by chance anyone there might be willing to babysit for a very rewarding hourly fee. No one could get there on such short notice. Time ticked by. Peter was watching television upstairs in the family room, like he was afraid to go near the basement door. Kate called Sara, getting desperate now, but she didn't want to tell her why she was asking.

"I got my schedule mixed up. I have an important meeting. I'm so sorry, can you come?" But Sara said the earliest she could get there would be five thirty, which was too late.

"Is Peter okay?" Sara asked. "You sound weird. Wasn't his thing this morning?"

"Oh, he's fine," Kate said. "I'll call you later. I still have to find a sitter."

Peter had to be checked in by seven o'clock that evening at the absolute latest. Or else he'd lose the bed.

"You could try Mom and Dad if you're in a pinch," Sara suggested.

"Oh wait. Mom went up to the outlets with that friend she goes walking with. They usually get dinner, too."

She told Sara not to worry about it, forget she'd called, she'd keep trying.

After another few fruitless calls, she felt Peter's presence behind her.

"Call my mother," he said. "She'll come."

It was true that Anne seemed to be back, perhaps because she knew the hearing was that week. Peter saw her walking the turnpike a few mornings earlier, waiting at a crosswalk for the light to change, and told Kate as soon as he returned home, wondering if he was supposed to do something about it. They'd spoken to her just once since the afternoon they had lunch together, when Anne showed up at the house to drop off puzzle books for the children, ask how Peter was doing. Kate had invited her in but she would only come as far as the front room and wouldn't sit down.

Anne Stanhope alone with her children. Kate tried to picture it.

"Can we be sure she won't hurt them?"

"Of course she won't hurt them," Peter said.

"Of course? No, don't act like the idea is absurd. You know, we didn't ask her many questions but I'd like to know what medication she's on, whether she's seeing someone regularly."

"She seemed okay the day she was here, Kate. We have no one else. This is why she came back. This exact reason. In case we need her." He crossed his arms and considered another option. "Or maybe I should wait a week or two. Until another bed opens up. Maybe this is a little too rushed."

"No," Kate said. "No, you're not waiting." Seven hours at the most. Six if she sped. She handed him the phone. "You make the call. If she's there, tell her we'll pay her. Or don't. I don't know. Say whatever you think is best. I'm going to change my clothes."

She'd barely gotten untangled from her bra when Peter called up the stairs, "She'll be here in ten minutes."

———

When she arrived, Anne received her instructions like they were hand-ing her the nuclear codes. She didn't ask where they were going or why, though Kate had the sense that she'd figured it out. She asked them both to stay put while she looked over the list—what they should eat for dinner, where their pj's were located, what time they had to head to bed. Kate tried to think of a way to let Anne know that at almost ten years old Frankie would report everything to them. Any weird thing that might happen, he'd be ready with it as soon as Kate walked back through the door.

"If it's okay with you," Anne said, her expression so serious Kate de-cided that if whatever came out of her mouth was scary, she'd bail on the whole plan.

"Yes?" Kate asked.

"Can I take them for ice cream after dinner? There's a Carvel on Hillside Avenue." Anne produced from her pocket a map she'd printed from the internet.

A trip in the car. It was supposed to rain. The air already felt heavy with it. Kate could pick up a gallon of ice cream and drop it back at the house before they left. She could pick up toppings and they could make their own sundaes at home. But that would take at least twenty minutes.

"Yes," Peter said, before Kate had a chance to answer. He took out his wallet but Anne waved him away.

"Are you sure it's okay?" Anne asked.

"Yes, are you sure?" Kate echoed.

"They'll love that," Peter said.

———

They set off around three o'clock like two kids playing hooky for the day. Anne walked them out and sat down on the front step to look out for the bus, even though it wasn't due to arrive for another forty minutes. Both Peter and Kate walked around to the driver's seat of Kate's car and she thought he'd argue with her about driving, suggest they could switch seats around the corner from the facility if she was worried about their policies. But he walked back around to the passenger door without comment. All the way down their block, Kate kept her eyes on the rearview mirror, watching Anne. When they got to the expressway, Kate told him he could sleep if he wanted to, but he stayed awake.

"Let's head to Mexico," he said after a while. "A few days on the beach and I'll be good as new. My mother will be fine with them until we get back."

"Oh come on," he said after a second. "That was funny."

Traffic was heavy near the airports and then cleared to almost nothing. They sailed by the northern end of Manhattan and over the George Washington Bridge.

"If it's like this all the way, we'll get there in no time," Kate said. There was peace between them, a sense of bubbling optimism that Kate wanted to swim inside. She turned south on the turnpike and though she knew the rolling hills to the west were landfills, they were grown over with grass and she thought they looked beautiful. Nothing had happened, yet, that couldn't be fixed. And now nothing would. Together, they were facing this thing and battling it, side by side. Next to her, fiddling with the radio, he seemed healthier already, like the switch had already been flipped. They'd vowed to remain together through good times and bad, and now look at them. If these weren't bad times, what were they? And they were doing fine.

She headed west, south, west again, the road unfurling before them and rolling up behind them. How could she ever have thought that they might not make it?

"So what happens when we get there?" he asked, pensive now.

"They'll assess you, decide whether you fit the criteria for detox, then when they decide you do, they admit you. A few days of detox and then you get to work. You come home to us in a few weeks."

"And then what?"

"I don't know. But think of it as an opportunity. How many people get a chance to start over again? You decided to be a cop at twenty-two. Did you really think out all your options? Do you remember when you told me you'd decided? You'd never, not even once, mentioned becoming a cop before that day. Be a pastry chef. Be a librarian. No matter what you'll still be a husband, a father," she said. "Those are the main things anyway."

"You realize we'll have a lot less money coming in."

"Yeah, maybe. But more money or less money, none of it matters if you don't get your act together."

"For them," he said. "They're great kids."

"For yourself, Peter. Not for them. Not for me. For you."

They drove down a local road that was thickly forested on both sides. They passed a row of farm stands, boarded up.

"Did you really think about leaving?" he asked eventually. "Do you think about it, I mean? It seems a little quick, don't you think? Considering everything."

"Quick?" she repeated, and tried not to let it darken the bright hope that had kept her foot on the pedal for over a hundred miles and counting. "This has been going on for a very long time. You haven't been sitting where I've been sitting. And also, life goes more quickly now. Have you noticed that? Everything that used to move at a normal rate is moving faster now." What she didn't say: Technically, you're the one who would have left. I would have stayed and kept those kids exactly where they are.

"And you haven't been sitting where I've been sitting."

"No, I haven't."

"Okay."

"Okay."

Anne had the kids color pictures but that took only fifteen minutes, so then she had them make paper airplanes. Then all the paper was gone. Frankie dropped a crayon on the floor and the dog ate it before Molly even had a chance to scream. Then they listed all the amazing things the dog had eaten in his life, then they asked Anne if she had a dog, and then they had her remind them once again of who she was, exactly.

Frankie disappeared upstairs with some sort of electronic device, and she didn't know if she was supposed to stop him. He could be watching pornography on that thing, and then they'd blame her, say that she hadn't been able to keep a proper eye on them for even a handful of hours. The girl watched a television show about elephants, but that was over in twenty-two minutes and Anne was still heating up their dinner. It was the first time in several years that she'd used an actual stove, and not just a microwave or a hot plate. When the chicken was done, and the potatoes had cooled a little bit, she called them in to the kitchen. They were just getting seated when Anne heard a car slow outside.

"Who's that?" Anne asked them. She checked the instructions Kate had written out. "Who comes around at dinnertime?"

The kids shrugged, their mouths full of chicken and milk. Kate hadn't said anything about visitors. Anne stood by the table, thinking about what to do, when the car drove off in the direction it had come. She had two seconds of relief before there came a pounding at the door.

"Hello?" a voice called. Someone was rattling the doorknob, trying to get in. "Kate?"

The kids all sat up taller to listen. "Pop Pop!" Molly cried after a second, and let her fork drop with a clatter as she raced to the door. She unlocked the dead bolt, pulled the door open. Anne heard all of this from the corner of the kitchen by the pantry. She pulled back as far as she could and tried not to breathe.

"Where's Mommy?" came his voice, and the kids spoke over each other to tell him their news, that they'd gotten off the bus as usual but instead of their usual babysitter guess who was there? Their daddy's mommy! And she let them watch a TV show even though it was Thursday and she said if they did a good job eating their dinner they could go out for ice cream later. And their mommy wouldn't be home until very late because she was dropping Daddy off somewhere for work.

"Whose mommy was it?" said Francis slowly, and Anne could hear him getting closer.

"Daddy's," Molly said.

"She has white hair," Frankie said. "Short like a boy's."

And then he was in the kitchen, and she was caught. She pressed her cheek against the cool of the wall and counted to three before turning to face him.

"Hello," she said.

"Well, I'll be switched," he said, gaping.

"Long time," she said, taking in his face, his cane. "They had an emergency. I was close by."

"Yes, that's why I came," he said. He took a step closer to her as if to see her better. "I took a taxi. Sara called me and told me Kate needed me. The taxi cost one hundred and twenty dollars. Plus tolls and tip." How odd that he'd told her that, Anne thought.

The kids adored him, Anne could see. He looked around the kitchen as if to discover what other secrets it might be hiding.

"Give me a minute," he said to the kids, who were hounding him, pulling at him, trying to get him to hear their stories. "Pop Pop needs five minutes."

He continued to stare at Anne.

"How long have you been back in touch?" he asked, finally. He was breathing heavily, as if someone had cut off his wind.

"Not long," she said.

"I thought you lived up in Saratoga."

Anne felt a flush rise to her cheeks. He knew about the halfway house then. He knew everything.

"Yes, I do."

He folded his arms. "Free as a bird," he said.

She had only to look at his face to remind herself that he'd earned the comment. And she was free, in a way, except for the tie she felt to Peter.

"How have you been?" she asked, her voice so weak and small it scarcely sounded like her at all. She heard how paltry the question was against all those years of not inquiring. The scar on his face was both silvery and red and reminded her of the thin end of a tenderloin that had to be doubled and pinned up against the rest of the meat in order to cook through evenly. Why hadn't he gotten fixed up? Wonders could be done now with plastic surgery. She watched a television program a few years ago where a man had gotten reconstructive surgery after a firework had gone off just a few inches from his nose. At the time she'd thought that's how it had been for Francis, that he'd gotten a new face and been sent on his way. Now she could see that she'd imagined wrong. And yet, once she got past it, he still looked like himself. It didn't take over his face, exactly. He looked younger than his age—mid sixties, like her, Anne guessed. He was trim, hadn't gotten fat like so many men seemed to. He still took everything in with that one good eye.

"Jesus Christ," he said instead of answering. "They could have given me some warning."

"I think they had to move quickly," Anne whispered. She should leave. He could handle the kids; they knew him better anyway.

"Where were they going in such a hurry?" he asked. "Is he going to dry out somewhere?"

So unpleasant, to just put things out in the open that would be better kept quiet. "Why don't I head out," she said, "now that you're here."

It was hard to fathom that this tiny woman was the same person he'd been angry with for so many years, the locus of all his trouble. He couldn't stop staring at her, even when she looked down at the floor, over at the cabinets, her cheeks growing red and mottled under his gaze as if she'd been slapped. She seemed not harmless, exactly, but not dangerous either. She had no secret weapon, no intent to do harm. He'd honed his sixth sense as a cop, and that's what it was telling him now. She was nervous, quavering, her fingers dancing down the front of her shirt as if there were buttons there to play with. He saw, all of a sudden, that she was never to blame, not entirely. Where the hell had Brian been? And why had Francis gone over there in the first place? He'd been puzzling over it for more than two decades. All he knew was that when he looked at her now she seemed so weak that it would be pointless to hate her. He wanted to say something, but he couldn't think of what. If she stayed, then it might come to him and he'd have his chance.

"You might as well stay," he said. "You've never experienced bedtime in this house. It'll take the two of us. Plus if you leave now, they'll think I sent you away."

"Which I'm sure they'd understand."

"Yes."

The kids raced back into the kitchen, armed with books and board games. They dropped everything at his feet.

"Are you trying to kill me?" he shouted at them as they squealed and giggled and forgot Anne was there.

————

He had a feeling. Before he saw her. Something Kate said on the phone a few weeks back, about help arriving from surprising directions. And then in the same conversation she told him a story about Frankie, that he'd recently tried to break his remote control airplane rather than share it with their neighbor's son, that it said something about him that would probably always be true.

And then she'd asked, "Do you think a parent always knows a child best? Even when that child is an adult?"

347

Francis had said, "A mother maybe." For himself he couldn't have predicted half of what his daughters had decided in their lives. Kate choosing Peter Stanhope over every other man in the world was a riddle he'd never be able to solve. And then more riddles on top of that main one: that his Kate, his bright girl, chose to pretend what was happening in her house wasn't happening rather than face it head-on.

"Leave the kids alone," Lena said when he tried to discuss it with her. She always said Peter had been a sweet boy, and when you thought about what he'd been through, it was a miracle he was as normal as he was. And he loved Kate. That's all that mattered to Lena. They'd hurt her when they'd got married like that, without anyone knowing. They were too bold. People didn't get married that young anymore. They'd come to Gillam and told them together, the four of them seated across a table, Peter's leg bouncing, so nervous he spilled his glass of water all over the bills Francis and Lena had been going through just before they walked in. There was something pathetic about a young man so tall and strong being that nervous, and Francis had poured him a drink. He thought about that a lot now. How he thought a stiff drink would hit the kid hard but Peter had put it down the hatch like it was no more than a cup of lemonade. He should have known then, Francis thought. There were a lot of things like that. He'd known Anne Stanhope was not right in the head but he hadn't really known. If someone had asked him if she was capable of shooting a person in the face, he would have said no. Anne, herself, would have said no. Everyone in the world would have said no. After Kate and Peter left that day, after Lena cried a little at the table and said she'd been robbed of seeing her daughter take the biggest step of her life, she'd gone out the next day and bought Kate eight bone china place settings because that's what she'd have gotten her if she'd had a bridal shower, a wedding. Kate had giggled when she unwrapped the boxes. One gleaming plate after another. Little cups and saucers.

"We don't even have a vacuum cleaner," she'd said.

"That you can buy for yourself," Lena had said.

Natalie and Sara had gotten her something, too, but Francis couldn't remember what. The point seemed to be not the thing itself—linens, maybe—but a way to tell Kate that they were okay with it, that they understood why they'd been left out. And, that they accepted Peter. That they wouldn't object just because of who his mother was. They went to Macy's, and spent too much money on some useless thing, and had come home and wrapped it in silver and white ribbons and presented it to her, as a way to say they'd love him since Kate loved him.

That's when Francis knew all three of them were a lot more like Lena than they were like him.

There was something about seeing Anne Stanhope there, in Kate and Peter's kitchen, that didn't surprise him. It was a shock and at the same time it wasn't. He was never, ever fully rid of her. Seeing her felt like something inevitable had come to pass. Mostly, it made him tired.

Now she kept stealing glances at him, at her handiwork, no doubt. He wished he'd left the cane at home.

Frankie appeared in the kitchen with a look on his face like he'd been wronged. "We didn't get ice cream." His bottom lip jutted out. Anne's stomach dropped. She didn't want her first promise to be a broken promise. But she didn't know what to do. Would Francis Gleeson come along? Would she drive them all in her car and all of them eat ice cream cones like old friends?

"I said if they ate their dinner," Anne explained. "Kate said it was okay."

"Frankie," Francis said, leaning over so that their eyes were on the same level. "It's pouring rain out there. We'd have to get it to go and that's not as fun. And look what I brought." Francis reached into his pocket and took out two Irish candy bars, selected from the stash Lena kept at home.

Frankie was reluctant to take the deal but the siren song of those Crunchie bars was too strong. "Next time you come here, ice cream," he said to Anne with warning in his voice.

When the kids finished their chocolate bars and went up to brush their teeth—step one of a ludicrous multistep bedtime process—Francis thought she might sneak out, but instead she looked at him and spoke.

"How does a person apologize for what I did? I honestly don't know."

It threw him. It was a good question. He didn't think she'd come out and say it.

"That's why I never tried. I don't know where to begin."

Her brogue had faded over the years. His had, too, he supposed.

He waited for her to make an excuse. To blame it on Brian, or mental illness, or something else. But she didn't. The kids came back down. She took Molly up to read books. He took Frankie, who preferred to read aloud to him. They brought water, brought tissues, answered questions. The longer Frankie went on about which would win if a shark battled a killer whale, the more surreal it felt to be under the same roof as Anne Stanhope. He was tempted to sneak down the hall and check whether it was really her. He remembered a tall woman. Strong. She used to pile her hair on top of her head and wear bright colors and was beautiful, really, when he thought about it. But this woman was washed of color, and could fit into Frankie's clothes, almost. Francis came downstairs first and waited.

Eventually, he heard her footsteps on the stairs.

"You know," he said, once she sat. "I always thought the right thing was to help people who needed help, but after that night I changed my mind. I thought one of you would get hurt over there. But after, I decided I should have let it happen, whatever it was. I should have called the police and waited like a civilian. I should have just kept Peter at my house and let whatever was happening at your house play out. Even if you'd killed Brian or he'd killed you. So if I'd been let back on the job, I would have been a bad cop after that. I would have let people kill each other before I'd go interrupting again."

"No, I don't believe that," she said.

They were quiet for a long time.

"A teacher in Ireland suggested I talk to someone once," she said. "My mother died unexpectedly and I was having trouble."

"And did you?"

"Well, he suggested a priest. This was the 1960s."

"Ah."

"So I said thanks but no thanks. It was the same priest who wouldn't even let my mother be buried in the churchyard. Why should I tell him what I was thinking? There was a wall around the churchyard and they put her just on the other side of it. Unconsecrated ground."

Francis remembered a suicide in his own hometown, how the local priest wouldn't allow a funeral and so the death had gone largely unacknowledged, unspoken. His mother had brought the widow a dozen hot cross buns. He never thought about where the man had been buried.

"And in America, after I lost that baby, I should have talked to someone. But I didn't."

"Well, it wasn't done, really."

"It was. It was beginning to be done."

"By some people. But not by us."

"Did you talk to anyone? After what happened?" Anne asked Francis.

"No. Never even considered it. Wouldn't even know how to find a doctor like that."

"Did Peter?"

"I doubt it. Well, the department shrink, but only after this recent business. And anyway, that's different."

"They'll make him, now. If he's going to the kind of place I think he's going."

They sat in silence for a while, as the rain lashed against the door and windows.

"Listen. There were plenty of people who should have talked to someone, and who didn't, and didn't end up doing what you did."

She looked over at him in a way that asked if he was indicting her or forgiving her. It was impossible to tell.

"You didn't know what you were going to do that night any more than I did, I suppose."

Forgiving. Anne brought her hands to her face and turned to the wall. Francis considered what Lena would do, but he couldn't just walk over there and rub her back or make her a cup of tea. Lifting the blame from her a little was enough generosity for one evening. And it had surprised him every bit as much as it surprised her. So he got up and stood by the window to give her privacy.

There were years when it felt important to hate her, but those years had passed, he realized now. He felt sorry for her, mostly. She had so little. Even knowing nothing about her life, he could sense the loneliness rising up from her skin and filling the space around her. And he had a lot. Three daughters he could visit anytime. Seven grandchildren. Lena. When he fell in the yard at the beginning of the summer, all four of them were there standing over him within the hour, deciding as one whether he should go to the hospital. Who did she have?

And while he lightened her burden, he felt he'd lightened his, too. It was the truth, what he'd said.

———

Kate pulled in just after nine o'clock and when she saw her father's shape through the window, she considered backing right out again. Of course, she thought, and saw exactly how it had happened: Sara had called him despite Kate telling her not to and he'd called a cab right away. Lena had given him hell last time he drove alone to Long Island, and he promised her he'd never do it again if she wasn't okay with it. He'd kept his promise. Kate considered turning around and calling to say she'd been delayed, that there was a storm that was too heavy to drive through. There really had been a storm. That part wouldn't be a lie. But then he was at the window, a silhouette against a bright backdrop, his hand cupped to the glass, peering out.

Where the drive there had been fragile with hope, a crystal ball they handled tenderly as they tried to make out the scenes inside, the drive home was hazed over with sadness, and there were times when her chest felt so heavy that she considered pulling over to catch her breath. When the rain came down too hard for the wipers to keep up, she stopped at a donut shop to get coffee but didn't have the energy to get out of the car. He'd kept it together through the assessment. He'd answered all their questions honestly and he'd asked that she be allowed to stay. Some of his answers had chilled her, and she didn't realize she'd started trembling until a counselor took her hand and squeezed. Among the questions: had he ever thought of harming himself? A pause so brief only she, the person who knew him best in the world, would notice. "No," he said, and they didn't doubt it, she saw, even as a vast, terrifying crevasse opened up under her ribs. They had Kate and Peter step out for a moment while they discussed his case, and he was calm in the little waiting area, spent from answering so many questions—not just those she'd witnessed, he reminded her, but the questions of that morning, and of the past twelve weeks—that he seemed almost sleepy, but then when they came back out and handed him the paperwork that meant he'd be admitted, he'd turned to her like an animal caught in a snare and she'd almost, almost, taken him by the hand and led him back outside. It seemed like a thing that they could work out together, just the two of them, and now that he was saying all the things she'd wanted him to say—the truth, the details—maybe they really could. Maybe they didn't need these people at all. She'd take a leave from work and they'd come up with a plan. They'd take out a second mortgage on the house while she locked him in a room with her and they figured the whole thing out.

"Kate?" he said, his hand poised over the signature line, and next thing she was ushered out, and a woman named Marisol tried to console her by telling her that they wouldn't take his bullshit there.

"Don't talk about him like that," Kate said. "You don't know what he's been through. You have no idea." She hadn't read enough about this specific facility. She'd done a quick search, read a little online, but it was the only bed available to them within two hundred miles and partially covered by insurance so she'd jumped. Now she wished she'd paused. He'd never been unkind to anyone in his entire life. He was generous, and fair, and patient, and he didn't deserve their unkindness now, if that was the approach they were going to take.

And then she remembered that someone could have gotten killed when he fired his weapon. A fellow officer. An innocent bystander. A child.

"Hey, hey, hey," Marisol said, rubbing Kate's arm. "First time? First time is the hardest."

First time? So they all assumed there'd be a second time? And they'd just given him a speech about setting up for failure? She wanted to rake her fingers across Marisol's face. Instead, she turned and pushed through the doors, walked through the rain to her car, and sat there for fifteen minutes looking at the lights of the building to see if a new one would go on that had been previously dark, so she'd know which room was his.

———

In the hour since the kids had finally fallen asleep, Francis and Anne had talked about Ireland, about the mild winters there compared to New York, the cool summers, St. Stephen's Day. They sat stiffly at first, Francis in the armchair, Anne on one end of the couch, but then they relaxed into the memories. They'd both dressed up as wren-boys. They'd both traveled to and from Mass in a horse and trap. They both remembered food tasting different there, especially butter, milk, eggs. They were both lonely for Ireland in some ways, or maybe it was loneliness for their own childhoods, before they knew decisions had to be made, before they knew regrets would pile up. Francis could see that same nameless grief in her—not homesickness, exactly, more like a low fury at having to leave in the first place, and with so little money or wisdom, and to be in a place for so many years that was not home, though neither was home still a home, so where did that leave them? Anne was from Dublin, yes, but not Dublin City, as Francis had always assumed. They'd each had a dog named Shep. Neither of them had ever gone back. When Kate walked in they were talking about all the Irish who'd come to America fifty, sixty years ago but chose to be buried there when the time came. Francis remembered his uncle Patsy for the first time in probably a decade, the expense it had taken to ship his body to Connemara.

"You won't be buried there," Anne said. "Will you?" It struck her again how odd it was that they were sitting there together. Thanks to her, he'd almost been buried years ago.

Kate apologized for being so late. Were they really talking about dying? Being buried? The rain was biblical. There was a bad accident on the turnpike. For part of the drive home she tried to understand how the scariest person from her childhood was at that moment sitting in her living room, waiting for her, and that their worry for Peter, the person they each loved most, bound them, put them in the same boat together, and they could either row hard as one or else drift while he drowned nearby.

As soon as Kate walked through the door, Anne stood, looked ready to bolt.

"How's Peter?" she asked, and Francis looked up with the same question in his face. He saw his girl had the pale, dazed look of someone who'd been through it.

"They admitted him," Kate said. "So I guess we'll see."

So it was done, and she could go now, Anne thought. She could leave these people alone. When Peter returned she could return, too. Until then, the house was Gleeson territory, probably Lena would come and the sisters, whatever their names were. But then she thought of the children, upstairs sleeping, carrying her whole history in their blood along with Francis Gleeson's, Lena Gleeson's, Brian's. Anne thought of her first nights at the hospital, how strange it had been to sleep with a light on in the hallway as nurses walked through her room at all hours, pulling up her bedsheet sometimes without telling her why, rolling her from one room to another identical room without giving her an explanation. She wondered if they'd give him medication, and if they did, she prayed he'd take it and not hide it under his tongue or in his ear or drop it on the floor and kick it. The ones who did okay were the ones who gave over almost immediately, who showed up to group and participated and tried their best, and when she thought of the earnest young boy Peter had been, she knew he'd be one of these. He'd do everything they told him to and he'd be fine.

Francis said, "You have options, Kate. Just remember that. You and the kids want to move in with us for a while, we'll figure it out all together. Don't forget that. Your sisters have said the same. We all have room."

Anne turned on Francis like a whip. You shut your mouth, she wanted to say, and remembered once again what had bothered her so much about these people—their reckless way of talking, and advising, and being in other people's lives. And what was Peter's other option? Anne wondered. Me?

And then the thought she hadn't seen coming, a cry from so deep within that she felt weak with it, had to sit back down. Don't leave him, she begged Kate, silently, desperately. Do not leave him. He's been left too many times already.

twenty

ONE MONTH. A PAGE on the calendar.

When he left, the trees were still green and full. But during that month the leaves turned colors and fell, and the kids gathered piles of them to their chests and, shrieking, flung them into the air. The air turned cold and, overnight, Molly had two lines of chapped skin between her nose and lip. Two Saturdays in a row Kate raked the leaves onto a sheet, dragged the sheet to the curb. Frankie took one corner and lifted it so that the leaves wouldn't spill out. "Where's Dad?" he kept asking. And once: "Where's my father?" His face was pinched with the beginning of grown-up worry.

One morning as they were about to leave for the day—breakfast dishes scattered across the counter, jackets and hoodies in the same pile in which they'd been dumped the evening before—they heard a loud thump at the door and when they opened it—all together, all curious to see who might have come calling so early—they found an injured bird on their welcome mat, one wing still fluttering. The kids had to get to the bus stop, Kate had to get to work, but they all stopped, dropped their clutter of bags to the ground, and looked at it. Frankie brought a few seeds from the bird feeder and laid them by its beak. Molly went inside to get a tissue to be its blanket. Kate thought about how she'd get rid of it without them seeing—it was a goner, clearly—when next thing it scrambled to its tiny bird feet and blinked. Molly reached out a finger and stroked its wing and it hopped once, twice, and then zoomed past their faces and into the over-grown boxwood on their neighbor's lawn. They cheered, gathered their things. All three would spend the day telling the story again and again.

Backing out of the driveway, Kate said, "I thought I was going to have to bury it and then tell you guys it flew away."

Molly said, "Would you have told us a lie?"

"No," Kate said, but in the rearview mirror both of them looked dubious.

———

All day, all week, all month felt as if she were expecting news, but then the news, whatever it was, never arrived. The kids had apples for dinner. She let them skip their baths. She let them watch TV. If their clothes were cozy—sweats, not jeans—she let them sleep in them instead of changing into pajamas. At Frankie's Little League games she chatted with the other parents, and when they asked for Peter, she said he was so disappointed to have to miss this game but would definitely be at the next. Then at the next game she said something else.

When she spoke to Peter the conversations were forced. Things were going well, he said. He felt good. He missed them. He was looking for-ward to coming home. Kate clutched the phone and tried to decode secret messages. She told him that she wanted to picture where he was, the room, the windows, the blinds. Were there people listening? Was he allowed outside? She told him anecdote after anecdote, like throwing stones into a lake to watch the ripples rush toward shore.

"Let's talk in a few days," he always said as a closing. He didn't want to talk to the kids.

A freak October snowstorm came, and school was canceled for two days. The radio reported record-breaking low temperatures. Downed trees took out power lines all over town, and Kate started worrying about the pipes. She hustled the kids into the car and went to three hardware stores before she found a generator. "Don't turn it on inside," the salesman warned her after loading it into her trunk, handing over the manual like he still wasn't sure she wouldn't accidentally kill her whole family. "You have help? Someone to lift it out when you get home?"

"Oh, yeah," she said, waving his question away. At home she sent the kids inside while she contemplated the hundred-pound machine and came up with a plan. She went into the garage and brought out a hand truck. Then she braced one foot against the rear bumper of her car and pulled until her whole body shook. When she got it up on the lip of the trunk, she balanced it there for a minute to gather her strength again. From there all she had to do was give it one mighty heave and swing it down.

Sara visited. Natalie visited. They asked for Peter but they didn't push when they could see that Kate didn't want to say more than the plainest facts: he wasn't home, and he'd be gone for a few more weeks. Anne Stanhope had returned to Saratoga. She called once a week but their conversations were always brief. Francis called every night after the seven o'clock news. Kate answered only every third or fourth time.

She watched garbage TV at night after the kids fell asleep. One night she went down to the basement and sat on the couch she thought of as his. She ran her hands over the cushions where he often slept. She buried her face in the throw blanket down there and waited for tears. When they didn't come she climbed back up the stairs.

———

He was discharged on a Tuesday. He called the preceding Sunday to let her know. "Sorry you'll have to come all the way back," he said.

"Not at all!" Kate said. She did the math. Thirty-three days. The longest they'd been apart since the years they were apart. Whatever the bill showed it would be a little price to pay for a life returned to the rails.

She took the day off work. She kept the kids home from school and packed their lunch boxes with snacks for the car.

Traffic was heavier than it had been on the afternoon she'd dropped him off. Every ten minutes the kids demanded to know how much longer. The row of boarded-up farm stands they'd passed that rainy night in September were open, and Kate pulled over, wanting to get something she'd be able to keep, something with the name of the town on it so she'd never forget the place he'd come to save himself. Back at the car she unscrewed the cap to a jar of honey and let them each dip a finger to the first knuckle.

———

He was waiting outside, sitting on a bench under a maple that was ablaze with color, the bright red embers lying at his feet. He stood when he saw the car, and when he saw that the kids were in the back, fidgeting, applauding, his face broke open with joy.

"Hey," he said to her over the tops of their heads as they hurled themselves at him, told him everything at once.

"Hey," she said, but found she couldn't bring herself to move closer to him. It would be good to go through the motions, she knew that and scolded herself, but paralysis had set in. She should fling her arms around him like the children had. She should kiss him and squeeze him and tell him it would all be fine. Instead, she felt something withdraw—some of the warmth and hope and urgency she'd been feeling since she left their house, dinner in the Crock-Pot to be ready for them when they got back.

"You look good," she said. "Do you feel good?"

"Yes," he said, looking away.

Later, several months later, she understood that what she meant to ask was: "Are you cured?"

Anyway, he still would have said yes.

She'd scrubbed the house for his return. Made everything shiny, opened the shades so that the light would be there to greet him. She filled the fridge with fresh fruit and vegetables. The kids made cards and a giant banner. Still, for days and days and days, it was difficult to put her body near his. It was difficult to look at him head-on, in case he might know what she was thinking, in case she saw similar thinking working inside him. While he was gone she'd taken out their wedding album. Far from the linen-tufted and ribboned album Sara and Natalie had purchased of their own wedding photos, Kate and Peter's was a dollar-store album containing snapshots they'd asked strangers to take on their way to work. There was Kate, in a pale pink dress that barely covered her thighs, a lilac twisted into her hair. There was Peter, skinny and tall in a suit that sagged at the shoulders. Their arms around each other. Triumph in their faces.

He seemed so busy during those first days at home, when she expected he'd feel bored and lost. Mornings he spent on his laptop, then he went to the library, then he returned to his laptop. When she asked what he was doing, he said, "Nothing," without taking his eyes away from the screen. Benny called to tell him his pension hearing was scheduled, but he barely seemed to care. He took a call while pacing on the sidewalk, and Kate watched him from the window. He'd started drinking herbal tea while he was "in New Jersey," as they'd come to refer to it, and now he had ten, twelve, fifteen cups a day. She found the mugs around the house with the soggy tea bags inside like she used to find empty bottles. She almost complained about it—he could at least dump the bags, stick the mug in the sink—but then in a rush of remorse she stood in the middle of their living room, two dirty mugs in her hand, and vowed if he stuck to tea she would never, ever complain again.

Finally, after two weeks back at home, he told her he wanted to be a teacher. Specifically, he wanted to teach high school history. He'd had the idea when he was in New Jersey, and he'd begun putting feelers out. He didn't have a master's degree; he wasn't certified. But a parochial school might consider him. The deputy chaplain of his old precinct put him in touch with a Catholic boys' high school not far from where they lived. He had an interview scheduled for the Wednesday after Thanksgiving.

"Amazing," Kate said. "I can see you really liking that, Peter. Such a good idea." She was happy for him. Delighted. Relieved that this was what all that busy industry had been about. But it felt apart from her, and even as she agreed and kept agreeing that he'd be happy, that it was exactly the kind of total change he needed, she felt a shifting of plates, a fault line down the middle, him on one side and her on the other. All those blank phone conversations and he'd never once mentioned this. She was hurt but feeling hurt also felt selfish, so she tried to brush it away.

He woke early now, helped get the kids out to school. She could see him trying, willing himself to health, to happiness, and felt a swell of love for him. As she showered, as she dressed, as she backed her car out of their driveway, she listed over and over the things that made her lucky. It was a trick her mother had taught her for when she was down, and until now it had always worked. She tried to make herself understand how it must feel for him to have been something for so long and then to not be allowed to be it anymore. But on other mornings, when his enthusiasm for domestic life showed signs of wear, she felt all that sympathy collapse and she wanted to turn on him and ask if he had any idea how great she was, how great the kids were, how there were a million people in the world who'd love to be standing exactly where he was standing.

"Was it really so important to you? Being a cop?" she demanded one morning when he was wearing his concerted effort too close to the surface. Even as she said it she knew she was purposely overlooking some crucial details, but life went on, didn't it? Chapter over. Next. What was the point of being so broken?

He looked stricken, walked out of the kitchen, but returned not five seconds later. "You're harsh, Kate. Everyone says you're so strong, but what you are is harsh."

Practical. Level-headed. Mentally sound. Not harsh.

Blunt, maybe. Honest. Not harsh. How dare he.

They went on like this for weeks, two steps forward, one step back. But slowly, slowly, days seemed to pass more easily and Kate felt walls crumble. She tucked in closer to him at night. She put her hand on his back or his chest when they swapped places at the kitchen counter. One evening when he touched her shoulder, she turned and took his hand in hers, kissed his palm.

To save money they cut out the after-school program for the kids, and when Kate was at work he took them to the library for Lego Club and music. Molly announced at dinner one night that *allllll* the mommies liked to talk to her daddy, and Peter grinned at Kate over Molly's head, his face alive with mischief. He had dinner ready most evenings when Kate got home from work. He started going to AA meetings, telling Kate exactly where a particular meeting was, what time it began and ended, even though she'd never asked him to do that. When he came home he'd sit close by her on the couch and ask about her day, tell her about his. She'd grill him for gossip about the people at the meetings, make him swear he'd tell her if someone showed up who would shock her—Frankie's teacher, for example, or their local state senator—and he just laughed, said he'd be put in AA jail if he ever did that.

One night, finally, he moved her hair away from her neck and kissed her throat, and then her mouth. He drew back when he felt her trembling, and held her tight for a long time and told her it would be all right, everything was going to be all right. When they slept together now it was on a shore so distant from the one they'd set out from that Kate found herself looking over her shoulder, looking back at the blinking light of their beginning to compare over and over the way things were then and the way things were now. What used to be fluent between them felt incomprehensible lately, far more difficult to translate. But things are meant to change, Peter said. Because life changes and people change. As long as we change together, we're okay.

On the day of his interview at the high school, just six weeks after he got home from New Jersey, he put on the same suit he'd worn to his hearing.

Kate could imagine how well the interview went. He knew everything about history, all the angles, the complexities. The boys of that high school would be lucky to have him, and it turned out the administrators agreed. They had him back for a second interview and then they offered him a job. He needed to learn how to plan classes and organize the units around tests, but they told him he could start after the Christmas break, when one of their teachers was going out on maternity leave. She taught American History II, so that's what he'd take over, but the following September he would teach Modern European History. Summer would be spent doing professional development. If he wanted to, he could coach the track team. After the second interview, the head of the history department, a man named Robbie who was roughly Peter's same age, walked him out and said that he remembered Peter from high school track meets, that in fact they'd run against each other. "Well, we were in the same heat a few times," Robbie said shyly. "There really wasn't any chance of beating you. Maybe you remember me? I ran for Townsend Harris?"

"You know, I thought you looked familiar," Peter said, though he had no recollection of anyone from Townsend Harris's team.

———

At Christmas, which Kate and Peter always hosted, Kate called around to her parents, to Natalie and Sara, to tell them that there would be no booze that year, but she knew that was depressing so if they wanted to go somewhere else she totally understood. She wasn't interested in answering their questions, but she knew they knew—Francis had no doubt told them and they'd all discussed together—so she figured she might as well let them know in advance. They all came—arriving early and leaving early—and Peter, though he insisted he was fine with them all coming as they always had, was awkward, uncomfortable. When Kate asked what was wrong, he said only that he hadn't realized they all knew.

He began to say it was fine, but he stopped himself and said instead that he wished she'd told him, that it felt like something private, his own news to tell, not Kate's, that was all. Kate could almost hear the therapist's voice in his words, encouraging him to say what he felt.

"I didn't tell them. I never discussed it with any of them. But you were gone for a month, Peter. They're not idiots."

———

Anne waited until Peter came home after his thirty-three days and then she stopped by the house, refused to come inside, and told Peter that she just wanted to see him in person, make sure he was okay. She told them that she hoped they'd come visit her sometime, all of them. She'd lived there for so many years and not once had she ever been to the races. The kids might like to see the horses run. "That would be nice," they both said, and as Peter walked her back to her car, Kate thought, I will never ever be visiting you in Saratoga.

And then, on the night before he was to begin his new career—three new pairs of khakis pressed and hanging in their bedroom closet, a new pair of shoes—he came home from an AA meeting and went straight downstairs. When Kate passed by the basement door she thought she heard a clink of glass on glass.

"Peter?" she called down into the dark. "What are you doing?"

"Nothing," he called up. "I'm just looking for something. I'll be right up."

She stood perfectly still. She held her breath. She could feel his still-ness, too.

"Why are the lights off?" she called down.

"I don't know," said Peter. "I'll turn them on. There."

The room flooded with bright light and he was standing at the bot-tom of the stairs, looking up at her.

After what felt like a long time she turned away from him, went up to their bedroom, shut the door behind her, and crawled under the covers.

The next morning—after he rushed around the house like a maniac searching for something that he wouldn't let anyone help him find, after he cursed to see the coffeepot had never been turned on, and after he finally drove away—she heard Frankie calling her, and she looked up to see a car she didn't recognize pull away from the curb.

"There you are!" Frankie said when Kate appeared. "A man dropped off Dad's wallet. He said Dad left it on the bar. He opened it to find out the address."

Kate held the wallet, and calmly, rationally, she recalled exactly what he'd said: it was a ninety-minute meeting, fifteen minutes away.

He'd been gone for over two hours and when he returned, just before he headed downstairs, he said he was going to get fat with all the donuts and junk people bring. "These addicts," he said, "they replace one thing with another."

"Uh-oh," Kate had said, easy in her heart now that he was home. "Don't say that, they'll send you to AA jail."

She remembered the clinking sound she thought she heard coming from the basement the night before, the expression on his face when he flicked on the light. She descended the dark stairs and saw immediately that the little blue cooler they used in the summer to take sandwiches to the pool had been moved. She opened it and found three little bottles, hidden under an old PennySaver.

She called up the facility in New Jersey first, as if she might be able to demand a refund. What kind of science did their approach rely on? Who were the doctors there? What were their credentials? Questions asked several months too late. She asked to speak to Marisol, the woman who'd first let the possibility of failure into the air and so the person completely at fault. But Marisol was unmoved, and her tone implied she'd gotten thirty similar calls already that morning. Then she called Peter's sponsor, a guy named Tim who'd scribbled his name and number on the title page of the Big Book. No answer. Then she called her father, who said he wasn't the least bit surprised, it was too much to ask a guy to go cold turkey, it was both unrealistic and unnecessary, and he never saw Peter getting on board with all that higher power stuff anyway. What he should do now is a quick dry-out again, then switch to brown liquids, only between seven and nine at night. The guys who had it real bad always drank clear. That should have been their first clue.

She called George, but before she could tell him anything he asked if he could call her back later because Rosaleen wasn't feeling too good and in fact had been admitted to Lenox Hill the night before.

"Yes of course!" Kate said. "Is everything okay?"

"Her heart," George said. "I don't know. I have to go." Kate hung up quickly, feeling immediately how paltry her response had been.

And then she saw it all so clearly, the whole trajectory of their lives, a twin flare of lights against the gunmetal winter sky: we're born, we get sick, we die. Beginning, middle, end. She saw her life as if held aloft by her own hand, and in an instant it spun away from her. Where did she want it to land? She was in the middle. The exact middle. Peter, too. How could she have failed to notice that the beginning had come to an end?

She couldn't wait until he got home. Instead, she got in her car and went to find him. In the parking lot of his new life, standing beside his new leased hatchback, she waited for him to walk out and see her and know that she knew. She had considered, very briefly, not calling him on it, not on his first day, not until he'd gotten a hang of his new job, but she quickly acknowledged that sort of discipline was beyond her.

"You want to see harsh," she whispered into the frigid air, the doors of the school as forbidding as a prison. She felt wraith-thin, old.

She thought of Frankie and Molly, who would carry their pain—hers and Peter's—for the rest of their lives if they weren't careful.

And then the doors opened, and mobs of people spilled out, and he broke away from the crowd and walked toward her.

twenty-one

APPROACHING HER, HE WONDERED how many thousands of times in his life he had looked out to find her waiting for him. How many times in his life had he turned to tell her something only to realize she already knew? That morning, coming out of the shower, her shoulders and back scalded red, she'd twisted her hair into a threadbare towel as the water ran down between her breasts. She said she was sorry she'd taken so long, she'd forgotten he'd need to get in there, too.

He cursed when the water ran tepid. He raced to rinse himself before it was ice cold.

"Sorry," she said again when he got out. She was making their bed in her underwear, letting the cream she'd rubbed all over her legs and arms soak in a little before dressing. He'd never, not once growing up, seen his own mother in her underwear, but their kids saw Kate all the time. They wandered in and out asking for things, for help, as if she were fully dressed.

But now he was the one who was sorry. He'd been almost unbelievably nervous for his first day, considering he'd been a commanding officer and thought nothing of it, but this was different. Who could spot a faker better than a class of eighteen teenage boys? When he began speaking to them, he'd looked out at eighteen sets of drooping eyelids, hanging heads. But he said what he'd practiced alone in the basement the night before, and one by one they perked up, cocked an ear to listen more closely. History isn't about memorization, he told them. It's not about studying, burying your head in a book. It's in our daily lives; it's now, living inside us. And he'd spend the rest of the year proving it.

He saw she was holding his wallet. He saw that she knew where he'd been the night before when he told her he'd gone to a meeting. This woman, the one who knew all the secrets of his life, was the one he'd lied to.

She handed the wallet to him in silence, her face pale under her thick winter hat.

"I'm sorry," he said. "It won't happen again." He meant it. But he also heard how cheap it sounded. All around them, car doors slammed.

Her eyes searched his. She'd come ready for a battle and now she didn't know what to do.

"Was this the first time? Since coming home from New Jersey?"

"No."

She hugged her stomach and dropped to a crouch.

"It was the third time. Just this week, Kate. I've been feeling so good I thought it would be okay to go to a bar like a normal person and just have two pints. Two. Just beer."

It was true. He'd had two pints, paid his tab, and left. He'd felt so proud of himself. But then, the very next day, he'd been standing in the kitchen doing nothing when the need to do it again set in. He felt it across his scalp, through the crook of his jaw. He felt the burn in his throat, the warm heat filling out his chest. So he went, again. Just two, again. Then the next night. But on the third night, he stopped at a liquor store on the way home to buy a few of the little airplane bottles of vodka they kept by checkout. A cop habit: he kept his cash in a clip and didn't notice he'd forgotten his wallet at the bar until that morning. He'd spent

370

all day wondering why he'd done it. He hadn't enjoyed it, and it meant stepping right back into the same rip current he'd worked so hard to swim away from. Even before she showed up he'd decided to never do it again, he told her.

"How do I know that?" she asked, and he could see that the question wasn't rhetorical. She wanted an answer with specifics, a plan of action. "How do you know that? Why should I believe you?"

When he couldn't answer, she got into her car and drove off.

———

At dinner that night and for the next hundred nights, he tried in every way to let her know it was all over now, it was all better. The need hadn't gone away—anytime he wanted to he could close his eyes and imagine holding the nimble little airplane bottles in his hand—but every day and night, he fought that need, and won. She did all the things she'd always done, except she didn't look at him, and whenever he caught her eye she looked away. She asked the kids for stories and responded to them. She asked how his day was and made appropriate responses when he told her. When he went down to the basement or into the garage for any reason at all, she listened to everything he did, every move he made, and when he returned she went about her business as if she hadn't been terrified. She cleaned and cooked and studied and rushed around looking for her keys. But now she did all of those things from within glass walls, and when he spoke to her, he felt as if he was pushing his words through a chink in the glass. He'd wobbled for a few days, yes. Yes, that night when she'd caught him downstairs in the dark, he'd lied. But he was not his father. He was not his mother. He was himself, and it was taking longer than he expected to decide what being himself meant. It was taking more than thirty-three days. She listened to everything he said, but for a long time she didn't react to any of it.

"What can I do?" he asked her one night, grabbing her wrist to stop her from following the kids up the stairs. Instantly, her eyes were full of tears and she yanked her wrist away.

"I don't know," she said.

He decided the only thing to do was be with her as much as he could. He started going up to bed at the same time as her again. On nights when she stayed up to study, he made tea and kept her company in the kitchen, reading the paper or preparing lessons. When she sat on the couch and tried to find something good on television, he sat next to her. She began looking at him again, sometimes just long enough to let him know that she knew exactly what he was doing. When he had to go through his boxes of old books to find something for his students, he brought the boxes upstairs and went through them in the kitchen.

"If you tell me what you're looking for, I can help you," she said, and together they sat on the floor, legs splayed, and flipped through book after book.

It wasn't that she didn't love him, he knew. It was that she loved him so much that it frightened her, loved him so much that she worried she might have to protect herself from it. He tried to let her know that he'd figured that out, finally, that there was no need to explain, but then he realized that she might not know it herself.

———

The school year ended and the long, empty summer stretched out before them. He took classes and selected only the ones that met in the mornings. He learned how to pace and map out a course, how to best deal with wayward students. Some of what he learned wasn't all that different from the advice he'd given to young cops. Kate had finished her thesis; all that was left was to defend it and then she'd have her master's. Before, when he was at the precinct all the time, he hadn't seen how much work she put into it. He hadn't really understood how important it was to her.

And then came one summer night in early September, their wedding anniversary, just three days before the start of a new school year. They'd gotten married so young that he kept calculating and recalculating to make sure he hadn't gotten it wrong.

It was a Saturday. After he came home from coaching cross-country practice, he helped Kate pack lunch and they spent the day at the town pool with the kids. But she seemed to be turning something over. Finally, when they got home, the damp towels stuffed into the washing machine, the kids in front of the TV because they'd earned it with all those hours in the sun, she asked, tentatively, if she should find a sitter so they could go out to celebrate. Fifteen years was no small thing. And they hadn't gone out to dinner in ages.

"It would be nice, wouldn't it?" She picked up his hand and placed hers against it, palm to palm.

"Yes," he said. "I'd like that."

"You think you can handle it?"

"Yes," he said. "Absolutely."

She smiled like the old Kate, and he saw that she'd been afraid he'd say no. A few minutes later he heard hangers sliding back and forth as she pushed around the clothes in their closet, deciding what to wear.

He chose the restaurant, one they both thought of as new because it had opened during those dark months leading up to his hearing. It looked out over the sound, but they didn't arrive until after dusk and missed the sunset. Walking from the car they could hear water lapping the shore. Once seated, a bottle of Perrier on the table between them, they discussed the kids for a while, the house. They talked about whether Kate's position at the lab would change. They talked about the school where Peter worked, and whether he should have become a teacher after college, whether he regretted not considering it when he was in his early twenties, when he spent all those months casting around for an idea of what to be. Since they were already on the subject, and as they were finishing up their meals, they wandered into other regrets. They began small. They began safe. The classes they wished they'd taken. The places they wished they'd been.

"But big ones?" Kate asked. "I've never really thought about it. What's the point? I guess I should regret sneaking out with you that night."

"But you don't?"

"I'm sorry about everything that happened after, but if we hadn't snuck out that night, maybe we wouldn't be together now. Frankie and Molly wouldn't be here."

Peter thought about that.

Kate picked up her napkin and folded it neatly before her. She smoothed the edges and then tucked and retucked a lock of hair behind her ear.

"I'm not sure it's a regret but there is something I have to tell you." She looked over at the table next to theirs, at the people sitting there. As Peter watched her struggle, he felt something inside him cave in. Her lips were pursed. A vein in her neck throbbed.

"What?" he said, and just like that the ground beneath him felt more precarious than it had in months.

"Your mother. When she showed up that night looking for you, it wasn't the first time. I spotted her years ago, when we were still in the city. Before we were married. And after. And a few times at the house."

"And what? You sent her away?"

"No. Not exactly. I just knew she was there, watching. Checking in on you. And she knew I knew. She didn't approach and neither did I. Until that night. I went out to her car because I felt like I needed help. I needed to talk to someone who loves you as much as I do, who was looking out for you first. So I lied about that. She didn't come to the door."

Peter leaned forward over his elbows to better understand what she was saying.

"All those years when I thought you were better off without her maybe you could have used knowing that she was there. Maybe it would have made things easier for you. To know she hadn't forgotten about you, that she did care about you. Maybe if you'd known that she was out there fifteen, seventeen years ago, you wouldn't have ended up feeling so lost."

It was news, yes, but not at the level she thought it was, clearly. As he'd tried to explain to her before, he never doubted that his mother loved him. But as Francis Gleeson had once told Kate, love is only part of the story.

"I used to tell myself that I was keeping it from you to protect you, but I'm pretty sure I was thinking more about myself." Kate was looking at him closely now, to see how he was taking all of this.

"Okay," he said. What would he have done if he'd known? Maybe nothing, just as she had done nothing. He felt lost long before his mother left his life, he wanted to tell her, but it would ruin their dinner, their night. He thought of Frankie and Molly doing their homework with music and talking and laughter in the background. The doorbell ringing, kids stopping by, Kate on the phone, pots boiling over, everything a chaos of love. Then he thought of himself at their ages, alone in a silent house, listening for a creak on the stairs.

"You're not angry?" she asked.

"No." He checked himself to make sure it was true. "I have to think about it more, but, no, I'm not angry."

He watched relief pass over her face, her shoulders relaxed.

"I have one," Peter said. He went back to the day they decided to get married.

Kate sat up straighter in her chair and listened so closely it was as if she'd shut an actual door against the noise of the other diners, against their chatter and the tap of knives on plates. Her hair fell over one of her shoulders and he thought about how lovely she looked that evening. He'd been looking at her face for so long that sometimes he forgot to notice it.

He'd been thinking about it a lot lately, he told her. That they'd just slipped into marriage, maybe because it was a fantasy they'd had as kids.

But he hadn't even had a ring. Why had she said yes? He always said he'd get her a nice ring one day, but he never had. She still wore that seventy-five-dollar band they bought on Bleecker Street. So he hadn't properly asked her, not really.

If she'd married anyone else, that person would have planned the question as an event, would have presented her with a beautiful diamond. He wished he'd done that.

She listened from across the tea lights at the center of their table, and then she threw her head back and laughed.

"So you don't regret marrying me, you just regret the way you asked? Oh, Peter, I can think of so many other things you should regret."

"Yeah." He looked down at his empty plate. "Probably."

"Hey. Come back." Kate covered his hands with hers. "If you regret it so much, ask me now. Ask again. Properly, this time."

But what would she have said, truly, if there'd been a way for her to glimpse everything that was coming for them? For the second time that night, he felt something at his center go unsteady.

The waiter came, cleared their plates. Still, she didn't look away.

"Things are better now, they feel like they're getting better—don't they? But there might be more coming. This might be the least of it. Have you thought about that? We knew nothing about what it meant to grow up, to be partners, parents, all of it. Nothing. And maybe we still don't. Would you have said yes back then if you'd known?"

"But I know now. So ask me."

But he couldn't find the right words.

"I'll give you a hint," she said, squeezing his hands until he looked up to meet her eyes. "Then and now, I say yes."

twenty-two

A YEAR PASSED SINCE PETER got home from rehab, since Anne drove away from Floral Park and headed back upstate. Anne didn't have a phone, so she left them the number at the nursing home, just in case they wanted to reach her for anything. Every time she arrived for a shift she checked the messages at the nurses' station. Peter called on Christmas Day and was surprised that she was there, working. She told him she was going to Christmas dinner at a friend's house that evening. That she was just putting a few hours in but then she'd head over. She told him that she was in charge of bringing a vegetable. She told him the friend was named Bridget.

But then she didn't hear from him again for months and months. Maybe she should have sent presents to the kids, but what would they have liked? She could have sent them each a twenty-dollar bill in a glittery card tucked inside a bright red envelope. Every year, when she sorted the Christmas mail for the residents, she got a pang seeing all those colorful cards, like ornaments sent through the postal system, and that year, just a few months after meeting her grandchildren, she received one: a green envelope that had gold leaf lining the inside. It was a picture of the children and on the back, the dog. She would have liked a picture of Peter, too. She put the card on the fridge and kept the envelope open on the counter until mid-January because the light from the streetlamps glanced off that metallic liner even in the middle of the night.

She wanted to go back down there but now it would be different. She couldn't just park and check up on him in secret. She'd have to go to the door, and doing that would be inviting herself, and maybe they didn't want to see her now that the crisis had passed a little. It was hard to know what to do. Kate had asked for her help that time but she hadn't really done anything, not really. Maybe Kate regretted asking.

Peter called again in May, just to check in, as he put it. He told her about the kids he was teaching, and about Frankie and Molly. Kate had written a very long paper and had gotten her master's degree.

"Everything is going okay otherwise?" she asked, not wanting to push. "You feel good?"

"Yes," he said. "And you?"

"Yes. Doing very well."

Before hanging up he asked when they'd see her again, but she didn't know if he was asking because he felt like he had to or if he really wanted to see her.

She knew he'd never tell her if things weren't going well, not over the phone. And he hung up thinking the very same thing.

And then, the week after Thanksgiving 2017, a Tuesday mid-morning, she stood at the window of her apartment and decided that she *would* send the children a card that year, each their own, so she wouldn't have to choose whose name to write first. City workers were outside on cherry pickers, hanging wreaths on the tops of lampposts. She'd write in their cards that she'd like them to pick a date to visit, but how would she put it so that it would feel welcoming but also let them know that her place was too small and they'd have to stay in a hotel? And in the very same second that she wondered whether it was safe to send cash through the mail, the super of her building knocked on her door and, when she answered, handed over a thick yellow envelope that was too big for the mailman to cram in her mailbox.

"What is it?" Anne asked.

The return address was a place in Georgia that Anne had never heard of, and above the address it read: "Attorneys at Law."

"Gotta open it to find out," the super said.

Georgia, Anne considered. Brian had once asked Anne if she knew there were little islands off the coast of Georgia. The Golden Isles, she remembered. He wanted to go there after the baby was born because they hadn't had time for a honeymoon. But then they lost the baby.

She placed the envelope on the counter and looked at it while the water in the teakettle began to thrum. He was either divorcing her, finally, or he was dead.

"Well," she said aloud to her empty apartment once she was ready.

———

After reading the documents through, she picked up her keys from the counter and drove over to the nursing home, the papers on the passenger seat. Once, before they got married, they'd agreed to meet up on the corner of Eighteenth Street and Fifth Avenue. She got there first and watched the throngs of people pass by. She didn't know what direction he'd be coming from and then she saw him, so far away he was only a human shape bobbing along with so many others—their coats and scarves flapping, their bags weighing them down—but there was something about the way his particular shape moved that she knew it was him, long before she could make out his face. That one is mine, she thought that day.

And when she remembered that, she was surprised. She had loved him. Maybe intermittently. Maybe not very well. But she had. She tried to remember what it felt like to put her key in a door and know there might be someone on the other side.

Mary Beth Keane

When she got to work she told the charge nurse that she knew it was her day off but she had a family emergency, so she was going into the private meeting room to make a call and she didn't know how long she'd be. If the phone call turned up on the bill as quite expensive, Anne would gladly pay for it. Someone just had to let her know how much it had cost. She'd read the documents through at home, but there were questions the documents didn't answer. How had he died, for example? She did the math—he would have been only sixty-five. There were sixty-five-year-olds who regularly visited their ninety-year-old mothers at the nursing home. Maybe that was skewing her sense of who was old and who was young. He'd died a whole month ago. She was listed as wife and beneficiary.

She dialed the number on the cover letter and asked for a Mr. Ford Diviny. The receptionist put her right through.

———

One problem was—and Anne caught from his tone that this was just one of many problems Brian had caused—what Brian had was a simple will. He should have had a complex will with disclaimers, codicils. He'd been living with a woman for going on ten years, but he'd left her not even one dime.

"He wasn't cruel," Mr. Diviny said. "It was just the sort of thing he didn't think about." He needed personal care these last few years, and that woman had provided it. He was a diabetic, and every single day she'd checked his feet and legs for discoloration, for cracks and wounds. She got him special socks. She rubbed cornstarch between his toes. Still, Brian's left foot had to be amputated in 2013. Did Anne know that? And he wasn't careful, even after the amputation. With his sugars and such. Anne thought that was a nice way of putting it.

"You seem to have known him well," Anne said. "Were you his attorney for a long time?"

380

"I wasn't his attorney at all," Mr. Diviny said. "I was his friend. We went to Louisville a few times. For the derby. Met him at a place down here called the Trade Winds. You been here?"

"No," Anne said.

Mr. Diviny went on. "I didn't know about you or about your son until he insisted I draw up that will for him, and by then I'd known him near twenty years. I know Suzie a little, so I felt bad about that. I had a feeling she didn't know a thing about you all and I was right."

It was looking like his other foot would have to be amputated when he died. Brian owned a home and Suzie lived in it, but Brian's was the only name on the deed and he left the house to Anne, and to his son, to be split fifty-fifty. He'd also left a sum of money and some personal items to Mr. George Stanhope, his brother. He left personal items to Mr. Francis Gleeson, too.

Anne dropped her head to her hands. "How much could he have had? I don't think he was even forty years old when he retired."

"Well, he worked down here until his legs got bad. And he had his pension. He had a lot by some standards. In any case, what's there is there. He didn't have debt, which kind of surprised me, considering how he was."

"How'd you find me?"

"I ran his social security number when he died. His old marriage license came up. Then it took a good three weeks to track you down."

"Poor Suzie," he sighed. "She's a good girl, really. What a shock."

"Have you informed the other beneficiaries?" Anne asked. "Are we all getting packages like this?"

"Should be. The notices and copies of the will all went out on the same day. Oh, and Mrs. Stanhope? The other thing is he wanted to be buried up north."

"Up north where?"

"Up there. New York. Near you all."

"Near who all? Me?"

"You, yes. And his son. His deceased mother and father. He spoke of his mother, in particular." But they couldn't hold him, Mr. Diviny explained. Who knew how long it would take to track down the family? So they had a little Catholic wake down there with an open casket and all, and then he was cremated.

Anne looked out the window to the parking lot but couldn't make sense of any of it. None of it. An ice cream truck went speeding by on Route 7, its music off. His mother who had never even acknowledged their wedding, or the fact that that first baby died. Anne had gone to her wake and funeral but had refused to kneel by the body.

"I haven't seen hide nor hair of this man in twenty-five years."

"Well," Mr. Diviny sighed. "As the poet said, every savage loves his native shore. I hear an accent in your voice. You don't feel the same?"

"No. Not really. Suzie can have the ashes. Is that her name? Suzie?"

"Nope. Doesn't want them. She's furious. Can't blame her. Besides, those weren't Brian's wishes."

"She can have the house then, as long as she keeps the ashes. I don't care."

Mr. Diviny was silent for a long time. "I understand you and Brian parted ways under difficult circumstances."

So he had told his friend a few things, Anne thought. Suddenly, a light on the phone she was using started flashing. She didn't know what it meant.

"I'm going to advise you to think about that, Mrs. Stanhope. And besides, half that house is your son's."

A young nurse came to the door of the office just then. She held her pinkie and thumb up to the side of her head and kept miming something until Anne told Mr. Diviny to please hold.

"What?" Anne asked.

"You have a call. Peter. He says he's your son? Should I put him through to this line?"

"Yes!" Anne said. "What do I do?" She rushed Mr. Diviny off the phone and was nervous all of a sudden that he'd change his mind, get sick of waiting.

But the young nurse came around the desk, pressed the flashing button, and nodded at her. And there he was.

———

In Gillam, a cup of tea in front of him, Francis read everything through for a fifth, sixth, seventh time before calling Kate. Lena read it through just once. Francis had seen her gaze run down the list of beneficiaries as if she might find her name there, too, since his was there, and when she didn't find it, she announced she was going for a walk. As he stood at the counter and listened to Kate's end of the line ring, he caught sight of himself in the stainless steel of the microwave door and saw a person who was haggard, a piece of driftwood left in rough waters for far too long. His hair was sticking straight up and he was wearing his eye patch again, the last prosthetic having deteriorated more quickly than the ones before. Less than three years old and a fine, dark ridge had appeared along the iris, and his eyelid blistered from closing over it a thousand times a day. He didn't want to order another. Every new prosthetic eye was a marker of time—how much his face had aged since the last.

"I knew it was you," Kate said when she answered. "Can you believe this? We were rushing around all morning and almost didn't open the mail. What in the world did he leave to you?" Kate wanted to know. She was breathless, as if she'd run in from the yard when she heard the phone ringing.

"Don't know. It's going to arrive in the next few days. Under separate cover, the letter says."

"What could it be?"

Whatever it was, Francis decided he didn't want it. If it had any value, he'd give it to Peter. If it didn't, he'd just throw it away.

"How's Peter?"

"Fine," Kate said, lowering her voice. "Seems okay. Surprised, I guess. He never expected to see him again but he didn't expect him to die either."

That was exactly the way Francis had felt about his own father, hearing about his death from so far away.

———

He didn't want whatever it was Brian had left for him, but still, he found himself glancing at the clock more than usual, waiting for the mailman. Wednesday and Thursday went by. On Friday a package came but it was subscription vitamins Lena ordered.

Finally, on Saturday, a small cardboard envelope arrived from Georgia. Francis was expecting a box. Maybe a large box. An envelope meant it was more likely a check. Or the deed to something he owned. Or the key to a lockbox somewhere he figured Francis would be able to find. He probably didn't even know his own son had been a captain in the NYPD.

And then he thought, Oh Christ, what if it's a letter?

Lena wasn't home, so Francis called Kate.

"Did it come? What is it?"

"It came but your mother isn't here."

"So open it now. I'll stay on the phone. Or, you know what? We could go there, open it together. Oh wait, hang on." She turned from the phone and he heard the low register of Peter's voice in the background. Then Kate's, muffled because she was covering the mouthpiece with her hand.

"Dad? Can you wait an hour? We'll come there. Then Mom will be home, too. Tell her not to worry about cooking. We can get a pizza or something for the kids."

———

Peter wasn't there entirely willingly, Francis could see as soon as he walked through the door. He looked healthy lately, younger than he had a year before. But on that day he had some of the same expression he'd worn when he and Kate came to tell them that they'd gotten married, a wild, skittery fear around his eyes.

"What could it be?" Francis asked, holding up the envelope, and Peter recoiled from it a little as if he didn't want to know. Kate had already told Francis the value of the house in Georgia, the stocks, Brian's meager life insurance, purchased, presumably, before diabetes set in. But there'd been no personal note to Peter, and privately, Kate said to Francis, she knew Peter was disappointed. He didn't imagine he'd get an apology or anything, but maybe some sort of acknowledgment that things had not been ideal. An acknowledgment that Peter had done well with his life, despite everything. But how would Brian even know that? Kate wondered aloud. He didn't know a thing about Peter as an adult. There was a woman down there who lived with him, took care of him, Kate told Francis, and Brian left her nothing. Not only that, but he'd never said a word about being married, having a son.

Francis made a sound of disgust. It was always the same. People didn't change.

"So between them," Kate continued, "Peter and Anne decided to cut her in for a third."

That surprised him. Shocked him, even, and he didn't know he could be shocked. "That's very decent," he said. He wondered if he'd have been as decent, if he were in their shoes.

"Okay!" Lena said, putting a plate of cookies on the table. "Let's not drag it out any longer."

So they pulled up close to the table, all leaning forward to see. Francis pulled the tab of the envelope across the top and flipped it over, tapped it on the table until the contents slid out: three photographs, and one prayer card, Saint Michael the Archangel. All four of them held perfectly still as they looked and tried to understand. The first photo was a snapshot of a pretty blond woman with a long, slim neck. The next was a photo of two sunburned young men sitting in the bleachers at the old

Shea Stadium. And the third photo was of Peter, around kindergarten age. All of the photos were yellowed and stained.

"Are you sure these were meant for you?" Lena asked after a long moment of silence. "Is that lawyer sure?"

"What happened to them?" Kate asked, picking up the one of Peter. "Water damage?"

"Sweat stains," Francis said. "I've seen these before." The day came back to him. The heat. The smell of the Bronx burning. The sound of the alarms ringing and clanging and buzzing every minute of the day. They were crazy years, and looking back sometimes he wondered why he'd gone at the job so hard. He often thought of himself giving chase, pursuing subjects down alleys, into dark lobbies, up stairwells. Why hadn't he just pretended, like some others did? Why hadn't he quit and then said simply that the suspect had gotten away? Everyone would have believed him. Only later, years and years later, did he look back at some of the situations he'd been in and see he was lucky to be alive.

He picked up the photo of Anne, and turned to Peter. "He showed me this one in 1973. July. We were on patrol. He kept it in the lining of his hat." He touched the prayer card, and the photo of Brian and George. "These, too."

"This one he must have added later," he said, picking up the photo of Peter. Francis remembered Peter at that age: a weird kid, always sitting on the rocks out back with soldier figurines, whispering to himself as he made them battle each other. A weird kid, maybe, but his father had loved him, had tucked him into the lining of his hat so that he could look at him when his patrol car was idling, or when a day was hard, or maybe when he felt afraid.

"Why did he send them to you?" Peter asked. "And not to me?" He was staring hard at the photo of himself.

"I don't know," Francis said.

Maybe he sent them to Francis because he believed Francis alone would know what the photos meant to him, and he would tell Peter. The young cops today probably kept all their photos on their phones, kept the linings of their hats empty.

Or maybe Brian was saying he was sorry to Francis, for whatever part he played. Maybe he was saying he should have done something more, seeing how they'd been partners, once, for six sweltering weeks in the summer of 1973.

Or maybe he was saying, simply, that he remembered. That he'd not forgotten, even from the distance of so many years and so many miles, that he'd had a different life, once.

Or maybe he wasn't saying anything at all, but simply wanted to mail the photos to someone who wouldn't be upset by them because he didn't want to throw them away, not after their having protected him through all his tours. This slim-necked woman was the woman he'd married. And this boy was the boy he'd made with her. And maybe he had to get their images out of the house in case Suzie came in to rub cornstarch between his toes.

There was no accompanying note, and anything that had once been written on the back of the photos had long ago been smudged away.

"What'll happen with the ashes?" Lena asked.

"They're being shipped to my mother," Peter said. "She's going to bring them down here and we're going to have them buried with his mother. George suggested that."

"It's pretty easy," Kate added. "They just open up a little spot in the same plot."

Better than sitting on someone's shelf, Francis thought.

Slowly, everyone began to move from their places. Lena got up first and took a few pork chops out of the fridge. She took down the bread crumbs from the high cabinet, brought out the eggs. After a minute, as Kate continued to look from one photo to the next to the next and then back to the first again, Peter got up to help Lena. Without being asked he grabbed a few apples out of the bowl. He sliced them and dropped them into a pan with butter to soften for a quick sauce. He ducked his head to glance out the window at the kids, who were out playing on the rocks.

"Kate," he said over his shoulder, and lifted his chin to indicate something that was happening outside. They looked at each other quickly, and smirked. Some private pride about one or both of the kids, Francis knew.

And then he saw what he'd never seen before, which was that Peter was fine. And Kate was fine. Lena was fine. And he, Francis Gleeson, was fine. And that all the things that had happened in their lives had not hurt them in any essential way, despite what they may have believed at times. He had not lost anything; he'd only gained. Was the same true for Peter? For Kate? Yes. And yes. Would they be somewhere more magnificent than this were it not for everything that had happened? Would their lives have been fuller and happier? Looking at them now, he didn't see how it would be possible. For the very first time, he felt that Peter was his blood.

"Hey," Lena said, coming up behind him and putting her hands on his shoulders. He could feel her looking at the pictures again, so he looked, too.

"You know what I think?" she asked.

"What?" Francis asked.

Lena tightened her grip. She leaned down so that he could feel the warmth of her face against the crook of his neck.

"I think we've been luckier than most people."

He let that swell over him like a wave, and when he bobbed up from the black water, his chest full, his body tired, the sky looked more blue than when he went under.

"What do you think?" she asked, the softness in her voice belying the strength of her hands.

"Yes," he said. "Yes."

acknowledgments

I'm deeply grateful to several trusted readers and friends who took time away from their own novels and other obligations to read early pages of *Ask Again, Yes* in very rough form, and whose questions helped me see these characters more clearly. Many, many thanks to Jeanine Cummins, Mary Gordon, Kelsey Smith, Callie Wright, and most especially to Eleanor Henderson and Brendan Mathews, who read several drafts and kept urging me forward.

To the John Simon Guggenheim Foundation for selecting me. The fellowship bought me additional writing time while I was working on this novel, but more importantly, it gave me confidence when I needed it most.

To Lesley Williamson and the Saltonstall Foundation for twice providing me space and quiet to work with very little notice. I get more done in one week at Saltonstall than in three months of my real life. I wrote the last two chapters of this book in the downstairs studio there.

My deepest thanks to the NYPD officers, both retired and active, who sat with me and answered what were probably very dumb questions without flinching or rolling their eyes. I owe particular thanks to Artie

Marini, Austin "Timmy" Muldoon, and especially Matt Donagher. For insight into disciplinary procedures within the NYPD when there's a mental health concern about a police officer, my thanks to Dr. Sheila Brosnahan. Also, thanks to Dr. Howard Forman for chatting with me about forensic psychiatry when I was just beginning to think about this book, and knew absolutely nothing. Anything I got wrong is entirely on me and not on them.

To Nan Graham for acquiring this novel, and to Kara Watson for her careful edit. I'm so grateful and proud to be at Scribner once again.

To Chris Calhoun, my agent and friend, for insisting I was not yet at my limit.

And above all, thanks to Marty, for teaching me a long time ago that the only secret to love is kindness.